SNYDER'S WALK

Books by Thomas B. Morgan

Friends and Fellow Students
Self-Creations: Thirteen Impersonalities
This Blessed Shore (novel)
Among the Anti-Americans

SNYDER'S WALK

A NOVEL BY

Thomas B. Morgan

A DOLPHIN BOOK

DOUBLEDAY & COMPANY, INC.
GARDEN CITY, NEW YORK
1987

The characters and the events in this book are fictitious.
Any resemblance to living persons or actual events is
unintended and entirely coincidental.

LIBRARY OF CONGRESS CATALOGING-IN-PUBLICATION DATA

Morgan, Thomas Bruce, 1926–
Snyder's walk.

"A Dolphin Book."
1. Vietnamese Conflict, 1961–1975—Fiction.
I. Title.
PS3563.0871496S6 1987   813'.54   86–16224
ISBN 0-385-23637-9

For Mary
and the children:
Kate,
Nick,
Geoff,
Mike,
and
Sabrina

CONTENTS

CONTENTS

Goodness, armed with power, is corrupted;
and pure love without power is destroyed.

— Reinhold Niebuhr, *Beyond Tragedy*

ERLANGER

ONE

Pilgrims' Progress

I

In the early darkness of a cold evening in January, 1986, the spire of St. Patrick's Cathedral pointed heavenward like a hectoring middle finger before the old eyes of Bruce Erlanger, who looked down on it from his office window in midtown New York. The man was in his mid-sixties, portly and bald, except for a little gray trim behind the ears. His suit was blue sharkskin, well tailored, with lap stitching on the lapels, but he wore an ordinary maroon cardigan underneath and a green tie, all wrong. He looked like an Eastern bloc bureaucrat. In truth, he was in his fortieth year as chief editor of the popular general magazine now known as *Harrington's World Journal,* still too busy to think about writing his memoirs, but troubled by a certain memory going back twenty years to 1966. He had stepped to the window to meditate on it.

Yesterday's snow was blowing, Erlanger noted, but the sky was momentarily clear up to the moon. There was a chill in the office. It would soon be time to leave. He was comforted by knowing that his four-year-old Mercedes-Benz turbo-diesel sedan with a driver at the wheel waited fifteen stories below on East Forty-ninth Street to take him home to Mount Kisco, Westchester County, New York. Still, the building should provide more heat. It was one of those wedding-cake terraced skyscrapers that had amused Manhattan builders in the early fifties. It had no name, but a Madison Avenue address. He made a mental note to ask his executive secretary, Felicia Selby, to complain about the heat in the morning.

Erlanger resumed his seat behind the high, square antique foyer table that served him as a desk. In the chilly glow of overhead fluorescent light, he studied his wrinkled hands, spread flat, palms down, over a small pile of letters and a one-page memo from Selby. He could have been blessing the pile or sounding it for vibrations. He shook his head as though rejecting some inner advice.

Oh, of course, Bruce, he was thinking, you can let Selby file the letters and her memo and you both might forget the whole thing. But then, tomorrow, you could ask to see the "Snyder/Walk/66" file again, and two weeks from now, and so on, because curiosity, or even remorse, had demanded it. Destroy the letters, man. You would, were Snyder alive.

Jacob C. Snyder was ten weeks dead, stopped cold on November 7, 1985, at age sixty-one years, five years Erlanger's junior. It seems impossible that he is gone, Erlanger thought. Snyder should be there still, his looming presence (six-three? six-four?) right there on the adjacent terrace. He should be down the hall in his smoke-filled cubicle. He should be working, late as usual, initialing corrected proofs: "JCS." He should be persevering, still writing one of his "World Class" (that old pun!) articles for *Harrington's WJ*, monthly heir of the once-great national magazine *Harrington's Weekly World*. In the trade, they had said that he was your man, the quintessential magazine journalist, that he wrote so long for *Harrington's* because it was "a writer's book," that he was your best find in all your time as editor-in-chief. If they only knew the truth, that for all those later years Snyder wrote articles as an atonement, rejecting promotion and with it the prospect of succeeding you (who expected you to last so long?). Now imagine! Even Snyder, it turns out, never knew the whole truth. If he had, he might never have written again.

Snyder was forty-two in 1966. Somewhere George Bernard Shaw proclaimed that no man (unless irrational, incompetent, or unlucky) should be turning out pieces of journalism after age forty. Shaw must have meant that it was a boy's game, like professional baseball. He may have been right. What does that make you, old Bruce, the Stengel of magazines?

Well, yes. But better than anyone, you've understood there was more to Snyder's perseverance than mere defiance of Shaw's law.

Erlanger nodded, approving his rising recollections. The word "perseverance" was decidedly the right one for Snyder. Years back,

Snyder had taken some substantial times out, but months, not years, first to work on a moderately successful fact book about history's Arctic and Antarctic explorations, tied to the International Geophysical Year, 1957–58; later to take care of some unpleasant family matters; and once, after 1966, to treat a bad case of the shingles. But allowing for those gaps, Snyder had been the magazine's continuity for a generation and more, your star and most prolific staff writer of fact pieces, producing seven or eight features, averaging five thousand words each, every year for nearly thirty years. Think of it!

Bruce, do not kid yourself. Of course, you have run the place like a noble little kingdom, a place where each knight (male and female) can choose his own windmill, take the travel and research time he needs, and return to write those seven or eight features a year, knowing you will always publish him, so long as he has a story to tell and practical opinions, not too left, not too right, grounded in the Americanist middle of the middlebrow middle class. But over time, your counterparts at *Life, Look, The Saturday Evening Post,* and *Collier's* all did that. It was for Snyder alone that you permitted a kind of open-ended security that is otherwise unknown in our timorous, deadline business, a moral incentive beyond mere survival and beyond the fix that every journalist gets when he sees his name in print.

And yet, once you had nearly lost him—what possessed him, what made him so professional—to the war in Vietnam and one extraordinary assignment, his "Pilgrims' Progress—Profile of a Peace Walk," published as the cover story late that sad summer, now these twenty years back. It was the magazine's all-time best-selling issue, and the pivot of his life, the still point of ambition past, present, and future, after which keeping on was the only endurable answer to his conscience.

It was your luck, Bruce. And wouldn't you give a lot to hear his comment on today's mail?

But Snyder died back before Thanksgiving.

Next morning (will you ever forget?), his obituary in the New York *Times* was only four column inches long. No one here at the magazine, from which to the *Times*'s obit desk during those last, dying days had been sent a three-page, single-spaced résumé of Snyder's career, knew why so short. It could have been much longer.

Clearly, the *Times* meant, hell, he was only a magazine writer. Damn the *Times* anyway!

The obit left out, for example, that before *Harrington's,* Snyder had worked in the Atlanta bureau of the Associated Press. His byline was J. C. "Jack" Snyder then, and his coverage of the Montgomery, Alabama, bus strike, which introduced Martin Luther King to America, would win one of the big annual journalism awards. This was in December, 1955, before television really started to hit and the citizenry got their first inkling of most news from the wire services. It had brought him to New York and *Harrington's* before that winter was over. He deserved remembrance for it and got none.

The obit also left out any measure of his struggle, any acknowledgment that gathering information for two hundred and sixty-seven *Harrington's* articles was an achievement, that it usually required a hard journey, was sometimes dangerous, and could be occasionally frustrating, as when a story would change or even, if rarely, abort somewhere along the way from approval of the idea to publication. The man didn't just survive that struggle, he prevailed. He never lied. Surely, the comments of his peers on that subject would have been worth a few phone calls and an extra paragraph. Instead, the *Times* took up space with a three-inch photograph, circa 1979, from the book jacket of a collection of Snyder's articles published that year, showing Snyder at his office typewriter with his right hand on the roller arm and his left hand holding his eternal cigarette. Less picture and more words about the man's works would have been a hell of a lot nicer—the picture did not look like him, anyway, the red hair and the red mustache in black and white.

Not that any of this would have bothered Snyder himself.

"There are no immortal magazine writers," Snyder said just before he died.

He was right, you know—nothing immortal about magazines, either. How long can *Harrington's* last? Wisconsin brewery money financed the first issue on sepia paper in 1908 to give an American voice to the anti-British side should war come. The major holder of voting stock and founding editor, Charles C. "Duff" Harrington, a Roman Catholic with both Irish and German roots, shifted the offices from Milwaukee to Manhattan in 1919, and his opinions on foreign affairs as well. He became a leading spokesman for U.S. membership in the League of Nations and, when the time came, in the United Nations. Duff made himself emeritus in 1946 and moved you up from managing editor, at age twenty-seven. You were good, and you were available, having missed World War II, for a health reason—the one deformed foot. In 1974, after sixty-six years of publishing as a weekly, fiscal logic forced *Harrington's* to go monthly with drastically reduced circulation and a new format. You downsized her from an imperial eleven by fourteen page to a brassy, more contemporary eight by eleven. The result has been a new lease on life, if in markedly reduced circumstances. But for how long, dear God?

And, face it, these days are not the heydays of the late fifties through the sixties, when the magazine was ubiquitous. Six million Americans used to spend nearly $2 million every week to read *Harrington's* and corporations paid over $100 million annually to hawk their wares among its features. Shoppers knew subliminally that the phrase "As Advertised in the *World*" meant *Harrington's Weekly World*. And even non-readers were kept up with each new issue, with the news wire services routinely moving *Harrington's* stories as major news for local newspapers, radio, and TV. Almost everyone in the land seemed to be aware of something *Harrington's* had just said. Such penetration, as the ad boys liked to call it, gave *Harrington's* a powerful voice as it spoke to the nation about anyone, great or small, trying to be heard. That's the way it was in 1966. *Harrington's* had clout. So, Snyder did.

We lost it together, almost overnight, when network and cable television conclusively took over the media frontier. Then the glory days of general-interest magazine journalism passed quicker than those of the Old West.

Yes, into the eighties, absent former power and old prestige, *Harrington's* survives on the monthly fringes of electronic civilization. And any impartial observer will agree that its features have been no less stimulating and sassy than they were in the great years. But it has not been the same, just less bad than it might have been because, for one thing, Snyder continued. If he had become less important in the democratic process than he once was, his work still counted for something and so did his example for the younger writers. You knew how they felt. The effort to maintain one's professional discipline and write well would seem absurd sometimes. But then, there was

Snyder still at it, when long since he could have been managing editor, or exec, poised for old Erlanger's retirement. Who says Buffalo Bill's defunct?

"I suppose I'll keep on doing it," Snyder told you across the street at Click's Bar last February, with a squint-eyed look at his Marlboro, "until these things kill me." He knew you knew why.

2

The cathedral bells struck eight. Erlanger's driver was waiting. There were snow clouds gathering. Erlanger picked up the telltale letters and Selby's note and tossed them into his briefcase on top of a pile of manuscripts. Then he turned out the light. The city outside seemed morose without its Christmas decorations. Erlanger let himself out of his office and into Selby's. Everyone had gone home hours ago. In the gray dark, Erlanger left Selby a note, pushing back the regular Tuesday-morning editorial meeting to the afternoon, on account of the weather. Then he took the roundabout way to the elevators, limping on his irreparable right foot down the long corridor to the editorial bullpen and along the cubicles to Snyder's old room with the terrace.

Erlanger had not wanted to think more about Snyder after the binge of ten weeks past. But here he was standing in the door trying to remember the pictures and posters Snyder had kept, Adlai Stevenson with the hole in his shoe and Martin Luther King in Montgomery and Brigitte Bardot and Secretariat and a lot more, all gone now, many moved to other offices and work spaces as mementos of the well-respected man. Someone had even taken Snyder's typewriter. But still Erlanger delayed reassigning the office. Something will have to be done, he thought, moving on to the night elevator, but not just yet.

Christ, Snyder was your man for thirty years, so you cannot just move out every last trace.

It is all so strange, Erlanger thought. You didn't even know him well. You really cannot say that you knew him well, except when it came to the business. Could that have been all there was to him? He was obsessed by professionalism. Once, by accident, you'd overheard him mentoring Phil Zimmerman (gone, too!). The job is closer to police work and the priesthood than medicine or the law, he was saying, and so's the pay, on the average. (Ha!) Journalism schools talk about practices and procedures, he said, but the real worries are about tainting your information by your own involvement with it, about maintaining a certain discipline even in moments of great intensity, about being manipulated by others for publicity, about the sins of omission as well as commission, and about telling no lies. That was before Snyder's Walk, when none of it worked.

Really, we weren't even friends, Erlanger admitted to himself. You did a great deal of business together over the years. But the office relationship was too structured, King Arthur and the Round Table, trail boss and outriders, nothing too personal even though only five years separated you in age. Outside the office, you would have a lunch two or three times a year at Christ Cella's, and drinks every couple of months across the street at Click's. Otherwise, recall, Snyder and his Scottish wife, Paula, visited you at home in Mount Kisco exactly twice. And just once, you entertained him with the Jewish girl from the Walk, who had come from Chicago to be near him and, after two years, unwilling to marry a man who would never leave the road, went home again. Somehow, further social exchanges never occurred to either of you. It might have been different had you rented a place in town. Selby had opposed that.

And, come to think of it, you never heard much from Snyder about himself, either. Obviously, his best friend among them had been Phil Zimmerman, the four-foot-eleven-and-one-half-inch runt who joined *Harrington's* at age twenty-seven in late 1956 from the Associated Press in Tokyo, came under Snyder's wing (like Mutt to Jeff, it was said more than once) for a year or so, and rose to bureau chief in Saigon, Vietnam, 1965–66.

Well, then, the crisis year was 1966.

It happened that you sent Zimmerman on two tours to Vietnam, the second one fatal. The worst luck! Little Phil became *Harrington's* only casualty in the four major wars of this century.

It might have been Snyder's lot had not Zimmerman persuaded Snyder to persuade you to let him be the first to go. In fact, World War II had made Air Corps Captain Snyder something of an authority on the kind of aerial bombardment that President Johnson's advisers were pushing for a quick end to the war in Vietnam. Then, after Zimmerman's death, Snyder wanted to go, but you said no because your new policy was to send men without wives or children.

At the same time, even though *Harrington's* editorial page was still supporting the war policy, you gave Snyder the other assignment, the Walk he so badly wanted to cover just then. You had your reasons. He had his. It was about a peace march protesting the war in Vietnam, a handful of activists on a 750-mile trek across mid-America from Chicago to Washington, starting May 11, 1966, and ending —ending? Snyder's Walk only just ended.

3

Through snowing darkness, the driver moved Erlanger's sedan smartly up the Sawmill River Parkway, then along a narrow, two-lane country highway to an even narrower gravel road. Moments later, Erlanger was home. The sprawling Cape Cod bungalow in the darkness of pines and night sky had light in several rooms.

Avoiding housekeeper and dog, he carried his briefcase straightway to the den, where a fire had been laid on the stone hearth. He lit the fire, replaced the screen, and, still in his overcoat and hat, mixed bourbon and water. The cigarettes, he was thinking, killed Snyder at Mount Sinai Hospital in early November; his head was close-shaved then, but somehow his mustache had survived chemotherapy as rich and deep red as ever. And you stopped the presses in Rutland (where the bastard printing-tradesmen of Vermont were greatly outraged) to include a eulogy for him in the Christmas '85 issue. The issue went off-sale at the end of December. You were able to squeeze in some readers' mail about Snyder for the January issue. Then yesterday, an envelope arrived addressed "To the Memory of Jacob C. Snyder." It was postmarked Decatur, Illinois. It contained a news clipping announcing the death at twenty-three of Reed Herndon, son of Mrs. Adele Herndon and the late Hobart Herndon of Decatur, on that summer's protest walk so many years ago; some letters from Herndon to his mother; and a covering note. Over the feeble signature of Adele Herndon, the note merely said, "Reed would have been forty-three this birthday."

It was the dead boy's letters that dismayed you. And you finally came to tears as Snyder's encounter with its author on that peace walk of 1966 was revealed to you in new detail. Still, the purpose of Herndon's mother was not clear to you. You smelled a lawsuit. Why should an old woman send her son's precious and private letters to a stranger? What did she expect? Was it her purpose just to let you find out that it was all about Snyder? How bitter, now that Snyder was dead, too.

You asked Selby to call Decatur, Illinois, and give you a report. And just at closing time, you had learned that Adele Herndon, a very old and now childless widow, had sent the letters from her own sickbed, writing the note virtually with her last atom of energy. A friend had mailed the envelope for her. The nurses would not let her speak. No one knew her mind or, in fact, had ever heard of Snyder. The timing of the mailing seemed related to the readers' mail rather than your eulogy of a month earlier. Perhaps the old woman had missed the Christmas issue. Nothing in either issue referred to Vietnam. Pathetic! It was as though Adele Herndon, herself dying, believed you were now the one other person in the world who would really remember her son. An old woman was dying and did not want to take her only child's memory to her grave. "Reed would have been forty-three this birthday," her note said, addressed to the memory of Jack Snyder.

You try to understand.

In the mother's mind, Snyder's death meant the end of his memory of Reed Herndon, a memory more important than any other because it gave a meaning to her son's dying all the more terrible for the loss of what he might have become. Now you were the last connection between Snyder and Herndon. Snyder was dead at age sixty-one and Adele Herndon was going, too, and the letters needed some disposition. So you were chosen.

To read Herndon's few letters was to imagine how the mother must have restrained herself not to have sent them to Snyder long ago. They would have almost certainly changed Snyder's life, his self-image, his self-respect. How could his way of atonement have been enough had he known the whole truth, that his fault lay not only in ambivalence but in presumption? Never assume a goddamn thing, Snyder always said, but he did assume, just this once, and that had made the terminal difference, of which he lived and died unaware. Well, on second thought, perhaps Mrs. Herndon had done Snyder a favor, and you, too. This way, you got a writer. That way—but then, you can't know, can you?

Erlanger finished his drink and poured another as the fire mounted behind the screen. Then abruptly, and very fast, before compulsion could overwhelm common sense, he pocketed the letters and left the room. He knew that he might otherwise throw them (especially the last one) into the fire. Such, he thought, would not be fitting. The letters are history.

And someday you might use them in your memoirs.

ZIMMERMAN

TWO
Birth of a Story Idea

I

There was a memorandum from the Saigon bureau in the interoffice mail for Jack Snyder at the end of February 1966. Phil Zimmerman had written it after two months of his second tour covering the war in Vietnam for the magazine. First to read it was Lilian White, one of the staff writers' pool secretaries, in the editorial bullpen on the fifteenth floor.

". . . take it from me [the memo said], this war is one our side is not going to win soon. Pessimist or optimist, hawk or dove, you have to admit that the South Vietnamese and 150,000 Americans aren't going to win this year or next, and maybe never. The Vietcong and the North Vietnamese are simply too much for us at current force levels. Off the record, people are saying maybe a million Americans with a killer like Ulysses S. Grant to lead them can win it someday, and maybe not if the Chinese want to play. Do we want to win that badly?

"The kind of a massive commitment required to stop the Communists here seems less and less likely every day with opposition to the war rising in your opinion polls at home. Will we pay the price? If not, is it right to continue?

"Don't ask me how far the current escalation will go. I'm trying to find out. Rumor has the top at 200,000 troops by Christmas, maybe more once LBJ has analyzed Nov. congressional election returns. But won't we peak long before we get to a million men on the ground over here? So then what?

"Do we negotiate a stalemate? Do we withdraw? See, we've got no principle here, just a policy on the cheap. It's unreal. You're a dove—you should do one on the peace movement. I'm liable to become a dove myself, at any minute. Boy!"

Zimmerman's memo would not be seen right away by Snyder, who was on assignment in Paris. Ten days earlier, Erlanger had asked him to profile Jean Monnet, father of the Common Market, which seemed to be faltering on its way to the creation of a United States of Europe.

Lilian White, having read the memo, decided it could wait. She filed it in Snyder's mail folder pending his return. He was due back in New York third week in March.

"You should do one on the peace movement"—this was the first germ of such an idea for *Harrington's Weekly World,* which, in the year since the bombing of North Vietnam had signaled the Americanization of the war for South Vietnam, had continued to support the Johnson administration's war policy. Though lacking a carrier and a host, it was still the kind of germ from which important assignments and pivotal magazine articles grew.

2

Thursday of the third week in March, spring was on schedule, blossoming around Central Park and in Mrs. Lasker's daffodil beds on the islands of Park Avenue. By noon, the warmth of the sun had brought the pre-Easter crowds onto Fifth Avenue around St. Patrick's Cathedral. A troop of ragged mimes in camouflage suits played dead on the cathedral steps protesting the war in Vietnam until two policemen moved them along. They cavorted eastward, along Forty-ninth Street across Madison Avenue, some limping and others carrying their pseudo-wounded.

A young woman, who had been following the mimes at a distance, turned into the nameless skyscraper on Forty-ninth Street east of Madison. *Harrington's Weekly World* occupied five floors here, fifteenth through nineteenth, editorial, advertising, circulation and accounting, and publishing, respectively, with offices on the nineteenth floor linking the magazine to other segments of the company's media empire, three midwestern television stations, the chain of radio stations in the Southwest, and the newspaper syndicate. There were two armed guards at a station in the rear of the main-floor lobby, but no doorman or information desk. Other companies in the building did business in oil, real estate, tobacco, and heavy railroad equipment. The young woman scanned the office directory, located the editorial floor, and boarded a crowded express elevator.

She debarked at the fifteenth floor, entering a bleak hall of gray walls and blue linoleum floors with closed doors at each end. In a windowless alcove facing the elevators, there was a reception desk for visitors to the editorial department. A life-sized, full-length color photo of a smiling old gentleman wearing a trench coat and a 1940s felt hat filled the wall space behind the desk. From the moment a visitor stepped off the elevator, he or she was thus obliged to pay respects to the founding editor of *Harrington's Weekly World,* C. C. "Duff" Harrington, as portrayed by the photographer Alexander Caldwell. Like most of Caldwell's pictures, it had something extra to say about its subject. This one showed its man in 1945, at the time of his retirement, holding a copy of his magazine with a cover photo of himself holding a copy of his magazine with a cover photo of himself. The newly arrived visitor could not have identified the old man, but Caldwell's message about his power left no doubt in her mind that he had once been boss. Bemused, she found herself third in a line at the reception desk, behind a messenger boy and a long-haired man weighted down with a large envelope and a portable typewriter.

The young woman's name was Rachel Abraham. She was tall and strikingly pretty, in her late twenties, with olive skin and long, straight hair the color of pine cones. Her beauty was all in angles and planes rather than curves and valleys. Still, beneath her jacket and sweater, there was the suggestion of fullness and her miniskirt showed good legs and flawless knees. Most men and not a few women would have spotted her lanky figure in a crowd. The long-haired man had turned to admire her, but moved quickly to the door behind Duff Harrington's picture when the receptionist buzzed him into the inner sanctum. At first glance, the receptionist seemed to think Rachel was a model, which would also have accounted for her oversized shoulder bag, and gave her a smile as to a fellow working girl.

"Studio?"

"To see Mr. Snyder," Rachel said. She noted the identification badge on the woman's blouse.

The receptionist's name was Niya Samerjan. She looked middle-aged and masculine. Her manner was brisk as she logged in Rachel's name and affiliation: World Institute for Survival Education, 3707 State Street, Chicago, Illinois.

"I spoke to a Miss White in Mr. Snyder's office Monday and again yesterday," Rachel said. "It's about a story."

"Lily White? Don't you love that name? What did she say?"

"First, call back. Then, come by. I'm Maude Abraham's sister."

Niya nodded, skeptically. She would know that Maude O'Neill Abraham was the byline of a *Harrington's* staff correspondent who regularly wrote on European arts and fashions from the magazine's Paris bureau. But all one would have to do was make up a name to match hers and try a bluff to get inside.

"Sister-in-law," Rachel said, correcting herself. "Maude was once married to my brother. She still likes the name."

"It's a nice name."

"She was to speak to Mr. Snyder for me."

"In New York?"

"Over there. My understanding is that Mr. Snyder has been in the Paris bureau for the past several weeks, expected back today. That's why I'm here."

Niya frowned, unmoved.

"We have this policy, miss. If you haven't an appointment, I take your phone number and tell you someone will call. It's the new security, because of the articles we run, statehood for Puerto Rico, Black Power, what it all means, you know, we get crazy threats."

Rachel nodded her understanding of security. Help me, Niya, she was thinking.

"I explained everything to Miss White."

Niya pressed an intercom button, turned away from Rachel, and spoke inaudibly into the mouthpiece. After less than a minute, she hung up.

"No Lily today," Niya said. "Out of the office, sick. The typist is taking the calls. She's a Turk like me. She says Snyder's calendar shows no appointments, so I know that's true."

"But he's here?"

"He's in with B.E.—Mr. Erlanger, Bruce—came in this morning, red-eyed and wrinkled, bag and baggage right off the plane."

Rachel looked up at the Caldwell photograph on the wall behind the receptionist.

"That's Mr. Duff, old C. C. Harrington," Niya said. "After him came B.E., the prodigy. Two editors in fifty-eight years. That's something, hey?"

Rachel had once thought it might be best to seek an appointment with the chief editor, but Maude had assured her that Snyder was her man.

"May I wait?"

"You can wait, but you'd better call him through the switchboard, and see if he picks up. Chances are you'll get the typist. Okay, hon, you can leave your story idea with me. Do you have something in writing? I'll see that it gets into the interoffice mail. . . . How long does that take? As the mail boy flies? Will it keep until tomorrow? Would you take Monday?"

"I'm due home Monday. Chicago."

"You're really Maude's kin?"

"Formerly."

"Not a press agent? We shoot press agents."

"Not a press agent. I've never done this before. I go to school, Northwestern. I model, Marshall Field's."

"I get it! College model! Is that your story? If you'll let me say so, a model goes to Northwestern or Radcliffe or Tulane is more like *Look* magazine. At *Life,* it's parties. With *Harrington's,* it's child geniuses. Ever notice that every two, three weeks, *Harrington's* runs yet one more story on this or that whiz kid who just invented a substitute for blood or something? I sit here and I read all the big magazines. I used to have this job at *Life,* the same job, editorial receptionist. Here, the pay's a little better, the book's a little classier, and the editorial floor, it's not so hectic. In this business, deadlines set the mood. A magazine like *Life* closes later for breaking news. *Harrington's* closes earlier for a more regulated pace. It makes a big difference in the tension, the atmosphere, yes? Nothing like *Front Page* around here. Anyway, what in hell is the, uh, World Institute for Survival Education? Did you make that up?" Niya laughed.

"No, it's real."

"You're not carrying a bomb, are you?" Niya laughed again.

Rachel patted her shoulder bag to show that she was unarmed.

"You are a little past the college age, in fact," Niya said, her smile lingering. "Don't take that the wrong way."

"I tried New York for a few years between semesters."

"Show biz, I'll bet. Well, see, that's more interesting, hon. Now, you don't have to tell me anything about your story, but maybe you'd like to tell me a little. I'm curious."

Niya interrupted herself to take a package from a messenger and to call in a visitor for the secretary to Bruce Erlanger, Miss Felicia Selby.

Rachel felt weightless, small, almost ludicrous. Still, Niya wanted to be important. She might help.

"I'm not here for myself," Rachel said. "I've volunteered a week to help a cause I believe in. The story I'm proposing has nothing to do with modeling. Not at all. It's about the war in Vietnam. It concerns a long march."

"Oho! In Vietnam?"

"No, right here, in America, seven hundred and fifty miles, sponsored by the World Institute for Survival Education—WISE, as we call it. That's what the Institute does. It educates people on life-and-death issues."

"You don't say."

"Seven, almost eight weeks, a group sponsored by WISE will walk all the way from Chicago to Washington—May eleventh to the Fourth of July—protesting the war."

"Is that the story, hon?" Niya's expression turned incredulous, then disappointed. "Mr. Erlanger won't like that—"

Rachel persisted. "Chicago across Indiana and Ohio and on down to Washington and the White House with a petition calling for peace talks. The story is about people trying to do something to get peace talks started and the war stopped. We thought *Harrington's* would—"

"A beauty like you is going to do this?"

Be calm, Rachel was thinking, you need her help.

"Actually not me, because of my work and all, but other people, more or less like me in how they feel about the war. They will be from everywhere, all ages, all kinds, maybe fifteen or twenty to start, maybe lots more before it's over. That's one point we want to make. The war's an outrage to all kinds of people, not just radicals and rock stars."

"So, tell me about that," Niya said, eyes glazing over.

Help me, Rachel badly wanted to say. She turned a hundred-watt smile on the receptionist.

"Maude says it's Mr. Snyder's kind of story," Rachel said. " 'Endurance stories,' she calls them. Expeditions, journeys, political campaigns, missions of one sort or another—last week, I looked up half a dozen by him—migrant farmers, the Antarctic—"

"Oh, yes. He's a traveling man, all right."

"Maude says—" Rachel waited, sensing that she had somehow lost Niya forever.

"Yes, he is," Niya said, abstractedly, "but I just keep the daybook here—make calls, and do my nails, do you understand? There are channels. Interoffice mail. The whole bit."

Something happened, Rachel knew. You said something wrong. Do you do tears? What more do you say?

Day four in New York, she was thinking. Four days' contribution to the Walk, taking flat rejections from contacts at four other magazines. There was Sunday afternoon at *Time,* a reasonably attractive senior editor advising you to "save your pitch, dear, we're for our side." He offered you an invitation to come by that evening for drinks, which you knew you might have accepted had he been more helpful. There were morning meetings Monday at *Life* and Tuesday at *Newsweek* that produced quick nos, respectively, from two feature writers, both women and both actually against the war. The Walk is a good idea for a story, both agreed. But "not our dish of tea," said *Life.* And "not enough space to do it justice," said *Newsweek.* And there was Wednesday at *Look,* most frustrating of all. "A week ago, we might've been interested," said the senior editor, explaining himself in the time it took for a frantic eleven-story ride in a down elevator at the end of his day's work. "We're doing the peace movement another way," he cried, running (he had said) for his train. And you realized that the imminent return of *Harrington's* Jacob C. Snyder is all there is.

Rachel saw herself slinking home to Chicago without a single expression of interest in the Walk.

She also saw herself dressing early that morning in her room on the seventh floor at the Roosevelt Hotel overlooking Forty-fifth Street with heart-pounding concern (all wasted!) for her first impression on Snyder. She put on the nubby wool sweater and the gabardine miniskirt from Marshall Field's (to suggest you're no greenhorn), low shoes (in case Snyder was short), and a Navy pea jacket (for the populist touch). Then, still anxious, she called long-distance to Samuel Lucas, director of WISE, and reviewed her failures thus far. Lucas was so Lucas, the bubbling optimist, always and still at fifty-two glutted with the confidence she herself lacked. The smile she imagined on his round, bearded, food-happy fat man's face had been a tonic. Lucas assured her that *Harrington's* would buy the story. "I always said it was their story. So did Maude," he told her. Yes, but then, she recalled, Lucas added his own little piece of bad news. A friend of WISE, calling from Philadelphia, had reported that their story had stirred no breath of interest at *The Saturday Evening Post,* either. Like *Time,* the *Post* was going with the government. *Et tu, Harrington's?* "Don't give up!" Lucas exclaimed, but croaking hoarsely, as though his age and one hundred pounds of excess weight had suddenly caught up with him.

"What's your pleasure?" Niya asked.

Even the morning's outfit fails, Rachel despaired, the sweater too bulky, the skirt too short, the pea jacket's Army-Navy surplus chic too much for the whole ensemble. In an effort to look both well and serious, you dressed like a seagoing bird. Surely, Niya Samerjan thinks you are an impostor. She is stalling until the guards come for you.

From behind, Rachel heard the elevator doors opening; then quick, startling steps, the squeak of brogans, the click of high heels; and then a renewed, but heavier silence after unseen people, presumably with special access, disappeared into the mysterious passageways behind the doors on either side of the elevator hall.

Access!

Sam Lucas says access is the real essence of democracy. Without it, you can only talk to yourself.

So many depend on you, Rachel told herself, you keep smiling at this woman.

"Help me," Rachel said.

"I can just take your phone number, miss," Niya said, "and I can put any papers you have through interoffice mail. The typist says Snyder's on deadline, so he's not going to take calls below the Secretary of State."

Rachel studied Niya's dark, square face, narrow eyes over wide cheekbones, a short nose and wide mouth with just the hint of a mustache in between. Maude had warned her; you don't offer a copy of your story memorandum and the WISE press release to anyone, except as a last resort, the way it had happened at *Time,* where you knew you had had no chance anyway. Talking a story is always best. Even the telephone works better than a memo or a release. When we buy, Maude said, we're buying you, at least by half.

But the doors were closing, Rachel knew. Your hotel-room phone number might not reach Snyder for days, depending on when a secretary with the unlikely name of Lily White should arise from her sickbed. Better, then, to leave one of the Institute's information packets—the Walk press release, the map of the route, several Chicago newspaper clippings, and the sheaf of testimonial letters praising the work of Sam Lucas, all neatly organized in folders waiting inside the shoulder bag.

Rachel handed a folder to Niya, certain that it would be a long time reaching Jacob C. Snyder.

"Snyder may have a deadline, you understand," Niya said. "But sooner or later, he calls people."

"You're very kind," Rachel said. "I understand."

Later, at the security desk in the lobby, Rachel discovered a Manhattan telephone directory and copied the only listed address for a "Snyder, J. C." Then a taxi drove her up Madison, through the Central Park transverse, and across West Sixty-seventh Street to number 38. Facing a pair of elegant Stanford White apartment buildings on the north side of the street, 38 was a nondescript brick high rise with a locked glass door guarding an orange stucco lobby. Rachel roused the superintendent and confirmed that his tenant was indeed the journalist Jacob C. Snyder. He accepted her dollar and promised to deliver the Walk press kit to his door. She scribbled a note on the cover, telling of her relationship with Maude Abraham and promising to remain at the Roosevelt Hotel all day Friday and Saturday and until her departure time Sunday in hope of a call.

THREE

Some Wars Are Better

I

At *Harrington's* on the fifteenth floor that night, it was almost ten o'clock when Jack Snyder, who had slept six hours in the past forty-eight, switched off the fluorescent ceiling box that lit his office, struck a match for the last cigarette in his pack, and stepped outdoors. His office boasted a brick terrace that, though small and grubby, made it unique among the staff writers' cubicles surrounding the editorial bullpen like so many stalls around an exercise ring. The fifteenth-floor setback provided both a very grand terrace for Bruce Erlanger's executive editorial suite and, almost as if by an afterthought, a brief extension beyond a high brick wall on the editorial staff side. The space in the extension barely allowed a canvas deck chair and an aluminum end table. But it provided a fine, clear line of sight south and east toward the United Nations building, and a place to go for a smoke. In 1958, Snyder had won the office in a staff lottery after *Look* magazine hired away its previous tenant, Gordon Mandelbaum, the veteran entertainment writer.

Snyder sat down in the deck chair. It was one of those brooding nights in New York when the stars hide behind very high, black clouds. His thoughts flashed to a woman friend named Bliss Carpenter and back again to his most inexhaustible concern, the work, the Monnet–Common Market piece, and the next job, on the urban crisis. He then thought, yes, there may be something for later in Phil Zimmerman's idea about home-front opposition to the war in Vietnam. How strange that Maude Abraham should have pitched an idea on the same subject in Paris, for her ex-sister-in-law no less!

Yawning, stretching against a wave of fatigue, he now leaned on the parapet and looked over and down to the top of a low building on East Forty-eighth Street. Work-to-the-last-minute Snyder, he was thinking, spent the previous evening going over notes with Jean Monnet at his apartment on Avenue Foch, where at virtually the last minute Maude Abraham and her French beau swept you into her tiny Citroën to race for the New York plane leaving Orly at 1 A.M. Then, landing at Kennedy, given the effort invested in Monnet and Paris, with side dashes for interviews in Brussels, Geneva, and London, you should have gone home to bed. But it is so typical to be here, defying the long plane ride and the certainty of a working weekend ahead. And for what? To check a few facts, which the copy checkers will recheck anyway. Crazy, man.

Behind him in his darkened cubicle, before Esther Wilmeth had even tapped on the door open to the terrace, Snyder sensed her approach. She was new since Snyder's departure, a bright, young Negro researcher assigned to help him fill the gaps in his story. The work he had intended to finish after the morning meeting with Erlanger had kept them both in the library well into the evening.

"Are you going home that way, Mr. Snyder?" she asked.

"Yes, on account of all the questions I forgot to ask Monnet."

"Please don't jump yet. May I come out? I brought you the rest of the British data."

"Admission is one cigarette, Esther."

"Left mine. I'll get them."

"Actually, I'm too tired to jump or smoke. More British data is just what I need to wake up. Thank you so much. Also, listen, please don't call anyone 'miss' or 'mister' on the fifteenth floor."

"Not even Mr. Erlanger?"

"If you think Bruce is a funny name, he answers to B.E."

Esther Wilmeth turned on the office ceiling light and began a sweep of Snyder's desk for the British data folder. She was twenty-five, stood five-six, stocky and handsome, with skin the color of dark coffee. Bending over, she patted Snyder's papers for the folder hidden underneath. She had long fingers and well-kept nails. A full ashtray surfaced and she emptied it into a wastebasket.

Snyder startled her as he stepped out of the darkness and down into his cubicle. Standing straight up and well lit, he seemed to come as an unexpected pleasure to her. He was nearly four inches over six feet tall, rather broad from side to side, but thin from back to front, with a slightly hovering posture, like a leaning tower. His head was large and sat egglike on a short, strong neck. His nose was a long straight wedge, large for his face, but balanced by a lantern jaw that he tended to lift, like that of a jeweler trying to defy the sight of his own eyes. Snyder's arms were not overlong for his torso, but he gave the impression of a gangling man, perhaps a former basketball player, or someone who used to tap-dance.

In fact, as Esther Wilmeth had found out for herself, baseball had been Snyder's school sport, and he could dance and sing, having performed creditably on the amateur stage, all according to his senior class listing in the 1948 yearbook of the University of Kansas. She had found a Thermofax of the listing in his bio file in the library. Other clippings and company forms also gave her, among other things, his birthday (September 9, 1924), birthplace (Topeka, Kansas), religion (Jewish), college major (English), and marital status (divorced: ex-wife Paula née Donaldson and seventeen-year-old twins, Eve and Andrew, living in Edinburgh, Scotland). He rather looked more like a Wasp, she had mused, than the mere ex-husband of one.

At that late hour, the attraction of all this for her was now intensified by other physical features, some as startling as his altitude and, again, seen as though for the first time. His complexion, though presently grizzled, was extraordinarily fair and pink where it was not freckled. He had the light-sensitive skin common among red-haired Europeans. His eyes were barely screened by the palest, yellow-white lashes imaginable. This peculiarity, along with rimless glasses, gave him an expression especially wide and inquiring, and contributed to a manner that seemed both guileless and insistent. Finally, although the hair on his crown was thin, close-cropped, and ginger-colored, a thick mustache covered his upper lip with hair so red-dark as to be virtually black. It partially covered a three-ridged surgical welt from the nostril into the lip on the left side. When Snyder smiled, the mustache would turn up, revealing notably big teeth and the welt ending abruptly, like a wound scar, rather than the correction for a harelip. It was, at last, the focus of one of the busiest faces

Esther had ever seen, busy on the surface and busy behind the eyes, unquestionably too busy for her, at least in the long run.

With another great yawn, Snyder sagged against the desk. He put on a narrow-brimmed felt hat, drew his suit jacket from a wall hook to the crook of his arm, and hoisted his B-4 bag and briefcase into a carrying position. On second thought, he opened the briefcase and tossed in the six four-by-five spiral notebooks from the Monnet–Common Market story, just in case a Great Inspiration needing confirmation or exposition might come to him during the night and blessedly shorten the process of writing his piece. Then with a tilt of his head, he indicated his full readiness to escort Esther out, to her office, the elevators, even a taxi, anywhere but to his own home, or hers.

Esther stood her ground.

"I stayed thinking you needed the British farm data," she said.

"You skipped dinner?"

"I thought you needed the data."

"You're very diligent."

"The library employs seven women researchers, all more experienced than me, that I'm trying to get ahead of."

Esther lifted her face to the light. She was still smiling, as though determination had frozen her last expression.

Jesus, she wants you to kiss her, Snyder thought. He met her look with a smile of his own. In that angle of light, she had lost the shadow under her fine cheekbones, but gained light on her mouth.

"I don't have any doubt you will make it, Esther," Snyder said. "I just can't do the British tonight."

Esther retreated in reasonably good order, stepping back to the door leading into the bullpen. His message received, she relaxed her face.

"What happened to your lip?" she asked. "Do you mind my asking?"

"Most ladies do, but they usually wait till the second date. I bit it."

"That's fine."

"It's true. There was a plane crash and I was in it."

"I shouldn't've asked."

"Really, in the war."

"Vietnam!"

"No, Germany."

"You don't seem old enough."

"At forty-two? Oh, yes, it was a very good war."

"Not like this one."

"Not at all—here or over there."

"Have you been to it?"

"There? No. We've got a man in Saigon."

"Philip Zimmerman?"

"My friend."

"He's very good."

Snyder smiled.

"Well," he said, "it's time. I'm dead."

Esther backed toward the library, which was entered through a narrow arch on the far side of the bullpen, near the corridor to the reception desk. In the bullpen itself, desks, tables, typewriter stands, and file cabinets had been shoved to the center of the room for an overnight spring cleaning. Two very stout women in blue uniforms were sweeping the winter's debris into a huge burlap bag. They exchanged winks and chuckled at the sight of Esther gliding away from Snyder's office with Snyder in apparent pursuit.

It was not unusual for *Harrington's* writers and library researchers to spend time together after office hours. As the deadline approached, it was essential to the magazine that they collaborate to get a story processed on schedule in its best form. Since most researchers were women and most writers were men, these working relationships frequently led to brief affairs and, once in a great while, marriage.

The one still most talked about was that between Felicia Jaffe, then a researcher, and William Selby, then a *Harrington's* sportswriter. They were married in 1959. Months later, Felicia took the job outside Erlanger's door as executive secretary, and her husband wisely followed an opportunity at the New York *Herald Tribune* to apprentice with that newspaper's thoroughbred horse-racing columnist. Felicia became known in the office ever after as Selby, jealous guardian of Erlanger's inner sanctum and, always linked to Erlanger, the subject of boundless, if discreet, gossip.

The very triteness of office romance discouraged some likely couples; so did the same long assignments and writing difficulties that plagued *Harrington's* marriages and other relationships outside the office. And the workplace dictum, thou shalt not defecate where thou dinest, gave pause to all but the most determined. Still, there were irrepressible attractions almost certain to arise in the process of fact checking and rhetorical analysis shared by any male writer, single or married, and any female researcher, more often than not young, attractive, and single. Everyone understood this. And since it was all in the family, so to speak, affairs among writers and researchers, or, for that matter, any other couplings among the two hundred eighteen employees in all departments who produced *Harrington's* every week, would really be nobody's business, usually ignored, and never equated with behavior in the outside world that might be considered truly scandalous, or even shameful.

Nothing concerning love among the staffers, for example, promised guilt even remotely comparable, for example, to the taboo against a romantic relationship between a writer and his or her subject on an assignment. *Harrington's* unwritten code of professional honor and duty, of course, prohibited all conflicts between public and private interest. But some violations were considered more heinous than others, none more unequivocally wrongful than bribery, which assumed that any exchange of money or sex or other favors on assignment gave the appearance of conflict regardless of any extenuating circumstance. Needless to say, no one should take cash or fall in love. And if one did fall in love on an assignment, presumably one would abort the story or resist the affair.

Professionalism had so imprinted this score on the psyche of *Harrington's* journalists that only two violations had been known to occur under the Erlanger regime. One concerned money, the other sex, and both had been punished by dismissal for the writer and death for the story. The tale of greed concerned a writer and a press agent promoting a Mexican uranium find in the late forties; the tale of lust involved a writer and the daughter of a Texas lawmaker in the late fifties. Snyder had known the hero of the latter; the man had actually got the girl (pregnant and married), but no new job to speak of until Lyndon Johnson had become Vice President of the United States and arranged something for the father-in-law's sake in public relations with one of the agencies in Washington.

Under the circumstances, the cleaning ladies' assumptions notwith-

standing, it was therefore neither repression nor anything like a taboo that prevented an attempt by Snyder just then to seduce Esther
Wilmeth. Rather, it was honest fatigue and a prior commitment.

At the door to the library, Esther ducked in and quickly reappeared with a cigarette for Snyder.

"Good night, Mr. Jack," she said. "You owe me a dinner."

"Yes, for sure," Snyder said. "Good night."

2

Snyder arrived at number 38 West Sixty-seventh Street just after
eleven with his Paris luggage, briefcase, and a bag of groceries.
Brodz, the building superintendent, gave him a shoe box full of mail
and the last four editions of the New York Sunday *Times*. Snyder
toted his cargo up two flights of stairs and let himself into his apartment, a "junior three" that rented for $280 a month plus utilities.
The place smelled of stale air and the cleaning lady's perfume. Turning on lights as he went along, Snyder stowed the groceries in the
galley-sized kitchen, then his gear in the bathroom laundry bin and
the bedroom closet, as appropriate. He shoved the bags into the
plywood cabinet that supported his innerspring mattress, which together comprised an oversized bed that virtually filled the room.
Then he dumped the newspapers and the mail on the plaid couch in
the living room, which was the only area of any size in the apartment. Bookcases and cabinets filled three walls; a dining table,
chairs, and a TV set lined the fourth wall under a large north-facing
casement window. Snyder tuned in the TV and poured himself two
ounces of Scotch whisky. He drank an ounce and added an ounce, to
which he added bottled soda water.

By then, the TV had brought up a gray-haired man rereading
tomorrow's headlines to conclude the nightly late news, a fifteen-
minute program from NBC. The economic indicators and Friday's
weather looked promising; the Vietnam War, a Black Power rally,
and a UFO sighting over Ann Arbor, Michigan, seemed ominous;
and major-league baseball was reassuringly imminent. Then the
credit titles rolled, listing B. Carpenter as assistant producer. The
broadcast emanated from a studio in Rockefeller Center; by the time

the news staff had wrapped up for the night and the studio car had dropped her off, it would be midnight.

Snyder tuned out the TV audio, turned on the phonograph, and set up a stack of records with Sibelius first. He liked to watch the Johnny Carson show as though it were a silent movie with background music. Drowsy, he thought about coffee. He brewed it slowly, listening to the tearful theme of the Second Symphony. Back in the living room, he added the whisky from his glass to his coffee mug, a reference to the belief widely held in the Midwest that the combination made the best stimulant for the late hours. Then he paused to look beyond his windows to the tops of the indomitable ginkgo trees that lined Sixty-seventh Street. He noted that their buds had become spring leaves in his absence. They seemed valiant in the yellow-green glow of the city's lamplight. You have to admire them, he was thinking. They never sleep.

Snyder sat down on the couch with the mail in his lap and his tired glance fell almost immediately on his own name and that of Maude Abraham in a note written across a large brown envelope; the note had been signed by Rachel Abraham. This would be the hand of the sister-in-law (former sister-in-law, his memory corrected) of whom Maude had spoken that morning on their dash to Orly.

Maude had begun, he recalled, begging forgiveness for having given your name to an "amateur publicist," Rachel Abraham, notwithstanding her status as a onetime relative. Smart, plump Maude insisted she had violated this section of their code only after the third phone call from Chicago, and then only for good reasons—first, because she, Maude, so hated the war in Vietnam and, second, because her ex-sister-in-law had an idea for a *Harrington's* article about the war that sounded all right, even a cover story if Erlanger could be brought around, and especially right for you. Even then, she had waited "until the last minute," to which you added, half jokingly, "until you have me trapped in a car." Sensing you might resist, Maude struck a fast bargain. If you would listen to the proposal, perhaps make a few notes, she would not ask you to see the sister-in-law (former) in person, only read her material, and decide.

"Okay, all right," you said.

Snyder studied Rachel Abraham's note. The script was impressively well formed and the letters invariably connected. The writer would have been a good girl in elementary school, diligent in her practice of the whirls and circles of the Palmer Method. In any case, given his eight-year friendship with Maude, not to mention her recent assistance during his stay in Paris, it transmitted material that he was obliged to read and to answer. Moreover, he acknowledged to himself that the story idea, as described by Maude, had aroused his curiosity, later intensified by the querulous Zimmerman memorandum.

Still, were Bliss Carpenter not en route from Rockefeller Center, he would have set aside the material to read in the morning. It was having to stay awake anyway that moved him to begin the process of generating a new assignment. A charge of adrenaline, unnoted but effective, refreshed him. He opened the pregnant envelope, then held it under his chin to fish from his briefcase a notebook from the Monnet–Common Market story which, when turned upside down and to the back, opened to the notes he had taken on Maude's Orly-bound monologue. He read:

"Maude: Everyone in Paris against the war, because the French were in Vietnam even under the Japanese. They knew when to get out. . . .

"Maude: How long can Phil Zimmerman endure filing Saigon dispatches for *Harrington's* like a sportswriter traveling with the home team? It's Bruce Erlanger making him do it. Bruce surely knows the Administration's program in Vietnam isn't right, but he's with it just the same. That's why the war can only be stopped in America. Human interest from the heartland is the answer! Washington proposes—the Midwest disposes. . . .

"Maude: The story is about bringing out of the Midwest on a protest walk activists of all ages from everywhere, proving that a united national movement against the war is possible. . . .

"Maude: Inspiration and leader is Samuel Lucas, Congregationalist minister, serving University of Chicago campus, founded World Institute for Survival Education (early fifties). Quotes Tolstoy, Gandhi, A. J. Muste, Martin Luther King. Also an admired friend of Maude's ex-family.

"Maude: WISE/Lucas intended to help build a liberal center-left constituency against nuclear weapons and international hubris, now

Vietnam, somewhere between SANE and Students for a Democratic
Society. . . .

"Maude: Who Rachel? Chicago family. Russian-Jewish father,
drama professor, University of Chicago. Irish Catholic mother,
housewife, former band singer, Mel Tormé's orchestra. Older
brother, Henry, Maude's ex, teaches international relations, Tulane.
Rachel withdrew from Northwestern University 1958, junior year,
for summer theater, then New York, with some talent, interesting
face, energy. Five years, Equity card, but few credits, and many hard
times later, Northwestern again. Now going on twenty-eight, un-
married, master's candidate in American history (U.S.-Indochina relations), part-time department store model, and member—along
with her mother—Women's Strike for Peace. Fine girl. Volunteer
worker for WISE, but schoolwork precludes walking. Too bad.
Good legs. . . ."

Snyder's eyes snapped open. He had dozed. His mail and the
notebook had fallen to the floor. He picked up Rachel Abraham's
envelope, registering for a moment that someone must have dropped
it off at his apartment rather than at the office. Then he read the
World Institute for Survival Education press release, its clippings,
and the letters of recommendation.

Only one item added an interesting footnote to Maude's day-old
outburst of advocacy. It was a publicity photograph of "WISE Director Samuel Lucas," showing full-length a fat, dark-bearded man who
did not look as though his bulk would endure seven miles on a
sustained walk let alone seven hundred fifty miles in seven weeks. A
brief biographical sketch attached to the back of the photograph
listed Lucas's year of birth as 1914. He was fifty-two, and looked like
Man Mountain Dean well past his prime.

Now Snyder slept.

He awoke at the sound of the intercom buzzer. He had pulled up
one leg to the couch and still clung to Lucas's photograph. A Cop-
land dance played on the phonograph behind a visit by Mayor John
Lindsay to the Johnny Carson show.

Snyder lurched to the hall door and seized the hand phone. Then
he pressed the talk button to open the line to the entry foyer outside
the locked lobby.

"Come up!"

"Do you know who this is?"

"You're the nice lady who works in television."

Snyder pressed the security button unlocking the lobby door. He opened his own front door and stepped off to the bathroom. Bliss Carpenter always ascended to the third floor by the elevator, which was slow at best. Snyder was at the door again when she came down the hall. She was a big Scandinavian woman with dark blond hair, athletic shoulders, and a rounded figure. She wore a dark tailored suit and carried a white raincoat, briefcase, and the bulldog edition of Friday morning's New York *Daily News*. She's even tougher than she looks, and more invulnerable than even your own ideal self, Snyder was thinking, so for nine years you can be lovers and still friends without explanation.

Bliss had been age thirty-nine for the last three of those nine years. She remained fit despite a hard-drinking life in a male-dominated world, so determined to be the next woman producer of network news documentaries that neither love, friendship, nor common sense could interfere. A Roman Catholic, she carried the name of and remained married to a man she had not seen since he took off for Alaska in 1951; no further information available. She met Snyder soon after she joined *Harrington's* staff by way of the Boston *Globe*, where she had shown early foot as a medical reporter. They became partners in an adulterous affair, his first, foreshadowing the divorce that would come seven years later. Their passion lasted less than a year, partly because Bliss changed jobs again, this time launching herself in television news. Still, she remained his friend, adviser, and favorite critic long after the lovemaking had become infrequent, not to say incidental. He had not seen her since the Christmas farewell party for Phil Zimmerman, nearly three months past. Now Snyder enfolded her in his arms and, for a moment, held on for dear life.

"I'm back," Snyder said, and kissed her full on the mouth. He knew, by taste and smell, that she had stopped at Hurley's Bar on Sixth Avenue before coming north.

"My, have we been away?" she asked, smiling.

"Can't you tell?"

Bliss returned his kiss, probing between his lips with her tongue. She pressed her body tightly against his.

"Yes," she said. "I can tell."

"Shall we stay in the hall?"

"Let's go inside. I need a drink, Jack."

Snyder's scattered papers, the cup and the whisky glass on the carpet around the couch amused her.

"Tell me you weren't working."

"I fell asleep planning the summer."

"Hold me. I don't feel loved."

Snyder embraced her again.

In his arms, she said, "How's the piece?"

"Tedious. Actually, I was just sleeping on an idea."

"Of course. Vodka, now."

"The whole story of one peace demonstration."

As Snyder described the WISE walk, Bliss eased herself into a chair beside the TV set. She turned the channel selector slowly through the seven available channels.

"I get it," she said. "Do it."

"Erlanger won't. Can't you hear him? 'No focus,' he'll say. Or: 'Despite the demonstrations, the war's still popular.' "

Bliss thought about that.

"He'd have a point," she replied. "Reason: no Martin King to make the anti-war case and embody it at the same time. Fifty thousand people protested at the White House last November, but the biggest name in the group was only Benjamin Spock. Who is Benjamin Spock, asks Lyndon Johnson, who? It's names that focus the news, Jack. No vodka?"

"Bruce can have a million excuses, all to hide the one big excuse, he's going with the mainstream. What do I do? All I've got is Scotch."

"Make leaderlessness the angle, silly—a rising protest looking for a leader. Maybe this great leader is among the handful of people on your seven-hundred-and-fifty-mile walk. There's your angle—you're Stanley looking for a Livingstone in Darkest America. Think while you pour, dear man."

"I'm thinking."

Snyder moved into the galley. Bliss stood in the doorway, watching.

"You can make Erlanger assign it, Jack. Threaten him."

"So I wind up at *Life*. They won't do it either."

"He won't let you quit."

"I can't test him. I've got other stories to do."

"Listen, there is no other story. Look at television. The networks've got a big stake in covering Vietnam itself. The protests are still a sideshow. But you let *Harrington's* and the other big magazines publish major cover stories on the peace movement, identify its leaders, not necessarily sympathetically, just straight and serious, and television will blow on the flame. The system feeds on itself. NBC White Papers! CBS Reports! Chet Huntley! Walter Cronkite! Ed Sullivan! You want a movement, you cover it and, first thing you know, you'll have a peace candidate running for President." Bliss spread her arms in supplication. "Big stakes, Jack! I say try, boy! Give it all you've got! Now may I have my drink?"

Snyder had begun to laugh.

Over his tiny sink, he fixed Bliss's drink, Scotch with water and no ice, the way she liked it, and presented it with a flourish.

"I'm not a propagandist," he said.

"Purpose ain't propaganda," she replied with spirit. "I recall, a year ago, you went down to the Washington Monument for an SDS demonstration. You're entitled. You vote."

"It was research. Zimmerman was just back from his first tour in Vietnam and wanted to see it. He and Harriet and I drove down. We didn't march. We watched. How Phil hated those students! He'd been covering the first contingents of American combat soldiers in Vietnam and here were boys the same age, all nicely dressed, nicely behaved, nicely deferred, saying no."

"That's Zimmerman."

"That was Zimmerman. He's turning now."

"So! So you've both got feelings. You can't help it. But still you're a professional journalist. Both of you, dammit."

"You're getting testy."

"I want you to do this story."

"Don't take it out on me. Bruce is the problem."

"He can't turn you down."

"Bullshit, dear. He knows—he runs this story, he spells the names right—he knows he escalates the peace movement, teach-ins, draft resistance—those two kids who immolated themselves last fall."

"Don't tell me. Remember, I edited the footage from the Pentagon—and the burning man was no kid, he was thirty-two, a Quaker named Norman Morrison. He burned right up, so awful, we showed about ten seconds of it on the late news—"

Bliss clasped her throat with her free hand for emphasis.

"Really awful," she added. "And it's going to get worse. The story's not going away, Jack. B.E.'s got to think of the competition. He must be afraid the *Post, Life,* or *Look* will grab this story or you, or both. I know you can make him afraid. Say, can another Scotch be done? I need the john."

While Bliss was away, Snyder poured a fresh drink for her and set about tidying up his papers. Then he heard the shower running, with Bliss humming throatily off-key.

He entered the bathroom and passed her drink around the edge of the shower curtain.

"I love you," Bliss sang out.

Snyder found cigarettes in Bliss's handbag, took one, and lit it at the living-room window. No ginkgo trees on his mind—he was thinking about business: the Monnet–Common Market article, followed by his next assignment, the team assignment surveying urban ghettos for the summer preview ("Hot Cities Again?"), could be followed by the WISE walk. The timing was right.

He was listening to the Sibelius once more when Bliss emerged barefoot in his candy-striped bathrobe, face shining clean, with a big towel wrapped around her hair. She tasted of his toothpaste.

"I'm into bed," Bliss said.

"You hungry?"

"I'll fix something."

Snyder bathed and shaved, and decided to ask Esther Wilmeth in the morning for a check on WISE and Samuel Lucas. Then he came to bed in a towel. Bliss had cut up an apple and some hard cheese. She was between the sheets with the dish on her stomach.

"Cheese is good," Snyder said. "Did I buy that?"

"No, I did. I stopped in the grocery. They said you'd been in, forgot cheese and cigarettes. I figured, 'He's gone a month, he must need cheese and cigarettes.' "

"A man has no secrets. Do I have cigarettes?"

"In the fridge with the cheese."

"I thank you."

"I thought I'd show off."

"To prove what?"

"I don't know. I've been missing something or someone. Maybe you, for Christ's sake."

"Come on, Bliss."

"I said 'maybe,' didn't I? I know you, Jack. You don't want to be missed."

"I liked being called in Paris."

"Maybe you'll call me next time."

Snyder kissed her and she embraced him. He felt her moving, setting the dish on the floor and slipping the sheet that lay between them to a point below her hips where, with a deft foot, she was able to remove it altogether. Snyder felt her familiar warmth against his legs. He made effortless love to her, holding the globe of one breast in his hand as, side by side, they moved together. She wanted very little penetration at the end, so she grasped his sex and held it just touching her. Her orgasm commenced in determined silence. It rippled on and on until one last contraction satisfied her and signaled his own as she allowed him to return into her depths. Snyder kissed her heavily and, almost immediately, fell asleep still partially astride her. He had last felt Bliss embracing him and supporting his long, wide plank of a body as though it were weightless.

When he awoke in midmorning, she was gone, a note taped to the bathroom mirror.

"Dear Jacob: Good morning. That walk is really a good idea. Call when you get work. Blissful."

FOUR
Sensitive Skins

I

When Snyder hit Sixty-seventh Street looking for a taxi that morning, he barely noted the sky above him where bosomy, white spring clouds slipped slowly along, west to east. They obscured the sun, but let through enough of the sun's more powerful rays to trouble anyone with sensitive skin and an awareness of the relationship between sunlight and skin cancer. Bliss Carpenter's piece on the subject had won one of the 1957 awards for medical journalism and inspired Snyder, ever after, in all weather, to protect his face with a hat or cap. Wearing something with a brim or peak became second nature to him. This day, for example, he had chosen for the first time a snap-brimmed Azores straw hat sent during the winter by his daughter, Eve, and stored in its original box, waiting for the change of seasons. On Snyder's mind, however, was the Monnet–Common Market deadline, with a subtrain of indecision about whether and how to present the anti-war walk story to Bruce Erlanger. The hat had simply come to hand. On the street, he was hardly more aware of it than the weather.

It was in the taxi heading for midtown, while sorting through the balance of his mail, that he discovered a lone photograph of Eve and Andrew, the Snyder twins, mailed by Eve herself from Edinburgh. There was no separate note, just "It's me and Andy. Hoot, Daddy!" in one corner. At seventeen, their faces were so achingly fresh, ruddy and dark like their mother's, long and chin-up like his. They looked both Scotch and Semitic, he thought, more the former after four years among the Donaldsons and MacPhersons, and all those

Methodists. With their last name changed to Snyder-MacPherson, they would be in New York in August, as they had been in each of the three Augusts since the divorce, but at no other time; this schedule was in the divorce settlement and still seemed the only plausible solution to the problem of visitation rights. He, of course, could have visited the twins in Edinburgh with Paula's permission, which, whether through excessive pride (why should Paula have such power?) or insufficient self-confidence (the annual month with Andrew's anger was already too much), he had never sought. Snyder returned the priceless snapshot to Eve's envelope, remarked the coincidence of the gift hat chosen and the gift photograph received, and slid the envelope into his briefcase on top of the WISE material from Rachel Abraham.

Then, his memory insisted, there were the twins at thirteen, on a cold night in autumn, when suddenly and surprisingly you learned that you were about to become single again. You'd come home to the brownstone duplex on West Seventy-first Street (controlled rent, but no taxis) filled with Paula's Shaker country furniture and lace curtains—coming home after two weeks spent in Washington researching a think piece on the presidential style of John F. Kennedy then captivating the nation (while, you would note, his Vietnam chickens came home to roost)—and there by the fire, in poses of sweetness unimagined even by Norman Rockwell for *The Saturday Evening Post,* you beheld standing together your dark-haired, apple-cheeked, immigrant Edinburgh nurse-wife, age thirty-seven, your pubescent melancholy daughter, her still childish pudgy twin brother, and their loyal old black standard poodle, who, as a puppy in 1948, was the Donaldson clan's personal wedding gift to their departing daughter (not to the son-in-law, who, no matter how non-devout he truly was as a Jew, was clearly a non-Methodist, too), a winning quartet, Paula, Eve, Andrew, and the poodle, named Françoise, all packed and ticketed for Scotland, obviously never to return. Paula's brass-trimmed steamer trunk, the one she'd first brought to Topeka, was the killer, until superseded by daughter and son's night-long silence.

It turned out that on her last biennial visit to Scotland—early fall 1960, after Erlanger sent you on the road with Vice President Nixon's presidential campaign (and Zimmerman with Kennedy's)—

Paula had met an old beau. Chemistry! A correspondence followed and here she was going home to marry the man, a Scot named Mac-Pherson, in apparent response to certain romantic expectations you yourself had never fulfilled, because she hadn't fulfilled yours, and vice versa to infinity. The Snyder-Donaldson marriage of fourteen years, from the bride's first kiss, your family's grudging wedding party, her family's resentment toward the presiding (Jewish) judge, etc., etc., was all a great and egregious misunderstanding, motivated by your romantic gratitude (was she not your nurse, the Catherine Barkley in your life?) and, frankly, her sentimentality (were you not her Jewish lieutenant, appropriately wounded, not in the legs, but the mouth?). It was an earthly match that could ne'er succeed, and had merely persisted between assignments until she realized that she had paid too high a price to come to America.

Say, who was the other man? Malcolm MacPherson was the name, obstetrics and gynecology was his game, and Edinburgh his ace in the hole.

That conclusive cold autumn night, there was no fight. Actually, it was relief that sparked your synapses, immediately followed by shock waves of guilt for the relief you were feeling. Paula's farewell address was superb; it bespoke not the complaining, long-suffering Paula, who must have suspected a Bliss Carpenter in your life, or one of the half dozen or so successors (by then) to Bliss Carpenter, but the occasionally dauntless, ambitious Paula, who would never have left you had she not believed she was getting a better deal from Doc MacPherson. And your own cuckold's acceptance speech wasn't bad either. You sought neither vindication nor reconciliation; you were rather a commentator on your own life's worst debacle, the first divorce so far as you knew in the Snyder family's history, and as the night wore on, you'd been rather more interested in reflecting on your role as a victim-benefactor of the sexual revolution (my God, she is taking the children!) than in discussing the problems of the transition to child support, alimony, and bachelorhood.

Still, over the long run, to this very morning, the most painful hurt of the act of separation was the twins' silence as they had witnessed your humiliation. Time and their visits notwithstanding, to receive the gift of a photograph from Eve on a day of no consequence, neither a holiday, birthday, nor anniversary, for no apparent reason other than a passing thoughtfulness and, coincidentally, on the very same spring day that you'd chosen to wear her gift hat, that is surely a sign of hope! The gods are at home! As he reached *Harrington's,* Snyder judged himself in such luck that he would press Erlanger before the end of the afternoon with the idea for the peace walk story.

Thus motivated, with a winning tip of his hat to Niya Samerjan at the reception desk, Snyder hurried through the usual hellos in the crowded bullpen and disappeared into his cubicle. He lowered the blinds against the sharp gray-yellow glare of the cloudy day and turned on the overhead light. You need, he advised himself, more information. In minutes, through Lilian White directly to Esther Wilmeth's attention in a big library job envelope, he bucked the WISE press release, Lucas's fat-man photo, the notes on Rachel Abraham, and the rest of the peace walk data. The envelope would bypass the office of the research director, ensuring Esther's first licks at following up its contents on a drop-everything, back-on-the-run basis— good for him, good for her.

While he waited, he pecked away at another first paragraph, his fourth, for the Monnet–Common Market piece. He had long since learned to think on the typewriter, building by the hour the tension that, before too long, generally found release in the discovery of a single sentence that defined his purpose. Abstract, thumb-sucking thought merely stole time from the hours until deadline; you write by writing. Just then, the message that seemed to be coming would not make Monnet happy; the failure of the Common Market to evolve into a United States of Europe was not such a bad thing for world peace and prosperity after all. One big European nation would probably mean one more insecure superpower for mankind to contend with, the piece was going to suggest.

2

About two-fifteen, Esther Wilmeth appeared in Snyder's doorway with two coffees, Rachel Abraham's papers, and the memo she had written about WISE. She wore a snug yellow sweater and a yellow ribbon in her hair. Snyder waved her to the cubicle's guest seat, a straight-backed steel chair with a straw-and-leather cushion. He tipped back in his own wooden swivel chair, cleaned his glasses with a tissue, and commenced reading her memo, taking a pencil to underline as he went along.

"WISE is a non-profit organization, as defined by the federal tax laws, without partisan political or religious sectarian affiliations. Its resources are, first, a mailing list of three thousand, being the names and addresses, nationwide, of subscribers to *Peacetime,* a monthly newsletter on world tensions written and published by Samuel Lucas from a liberal-libertarian viewpoint (maximum U.S. foreign aid, minimum foreign intervention) and, second, the largess of wealthy citizens, familiar funders of goo-goo causes, especially civil rights, civil liberties. Vietnam is moving the latter toward coalition with international disarmament and peace groups, such as WISE. . . .

"Lucas: An old-fashioned midwestern progressive preacher, favored interventionism only after Pearl Harbor, 'on December 8,' he once said. After the war, in his thirties, doctored in religion at Chicago and set up his ministry among the students. Korea as chaplain 1952, received minor wounds while conducting a Christmas service for Chicago GIs near Seoul. Convalesced in Japan, made repeated visits to Hiroshima and Nagasaki, interviewed survivors, and wrote a 35,000-word peace essay, self-published as the book *We Bear These Burdens,* a best-seller in the fall of 1955. Publication coincided with the tenth anniversary of the dropping of the atomic bomb and incorporation of WISE. In an interview at the time (see clipping, Chicago *Tribune),* he said, 'The cold war makes surrender unthinkable, victory impossible, and honorable peace through international agreements the only rational goal in the atomic age.' He described himself as a ' "peace activist," rather than a "pacifist," with faith in nonviolent resistance and civil disobedience, if necessary to achieve that goal.' Shades of Martin King. . . .

"WISE occupies three basement rooms in Lucas's home on Hyde Park Avenue, on the South Side, with a paid staff of three, including the co-director, Molly Hamilton (Lucas's wife), many volunteers. Also, five okay-board members, all Chicagoans, two lawyers, a businessman, a college professor, and a Chicago 'housewife' named Cecile Abraham, who was once mother-in-law of Maude Abraham in our Paris bureau. Is this a conflict? I think not. Her daughter is the

Rachel Abraham sitting over at the Hotel Roosevelt waiting on you. . . .

"IMPORTANT: Until the proposed peace walk, the most noteworthy cause for WISE has been a lost one, going back to 1963–64: WISE challenged the conviction ('illegal, violates due process') and four-year sentence ('cruel and unusual punishment') of a young man named Reed Herndon for draft resistance. Its lawyers (unpaid) appealed as high as U.S. District Court. They lost, hearing denied. Lower court (Springfield, Illinois) upheld, saying: draft resistance simply violates the Selective Service Act, since Herndon did not claim a religious exemption, merely a 'right to conscience.' No constitutional issue, period. . . .

"Herndon, twenty-one, a resident of Decatur, Illinois, began serving his sentence in April 1964 at the federal maximum-security prison in Leavenworth, Kansas. After nearly two years, he is about to go free, subject to the conditions of a parole—my source says WISE badly wants him on the peace walk, but can't confirm."

The Reed Herndon paragraph ended Esther's report. Snyder looked up from the page with a frown.

"You like?" Esther asked.

"It's fine," Snyder said. "Any more on Herndon?"

"He'll have a story to tell you."

"That's what I'm thinking, if he walks. Who was your source?"

"Called a Chicago friend at the *Tribune,* got out the clips for me, even knows Lucas. Herndon paroles next month, no travel restrictions, regular reporting to an officer, the usual thing. There's some caveat, unclear, a question about the parole. And one more thing—Lucas took heavy flak from the American Legion on the Herndon case, 1964. And then, just last month, because WISE supported a sit-in by Students for a Democratic Society at the Great Lakes Naval Station, an editorial writer zinged him, quote, 'for using tax-deductible contributions to undermine American resolve in Vietnam,' end quote, and brought up the Herndon case again."

At last, Snyder smiled. Esther met his eyes and beamed.

"So, now what?" she asked, like a pupil.

"We sit here and meditate."

"I see."

"Then in about a minute, we type a memo for Bruce Erlanger.

First, we need a working title, say, 'The Longest Protest' or 'Anatomy of a Peace Walk' or—what?"

"How about just 'A Profile of a Peace Walk'?"

"Not bad—but start with 'A Message for the President.' "

"I like that, too."

"So it's done. Can't miss, Esther! Let the Establishment beware!"

They laughed together. Snyder enjoyed her face; their joint brainstorm seemed a pure delight to her.

"So, now," he said, "we do a short memo for B.E., and wait for the sunrise. Normally, that's a week off—but give him a reason, like Maude's ex-sister-in-law at the Roosevelt, we might get an answer today."

"What do we do if he says no?"

"It depends on how bad we want it."

"Would you quit?"

"I've never wanted a story bad enough to quit, Esther."

"Now that's interesting!" she said, with great intensity.

"What do you think that means?"

Esther stood up. For a long moment, she held her breath and stared at Snyder. Then with both hands on his typing table, she leaned across his typewriter and kissed his cheek. Snyder felt her breath on his ear and his face uncontrollably reddening.

"It's because you've always been lucky," she said.

"How do you know?"

Esther receded with a grin. Her teeth were small and very white.

"Look at your life," she said. "Who wouldn't want it?"

3

It was nearly five and raining, with the Monnet article beginning to take shape, when a call from Felicia Selby in Bruce Erlanger's office broke Snyder's concentration. The jury was in already on the case of "A Message for the President—Profile of a Peace Walk."

"What's the verdict?" Snyder asked.

"Don't ask me, it's you he wants to see," Selby replied.

Snyder pulled up his tie and his socks, drew on his jacket, and finished a cold coffee. From the bullpen, he took the left corridor into the executive suite. Here there was a space for Selby, an inner storage room for file cabinets and supplies, a butler's pantry, and a very large office for Erlanger wrapped by the fifteenth-floor terrace with its view of St. Patrick's Cathedral. At the corridor entrance to the suite, the floor covering changed from blue vinyl tile to beige carpet and, inside, Selby's furniture was a cut above the standard issue.

The message of these changes in decor had long since been assimilated by Snyder, and so went unnoticed by him, but clearly it was intended by Selby, who controlled such matters, to assert her authority at the magazine as well as Erlanger's. To the alert visitor, it warned that she was more than a secretary, or more of a secretary in the original sense of the word, a keeper of secrets. There was little, perhaps nothing, going on at *Harrington's* about which she did not know or would not soon hear. Moreover, you knew she had Erlanger's ear, at least.

Like Erlanger, Selby was a few years older than Snyder. When, some years back, she had married and taken herself out of the researchers' rat race to become Erlanger's executive secretary, office gossip predicted she would not last. Her predecessors had been a series of much older women, all over fifty, all inclined to motherliness toward Erlanger and the staff, and all doomed to short terms in the chief editor's office by Erlanger's dauntless pace, at the office twelve hours a day, six or seven days a week. As it happened, Selby's qualities matched those of her predecessors—with stamina added, as Erlanger must have foreseen. She not only survived but quickly expanded the influence of her position, emphasizing the first word in her title, executive, as well as the second, secretary.

Selby now played a role in Erlanger's editorial decisions almost as influential as that of Jesse Rosenheim, *Harrington's* managing editor. And she had the one advantage that neither Rosenheim nor any other staff member could have, total access to Erlanger, night as well as day.

Office gossip speculated, conversely, on Erlanger's access to Selby's private parts; but without public evidence, no conclusion could be reached. If they were lovers, they were supremely discreet. Speculation continued because, on the one hand, clubfooted, childless Erlanger, a widower since his late twenties, had no public social life in the city or the suburbs and, on the other hand, Selby's marriage to the accommodating Bill Selby continued as it had begun, in a two-room apartment in Greenwich Village, childless as well. Speculation also continued because, on the one hand, Erlanger was not altogether a fish and, on the other hand, Selby was not altogether unattractive.

She was an even-tempered, snub-nosed, bright-eyed little woman who had only recently begun applying a blue tint to her graying hair. Winter and summer, she dressed in loose-fitting suits in the colors of the female sparrow. Only occasionally, jacketless in her customary brown or gray silk blouse and ramrod straight in her typing chair, did she reveal superb melonious breasts cantilevered over a trim waist. On such an occasion, were he present, Snyder would marvel at her figure and the style chosen to conceal it, so much revealed, so little suggested. It was all there, but no therefore. Sometimes he would even wonder about Erlanger; Snyder had never, ever, seen Selby looking like the morning after anything but a night's rest.

Fastidious Felicia! Upon his arrival, when unasked she tossed him two cigarettes, not his brand, but smokes all the same, he believed his luck was holding.

"Won't be long," Selby said. "Jesse Rosenheim is coming out."

"What's the mood?" Snyder asked, suddenly sensing a reversal.

"Bad, old dear," she said, using the intimacy reserved for Snyder and only one or two others on the far side of the corridor wall.

"Why?"

"Do I know? You can't say the magazine's ignoring your side—the Fulbright anti-intervention piece, the teach-in forum, the row between Gavin and Rostow."

"But overwhelmingly we've gone the other way, with my pal Zimmerman beating the drum from Saigon."

"What do you want from us? Even the doves at the New York *Times* won't say absolutely quit Vietnam. The great Halberstam wrote *The Making of a Quagmire* and said stay on. Our list of hawks is longer than your doves, Jack, and good Americans, too. Bruce Erlanger is no fanatic. He just doesn't want to see the anti-war thing grow out of hand, you understand? The ghetto riots have made him sick of any street crowd over two people. It's his new non-violent politics, ha-ha! Do the coffee, will you?"

In the butler's pantry, Snyder poured two coffees into white mugs faced with the *Harrington's* logo in midnight blue. He placed both mugs on Selby's desk and remained standing. He gave a sigh, intended to disarm her.

" 'Get it right before you get righteous'—who said that, Selb?"

"The immortal Duff Harrington." She smiled, escaping his trap. "But Bruce isn't being righteous. He just knows what you know—that publicity goes only one way. The war resisters win if you just spell their names right, and Bruce is dug in on that, Jack. Look, he's got enough trouble, all of a sudden, with Zimmerman."

"I know—I'm delighted."

"Your little pal was so gung ho. Now he tells B.E. that he must focus his next piece on one typical combat patrol to prove, at the end of the day, that nothing's been changed, that it's all meaningless. You see that he's going for a goddamn metaphor?"

"Indeed, I do."

"Can't you imagine B.E.'s reaction?"

"It's high drama, Selby! Let's publish Zimmerman's story. I'll step aside for a hawk's conversion anytime."

"No, no, it's no joke, Jack. The problem is that Bruce can't stop Zimmerman from crusading in Saigon unless he orders him back home. Even then, tomorrow, Zimmerman could assign himself to his metaphor, cover it for a week, two weeks—how could we stop him? —and with luck write the damn story before he shows his ugly face in here. And should Bruce refuse to publish it, Zimmerman can resign, publish it elsewhere with attendant publicity, and initial a book contract in five figures. He's home free and famous, while *Harrington's* winds up chagrined in a column by A. J. Liebling."

"It hasn't gone that far—?"

"So far that Bruce ordered Phil to take ten days R and R in Bangkok and flew over Mrs. Z. to take his mind off the war. Harriet was due back yesterday—but went to Saigon instead. It's a mess."

"I meant to see her this weekend. I didn't know."

"Guess the alternative? Bruce wanted to fly you to Vietnam from Paris to reason with the little rat, but chose Harriet instead. You don't speak of this outside this office, or I'll have you killed."

"It's our secret."

"Bruce will ask you to call Phil sooner or later."

"I don't believe you, Selb—what for?"

"A personal favor, to bring him home with Harriet. Listen, when Harriet leaves, and that's any minute, Phil Zimmerman proposes to cover a surefire fiasco, next week, a joint U.S.-ARVN offensive of some kind, above Saigon, conveniently classified so Phil can't talk about it. Clearly, Harriet hasn't been able to pacify him—she'd be here now if she had. And Bruce wants to avoid a final confrontation, at least until Phil's had a chance to talk with you."

"Why does he expect him to take it from me? He knows Phil."

"Phil wasn't Bruce's first choice for Saigon, old dear."

"So I recall."

"And do you recall how hard you pushed Bruce for Zimmerman over all comers to go in your stead?"

"You're not playing fair. This is Phil's second tour. He's in Saigon because that's where he wants to be."

"You hold his biggest chit, that's all. I'm not Phil's buddy, you are —not to say mentor as well."

"And B.E. wants a favor from me, but first he rejects my peace walk?"

"Approximately," Selby murmured, with an elaborate nod of her head.

"Selby, tell me the walk story is not a good idea!"

"Let's just say, if you're right about it, so is Bruce," she said. "He feels as strongly as you do. You have to give him that. He's a believer, too, in the President and the President's advisers. He fears China in control of Southeast Asia. He's worried about India and Australia. And he believes America has a moral commitment in Vietnam and, win or lose, a commitment is a commitment."

"Christ, Selby, what about Lyndon Johnson's commitment to stay out of it? What about preserving us from unnecessary wars?"

"Are you sure this one's so unnecessary? You let the Communists win in Indochina, it's Munich all over again, Jack. You sneer, but Bruce really sees it that way."

"Who's sneering? I'm trying to make the case for a good story. Why shouldn't people know what happens on the longest protest march of the war? It's like not covering the Crusades."

"Wait, Jack—the fact is, Rosenheim and Selby took your case not twenty minutes ago. You know what Bruce said? He said, 'If we had troops in Egypt backing the Pharaoh this afternoon, I wouldn't let Snyder cover the Exodus.' It's a big no today, Jack, and especially big with Zimmerman in revolt. It's just a bad time."

Snyder felt a pain behind the eyes. The court of next-to-last resort had ruled.

"It's just a bad time, Jack—oh, my, there's the light. Rosenheim's coming out. Damn, we didn't get a chance to gossip about Maude and Paris. And the new girl in research."

"You're evil, Selby."

"Aren't we all?"

4

Snyder took a deep breath before entering Erlanger's presence; whether this act of apprehension was primal or personal, he did not speculate, but from the first, it had come to him every time he prepared to cross that threshold into the chief editor's office. The pine door from Selby's was paneled and painted, cream-colored with a dark blue trim, anticipating the decor beyond, also in cream and blue, *Harrington's* colors. Snyder opened it with slow consistency, almost as an allusion to his singular relationship with Erlanger; after twelve years, you still felt as though you worked for him, not with him. Your staff colleagues and their spouses were the core of your life in New York, especially the Zimmermans, Jesse Rosenheim, Alex Cantwell, Abe Ferris, and Bill Selby (gone to the West Side) as well as Felicia; not to forget Bliss Carpenter, or the newcomer, for that matter, Esther Wilmeth. Collegiality with Erlanger, however, entailed almost nothing approaching intimacy beyond the use of first names. It was defined by hierarchy, not friendship, and predicated on getting *Harrington's* work done week after week in relentless sequence. Erlanger made you feel lonely in his presence.

In Snyder's view, the answer-to-nobody power of Bruce Erlanger was enough in itself to isolate the editor from his staff, but an innate shyness and a physical reticence compounded its effect, so that the warm life of the magazine in the corridors and offices outside his door had no chance at all to reach Erlanger, except through Selby, of course. Early risers might be acknowledged upon his arrival, late workers upon his departure, but he never circulated. When you met, it was ad hoc, as needed, and only in his own inner sanctum. Rumors that, alone, he would prowl the fifteenth floor after hours, checking layouts in the art department and unfinished manuscripts in the bullpen, were not proven, but religiously believed. No one ever found a note or a telltale sign of such paternal comings and goings, but his knowledge of everything critical to every deadline was uncanny. So the legend of his ubiquity persisted, perhaps as a necessary antidote for his everyday remoteness. During working hours, Erlanger seemed to be no man's colleague, a private, single-minded, cold-blooded character fortunately blessed with a benign, almost weak voice, his saving grace. Lacking a heart of gold, it was the best he had to offer.

As such, he was still a man toward whom you felt a strange longing; the burnt-tobacco smell encountered at the moment of passage through his door pulled you in even as it put you off. It somehow reminded you that possession was nine-tenths of Erlanger's Law. He owned the presses, and took your talent and energy in pawn for a ticket to the world, subject to the conditions of professional journalism printed on the back. He could afford diffidence, a quiet style, and a tutorial manner, allowing himself only an occasional cruelty for the sake of good order.

Yet there was more, perhaps cued by the poignant note of personality in his daily apparel. His suits were expensively tailor-made, his look slightly rotund, but still dapper, fashionably correct down to his special shoe, but unfailingly offset by the wrong tie or the wrong sweater or the wrong socks, worn as if to show *them* who really was the boss. And then the border-state twang in his voice gave it all away, if you knew enough of his story, as told in inadvertent bits and pieces over the years by Selby. His strength of purpose was rooted in Kentucky, his body in the manure beneath a thoroughbred he couldn't mount, his foot in a boot that didn't fit. He was the crippled eldest son of a disappointed horse farmer and his scatterbrained wife, devoting his life after Princeton to showing the family how well he could run a magazine, if not a bluegrass estate. He had become more than the sum of his parts, tough like father, blithe like mother, and uniquely competent so that his handicap would seem an advantage, a trump in the games he played with the lives of others, so long as the magazine survived. He made you want to surpass his expectations.

"Show me" was the command with which he sent you off on your assignments. It was Erlanger's corny little saying, used ad nauseam, but thereby never forgotten. You abided with it—not because you feared him, but because you loved your power to show him. It was your work in his eyes that determined your success, which meant you could go on and on, free to try anything as long as he'd let you. It was not pure freedom, but it was the best there was. You could leave, but you knew you could not do better.

Entering now in the wake of slim, pale Jesse Rosenheim's silent exit, Snyder predictably discovered Erlanger straight up in his high-backed leather swivel chair and facing him head-on. Erlanger, sitting, seemed taller than his five feet eight inches. He was soft-looking but not overweight, hairless above his dark sideburns, with skin the color of worn chamois. He had slate-green eyes under a rounded ledge of forehead and brow, a small but puffy nose, and small, flat lips. There were pink bursts in his cheeks from clusters of tiny, sclerotic veins, at a distance suggesting robust health, but at close range quite the opposite. Erlanger was one of those middle-aged males who, through lack of exercise, seem attenuated, barely able to survive the day, but never miss work, and make a good bet to bury every last one of their contemporaries. His slightly bloated, bleached face smiled somberly at Snyder through a screen of smoke expelled in a cloud from a freshly lit dark-wrapper corona held at the exact center of his mouth.

Erlanger was in a defensive pose familiar to members of the *Harrington's* staff, who had often compared notes on the man's reluctance to dispense bad tidings except in his own controlled environment. As opposed to editorial criticism, which he would freely dispense by phone or in an office (his office) conference, his rejections, denials, cancellations, and terminations would always come first from Selby or, in her absence, from Rosenheim. Then he would follow up, invariably having pre-armed himself with one of his favorite scepters. These were either a No. 2 yellow pencil, a briar or meerschaum pipe, or a contraband Cuban cigar; that winter, Norbert Pfaff, chief of the Washington bureau, had replenished Erlanger's cache of Monte Cristos in Havana following an exclusive interview with Fidel Castro on the fifth anniversary of the Bay of Pigs.

Erlanger, on defense, would also decidedly place between himself and his visitor his desk, the oversized square foyer table, formidably cluttered with the week's collection of mail, memos, and manuscripts; layout sheets, stills, and color separations; and an assortment of reports from every sector of the company on the interaction of all two hundred eighteen employees of the magazine. On days of good news and routine meetings, a low-key Erlanger would be found turned away from the desk, inviting you to a seat on the couch by the terrace windows or on one of the chairs around the conference table in the farthest reach of the office. But in anticipation of a disagreeable, if not downright distasteful, interpersonal task, he would assume a precise, and even adamant, sceptered centeredness, which fixed the standing victim in midspace, directly across the vast desk, perhaps looking down on the memorandum that had been submitted by him, proposing an idea for a story, now with the fatal check mark in the upper right-hand corner of the first page. Thus confronted, one might be paralyzed between fight and flight or, given Snyder's years of experience, resigned to defeat, but unwilling to desist.

And thus Snyder lit Selby's second cigarette, with a glance outside. Rain was falling steady and hard, and the spire of St. Patrick's Cathedral appeared as a wet, gray shadow.

"I gather it's no," Snyder said, "from Selby."

"I can't approve," Erlanger said. "You'll be gone two months and another month to write it. I can't spare you."

"You've done it before. That's not the reason."

"It's the reason I'm giving you."

"We'd be telling their side, factually. What's wrong with that?"

"I've no quarrel with your ethics, Jack. Not the slightest. It's your priorities—you could do three pieces in the same time."

Snyder whispered "shit" in his mind, but could not say it. Arguing values with the editor is a certain loser; the last word can only be his. Try topicality.

"We can't ignore it, Bruce—the peace movement begins to add up to a third force in the war."

"I don't concede that. We're just getting into this thing. Lyndon Johnson isn't for damn sure going to preside over another loss to the Communists—whatever Zimmerman believes, that's reality! As far as I can see, there isn't a peace movement to speak of, really, because every time they burn a flag or throw a rock at a cop, Johnson's approval rating goes up in the polls. Come to think of it, I might even assign your, ah, 'Profile of a Peace Walk' if I thought you were going to make that little ironic point. But I know you, Jack—you'll be perfectly objective, balanced, *Harrington's* precision instrument— but still, the story will make more of the peace movement than it deserves. You see that, don't you? This is not politics. It's editorial judgment."

Snyder knew he was in check and reduced to one last move. He leaned forward against Erlanger's desk, looming for emphasis.

"It's our own citizens thinking about the war," he said. "They don't have to be changing the world to make that a story."

"It's too much ado over too little, a fraction of public opinion, that's all," Erlanger replied, with a smile to signal the end of their duel. "You've made your point, Jack. I'm still negative."

Snyder felt his ears and cheeks burning, his mind in wretched counterpoise between shame and rage. He was immobilized. You expected it, he was thinking, no slightest concession from Erlanger, let alone a trade-off, the assignment in exchange, say, for helping bring Zimmerman home. And yet you stand waiting on his pleasure. How truly professional!

"May I have one last word," Erlanger asked politely, "while you sit down, over there?"

Snyder hesitated, but could not resist. No one left Erlanger's presence without a sign. He folded himself into the end seat of the couch, next to a pane of glass streaked with rain. At the desk, Erlanger had begun leafing through a file folder, recognizably filled with clippings of Zimmerman's Vietnam pieces. A minute passed. Then Erlanger handed the file to Snyder, who brought it unopened to his lap. Snyder had read everything in it—as Erlanger would know.

Erlanger frowned. "The news is that Zimmerman has turned against the war. We've been on the phone, since you left, maybe half a dozen times. He's up to making an unpublishable case for immediate withdrawal, an 'end to aggression.' He's held back on his last assignment, a new pilot's first combat mission, until I approve his next assignment. And when I said, 'Take a vacation with Harriet and then we'll talk,' he said, 'No promises.' He's over the wall, Jack."

"Times are a-changing, Bruce."

"The man thinks he's Graham Greene."

"Is that bad?"

"Oh, yes, it's bad. I'll be frank with you. I want him back in the States, that's definite. If I order him back, he can still do one last story. I want to avoid that embarrassment, so I need your help."

"Selby said."

"Sheer bribery. He can have the Washington bureau, a good two years before he could have expected it."

"Pfaff's job?"

"And Pfaff to Saigon."

"Wow!"

"Right away."

"Then you'll have Zimmerman in Washington."

"I'll take my chances."

"Did you speak to Harriet?"

"Once—she wants him home, but not without his balls. Can you imagine she said that?"

"Harriet? She's fine."

"Well?"

"He's my friend, Bruce."

"I like to think I'm his friend, too. I could fire him with a telegram."

"How does he know you won't next week?"

"Fire him? I'll give him a guarantee against it."

"There is none."

"Yes, one—I'm giving my word to Jack Snyder."

Snyder whistled. His eyes probed Erlanger's grim face, then glanced downward, fastening on Erlanger's special shoe. It was ankle high, made of soft black leather, with a square toe and a four-inch sole and heel. Somehow, he was persuaded.

"And you think he'll believe me?" Snyder asked.

"Only you."

"In effect, I'm giving my word, too."

"You're giving *Harrington's* word. If he won't take it, you can promise him, he'll come home as yet another unemployed war correspondent with the pip."

Erlanger's scheme had left Snyder with only disagreeable options, but this gratuitous cruelty provoked a momentary rebellion anyway.

"How do I do it?" Snyder asked. "Giving my word on something I can't fucking control—"

"You control it here, Jack, in this office. And Jesse Rosenheim may be leaving. He's not well."

"I've heard. I'm sorry. But right now I'd have to resign to prove you don't want me to quit."

"If you put it that way."

"Indispensable unless betrayed—Phil will laugh at that, Bruce."

"But, he'll understand it."

"I wouldn't bet on it."

"If he does, he's home free, looking at all the windmills in Washington."

"What time is it in Saigon?"

"Saturday morning. You'll call?"

"Yes, I suppose so. I'm not religious."

FIVE

The Wise Exploitation of Mankind

I

Saturday at 7 A.M., after a cloudburst, there was a Pan American Airways flight from Saigon via Hong Kong to New York with Harriet Zimmerman aboard. She was due home Monday morning, in time for lunch with the latest wife of a wealthy client whose East Side apartment needed a decorator. For Zimmerman, in the departure lounge watching the 707's clumsy ascent, it meant that he was back to covering the Americanization of the Vietnam War for *Harrington's Weekly World.* By what plan, he wondered, or Whose, did you choose to stay behind, looking up the asshole of politics in order to see blue sky?

Moments later, in a self-critical mood midway between anticipation and resignation, Zimmerman set off behind a Sikh driver in a cushy Citroën taxi to return to the city. The suburbs had awakened earlier to goat cries and temple bells. Now their cranky streets filled with city-bound traffic, from homemade wheelbarrow to armored personnel carrier, transporting mostly Vietnamese humanity to post or business or school or Saturday's market. There were few Americans in the flow; it was early for them and a day off for many. But Zimmerman gave their innocent absence a sinister meaning, a sign of his countrymen's remoteness from the reality of Vietnam, and from the people on both sides who were more than the sum of their political differences. Determined to make up for his own time of patriotic detachment prior to his present state of grace and passion, Zimmerman commanded his attention to wander in the crowd until, approaching downtown, his taxi stalled in a jam so dense that it resembled a social gathering rather than a passing of strangers. For several minutes, nothing moved at all. Then Saigon abandoned its patented stiff-necked stoicism, with which it had long endured the inevitable; it set up a noxious clang and clamor of horns, whistles, and shrieked commands to which Zimmerman instinctively adapted. Cursed with hypersensitive ears, he had long ago perfected techniques of avoidance which, by now, were second nature to him. He rolled up his eyes and forced his senses skyward through the taxi's sunroof, open now to the fragmenting clouds, and into a state of self-hypnosis, where he found personal silence.

When he felt the taxi move again, Zimmerman was in no hurry to return to reality. His body was almost supine in the rear seat. The top of his head appeared just above the windowsill and both feet rested on the floor, which only his toes could have touched were he sitting up. Through the sunroof, he could see swatches of blue behind and above the clouds and utility cables and an occasional brown-green frond, still wet after the downpour.

Harriet, he was thinking, seems to understand your remarkable conversion from war lover to war hater. She would. She has no politics.

The hard part was arguing for your own inner consistency, how both positions, before and after, pro-war and anti-war, respectively, can represent a single concept of "doing justice," the meaning of justice to life, by Zimmerman out of Jack Snyder, who once defined it as "the wise exploitation of mankind." He and you came to that after many laced-coffee nights at the office, exchanging views on the uses of power, the inevitability of corruption, and the biblical imperative "to do justly," etc.—all B.H., Before Harriet, 1956, 1957, when the issue was still Korea and the United Nations and massive retaliation. Snyder had found those words for it, so pompous that they made you laugh and kept you from taking yourself too seriously, or Jack, either.

However, "justice is the wise exploitation of mankind" adhered to the back of your mind. Over the years, it helped cement some loose bricks in your thinking about God and the state, especially American democracy, and carried you through your moments of change, especially most recently, when it became your measure as to the justness of the war, which had been inexorably moving from winnable to unwinnable, and thus from "wise" to "unwise," from hope to futility in the exploitation of manpower, as well as mankind—in conclusion, unjust.

Oh, an invasion of the north by one million Americans backed by tactical nukes might do it, but even Lyndon Johnson almost certainly can't sell that to the American people, nor (remembering Korea) is it likely that the Chinese, whose containment is the only remotely rational excuse ever offered (Eisenhower, Kennedy, Johnson) for the present mindless pursuit of Communists in Indochina, will stand still for it. No, once you can't believe that a war is winnable by any reasonable commitment of conventional force, further killing in the name of victory becomes immoral, and an immediate settlement by political means becomes the only prudent policy.

Prudence? Is not that the cardinal virtue of your church? Yes, but what about the indivisibility of freedom that makes South Vietnam's fight our fight? Hey, what about that?

Certain defeat is no service to freedom, that's what.

Now, Zimmerman thought (after pausing for the flash and mosquito whine of three pairs of low-flying F-4 Phantoms on the rise from the Tan Son Nhut air base), you would sooner or later have been converted from hawk to dove by conscious observation and objective analysis; some thirty interviews in the past sixty days had already pointed clearly in that direction.

But, his thought train continued (after pausing again for a fourth pair of Phantoms and a moment's reflection on their probable destination, mere seconds into the countryside), that a particular dream—nightmare, actually—should have forced change upon you only shows that a man's ego stake in his past opinions and future credibility won't keep his brain from asking questions in secret. Nor will the answer permit repression; if necessary, the truth will appear in a hallucination straight from Hieronymus Bosch.

Remember how it came to you on another return to Saigon, not long ago, airborne a mere thirty miles back from the Iron Triangle by Skyraider (USAF A-1) among a gaggle of Skyraiders, after a morning and an afternoon on "A Day in the Life of Patrick X. Finley"?

You'd dozed for no more than a moment, but dreamt (never to be forgotten), unforgettably, of a sphincter closing about your neck, your head trapped in your own anus, while your excreted body dangled below, headless in limbo over a flaming jungle landscape, not in hell, but right out there in Vietnam, burning down to shores of sky-blue water in the bottom of a toilet bowl, in which both the horror inside and the horror outside were simultaneously experienced in a single montage.

With disgust, as he remembered the dream, Zimmerman exclaimed inwardly, "Beautiful!"

Then, he recalled, in reality, sitting (as only a little fellow could have sat) squeezed in behind First Lieutenant Pat Finley, a twenty-year-old pilot on his first mission and putative subject of that *Harrington's* profile. They flew in second position in support of an ARVN-Australian infantry attack, following the squadron's flight leader, whose approach suddenly and silently failed in a strange catapulting leap from air to ground to air and, once more, to ground and utter disintegration without smoke or flame, just a little dust. The dead man's name was Tsuru, Captain Henry L., USAF. He was Japanese-American and had drawn a bye for that day's mission, which he flew anyway so as not to miss the chance to get his family's name in *Harrington's Weekly World.*

Remember Finley's head turning. He had met your eye, caught your nod, and banked the Skyraider into the pattern of low-level attack. Had he spoken, you would not have heard, with the cotton wadded in your ears.

You dropped napalm, you two, on the targeted village off Route 239, northeast of the old Michelin Tire Company plantation, and on all that remained of poor Tsuru. And then as young Finley climbed and banked, you saw successive Skyraiders dive into the smoke followed by blossoms of flame that replicated your own.

"Beautiful!" Finley said, must have screamed into his mike.

He was a Roman Catholic, like you, and God had let war fascinate him, as it had yourself since Korea, only young Finley's trip had just begun and yours, as you would soon learn from the dream, had just ended. You had slept well that previous night in your own bed. You had enjoyed breakfast at the pilot officers' mess at Tan Son Nhut. You would dine with your young hero, on the *Harrington's* expense account, that evening on the roof at the Intercontinental. (And there, with dainty-fingered Saigon's twinkling, tangled night charm spread out below, Finley again cried, "Beautiful!") But still, on that flight back to base, you had not been able to resist the urge to sleep, without which there could have been no dream, no news from the interior.

So what was that dream of blood and shit, if not your immortal soul's condemnation of your own gratuitous collaboration with your country's unjust program on behalf of one side in an unwinnable civil war?

"Gratuitous" was the right word, Zim, so right! Such a nice, polite word for an American depositing fire blossoms along Route 239, leaving behind roasted people, only one of whom could not be called a complete stranger. Except for Tsuru, the dead were Vietnamese, some friends, some enemies, some neutrals, engaged in a war between the states of Vietnam. What difference would victory or defeat make for our national defense? security? interest? No one really says. What effect on the cause of freedom, or even anti-Communism? No one really tells. What's at stake here now besides our pride? No one really answers, for the price already exceeds any virtue. Lesson learned: when cost exceeds value, don't buy.

Still, there's a better argument, simpler, less ideological. Once a man concludes on grounds of military and political reality that no American force large enough to win the war will ever be committed in Vietnam, he can no longer support the war, period. Any defense of a war policy is immoral that coexists with the certain belief of its inadequacy and full expectation of its failure. And so to condone sending more men to kill and be killed is to condone immoral government, perhaps even criminal government. This now is the correct formulation. You did not arrive at it overnight, but having so arrived, you have had to act on it—ask Erlanger!

Did Harriet understand this? Of course, but she was also a pawn, a diversionary thrust. Ever the realist, Harriet.

Erlanger merely said he was sending her to help you rest, while he took some time to think about your memos, calls, cables, conclusions. It is thirteen days, Zim, better than any honeymoon. Do what you think is right, my love, Harriet said. But don't forget, she also said, B.E. runs the shop. Fair enough. She's always been for both sides. Ever the realist, Harriet. The job is not what I need, you said. No, she said, it's your balls, you need your balls, my love! It's what we all need, even Jack Snyder, you replied, and asked: Is there *Life,* ha-ha, or *Look* after *Harrington's?* Yes, but no change, she said. Ever the realist, Harriet. I love you, she said. I love you, you said. She cupped her hand around the issue. So long, Phil; come home safely.

What do you do now?

Wait for Erlanger's reply? You've had it already; it's implicit in Harriet's coming and going. The answer is no.

Do you then finish the Finley piece, calling it "Death and Defecation on Route 239"?

Do you, rather, stall? Write another memo, asking, "Well?"

Or do you ignore New York, and cover the Michelin siege on the ground, the story of the 1st Infantry Division, wasting good men, our best men, to do what the ARVN can't do—protect their own capital city?

It would not be long then, by death or by dismissal, before a new man for *Harrington's* resided in Saigon at the Hotel Elysée. Abe Ferris can't wait to make his bones. And that slime Bert Pfaff in D.C.

But, at least, little man, to be yanked back home with two salable stories—is better than skipping out with just one.

2

It was 9 A.M. in Saigon, and just past 8 P.M., the night before, in New York, as Phil Zimmerman's taxi glided to a stop at the curb in front of the Elysée, a modest hotel with a quiet American bar and a good Thai kitchen. Zimmerman leased rooms on the fifth and topmost floor. He had found the place on his first tour in South Vietnam and had paid a premium to lease it again on his second. His apartment was tiny, but comfortable, with three deep dormer windows looking back toward the Presidential Palace. It boasted antique French wallpaper depicting pre-colonial peasant scenes in yellow and green on the ceilings as well as the walls, and a shower with a glass stall. The Lilliputian sitting room had a desk and a typing chair, both of which Zimmerman had scrounged in the flea market, and a private, French-style cradle phone. A book rack on the desk held the eleven books of history he'd read about pre-modern Indochina, about the French era and the Japanese occupation, and about the American involvement since Dien Bien Phu. A box on the floor overflowed with a mildewing collection of embassy and mission press releases; the international editions of the American newsmagazines dating back to January 1965; and the past three months' supply of the airmail editions of the New York *Times*. His own research files and his special .45 caliber Army service pistol and holster were in a cabinet next to the refrigerator in the kitchenette. In all, this was the *Harrington's* bureau office. Its only seeming drawback was the single bed, to which Zimmerman had been attracted by his marriage oath.

Zimmerman sat himself in the typing chair and wheeled into the curtained dormer space, where he might catch the morning breeze. Then he read again the New York call message that Jack Snyder had left within the hour. He propped both feet on the windowsill. Obviously, Snyder was back from Paris. He has never called you in Saigon before. He would not be calling to say hello. More likely, based on your last month's memo, he wishes to welcome you to the nest of *Harrington's* doves. Or perhaps he's met a girl in Paris, and wants you to be the first to hear, again, that she's it!

Or none of the above, lucky little Phil.

Zimmerman dialed the overseas operator. Then Saigon put him on hold for New York. It was not that Snyder's night number at the office was busy; rather, there were no circuits at all to the States.

Waiting, Zimmerman bit his nails. He was a man of thirty-seven years, wrinkled in seersuckers, wearing a white tennis shirt and cordovan loafers without socks. His corn-silk hair was combed straight back from his forehead with deliberate defiance. He was pink-faced but severely pocked from adolescent acne and burdened with thick glasses on a bumpy nose. He was also afflicted with small, aquamarine eyes that turned blood red around the irises when, as now, he had been up all night and had tasted wine. (He'd drunk champagne in farewell to Harriet.) He was nearly ugly and, although almost ideally proportioned with broad, well-muscled shoulders and narrow hips, a very short man, the only child of small parents.

Growing up in Canonsburg, western Pennsylvania, he was the darling of an unlucky Catholic Bavarian couple named Von Zimmerman. His father, a consumptive survivor of the Somme, was a hapless traveler of back roads for a seed company who earned $3,000 in his best year and died of heart failure on V-E Day, three years older than the century. He always voted Republican. His mother, a diabetic, longed for Munich, which she had left as a young woman thought to have promise as an organist. With carrot (cocoa and cookies) and stick (a twelve-inch ruler), she taught piano at home for twenty-two years. Mourners at her funeral in 1946 (she was dead at forty-three) included more than fifty former pupils. They spoke of both her devotion and her discipline and seemed to have loved her more than her son had known. He strove to please her, despite an almost equivalent and competing need for status among his peers. At her urging, and unable to avail himself of the usual cultural opportunities (athletics, fighting, and girls) and, therefrom, to win respect in his old neighborhood, he graduated at the top of his high school class. With his parents gone, he became the first of his family or his crowd to acquire not only a bachelor of arts degree but also a master's degree (University of Pittsburgh, economics, 1950), all in four years. And still driven—notwithstanding night blindness, myopia, the tenderest eardrums, and numerous allergies (dust, tomato plants, wine)—he then applied for enlistment in the United States Marine Corps, requesting combat duty in Korea. The Marines turned him down, but for none of his ailments. Zimmerman's height at four feet eleven and one-half inches was half an inch too short for any service.

Two months later, however, in the fall of 1950, Zimmerman presented himself for enlistment in the United States Army and was accepted, his height just above the minimum five feet, at least momentarily. Over a period of weeks in a neck brace designed for whiplash victims, Zimmerman had hung himself from a doorframe chinning bar for a total of twenty-eight hours, three of those on the morning of his afternoon physical. He had gained the necessary half inch but narrowly missed rejection anyway, since the final stretching exercise had numbed the left side of his body and rendered him incapable of reflex when struck on the left knee with a rubber hammer. Fortunately, an excellent reflex from the right knee satisfied the examining physician.

Sixteen weeks' training made Zimmerman an infantry rifleman and another two weeks placed him in Korea with a mortar squad in deep trouble about halfway between the 42nd Parallel and the Yalu

River. Battle noise tormented him, but twice during the great retreat from the north, his sensitive hearing picked up night sounds of an imminent ambush and enabled him to alert his squad to danger. The second alert won him a Bronze Star.

During the stalemate, Zimmerman applied for the tank corps, only to be assigned as a chauffeur in the car pool servicing the Office of Public Information at Military Headquarters, Seoul. The possibilities of a lifetime career in journalism soon occurred to him and became manifest when, on submission of a copy of his M.A. thesis, he was promoted from corporal to buck sergeant and assigned to write summaries of the armistice negotiations for the *Army Weekly Gazetteer,* published in Seoul. His political maturity commenced about the same time. Zimmerman reached voting age and mailed home an absentee ballot for General Dwight D. Eisenhower. (In every subsequent national election, Zimmerman continued to choose Republicans. "Don't blame me for Vietnam," he had once said to Snyder. "I voted for Barry Goldwater.")

In time, as reprinted in *Stars and Stripes,* the *Gazetteer* pieces brought Zimmerman to the attention of Conrad McMenamin of the Associated Press, chief of the Tokyo bureau. On McMenamin's advice, Zimmerman took his discharge in Seoul, and remained as an AP stringer covering Korea. He dropped the "Von" from his byline and, after a year, moved up to the Tokyo bureau. McMenamin raised his salary from $67.50 to $90 a week. Impelled by need and inspiration, he interviewed Chiang Kai-shek in Taipei in anticipation of the signing of the U.S.-Taiwan mutual defense treaty of 1955 and wrote a piece for which *The Saturday Evening Post* paid him $1,000. Then he determined that his future would be in magazines, not the wire services or even the newspapers, because, as he told McMenamin, "I've got more to say about the war of the worlds than I can get into a lead 'graph." In translation, he meant that nothing less than writing for national consumption on the grand scale of the weekly magazine could possibly satisfy him. And McMenamin helped him with that, too. When Zimmerman transferred to New York, he carried a letter of introduction from McMenamin to *Harrington's* Jack Snyder, to whom McMenamin, as Atlanta bureau chief in 1949, had also given the first job of his professional career.

Zimmerman's initial meeting with Snyder took place on the fifteenth floor at *Harrington's* in Snyder's pre-terrace cubicle. There followed a job interview with Erlanger, arranged forthwith by Snyder. And ever after, now going on ten years, Zimmerman would believe that the best proof of luck in life was his relationship, thus begun, with Jack Snyder. Even a good marriage, begun two years later with the estimable Harriet Stewart, five feet five inches tall, would seem only second best, close behind although still (by her choice) without issue and (by his own admission) weighted down by his consequent chronic self-doubts and sporadic outbursts of jealousy.

At first glance, Zimmerman, born 1929 in Pennsylvania, had little in common with Snyder, born 1924 in Kansas, besides the ubiquitous Conrad McMenamin of the Associated Press. Zimmerman not only was five years younger (and fifteen inches shorter) than Snyder but also had lived through the depression at a different stage of youth, fought in a different war, and expected a different future: his, Catholic conservative pessimistic; Snyder's, Jewish liberal optimistic. While Snyder was already in the process of compromising his marriage, in and out of the office, Zimmerman still despaired of marriage itself, having yet to find a woman under five feet tall who would accept his proposals. Nevertheless, Zimmerman's heritage was not unlike Snyder's; both young men were driven by moral imperatives to do both well and good in print. And it was the force of complementary characters so shaped—the short and the long of it, so to speak, with Zimmerman's need for protection neatly suited to Snyder's desire to protect—that was destined to unite Zimmerman with Snyder, not only in friendship but also in the special dimension of pupil and mentor, even though Snyder had preceded him on the staff by less than a year. Indeed, that dimension all but defined the friendship for Zimmerman. His luck was that, as a novice eager to learn, he had somehow found Snyder anxious to teach.

To begin, Snyder taught Zimmerman the difference in form between the inverted pyramid of news dispatches for the Associated Press and the dramatic, often narrative structure of the magazine article.

"Article writing is an art form," Snyder insisted, "very minor—very, very minor—but an art form because there is a sense of the ending in the beginning."

Then Snyder volunteered to yes-no Zimmerman's story ideas before they were sent on to Erlanger. He lectured on research techniques never learned doing college papers. He shared his priceless book of telephone numbers. When several early anxiety attacks threatened Zimmerman's ability to transform thought into language, Snyder preached patience and courage, illustrated with horrible examples from his own personal struggles with writer's block. Snyder also offered in great detail his worldly knowledge of expense-account cheating, which *Harrington's* tradition allowed in lieu of payment for overtime. He even provided advice on office philandering, though not after Zimmerman's enviable marriage.

Finally, as Zimmerman's professor, Snyder discoursed on all of life, from alienation to xenophobia, but he was always best on how to do the work of journalism: above all, how to be (never assume); then how to conduct a private interview (first talk about yourself, be truthful, make yourself known, then ask questions); how to organize a magazine article around a single theme (any relevant idea with a verb in it will do, then modify it); how to retain long quotes without seeming to take notes (listen well, trust your memory, do your notes in the men's room); how to sustain one's focus (keep a journal on a prolonged assignment—summarize the drift of the story every few days); how to justify good writing that hurts good people (don't live for friendship; integrity lasts longer); how to respond to a subject after he has read about himself and hates you (remember, his game is self-promotion; ask him whether he would have had you lie—he's no friend if he would); how to live with your mistakes (admit them, say you're sorry, do better next time); how to live without praise (never expect it)—and on and on, defining the essence of his professional self in hundreds of axioms that Zimmerman secretly recorded in secretarial notebooks, of the narrow, back-pocket type favored by Snyder.

By 1958, Zimmerman was a *Harrington's* star in his own right, his first cover story a piece on the American response to Sputnik. He had also met the woman he would marry.

Harriet Stewart was a witty, curly-haired California blonde, not tall, but half a head taller than Zimmerman. She had very clear, tawny skin, almond-shaped eyes, and particularly full lips. Snyder very much approved. She was thirty, a year older than Zimmerman, and had lived long enough and hard enough to know a reasonable compromise when she saw one. Raised a Baptist by foster parents in San Diego, she had married at eighteen, divorced at twenty, and fled to New York at twenty-two. There, she parlayed a low voice and high breasts into advertising sales for a chain of trade magazines with offices in the Empire State Building. When the company was sold to a publisher based in Detroit, Harriet quit, and moved in with a girlfriend who covered fashions for the *Herald Tribune*. She applied her severance toward tuition at a school of interior design. A blind date arranged by Bill Selby, an office friend of her friend, turned out to be Zimmerman, a little man with little experience, whom she introduced that very night to the pleasure of fellatio. Best man at the non-denominational wedding was Jack Snyder, and although his relationship with Zimmerman necessarily expanded to include Harriet, she resented his bond to her husband.

Zimmerman sometimes protested to Harriet that Snyder was "only" his best friend. But mainly, he kept them apart and to himself his hope that he was Snyder's best friend. Sometimes he worried that he could not return the favor of Snyder's patronage, especially and above all his intervention with Erlanger for the initial Saigon assignment. But he felt he was doing his best to express his gratitude through loyalty, support (especially in the later years of Snyder's second bachelorhood), and information, as from Vietnam (given that Snyder had opposed the war long before Zimmerman's conversion). He loved Snyder.

And nibbling at his fingernails, he realized that Snyder would only call were he, little Phil, in deep shit with Erlanger.

The connection, bringing to his ear Snyder's cheery greeting, a routine concern for his health, and a quick report on Paris, echoed and overlapped uncomfortably, as though relayed between rooms of glass. Then suddenly, as though a switch had been thrown, it cleared and there, reassuringly, was the redheaded bean pole's Kansas twang that always seemed to emanate from his sinuses rather than his throat —asking after Harriet.

"Splendid, but gone home this morning," Zimmerman replied.

"Everything all right?"

"She has a job to do."

"Well, how was Bangkok?"

"A dream."

"What about you?"

"You tell me."

"Louder, Zim."

"Bruce is pissed, huh?"

"Give me a chance. I've got a whole speech to make."

"How about my Michelin story?"

"Listen, man, the 'immediate withdrawal' memo is a crusher."

"Nothing worse than a converted sinner, Jack."

"You woke up old Bruce, I'll say that."

"He'd pay attention if it came from you."

"Oh, yes? There's a peace walk from Chicago to Washington. He flat out rejected me. You're not alone, Zim."

"You mean you're with me on the story of the lost patrol?"

"Here's my speech, Zim. Can you hear me? Bruce wants you to take over the Washington bureau, with Pfaff next in Saigon. The trade-off is come home now, you understand? He thought you might want to fly back with Harriet."

"He can't wring my neck till he gets his hands around it, can he?"

"He gave me his word."

"You believe it?"

"Yes, I do. And Zim, he's bringing you home, no matter."

"You're sure?"

"One way or another."

"How about in a box?"

"You know what I mean, schmuck."

"I don't want Washington now."

"Washington bureau chief, that's his deal. There's more money in it, too, but I don't do overt bribery."

"I have the lost patrol to do."

"He won't print it, Zim."

"He'll have to, or get another boy. And I'll place it. Does he know that?"

"Yes, he knows that. He wants to avoid—"

"What did you say to him, Jack?"

"I said I'd call you."

"Will you quit with me now?"

"Quitting changes nothing—how do you influence Erlanger if you're not on the staff?"

"Don't you see? He won't let Jack Snyder quit! Harriet says Rosenheim is sick."

There was a long silence in Zimmerman's ear. The breeze picked up and fluttered the curtains on the dormer window. Zimmerman felt tears in his eyes. Don't you see, J.C., he was thinking, Erlanger's more afraid of losing you to the competition than anything in this world. You must see that. You have real power.

The connection crackled, breaking up Snyder's voice. Zimmerman felt pain in his ear.

"Say again, Jack?"

"I said, 'I'd like you to come home, and take the bureau.' "

"Well, fuck all."

"Be realistic, Zim. Where can you do better? The other books have a lineup of staff guys stretching round the block waiting to go to Saigon."

"I can free-lance. There's lots of monthlies, looking for writers."

"It'll take you a year to get anything into print, for sure. Working out of Washington, at least you can keep digging. Think of all the shit there must be. I'll help you. Even Erlanger says he'll take his chances."

"Obscenity, Jack. Obscenity! Do you care about me?"

"Care? Listen—there's a big Vietnam story in the States now, Phil. The war can be decided over here, in the damn streets."

"Please answer the question."

"I care about you more than you care about you."

Zimmerman lowered the phone to his shoulder. His throat closed as he swallowed. He felt the sphincter around his neck. Then, as from a great distance, Snyder's voice came to him.

"Zimbo, what do I tell Erlanger?"

Zimmerman sighed.

"Tell him I said no," he said, and hung up on Snyder.

If they're going to decide the damn war in the damn streets, Zimmerman was thinking, all the more reason for the story.

SIX

A Good Man Nowadays

I

Outside was an almost-spring night that almost smelled sweet, the rain gone, having left behind a momentarily washed-off city, breathing air which, for a change, could not be seen. The terrace door into Snyder's office was open. Snyder sat parallel to his desk under the blue-white fluorescent ceiling light, arms folded, legs crossed, facing his reflection in the cubicle window. He saw the image of his own exasperation in the language of his body, a tight, tense, angry thing with red hair and flushed cheeks, wearing a white shirt, buttoned-down but tieless, smoking a dry-tasting cigarette. He had not wanted to believe that Zimmerman would hang up on him, but there was no denying it. New York had restored his Saigon connection within minutes and a hotel clerk confirmed that his party was not taking calls.

In his mind, Snyder began replaying bits of his conversation with Zimmerman as though some one exchange would explain everything. Nothing came of this. Again Snyder's anger rose, then leveled off, and gradually drained into philosophy. An honorable journalist's resignation over a difference of opinion is comparable to an honorable soldier's refusal to fight, noble in conception, feckless in practice. No man is indispensable. Zimmerman knows this as well as you. He was not only asking too much but proposing nothing with half a chance for success. You do not bluff Erlanger, ever. And now, little Phil is not taking calls, undoubtedly at his hotel bar nursing a major case of friendship-betrayed-by-Snyder.

Snyder closed his eyes. He imagined himself towering over Zimmerman, arguing with him, appealing to his common sense, and finally persuading him to return home. But then, quite the opposite vision intruded. Zimmerman is standing up to him, asserting that the war is a matter of conscience to be considered irrespective of pious professionalism—pride, that's all professionalism is, anyway, a camouflage and a cover for bias, subjectivity, and corporate politics. Quitting the magazine, Zimmerman proclaims, is much more than an expendable employee's last resort in a dispute with his editor. It is a citizen's protest against the war itself, a principled public act, and all the more noteworthy if multiplied by two.

Snyder remembered the Monnet deadline; without it, he might just then have marched down the street to Click's Bar, where surely some of his colleagues would still be about, to chew together on Zimmerman's defection far into the night.

Still, he could not resist staring at the telephone. There is always the telephone, now staring back, asking to whom you wish to talk about politics and the journalist. Damned if you'll dial Mount Kisco. Erlanger can wait until Monday for a report on Zimmerman. You might talk to Harriet—no, she's in midair somewhere over the South China Sea. Bliss Carpenter will be out, working. Esther Wilmeth might be home, but that would be rushing things. Jesse Rosenheim is hopeless and perhaps worse, while Selby is too nosy (the same as talking to Erlanger). Unconsciously, Snyder lit a fresh cigarette. Then who?

He panned at random across his cluttered desk, over his notebooks, his typing paper, carbons and onionskins, over Esther's research on Monnet, the Common Market, and the British coal industry, and over last night's still intriguing brown envelope from the World Institute of Survival Education autographed by Maude Abraham's former sister-in-law, Rachel Abraham. His eyes stopped at his empty coffee cup. He remembered food, forgotten since breakfast, without hunger.

Then with a turn back to the telephone, he put through a call to the Roosevelt Hotel, asking for Rachel Abraham, who answered the hotel operator's first ring. Snyder identified himself, adding an apology for the late hour. There was unabashed warmth in her response, telling of a lost expectation suddenly found. And the next moment's exchange about Maude established the appropriateness of continuing their conversation on a first-name basis. At the same time, with the phone clamped between jaw and clavicle, Snyder opened a fresh notebook and scribbled down the date and two file words covering their subject: Peace Walk. Even if nothing was to come of the story, Lilian White would routinely save any exploratory notes, along with his idea memorandum and the WISE presentation, against some future need, a related idea, or even a second effort. You never knew.

In her room on the seventh floor at the Roosevelt, Rachel sat with the phone carriage in her lap near the head of the twin bed closer to the bath. She was barefooted, but still dressed for the street in a sweater and skirt. There was a TV set at the end of the bed, playing *Sullivan's Travels,* with Joel McCrea and Veronica Lake. The old Sturges movie was a favorite of hers, not least because of the laconic actor playing Sullivan; oddly enough, his flat, prairie accent was nearly a match for the voice of Jack Snyder, telling how he had found her presentation at home last evening. She almost mentioned it.

Snyder, too, remarked the woman's voice he was hearing, the sharp Chicago drawl softened at the edges presumably by the buffing of time, according to Maude, she'd spent elsewhere. He liked it, and the way she laughed after recounting her hapless meeting with Niya Samerjan and her decision to deliver the presentation to his apartment in the middle of the night.

"You were wise," Snyder said. "I'm in my office and Niya's copy isn't here yet."

"Oh, my," Rachel said.

"Worse—the news isn't good, Rachel."

"No?"

"Boss says no."

"How come?"

"He's got his reasons. I told him I couldn't think of a story I'd rather do."

There was no reply, only a faint buzz on the line. Half a minute passed in silence. Snyder thought of Zimmerman.

"Excuse me," Rachel said at last. "I was hoping—you understand —I'm not walking, so publicity was my contribution."

"I did my best—bad news at *Harrington's* usually takes two weeks."

"Everyone's saying no in record time. *Life, Look,* the *Post*—and *Newsweek* and *Time.* Now you. What does it mean?"

"The war's popular, and you're still on the fringe."

"Such a shame!"

"There's always television."

"Tried in Chicago. Producer said maybe, if we make the White House, we'll get fifteen seconds on the evening news, not more, unless somebody commits suicide. Very funny."

"Story ideas are a lot like new inventions. Sometimes the best are hardest to sell."

"You mean they laughed at Edison?"

"Something like that. At least you're laughing."

"I don't cry in public. At least now I can eat. And a good night to you, Jack Snyder."

Snyder knew he might then have ended their conversation. Instead, he chose to move back one sentence, as a favor to Maude, he might have said, but, actually, in response to Rachel's tone.

"Haven't you?" he asked.

"Eaten? Only my fingernails."

After a split-second pause, Snyder, who never lied easily about anything, said, "I was just going for a quick hamburger and a beer. Any interest?"

"Oh, my, yes—both."

"I'm on deadline. Do you mind coming up this way? A place called Click's?"

"Okay, thank you very much. I noticed it yesterday."

"I have Maude's description of you."

"I've one of you, too—same source."

2

Click's Bar was at the foot of a cast-iron staircase in the basement of a marble mansion protected by the city's Landmarks Preservation law. In front below street level, there was a Victorian mullioned window which provided the men at the long oak bar with a sporting view of the knees, calves, and ankles of some of New York womanhood's best legs. Beyond the candlelit bar and through a thickly plastered wall was a small, bright, oak-paneled dining room, with the kitchen hidden beyond. After nine, most evenings, under a single recessed spotlight, a trio of clarinet, bass, and piano set up in one corner of the bar calmly played jazz antiques, the best after midnight when the crowd had thinned to the regulars, a mix of male and female journalists, copywriters, and politicians who, as a subspecies of Manhattan life, still clung to their music in the age of rock and roll.

Waiting in the bay of the front window, Snyder acknowledged the nods and waves of several acquaintances further into the room who, with backs to the bar and drinks in hand, were listening to the music. When he saw the woman who was surely Rachel Abraham descending outside, he finished his White Label and moved quickly to meet her at the door, before she could have a chance to worry that she might have to stand alone at the bar waiting for him. Her eyes, almost blinkered by the high, upturned collar of her pea coat, brightened in recognition; his took in the triangle of Rachel's olive-skinned face, and her heavy Gaelic brows, sharp cheekbones, and wide, rougeless lips—"not a real beauty," Maude had said, "but a face of mixed emotions." Snyder closed the gap between them and they shook hands. He heard her thanking him for rescuing her from the Roosevelt Hotel café, which, she had just learned, was closing at that moment. Then she was apologizing for arriving five minutes late, the time lost on the phone with American Airlines making plans to leave on the morrow. Her expression struck a fine balance between disappointment and enthusiasm. Snyder felt as though he had known her for about twenty years.

He led her to a table in the corner of the dining room farthest from the jazz trio and gave her coat to the captain. She wore a tweed vest open over a white blouse, discreetly vented above her confident bosom and tied with strings at the throat. The freshness of the blouse let Snyder know she had taken the trouble to dress for him.

Over their meal, they had readily spoken three languages, his, hers, and the immortal third, the latter with gestures and signs and eye contacts all the more telling because both wanted to think that nothing more remarkable could come of their meeting than an hour's conversation with background music. She learned Snyder would be working all night; and he that Rachel planned to leave for Chicago, not on Sunday, as originally scheduled, but next morning to save Saturday's hotel room rent for the Walk. These very limitations freed them; instead of despair over the failure of their respective missions, his with Zimmerman, hers with the New York magazine world, they felt a kind of shameless relief as they briefed one another on their respective obsessions: her passion for her cause, his for his work. Further, over coffee, they were impelled by the particular chemistry of the moment to exchange private lives. So, after Snyder outlined his hard times with Paula, Rachel commenced a telling of her own more recent escape from an engagement to one of her father's young colleagues at Chicago.

"His name was Finbogassen," she said, "first name Jimmy, the terrific scholar of modern drama. He was about my age, clever and non-political, very promising and also amusing, an Icelander, a devout atheist. I'd bombed out twice as Marjorie Morningstar, both at Northwestern and on Broadway, yes, and wanted to find the real me, so I thought a two-hundred-pound nihilist intellectual might do the trick. I knew he wasn't Mr. Quite Right—but what is so rare as a right man these days? We met last July in Chicago; spent August—I mean, the whole month—on a lake in Wisconsin; engaged in September back in Chicago; and broke up in October on a return flight from Reykjavík. He was the King of Hearts all right, but only on amphetamines, all unknown to me until he failed to provide for himself when we stayed an extra week in Iceland visiting his parents. He tried iced vodka, but speed had spoiled him for mere alcohol, you know the song. So much for Jimmy Finbogassen, who has removed himself to Santa Fe, for the dried mushrooms, I have a hunch. And so much for the real me, whoever she may be—and you, you are not, by any chance, taking—it's none of my business, I know—taking anything? I don't mean notes."

They laughed together.

"Regular cigarettes, is all," Snyder said. "Are you?"

"No, just dreams," she said. "At twenty-seven-plus and counting, I think I'd like to be a married teacher, go live in Canada, raise some kids without worrying about the war."

Renewing coffee, they had smoked and talked about the peace movement and Vietnam and warfare in general, leading Snyder, for the first time in nearly twenty years, to account without jokes for the World War II scar under his mustache. He began by explaining to her that being wounded had left a small corner of doubt in his brain that he should have any right to be alive at all, which, in turn, gave him something that he had to prove over and over again, say, every day. As it happened, he went on, shrapnel had gouged out a large section of his upper lip in late 1944 on a bombing run over Düsseldorf. It was his eighteenth mission with the same pilot and crew, seventeen without injury to anyone on board. Several cosmetic grafts restored the lip, although cysts and periodontal threats to his upper teeth, which had been miraculously spared, continued to plague him.

"I don't need the mustache to hide the scar," he concluded. "It's really a tolerable thing. But I've worn it ever since the last graft, like a monument over a tomb, so I won't forget how we crashed in Scotland on the way home and, by sheerest absurdity, hardly conscious, I was one of two not killed, and the other is still a hospital wreck."

The surprise ending brought Rachel's fingers forward to touch Snyder's hand, which held a full coffee cup halfway between saucer and lip. Snyder flinched. Rachel's hand leapt back and Snyder brought down the cup without spilling. The safe landing amazed them and they laughed very hard.

"You see," Snyder said, "no faith, but still a lucky man."

Rachel was still smiling. "Bite your tongue," she said.

"What makes you think Anyone is listening?"

"It's the chance you take."

"Anyone we know?"

"I can't make Him out. Can you?"

"Not since I was a kid. I hear He died."

"But still, bite your tongue."

"There."

"Now you can have your luck."

Rachel blushed, as though sharing that childhood superstition too soon had brought them too close.

"I'll drink to that," Snyder said, too late recognizing that he might be too clever. It meant one drink already too many, with another White Label en route.

Rachel smoothed the tablecloth where he had set the cup. Without looking up she said, "I'm sorry about your crash, about your friends."

Snyder covered her hand with his. The back of her hand felt cold. "I didn't tell it right," he said. "I meant to say that being good doesn't account for who's lucky and who's not. That's what I'm trying to remember."

Rachel raised her eyes. "I guess everybody wants to believe in justice."

"Yes, on that, the whole world's Jewish."

It pleased him to see her smile.

"You're relentless," she said.

"How did we get into this?"

"You stopped telling war stories."

"You stopped me."

Rachel brought her elbows to the table, clasping her hands under her chin. "All right," she said. "I'm listening."

"What's to tell?"

"About the C in Jacob C. Snyder."

"For Charles."

"As in Chaplin?"

"Charles Evans Hughes. He was the greatest Republican of the age, next to Coolidge, and my mother could hardly call me Calvin. Charles was her idea of a real American name to modify Jacob. Her hero of heroes was the greatest Republican of them all, the martyred Lincoln, but she couldn't call me Abraham, either. Fortunately, Lindbergh came along, and I could live with Charles. Now you don't have to wonder why I always wanted to fly."

Rachel laughed with delight. "You mean flee," she said, "from your mother, of course."

"Watch it," Snyder said, grinning. "When you prick me, I bleed."

"Oh, I knew," she said. "Now begin with 'I was born.' "

Snyder found he could not resist, and did not want to. It is not only the White Label, he was thinking.

"I was born," he said.

"I'm glad."

"Oh, yes, Topeka, Kansas. I had a grandfather from Odessa. Deserted the Russian Army in the Caucasus. Walked to Belgrade. Then shipped out, the long way around the world. He finally landed in San Francisco, 1879. Changed his name from Tschacbasov to Jacob Snyder—and decided to stay."

"He was working on your DNA."

"A mighty man he was, or so I was told. Now he was thirty years old, and set off overland from San Francisco to New York, a sort of a reverse pioneer, to find himself a proper wife, whom, it turned out, he would meet in Lawrence, Kansas. Her name was Ida and they moved to Topeka. She died giving birth to little Jonah, my father. Meanwhile, Jacob started working Shawnee County, trading farmers' eggs for city folks' old chairs and tables. Before long, he had himself a secondhand furniture store. He put Jonah to work at age twelve and there was another son, named Noah, who died in a traffic accident on the way to the Battle of the Marne. He was in the store, too, until the Great War. When Grandpa Jacob died, 1921, Snyder and Sons was all firsthand merchandise, the best of everything from Grand Rapids, and the largest furniture store in town.

"Oh, Jake Snyder was a giant in his way, a front-page obituary when he died. My father always said I was lucky to carry his name, something denied my older brothers, David and Joshua, who were born and named while Jake still lived, and so he wanted me, more than the others, to go into the business when I grew up.

"That was until 1937, when all the customers stopped paying their bills and Snyder and Sons went broke. The bank took our big house and we moved to a small house on the street behind it. From then on, through the depression and the war, my father ran a tiny little furniture store, mostly secondhand stuff, on the edge of town, still called Snyder and Sons, and he endured. The wheel had turned full circle, and then some. Dad played a little cards. He also had to have a scam or two. Making a living in furniture was his life, so you can imagine what it meant to be hustling, besides. A man of integrity, too."

Snyder paused to light a cigarette and crossed his arms across his chest. He saw Rachel shift in her chair, while her eyes remained riveted on his face. She is the perfect listener, he was thinking, intense, yet half smiling, with a seemingly infinite range of nods and headshakes to encourage the most reticent speaker, let alone one whose trade is listening. You, who never tell any stranger a story, except to elicit a story, so why are you telling this story to this stranger now? And so eagerly!

"Don't stop," Rachel said.

"Just resting," Snyder said. "This is where the imperial Flo, Florence Walishinski, my mother, comes in. She was born in Warsaw, 1898, only child of a bicycle repairman, who died in steerage. With her mother, my grandmother, Flo went to live with a cousin in St. Louis. Grew up almost beautiful, with small hands and perfect teeth. She was a reader of books, especially Melville and Dreiser, went two years to business college, and marched with the suffragettes. She could sing 'Onward Christian Soldiers' without choking on the cross of Jesus because she knew who she was and, when both her mother and the rabbi objected, she said they were in America now and you could sing everybody's songs.

"Finally, they packed her off to a stenographer's job across the state in Kansas City with the Missouri and Great Plains Gas Company, where she met my father at a Purim party for local misses and any eligible Jewish males who could be found west of the Mississippi. He promised her wealth, status, and new furniture in Topeka ever after. So she went and, as I said, I was born.

"All fine, till the thirties. With the store in trouble, she took over as bookkeeper, but never forgave my father for promising her a rose garden. To get even, she told her sons, especially me, not only to get educated but to get out of town. No son of hers was going into the store, and no son did. One's a doctor, the other's a chemist, both in Seattle—than from Topeka, you can't get much farther. Except where I've been, from time to time."

Rachel interrupted. "But he must be proud of all three, no?"

"He was proud of us, for sure, although when he died, I was still working for the Associated Press in Atlanta. And after he died, when we were closing up the store, we felt pride in him for the first time, for keeping it going for as long as he did. Then she died in Seattle two years ago, and we realized they'd both persevered, and meant something in many lives, and what else can you ask of anybody, whether Anyone's listening or not? What do you make of that, Rachel?"

"Well, Mr. Tschacbasov, to produce you took more than luck."

"Yes, it did, didn't it?"

"Yes, it did."

"Yes. Two wars and a depression."

"Even more, maybe."

"Maybe."

"Okay, maybe."

Snyder found he could make no further argument. Rachel's eyes were too bright, even misty, so perfectly distracting.

Then it was 1 A.M. and Snyder signed the check. The waiter brought Rachel's coat and a plastic dish with Snyder's receipt. They stood by the table. Snyder placed three dollars in the dish.

"How's Phil Zimmerman?" the waiter asked.

"Coming home soon, Marty," Snyder said.

"With nightmares, I'll bet."

"I'll bet."

Marty, the waiter, left them. As Snyder helped Rachel with her coat, her blouse tightened across her chest. Snyder felt his damnable cheeks redden and momentarily turned from her lest she mistake his appreciation for a proposition. There had been, he thought, all too much intimacy already. Of course, technically speaking, she was no longer part of a possible *Harrington's* assignment. As a story, the WISE walk was dead. Thus, the rules against fraternization need not apply. But they restrained him nevertheless. Dinner with Rachel on company time, on the company tab, in the context of company business, a rejected story idea, acted upon him like a vaccination; it stimulated the symptoms of desire and, in the end, immunized him against promiscuity, his or hers. Feeling cool at last, he faced her again.

"Isn't Zimmerman your man in Saigon?" she asked.

"Phil Zimmerman, yes. Also my friend."

"I've read him, no comment. Coming home?"

"Yes, he's sick of it."

"I can imagine."

Snyder would have liked to discuss Zimmerman with her. She was, however, in this one instance, still a stranger.

They walked through Click's and climbed the stairs to the street. Above Forty-ninth Street, the iron-blue night sky was clear and specked with faint starlight. The air was still fresh. At the corner of Madison Avenue, they turned south toward the Roosevelt. The hour required Snyder to walk her to the hotel entrance, leaving her in safety with the doorman. He took her arm as they crossed Forty-eighth Street. They stopped for a red light at Forty-seventh Street. In minutes, she would be gone.

"So you'll be at Northwestern?" Snyder asked.

"Mid-June, my orals," she replied. "Then my master's thesis, Abraham Lincoln versus the Mexican War. It's to prove that the only winners in a bad war are those who oppose it."

"Lincoln didn't win. He had to leave the Congress."

"He got to be President."

"A war President—how do you square the Civil War with pacifism?"

"I don't. I'm not a pacifist. I'm a protester."

With a sudden movement, Rachel stepped between Snyder and the curb. She seized his hands at waist level and raised her face to his.

"Say you understand the difference," she demanded, with a smile.

"I am on your side," he said. "I swear it."

"I'm just making sure. Yes, I see it in your eyes."

Snyder might have kissed her, saw that she wanted to be kissed, but he did not. He felt her let go of his hands.

Rachel took a step back, teetering on the curb.

"You've got your deadline," she said. "I'll go quietly."

"Now you misunderstand me."

"Want another thesis? Very brief?"

"Sure."

"There are only half a dozen good men in the world. The rest don't count. So—if a woman should meet one of the six, she should let him know."

Rachel stepped toward him again.

They kissed through the change of the traffic signal, from red to green and back to red. Her lips were parted and felt wondrously soft on his. Her tongue fenced tentatively with his. Her arms rested firmly inside the knobs of his shoulders. Her right hand, warm on the back of his neck, seemed weightless and yet inescapable. A staggering passerby growled a suggestion and they released one another, helplessly laughing. Then Snyder stepped to her side and took her arm. They crossed the street and walked on.

"Oh, my," she said. "And it's not really the deadline, Jean Monnet and the nonsense about the Common Market, is it?"

"No."

"It's really me."

"No, Christ no. It's me."

"Okay, no explanation needed. Everyone has someone at the moment. But, well—here we are at the Roosevelt. You have nothing to fear but fear itself."

They turned in under the Roosevelt marquee facing Forty-fifth Street. A doorman in blue with a whistle between his teeth turned the revolving door and, boldly waving, swept them together through a single quadrant and across the threshold to the red-carpeted marble stairs leading up to the main lobby and the elevators. The café, off to their right, was dark. A printed sign on a brass stanchion suggested that night owls could drink until 4 A.M. at the Hyde Park Bar on the mezzanine. Beside the stanchion, there was a full newspaper rack and an honor box for coins. Passing quickly by, Rachel surged ahead of Snyder, up the stairs and under the colossal cut-glass chandelier, centerpiece of the great baroque lobby, to the reception desk. Snyder considered proposing a nightcap, a time to explain, but the truth involved an assumption, patronizing at the very least, which would make a mess of things greater than any misunderstanding. But, still— he was thinking fast.

Key in hand, Rachel returned, meeting Snyder directly under the chandelier.

"So, I appreciate everything," she said. "Thank you for dinner."

"The airport at seven A.M.? I'll come fetch you."

"One of the six good men in the world is keeping the faith. I don't know whether to laugh or to cry, so let's say goodbye here. I do really appreciate everything."

Rachel extended her hand. She frowned over their motionless grip.

"Where I come from," she said, "no one has faith in anything but politics."

"Good luck," he said, feeling the red flush rise again to his cheeks. It was impossible to explain, and too late anyway.

Behind Rachel, an elevator door opened and remained open on its night switch, buzzing impatiently. She glanced toward the sound.

" 'Luck,' he says!" Rachel said.

She brushed Snyder's cheek with her lips.

"Write well tonight," she said.

" 'Write well,' she says!" Snyder said.

There was a last, gray look between them. Then she moved with long strides into the elevator. As the door closed, she gestured, two fingers in a salute that could have signaled victory or peace or just "Okay, another time, perhaps." He believed she meant the latter, to finish with humor over regret. He liked that.

Snyder waved, a sort of confirmation, but the door had rolled shut. The elevator lights blinked in series, stopping at number seven. Snyder lit a cigarette and replaced most of the air in his lungs with smoke. At the bottom of the lobby stairs, he picked up a copy of Saturday morning's New York *Herald Tribune*. Reminded of Zimmerman, he looked for news of fighting in the Iron Triangle north of Saigon, especially a mention of the Michelin plantation, and found none. He thumbed through to the sports pages, noticing on the way that there were almost no advertisements in the paper. The wise men at Click's had been expecting the *Tribune* to fold at any minute. Snyder saw that they were probably right. Your luck turns sour, he thought as he started toward the revolving door. You don't know it's happening until it's happened, that's the trouble. Then it's too late.

SEVEN

The Secret of Lucky Phil

I

Monday morning, moments before first light, in the kitchenette where Zimmerman kept his clock, the alarm bell rang feebly as the hands moved off the hour; then the sound faded away. It had awakened him, naked and sweating, in need of coffee and nicotine. He mixed a spoonful of instant Nestlé's in a cup with warm water from the tap, and lit a Gauloise. His night fog lifted.

This week, Zimmerman would be defiantly watching another of the ongoing series of probes, called "search and destroy" operations, conducted against Vietcong guerrillas by American, ARVN, and Australian light infantry and supporting U.S. aircraft, all representing the 2nd Field Force of III Corps, in War Zone C, between the Iron Triangle and the Cambodian border, a few miles northwest of Saigon. In late 1965, "search and destroy" had been adopted as the Americans' basic tactic designed to grind up the Vietcong, who were threatening the stability of Saigon itself. By late March 1966, it had become Zimmerman's symbol for a command strategy that could never win. As such, in his latter-day mood of revulsion, it called upon him to witness one last operation before writing the definitive story of meaningless combat in a lost war. A working title had occurred to him during the night: "Oh, What a Waste!" Erlanger, he was thinking, will choke on it.

Inspired, he removed his .45 caliber pistol and holster from the cabinet. He slid the gun from the holster, emptied the clip, reloaded, and checked the safety. The gun satisfied him, although he had yet to use it in anger. In the field, early in January, he had attempted to fire a standard 5.56 mm M-16 automatic rifle which, on two potentially threatening occasions, had been thrust into his hands. The rifle jammed. Then he decided to carry a handgun that he himself would clean and care for. He bought the .45 from Eddie Mayes, a photographer for the Melbourne *Express,* who was going home for medical treatment. Poor Eddie had been nicked in the crotch and suffered an instant vasectomy. Zimmerman test-fired Mayes's gun at a civilian range on the road to Tan Son Nhut, but thereafter, though he attended four more combat actions, he had found no reason to shoot. He considered himself in luck, on a roll. You want to escape Vietnam with the safety on, he was thinking. You have no conscious death wish. You came to Vietnam to be in the war, not to die in it. Harriet! Jack! See?

In the bedroom, Zimmerman dressed quickly in brown, green, and gray camouflage fatigues with a correspondent's patch below the shoulder on the left sleeve. He put on two pairs of white socks and his boots, the very same pair of World War II Army issues he had worn in Korea. Then he deposited the gun and holster in the deep pocket on his right thigh.

The gun is always an optional thing, you know, he told himself. A correspondent might wear it on his hip, conceal it in his pocket or bag, or eschew it. You've considered the risks. On the one hand, for want of a weapon in a terminal crisis, an unarmed correspondent might lose his life, not to mention the respect of anyone assigned to protect him. On the other hand, unarmed, he might be recognized as a non-combatant and spared on appeal to an enemy. ("I am a journalist! Unarmed, see, an American journalist!") You choose concealment as a balance of those risks. A visible weapon makes you a target; an invisible weapon gives you an edge. Phil Zimmerman goes to war bearing arms, but not so that anyone will notice. With a little more luck, he concluded, this will be your last time and the gun, still clean, your gift to a deserving grunt.

Now Zimmerman stood concentrating in the center of his outer room. His boot heels lifted him an inch above five feet; the peak of a blue-and-orange New York Mets baseball cap added another inch. Upright and squared off, his posture lifted him even further. It brings you from bantam size to your real height, which, actually, has never been small, merely short. He asked himself: Are you ready?

He touched his pockets for sunglasses, cigarettes, lighter, notebook, ballpoints, paperback (with new vision, he was rereading *The Quiet American* by Graham Greene), wallet, III Corps area map, and rolled cotton for his ears. He rechecked his duffel bag for the helmet and flak jacket on issue from 1st Infantry supply. You don't, he thought, want to get hurt and give Erlanger the last laugh. Then he crossed himself, said *"merde"* aloud, and called the Hotel Caravelle for Stephen Laird, correspondent of the Dallas *Morning Star.*

"Are you on?" Zimmerman asked.

"Yes."

"Who else?"

"Two from NBC, one wire, and an Australian, that I know of."

"So many?"

"It's a p.r. show, you'll see."

"I've hired a taxi. Ten minutes."

"I've got this debutante here—fifteen, okay?"

"Oh, fuck it, Stevie."

"That's what I'm saying, man. I can't come right out with it."

"Okay, but I won't wait."

"With friends like you, I don't need the slopes."

"I'm not kidding, Stevie. I don't want to miss the first staging."

"Are you sure Ernie Pyle started this way?"

At half past five, Zimmerman's usual Sikh driver was waiting at the curb; the inside of his taxi smelled as though he might have been sleeping in it since Saturday. When Zimmerman ordered him, via the Caravelle, back to Tan Son Nhut, the driver tossed his head from side to side. He was interested, even amused, but not surprised. For days, there had been rumors of a big battle shaping up north of the Iron Triangle. The mere sight of the American magazine correspondent dressed in battle gear at dawn, having only just sent his wife home to the States, confirmed it.

2

"They're wrangling at *Time* and CBS, you hear? Plenty of staff want New York to come out against the war—you hear, man?"

"Zimmy, I was just telling Westmoreland at tea, 'Go north with the nukes.'"

"What'd he say?"

" 'One lump or two?'—" Stephen Laird laughed.

"You are an asshole, Stevie. Have any gum? Oh, oh—you hear that?"

The sound of gunfire came to Zimmerman muted from the north, but with a faint echo, proof that the shooting was not far off but nearby, among trees or from within buildings in the hamlet of Tri Ninh, suffused in the midafternoon heat, just up the road at the extreme southwest tip of the Michelin rubber plantation less than twenty miles above Saigon.

Since breakfast at Fire Support Base Casablanca, Zimmerman had trooped west with twenty-four American soldiers, their officer, a black lieutenant named Chester Faulk, of the 1st Infantry Division, an ARVN interpreter, and five other correspondents, including Laird, through a four-mile swale rising to a plain overlooking the Saigon River, slow-flowing from the Cambodian hills toward the South China Sea. Row upon row of rubber trees, untended for many seasons, and partly hidden by tall grass, overlooked much of the great swale. Faulk's mission was to provoke a Vietcong ambush from the high ground and, forthwith, to bring in from FSB Casablanca those units of the 173rd Airborne Brigade with sufficient firepower to guarantee a satisfactory kill ratio. However, the only action in nearly seven hours was a skirmish with a stray pooch who had rippled the yellow grass on the north slope. Four M-1 rounds were fired at his invisible presence. The dog screamed, but the grass rippled again as he fled and, when seen at last, he was running flat out over the ridge to safety.

On a narrow plain at the western end of the swale was the hamlet of Tri Ninh, through which a two-lane highway, Route 14, passed from north to south, adjacent to the river. And that afternoon, only two hundred yards before Tri Ninh and just off the east side of the highway, a dozen or so ragged women, with as many knobby children underfoot, were searching for salvage in the cold debris of a Michelin field warehouse which had taken a direct hit from a Skyraider within the week. Two of the children played with a teeter-totter, homemade with a strip of reinforced corrugated iron over a tin drum. It seemed to Zimmerman that the iron should burn their bare legs if it did not cut them, but their giggles belied all concern. For a reason he did not comprehend, he not only made a note of the teeter-tottering but also, on a separate page, sketched the children against the background of blasted ruins. He was more interested in his drawing than Faulk's interrogation of the women, which, carried out by the rules in the presence of the correspondents, would not produce useful information anyway. Still, he did not miss the ARVN interpreter gesturing south toward the Iron Triangle and further north toward the strategic village of Tri Tam and a woman nodding vigorously as though agreeing that someone had recently gone so many miles thataway.

At last, waiting for Faulk, Zimmerman joined Laird for a smoke, squatting in the shade of a charred fragment of the warehouse wall. In his view were the men of the company milling on the highway beside twin M-48 tanks in file which had come up by a plantation road to escort them through the village. The NBC television cameraman moved among them. A sergeant astride his hatch atop the lead tank shouted, "Take my picture!" The cameraman called back, "Smile!" Though Zimmerman was about fifty yards away, he heard the exchange distinctly. Then Faulk rejoined his company and, with a move-out sign to Zimmerman and Laird, led off toward the hamlet with the lead tank grinding ahead among them. The circle of huts known as Tri Ninh was said to be under Vietcong influence, but repeated American patrols since January had never been resisted. To receive permission to return to FSB Casablanca for the night, they had only to reach the other side. As everyone had been told, Division had already deployed a helicopter landing zone control party half a mile up the highway.

Meanwhile, the second tank remained in place, covering the amiable advance.

"Let's hitch a ride," Laird said. "I told you it would be a fucking boring p.r. show."

Almost casually, as they talked, Zimmerman let himself realize he was hearing rapid small-arms fire, the crack-crack of rifles answering rifles among the huts. It was too sudden, the passage from boredom to maximum interest. But there could be no doubt about it. The three men of the company who would have been last to enter the hamlet had turned and were waving frantically; in the next instant, they were scattering off the highway and running forward again.

Close at hand, Zimmerman heard a gasping roar as the rear tank geared into motion with all but the sergeant already inside the hatch. The sergeant hunched behind the shield of a .50 caliber machine gun on the right-hand edge of the tank roof aiming toward Tri Ninh.

Fastening their helmets on the run, Zimmerman on the left and Laird on the right came up behind the tank and fell in between the shrieking treads. Here they could keep up at a walk, with the tank as a moving shield and the gunner above as champion.

Zimmerman fumbled for his cotton, and tried to wet two pieces with saliva. The cotton stuck to his dry tongue. Then he wiped each piece across the fountain of his forehead and stuffed each ear. The noise pierced his sinuses nevertheless, and forced him to cover his left ear with his hand.

Over his right shoulder, Zimmerman saw that the salvage women in the warehouse ruins had hunkered down to watch. The children on the teeter-totter had disappeared. They must've known, he was thinking, and they did not warn us. With his right hand, he unbuttoned his thigh pocket and separated the gun inside from its holster.

A premonition, more powerful than any insight, warned Zimmerman to look to his left. About seventy yards west of Route 14, he saw the local garbage dump and a tiny painted shrine enclosed by a low wall of lavender stone backed against a stretch of coarse jungle. The sun glinted like an acetylene flame across the tops of the ragged trees. And emerging from the glare were two young men, naked to the waist and wrapped at the hips in white cloth, on a kamikaze dash from the shrine to the tank. At the same time, from the jungle behind them came rings of blue smoke, as from your father's cigar, accenting the covering fire that pinged against the tank's armor below the sergeant's cockpit. Sudden terror took the form of an enormous gob of spit that flooded Zimmerman's mouth and foamed at his lips.

"Stevie! Christ, Stevie!" he cried. "Wake him up!"

The sergeant sat slumped over his gun shield, a great black stain already forming under his helmet where a bullet had sliced through the base of his skull. A second bullet pierced the helmet itself, sending a stream of scalp blood like rusty water from a spigot into Laird's strangely upraised palms. Then, with a look of vacant horror, as though disgusted by his own reflex, Laird ducked to the right and sprinted forward, around and ahead of the tank toward a ditch near the first row of huts marking the entrance to Tri Ninh.

Zimmerman knelt in the highway, tearing at his thigh pocket. The tank moved off to his right as though following Laird to escape the imminent suicidal attack. Inside, Zimmerman was thinking, the crew must know.

An amazing silence enveloped him. He saw everything, but heard nothing. You see the two little gooks, running with clever, evasive leaps, missing the years' collection of broken bottles and jagged tins overflowing from the dump. They are crazy missiles in a soundless wonderland, racing to be first down the rabbit hole. But they are slow. Their legs wobble. You can bet their shit is flowing. They almost float, like sprinters in a race for the ambulatory disabled. So much for the world's record.

Ah, hey, something wet on your own knee!

The first runner lost his loincloth, stumbled in its folds, then vaulted the rise between the last swatch of sandy ground and the highway. Now he wore only a wide canvas belt, hung with small bulging pockets. His penis had disappeared into his pubic hair.

Aiming at the belt, Zimmerman fired one round from the .45 and the naked man exploded in a ghastly, noiseless flash of light. His flesh and bones carried forward on a silent blast, pelting the side of the tank as with the red debris of some awful blood storm, then flopping to the pavement, the torso and one leg connected and all else unidentifiable.

In the next moment, the second man reached the highway. He lifted gracefully above the mess below and glided to the top of the evading tank. Noiselessly, he opened the lid and dove in. Zimmerman saw the man's legs stiffen with a jolt. Smoke burped from the hole, and the tank, turning on a strange axis, headed off the road toward the jungle, its front cannon pointed toward the sky. A fury of smoke rings erupted from the jungle and continued even after the tank stalled at the edge of the dump, its treads turning silently and turning until, deep in the generations of refuse, they stopped.

Zimmerman arose from the road holding the gun at his side. You saw it all, he was thinking. You did see. Oh, the waste! And now, no more smoke rings.

Tasting his own bile, Zimmerman turned toward the warehouse ruin. In the shade, where Laird had joked with him, stood two women, one very old, the other young enough to be the granddaughter, both with solemn faces. The others had vanished. Laird was gone, too.

The grandmother held an antique bolt-action rifle across her waist like a pioneer woman of the Old West. The younger woman was balanced on a crutch, missing her right foot at the ankle, which was bandaged with white gauze and brown tape.

Without conscious intention, his mind divided by a sense of imminent hysteria and a rush of images replaying the exploding man, Zimmerman walked toward them. Now, to his left, black smoke rose from Tri Ninh. Where is safety? An inner voice, his own, told him that he had lost his hearing. With his left hand, he removed the cotton wads from his ears. An intense ringing struck inside, behind his eyes. No other sound came. The women, he was thinking, will help. You need help. You need some kind of help. Don't puke. Women can help. They can lead you to safety.

Snyder would know how to handle this.

Question: Did I show old Erlanger or did I show him?

Answer: You showed him.

Question: Does he appreciate me, grace under pressure, and all that, especially?

Answer: You can bet your butt he appreciates you.

Question: Did I survive and get my story, Jack?

Answer: You got it.

Question: What else is there?

Answer: Nothing.

Zimmerman saw the old woman raise her rifle. He lifted his arms, shoulder high. He felt the weight of the something in his right hand, thinking—oops! Palm extended, he let the .45 fall to the ground.

"Journalist!" he said, smiling in the shadow of his helmet. "Journalist. American, no harm done!"

Zimmerman pointed to the correspondent's patch on his shoulder. "Journalist, American journalist!"

Now he was within six paces of the two women. He saw the

younger woman looking past him to where the .45 lay on the ground.

The grandmother sighted her rifle, aiming at Zimmerman's face.

"Journalist!" Zimmerman cried. "Please!"

The grandmother squeezed the trigger.

In the split second before the bullet penetrates your forehead, you hear the report. Bang!

Bang, Zimmy! You're dead.

EIGHT
The Good Sport

I

Late Monday evening, in Washington, D.C., the duty officer at the national security crisis center in the White House basement bucked upstairs to the President's press secretary a hot copy of the priority cable from MACV, Saigon, about Tri Ninh. An aide alerted the secretary at home and the secretary awoke President Johnson because, not to mention an M-48 tank crew and an ARVN interpreter, the incident twenty hours earlier had killed a correspondent for *Harrington's Weekly World,* Philip Zimmerman of New York. A surviving colleague, Stephen Laird of the Dallas *Morning Star,* positively identified the body, which had been removed to FSB Casablanca.

Near midnight, at home in Mount Kisco, Bruce Erlanger took the news over the phone from the President himself, and wept. The President consoled him with praise for *Harrington's* sacrifice on behalf of the war effort and advised notifying Zimmerman's next of kin before the morning papers started ringing.

Moments later, in her Manhattan apartment, Selby heard about Zimmerman from Erlanger. She also wept. Then Erlanger proposed that he should call Harriet Zimmerman, while Selby spoke to Jack Snyder, without delay. Selby agreed, but first woke up her husband, Bill Selby, and asked him to hold her for a moment.

At the same time, Snyder was home asleep.

2

Over the weekend, the Monnet piece had come to Snyder in a rush. He finished a 3,700-word draft by early Sunday evening, slept five hours, and began revisions at dawn. He produced the final 4,900-word text minutes before the regular Monday editorial lunch, one copy to Jesse Rosenheim, who was looking better after a weekend's rest, and another, through Selby, to Erlanger.

Within the hour, Rosenheim sent for Snyder to discuss a new title (it was Erlanger's: "Europe's Monnet: Is the Common Market Coming Apart?") and a minor cut for space. Later, Selby dropped off a Thermofax of Erlanger's approval memo, which had already launched the piece into the copy-editing process, rush-rush for the April 27 issue, on sale April 19, three weeks hence. Erlanger had penciled in the new title at the bottom of the page.

Snyder circled in black crayon Erlanger's words "Coming Apart," and looked up at Selby.

"His own country's coming apart," Snyder said, "but he won't cover it—I mean the peace walk."

"Be a good sport," Selby said.

Snyder spent the afternoon clearing photos, helping lay out pages, writing captions and subheadlines, and proofreading, all of which he could have left to lesser editors, and never did. The end of a job was the time he liked best. It was absent all work anxiety while the adrenaline still flowed, giving him for his weeks of effort a tangible pleasure more satisfying than Erlanger's praise or *Harrington's* money. And as a bonus, it markedly improved the savor of music, food, and sex.

At the close of the day, the appearance of Esther Wilmeth with a final list of routine fact checker's queries made him feel twice blessed. The job was done and there she was. She mistook his euphoria for fatigue. She countered his invitation to Click's with an offer to bring food to his apartment if he would go home and rest; her report for Rosenheim would only take an hour. God is not completely deaf, Snyder thought.

Among the cardboard remains of a Chinese take-out dinner, the phone on Snyder's cocktail table rang minutes after midnight. In the bedroom, it awoke Esther on the second ring, Snyder on the third. Snyder carefully freed his left arm, on which her hard left breast lay, and swung his legs over the side of the bed. Between rings, he heard the phonograph still working on the stack of records she had chosen; the song was Tommy Dorsey's "I'll Be Around" with Frank Sinatra singing. Snyder remembered her sitting on the floor by the record cabinet, having kicked off her shoes and gathered her skirt high on her sturdy brown thighs. He took her to bed and, afterwards, she got up to play the same stack all over again. Sex with her had been quick and brittle. She was not an experienced woman.

Snyder let the phone ring on. "We're not here," he said aloud.

The seventh ring, by its very insistence, finally alarmed him. It seemed inordinately long, an operator's emergency call. Snyder thought first of Bliss, then Zimmerman. Then he bounded into the street-lit living room and groped through the clutter for a grip on the phone. With the receiver in midair, he heard Selby's voice calling his name, and knew everything in an instant. Outside, the ginkgo branches swayed in a noiseless night breeze.

"Does Harriet know?" Snyder asked.

"From Bruce, yes," Selby said. "President Johnson promised more information in the morning."

"But it's KIA, not just missing?"

"It's definite, from Military Assistance Command, Vietnam, via something called FSB Casablanca. Ambushed in a place called Tri Ninh."

"Is that Michelin's?"

Selby began to cry.

"Oh, fuck the war, Jack!" she said, and with a hard cough, hung up.

Slowly, Snyder lowered the receiver to its cradle. Muscles in his chest contracted, pushing outward against his skin. He felt his grief collecting in that area, leaving him light-headed. Amazing, he thought, you're about to cry over the late Phil Zimmerman. He covered his face with his hands. He wept, heaving great sibilant sighs in an effort to control even louder sobs. He did not want Esther to hear him behaving badly.

He sensed her presence behind him. You must be a sight, he was thinking, a naked man crying. He turned to her, as to a comrade. He realized she had never met Zimmerman.

Esther was naked, too, centered in the doorway, alarmed, yet uncertain of her function. Her body was now the color of dark chocolate, with broad shoulders and high, full breasts on an otherwise slight torso. Her smallness had surprised him.

Esther kept her distance. Then as Snyder subsided and commenced drying his face with a paper napkin, she put on a robe, brought another robe to him, and put her arms around him.

"Zimmerman's dead," he said.

They sat down on the couch beside the cocktail table, where Snyder's hands fixed two Scotches in empty cups. Snyder drank his and poured another. He smiled bleakly.

"Zimmerman's been killed. Selby says so, from MACV."

Esther gave a little gasp in disbelief and her eyes filled.

"Doing a story?" she asked.

"Doing a story, but not for us."

"Who for?"

"I don't think he knew."

Esther seemed to understand, but said nothing. She dried her eyes on a paper napkin. Then she busied herself cleaning up the mess from dinner.

Snyder watched her, mourning, watched himself. Inside, he was swaying in the night like the ginkgo between bitterness and despair. Then the long, black telephone wire snaking across the cocktail table and down into the baseboard caught his attention. At the other end of it, a few blocks north on the West Side, was Harriet Zimmerman, who had already been told, who would be waiting. Now he wished he was alone.

"Esther?" She was in the galley. "Would you stay there for a moment?"

Snyder turned up the volume on the phonograph. Then he dialed the Zimmermans' number, reaching Harriet on the second ring. He saw her blond and short, though not so short as little Phil, with everything well rounded under clear, tawny skin, with only a trace of middle-aged exhaustion in the squint of her eyes.

"You've heard," she said, her voice calm.

"I'd like to help."

"I'm through crying. Are you?"

"Yes. Are you all right?"

"Yes, so-so. Bruce Erlanger was tactless, but fine, really. He cried, too. Then the New York *Times* called, and the Associated Press, not so fine."

"I heard from Selby."

"Bruce asked about a Catholic service. I told him Phil would hoot at that, people saying mass! So then he suggested a *Harrington's* memorial service, because Phil went and died on a story."

"One that we weren't going to publish anyway."

"Oh, I know. I said okay because I want him remembered for all the other stories, the continuum, sixty-odd in eight years."

Snyder waited nearly a minute.

"Harriet?"

"I don't want to talk about Bruce, Jack."

"I'm sorry, Harry. Do you need company?"

"I'm coping, I think."

"If you need—"

"You and I, he loved us both, didn't he, Jack? Sometimes, as between you and me, you came first with him, though—that's true, isn't it? It's true, though not necessarily vice versa, as Paula used to complain. You gave advice and he gave love, isn't that true? He knew he'd never've gotten the Saigon bureau without you. It was yours to give. But he wanted it and I wanted him to have what he wanted, he was so short! We're all in this thing together, aren't we? So—no one's to blame, not even terrible Bruce. I know you don't agree. I can hear it in your voice. You'd like to blame Bruce, but you blame yourself. But no one could save him, not even you. Maybe that's why I visited? I don't know about that. I only just got home. Do I go back and claim the body? I don't know anything. I'm suddenly not coping so well, Jack. I hope you won't mind that I'm hanging up now. Sleep well, with whomever."

"Harry?"

Snyder heard a click on the line and a new dial tone. He listened for a while, frozen solid. Then he folded his arms tightly across his abdomen, the phone pressed against his ribs, and swayed with the ginkgos.

Esther emerged from the galley with the coffeepot and two mugs. She crossed Snyder's line of sight en route to the bedroom.

Snyder followed her with his whisky bottle.

They drank Scotch coffee in bed and, after a while, Esther fell asleep.

Snyder stayed awake past dawn, remembering Zimmerman alive, imagining him slain, accepting the fact of his death, trying out meanings, until the New York *Times* came to his door. There was Zimmerman's picture on the Vietnam jump page; the killing of an American journalist, even in a combat zone, was news, though it read as an obituary. The story subtracted three years from his age (Harriet?) and added a whole year to the length of his tour in Vietnam (Erlanger?). Still, it included a tribute to Zimmerman's courage from his colleague Stephen Laird, and a quote from General William Westmoreland praising "the persistent willingness of journalists to share the hazards of fighting men to report on the nation's wars." It almost filled a page-long column.

Snyder clipped the story for a memento. Luck, at last, for little Phil, he was thinking, a fine send-off, with nothing said about how a slight loss of professionalism killed him.

NINE

Cousin Kurt from Canonsburg

I

For six days, until the 1st Infantry closed out the Michelin operation, Zimmerman's body, enshrouded in green plastic, remained in the makeshift morgue near the helicopter pad at FSB Casablanca. Along with it were the four tankers who had died with Zimmerman and eleven other KIAs of the 1st, the week's total (fifteen, not counting Zimmerman, plus three MIAs) representing a kill ratio of one American per nine Vietcong. "Imagine," said Lieutenant Faulk in a summing up with Laird of the Dallas *Morning Star,* "at this rate, about four hundred thousand Americans have to die—that's more dead than in all our battles of World War II—just to kill the military-age population of North Vietnam, not to mention the Vietcong."

On the seventh day, with nine KIAs aboard (counting Zimmerman), a Chinook helicopter lifting off for Tan Son Nhut accidentally collided with a twin returning from a combat mission. The fighting ship tumbled safely into a tangle of jungle vines; the unlucky hearse fell back on the pad like an upended cricket and exploded, incinerating everyone and everything on board, including not only its hapless quartet of crewmen and the warrant officer from Graves Registration but also its cargo of corpses. Technical inquiries and forensic confusion took another eleven days—until a personal aide to General William Westmoreland, himself pressed on the matter by President Johnson, in response to a message from Erlanger via Pfaff, finally made some practical choices and entrusted a small pine box, said to contain

Zimmerman's remains, to a New York *Herald Tribune* reporter, who had been recalled to attend the imminent demise of his newspaper. To that doubly mournful trip, moreover, was added a two-day stopover in Rome, where the reporter had relatives, so that when Zimmerman finally came home, it was already mid-April.

Now, because Snyder was momentarily on assignment in Watts, Los Angeles, interviewing for the "hot cities" roundup, Jesse Rosenheim accompanied Harriet Zimmerman to John F. Kennedy Airport, where, without ceremony, she accepted the horrific box and ordered an immediate "second cremation." On the following Sunday at noon, a few miles east of Canonsburg, Pennsylvania, and flanked by a local priest, a state trooper, and Phil's cousin, a thirty-seven-year-old high school English teacher named Kurt Von Zimmerman, Harriet scattered a vesselful of fine, white ashes into the Monongahela River from a low place along the bank, where she had once taken a picnic with Phil on a visit to his hometown during the days of their courtship. Although Cousin Kurt wept bitterly, Harriet remained composed. Next morning, she approved Bruce Erlanger's arrangements for a memorial service, 11 A.M., April 18, in a religiously neutral place, Blake and Martini's funeral chapel, on Eighty-third Street off Lexington Avenue.

The date set for remembering Zimmerman was nearly a month after his death, due to no reluctance at the office, but to satisfy Harriet's wish that the proper disposition of her husband's remains should come first. Once it was firm, Selby took over, inviting, reserving, accommodating, planning, and ordering. Her call to Snyder early on April 16 found him packing in his room at the Los Angeles Biltmore en route to Detroit. The memorial program, in its entirety, she said, would be Erlanger's eulogy, with music before and after. "It's what Bruce wants," Selby added in answer to a silent query from Snyder, whom, she correctly guessed, would himself have liked to be asked to say a word about his friend.

Looking down on the palm trees in Pershing Square, Snyder felt Selby's impatience as he considered his options. He hated admitting, yet again, his dependence on Erlanger and the implacable conditionality of his life. Imagine Erlanger claiming exclusive rights to a remembrance for Phil Zimmerman! Yet, you cannot stay away, let alone (although the thought occurs) wish him failure; you are poor in spite.

"What about Saigon, Selb?" Snyder asked, stalling.

"It's Pfaff. Day after the service, we announce Bert Pfaff."

"Bruce never surprises."

"Bert's done a good job in Washington. No Zimmerman, but real good. I know what you're thinking, dearie, but he's probably less hawkish than Zimmy a year ago."

"The war's a year older, Selb."

"Be kind, Jack. Besides, you haven't volunteered."

"I still want the peace walk, Selb."

"I didn't mean that."

"I know what you mean."

"I have to hang up. Are you coming?"

"Maybe I'll carry a sign."

2

The morning of the eighteenth in Manhattan was perfect for mid-April, sunny and balmy, with enough breeze to fly kites, stir the new leaves, and flutter the blouses of coatless young women. It was one of those rare glittering times in the city when strangers smile and traffic moves and most New Yorkers complain because it won't last. Off the commuter flight from Detroit, Snyder stopped at home for his mail, then left early enough to walk slowly from West Sixty-seventh Street through Central Park to Blake and Martini's chapel. He arrived with ten minutes to spare, and found his name on a very short *Harrington's* list of Zimmerman's key colleagues, friends, and family assigned to a waiting room adjacent to the auditorium. It pleased Snyder to be so included, even allowing that it might mean to some that he himself had endorsed Erlanger's wish to eulogize Zimmerman all alone.

The waiting room was small, square, and windowless. A pair of sconces and the picture lights over six dark watercolors of the Maine coast cast a melancholy glow on the small crowd. A foursome of unknown, undoubtedly Canonsburg, ladies whispered in a circle of high-backed chairs, their husbands in a clot behind, smoking in silence. Somebody's little girl in a velvet dress sat on the floor. Jesse

Rosenheim and Felicia Selby stood apart over by the frosted twin doors to the auditorium. And between two solemn men on a couch sat Harriet Zimmerman, her face pale under a tiny black hat with a veil. Erlanger had not arrived.

Snyder kissed Harriet's cheek. She touched his hand. Then she stood to name the men with whom she shared the couch. One was the cousin, Kurt Von Zimmerman, the high school English teacher from Canonsburg, whom Snyder remembered meeting at Phil and Harriet's wedding. He was short and blond, indeed eerily familial, but unlike his late relative, petite to the point of effeminacy. With boyish enthusiasm, he seized Snyder's hand in both of his own and, given the brevity of their past meeting, radiated excessive joy over seeing him again. On the contrary was Harriet's other companion, Brigadier General Ray Weaver, official representative for President Johnson. The portly, beribboned old warrior, with two stars on his Purple Heart, accepted Snyder's hand without comment or smile. It was as though being used as an instrument of presidential patronage on behalf of any journalist, dead or alive, required all the forbearance General Weaver could muster; there was nothing left for civility. The two extremes seemed to propel Harriet toward Snyder. She hugged him in a brief, violent embrace, so forlorn that he thought she might be breaking down. She released him, however, without tears, and sighed through her veil.

"They're sending Pfaff in Zimmy's place," she said.

"I know."

"From—from Lyndon's lap to MACV's—such a joke!"

Snyder nodded.

"It gives Zimmy's life the wrong meaning, Jack."

"I know."

"Not as if it were you."

"It's too late, Harry."

"That's true, yes, you're right," she said, with another sigh, as though he had given her the key to a great mystery.

Just before eleven, Erlanger appeared. In one hand, he carried shell-rimmed glasses because he was going to read his eulogy and, in the other hand, a straight brown cane with an ivory tip because he would be standing longer than usual. He, too, kissed Harriet's cheek and, in a voice the whole room could hear, blamed his tardiness on traffic. Harriet did not embrace him, but compelled the enthusiastic cousin and the dour general to stand as she introduced them. Then she led him through meetings with the Canonsburg visitors, including the little girl, before letting him join, by himself, Rosenheim, Selby, and Snyder, who had merrily watched his embarrassed progression.

Erlanger limped into the company of his staff members with anxious dew showing on his forehead. He lifted a folded white handkerchief to his face. Then, in a whisper, he confided that he had actually been delayed just outside of the room, in the chapel foyer, by his own last-minute edit of the Zimmerman eulogy.

"It was good before," Selby objected.

"I cut out the political parts," Erlanger said. "A proper eulogy for a journalist is about journalism, not politics."

Pivoting on his cane, Erlanger lifted his broad face to Snyder, locking eyes with his star, as with a collaborator, adding, "You could do it just as well, Jack."

"You make the assignments," Snyder said, tactfully rejecting the compliment. You resign yourself to the process, he was thinking, the maker of assignments makes the eulogies.

A doleful silence fell on the room as an usher, a polished young man in a shiny black suit, bent over the couch where Harriet sat with the Zimmerman cousin and the White House general. Harriet accepted the usher's hand and arose without speaking.

"Yes, we're ready!" Kurt Von Zimmerman said, interjecting in a high, feisty voice, suddenly so reminiscent of little Phil's that, for a moment, it stopped Snyder's heart.

3

They entered the snug, white-walled chapel in single file, Snyder next to last, following Brigadier General Weaver, with Kurt Von Zimmerman behind, filling the front pew. There were sixteen pews, capacity about two hundred. Mourners claimed every seat and overflowed into the standing room, both behind the last pew and along the side aisles. Virtually every member of *Harrington's* staff was on hand, and many former staff members, like Bliss Carpenter and Bill

Selby. There were also dozens of magazine cronies from around town; the entire two-shift crew of thirty-four employees from Click's; and perfect strangers whom Zimmerman had touched somewhere at some time in his abbreviated life. Before all, centered on a low, narrow, stagelike platform against the front wall which ran the width of the chapel, was a modest oak pulpit and, next to it, a grand piano with a bearded man playing Mozart. Six little bottle-glass windows set high up in the rear wall let in a cool northern light. The chapel was non-sectarian, without cross or star or other religious sign, but in that light, it inspired a feeling something like reverence that few might resist.

In his seat, Snyder experienced an instant's vivid memory of Zimmerman, and another reprise of his greatest regret: had you known he was going to get himself killed, you might have found a way to save him. He was next aware of General Weaver shifting awkwardly, as though his undershorts had grabbed at his crotch. How the poor man must hate this, Snyder thought, this sharing heaven's space with a journalist, this chore for his Commander-in-Chief's image! But inasmuch as Lyndon Baines Johnson wants Bruce Erlanger and his magazine on his side, General, you sit still, and behave yourself. As, vice versa, I do.

A penultimate run up the scale and a minor chord ended the Mozart. The chapel rustled and coughed, then fell silent as, by cane and limp, Erlanger mounted the platform and took the pulpit. Magnified behind thick glasses, his disarmingly benign eyes scanned the body of mourners, as though the occasion were a staff meeting. He looked down at his script, over to Harriet, and back to his script, which then, dramatically, he turned face down.

"Phil Zimmerman wouldn't want this to take too long," he said to the assembly's quick laughter, and paused, a look of satisfaction flickering about his lips: calculated self-deprecation lowers expectations; the promise of brevity raises levels of attention; and humor recognizes the truth that life goes on—in essence, his message. It was a high-risk lead sentence, and won on all counts.

"General Ray Weaver is here," Erlanger continued, "representing President Johnson, in tribute to the late Phil Zimmerman, and the President is right. Phil Zimmerman deserves tribute. He gave his life for liberty as surely, in my opinion, as any of our fighting men who have been lost in Vietnam. I know I may sound presumptuous. We're just talking about a professional journalist here, a colleague who died on a job. Unlike a fighting man, he could go to work pretty much as he pleased, stand aloof or move in close, play it safe or take a risk, except, of course, as happens, when things got out of control. He was, let's admit, a privileged participant, an observer, a spectator, a researcher who was, in fact, under no orders except to collect information, organize it around a theme, and write it well—meaning objectively, that is, about the way things are, not how he might like them to be. That's the job. Objectivity is our substitute for victory. Do you see? We believe objectivity leads to truth, and that it, the truth, best serves the best causes. Truth is hope.

"And so, on his last assignment, Phil Zimmerman was, as always, searching out the truth about something important by experiencing it objectively. And whether, at the end, he picked up a gun to defend himself, as has been reported, is beside the point. What he was doing at Tri Ninh was not war, but journalism. Now do you see?

"Question: Why take such a risk for journalism? Of course, the usual answers: to make a living, satisfy curiosity, see the world, find glory—but above all, it is that finding a story and telling it to the rest of us—in a word, call it reporting—reporting is a very great reward, a primal reward all by itself. That's why, even though Phil died in war, he did not die for our side or the other side or any side, but for something else. Phil Zimmerman died in war but, I assure you, he died for this reward.

"In essence, then, journalism is about reporting. And above all, on this assignment, as on so many others, for Phil Zimmerman, reporting meant holding back a vital part of himself, the personal part—I can tell you, this is the hardest thing to do—holding back the part that worships and votes and dreams—in order to project himself as a reporter into the reality outside himself. It takes more than skill to take notes, record the scene, and list the facts. It takes an active separation of the private self from the professional self, the heart from the mind, the man of opinion split off from the man of truth, the independent observer detached from the engaged participant. For here we are at the soul of the ideal journalist—that he can be, foremost, an objective reporter, his story's truth seeker, not its manager, no matter the subject, no matter the theme. That was Phil

Zimmerman's ideal, I can tell you, to which he surely aspired to the very end, the very bitter end.

"On job after job, and on his last job, he ennobled our business: first, by striving to get the story and get it right, to the best of his ability and knowledge; second, by never playing God, never manipulating people or events to change the meaning of a story; and third, by admitting the limits of his power, personal as well as professional, to find and tell the whole truth about anything, anyway. Those are the virtues of our business—accuracy, restraint, and humility. They define objectivity, and they wouldn't be virtues if we weren't prone to error, manipulation, and arrogance. Zimmy staked his life on those virtues, and on the faith that it, reporting, the truth, makes a difference to us, to this community, this country, this world, in seeking liberty.

"Our Saigon bureau chief, Phil Zimmerman, like old biblical Job, against overwhelming obstacles, kept on believing that truth makes all the difference. And thereby, he chose where he would be and what he would be doing on the day he died. What more can a human being ask?

"The correspondent for the Dallas *Morning Star* wrote at the time that Phil had died defending himself from ambush, and for some readers this implied a violation of journalistic ethics. Some people say our kind should never carry guns—and I would agree, except wherein the alternative is suicide. But others will say then, you see, there is no truth in journalism, and only a fatal subjectivity, because all of us are private men and women with feelings, sympathies, and passions that can be repressed, but not really ignored. Ultimately, the enemies of a free press say, we do not deserve our freedom because we, too, become special pleaders, defenders of causes. We pick up a gun. But must sentiment so rule mankind that it renders the search for truth meaningless? Where would we find our jurists, our scientists, our ministers were not objectivity at least approachable? To be a hero of the truth one must believe that it makes a difference to freedom, that's all. One must strive on the job for that separation between man and mandate, humanist and professional, citizen and journalist, undaunted, as Phil Zimmerman did—not because one can always, or often, or ever, get away with it, but because one must try.

Zimmy died a truth hero. I hope he understood that at Tri Ninh. If not, I hope he knows it now. Thank you."

Oh, that was fine, Snyder thought. It was a grand eulogy. It set standards. It identified values. It discounted all but the highest motives. It paid tribute. It got down to basics, with no place for complexity, ambiguity, or apology. But no politics? It was fine—so long as you don't count that Zimmy died trying to turn *Harrington's* around on the war. That he died for a story that Erlanger wouldn't have run. That he believed in journalism as Erlanger believed—oh, the eulogy was fine, indeed!—and yet, had he lived, he would have had no audience and no reward. The eulogy, yes, was very good. But caveat emptor, lest you die in vain.

Erlanger took a moment to fold his unread manuscript. He was solemnly pleased with himself. He reached for his cane and, with a grunt, stepped heavily from the pulpit, moving along the front row toward his seat between Weaver and Harriet. The bearded man at the piano prepared sheet music to conclude the service with another Mozart. There were sounds of quiet crying in the chapel.

It was then, still within Erlanger's moment of appreciation, that Kurt Von Zimmerman raised himself into the outer aisle and quickly traversed the stagelike platform on his way to the pulpit. As he passed above Erlanger, the small man, so like his cousin, raised a hand toward the pianist, who sat addressing the keyboard, but waiting on a certain silence before he would play. The chapel stirred uneasily, but then came again to attention, ready to accept that programs do change, sometimes without notice. Cousin Kurt took Erlanger's position behind the pulpit and unfolded a single sheet of yellow paper. Erlanger himself had sat down and, in anxious relief, had begun the deep study of the backs of his hands; he was unaware of his successor until Harriet touched his arm. They exchanged bemused glances. Nothing, of course, was to be done.

"Phil Zimmerman was my first cousin," Cousin Kurt began, reading from his paper. "Before he died, I hadn't seen Phil in five or six years, except once when he came home with Harriet. But we've kept in touch. I had a letter not a week before Tri Ninh. He loved being a war correspondent and, finally, personally, humanly, absolutely, he hated the Vietnam War. He was determined to do everything in his power to stop it. He wrote me this, but in personal letters, so I don't feel I have a right to quote him here. Instead—well, I don't know whether he ever read Stephen Crane, but when I think of Phil, I think of Stephen Crane, and I want to read, in Phil's memory, a verse from a poem by Stephen Crane which, if you change wars, bears a message from both of them. It goes like this, and then I'll sit down:

" 'Then welcome us the practical men / Thrumming on a thousand drums / The practical men, God help us. / They cry aloud to be led to war. / Ah— / They have been poltroons on a thousand fields / And the sacked sad city of New York is their record. / Furious to face the Spaniard, these people, and crawling worms before their task, / They name serfs and send charity in bulk to better men. / They play at being free, these people of New York / Who are too well-dressed to protest against infamy.' "

Cousin Kurt folded his paper, flicked a cautious glance at Erlanger, and remained standing at the pulpit for another half minute. The audience sighed and whispered. There was a shuffling of feet, a kind of silent applause.

Snyder felt a kind of gladness, the feeling that overwhelms your own self-contempt when the bully gets his comeuppance. The images of the poem clung to his consciousness. At his side, he sensed General Weaver shifting, then knuckle-cracking angry, impatient to command the pianist to get on with his finale. Journalists!

A terminal decision took shape in Snyder's mind. Before leaving for Detroit, he thought, you must speak to Erlanger.

Afterwards, against the forward flow of the audience, Snyder took the side aisle toward the rear exit, avoiding all but Bliss Carpenter. She was on her way to Harriet. They shook hands. What was new? Her Texas documentary, approved and assigned airtime. His "hot cities" roundup, returning him to Detroit without delay. Both surviving.

"Imagine, a poem by Stephen Crane!" Bliss said, whistling low.

"Stole the show," Snyder said. "Never assume, right?"

"Bruce was good, too."

"Bruce was good."

"We're all well-dressed New Yorkers, though, aren't we?" she said.

"Yes, we are."

"When are you back?"

"Two weeks, maybe."

"I'm gone again by then. Cape Kennedy for the launch. Next for you?"

"I'm thinking."

"Well, luck, Jack."

"Ha!"

Bliss kissed Snyder, 'bye-'bye, high on the cheek.

4

Among the first outside, Snyder put on his hat and smoked half a cigarette in the sun. Then he saw Erlanger crossing Lexington Avenue alone, limping at a good clip toward Park Avenue, where taxis proliferated. Snyder trotted ahead on the opposite side of the street, hailed a Checker, and held the door for Erlanger. The driver jerked the cab forward, swerving into the southbound traffic. Erlanger raised his clubfoot to the jump seat, crossed his arms over his chest, and exhaled at length as though to purge the last of the air from Blake and Martini's chapel. Beads of sweat ran from his temples. Snyder waited in silence, wondering if the man at the other end of the bench seat, so close to him in age, knew himself or his needs or the limits beyond which others would not go in the service of his magazine. It was not until they were crossing Seventy-second Street that Erlanger unfolded, relaxed, and brought down his foot.

"Well, Jack, well, what about that?"

"Eulogy or epilogue?"

"The boy from Canonsburg who took me literally."

"Gives me courage, Bruce."

"What now?"

"Actually, it was the eulogy. You said some things."

"What will it cost me?"

"Zimmy's bureau, Saigon."

"Yes, Pfaff's going."

"I'd like to have it, Bruce."

Erlanger concentrated on the nob of his cane. Then he fished in his side pocket for cigarettes and matches. He brooded straight ahead through a fresh cloud of smoke. The cab passed St. Bartholomew's

Church, then encountered a jam at Fiftieth Street. There was a line of limousines, squad cars, and network panel trucks at the side entrance to the Waldorf-Astoria. William V. S. Tubman, President of Liberia, was in town. The cabdriver swore and slapped his brow. Erlanger inhaled noisily. The answer is no, Snyder was thinking, but for cooking the rationale of a definitive no, a non-political no—an irresistible no—the man needs time. Then what?

"I'm not going to ask you why," Erlanger said. "I'm going to tell you why it's Pfaff. It's because he has no children and no wife. That's the new rule. From now on, no married men and no fathers can qualify as war correspondents for *Harrington's Weekly World*—not so long as I'm editor."

"My children are seventeen. I have no family."

"That's family."

"I'm volunteering, Bruce."

"You can't volunteer."

"Pfaff is too obvious, Bruce. You know that."

"It's not just politics."

"I'm making it a quitting issue, Bruce."

The cab started again, spurting into the turn at Forty-ninth Street. Enforcing silence, Erlanger tossed his cigarette butt through the window. Then he twisted at the neck, bringing his face close to Snyder's, so close that Snyder could see the faint marks of some long-ago pox.

"You said I do the assignments, Jack."

"I owe Zimmerman something."

"Not to threaten me."

"I never told you, Bruce—that last weekend, he wanted us both to quit over policy."

"But you didn't and he got killed, is that it?"

"I told Zimmy I didn't want to. And I was coping with that until I made the mistake of listening to your eulogy."

"Sugar for the ants. You weren't Zimmy's keeper."

"Followed by Stephen Crane."

Erlanger sat back heavily, then lightly tapped the toe of his special shoe with the tip of his cane. The cab had pulled up at the *Harrington's* building. Erlanger opened the door on the curb side.

"Zimmy's my responsibility," Erlanger said. "Jack, I sent him to Vietnam, twice."

"I'm quitting, Bruce, if I don't have a choice."

"Well—that reverses the question to: do I want you to quit?"

"You wanted me to cover the war nearly two years ago."

"I won't send you now, Jack."

"I haven't got a choice, then."

"You do, yes. Do the World Institute for Survival Education peace walk. When is it?"

Startled, Snyder caught himself frowning. At the chapel, his determination to do Vietnam for *Harrington's* or to free-lance the peace walk had risen on a wave of sudden idealism; now Erlanger's riposte made doing the peace walk for *Harrington's* seem venal, tainted as in blackmail.

"May eleven, through July four."

"You agree?"

"I don't know."

"I'm making one blessed assumption, Jack. That is, I'm assuming you won't fall for them. I don't want to kill a story that takes you out of town for eight weeks, and another month to write. But I'll do it if you don't go by the rules. Just remember, I'm sick of fucking engaged journalists. I don't want a story about how bad the war is, but about whether the people who think it's bad are any good. Our poor benighted readers want warts and all, Jack, and no apologies. If the truth hurts, so what? It's casualty lists, not crusaders, that decide wars, anyway. Am I clear, Jack, about falling?"

Snyder nodded, frowned, smiled. Jackpot, he thought, with your last quarter.

"You're very clear, Bruce."

"You'll have to show me."

Erlanger braced himself on the open door and began his usual exertions for climbing out of an automobile. Before his last upward heave, he paused to demand a final word of assent from Snyder. He was a man who liked things tidy.

"Leave for Chicago, May tenth?" Erlanger asked.

"Soon enough," Snyder replied. "All right."

Victorious, Snyder did not feel as though he had just won a prized assignment, but had rather acquired a fear of falling.

LUCAS

TEN

First Impressions

I

From his room at the Detroit Hilton on the morning after Erlanger's reversal on the Walk story Snyder wrote on *Harrington's* stationery to Rachel Abraham, care of WISE, Chicago, to announce that the magazine was covering the story after all. It was a formal letter, brief and to the point, with no mention of Zimmerman. He had thought to call and thought again. Routinely, you confirm out-of-town assignments by mail. A letter minimizes misunderstood arrangements and wasted trips. It also implies your professional stance precisely because it is not a phone call. In the same spirit, he had addressed her as "Dear Miss Abraham."

Snyder posted the letter in the chute by the hotel elevator and went off to a noontime rally sponsored by a Detroit affiliate of the Congress of Racial Equality. The schedule of speakers included two Negroes with national constituencies, Dick Gregory, the comedian, and James Meredith, the activist who, four years past, had been the hero of a desegregation showdown at the University of Mississippi.

A week later, a letter from Rachel, care of *Harrington's*, reached Snyder at yet another Hilton hotel, this one in Philadelphia. Except for her salutation, "Dear Jack," it was all business, returning Snyder's impersonality with her own, as might befit communications between the male journalist and the female publicist had they never met.

Rachel had divided the letter into thirds. First, she reported on recruitment. Still hoping for twenty starters, WISE had enlisted fourteen "certains," whose names and brief bios—age, hometown, and identification—were attached on separate sheets. Second came logistical news, including word that a Chicago auto dealer had loaned a 1963 Ford pickup truck to carry luggage and supplies, which the contributor's handicapped son, one Arley Broyle, thirty-one, would drive. Third was an invitation to Snyder for the length of his pre-Walk stay in Chicago to be the guest of Sam Lucas and his wife, Molly Hamilton, at their home on the South Side; they lived close by Jackson Park, from which the Walk would eventually start.

Snyder read this last knowing he could not accept. The magazine's code limited favors from subjects to the necessary or the unavoidable: food, shelter, and transportation on certain assignments; an occasional lunch with a political or corporate public relations man (when it was his expense account vs. yours); or an inexpensive gift (nothing over twenty-five dollars retail, according to an Erlanger edict). But he was not expected to flaunt it, insulting the motives of others with the pieties of *Harrington's Weekly World;* instead, a harmless, plausible excuse would do. By return mail to Rachel, he decided, he could reply truthfully that his current assignment would trap him in New York until the last possible moment.

Then, on the morning of May 8, with three days left before the Walk was to begin, a second letter from Rachel reached Snyder, who was, in fact, trapped at the office rewriting his share of the "hot cities" roundup. "We are now seventeen," the letter said, commencing an update of the roster of walkers, "including four new recruits, minus one who has dropped out." Stricken was the name of Nils Fredrik Rolans, a twenty-three-year-old Harvard exchange student from The Hague, Netherlands, who had withdrawn "in fear that he could forfeit his State Department visa in a hassle with police if, at some point along the way, the walkers cross the line between peaceful demonstrating and civil disobedience." Added were "the following walkers, listed for you in order of interest": Reed Herndon, twenty-three, the paroled draft resister from Decatur, Illinois, now a "definite starter"; Dorene Quink, twenty-four, from New York City, a Hunter College graduate and a charter member of Students for a Democratic Society, the four-year-old national organization of New Left campus activists; Frank Dunne, fifty, a carpenter employed by the Pacific Shipbuilding Corp., Wilmington, California, and a union shop steward for the International Brotherhood of Shipyard Workers, whose members were paying his train fare, round trip, Los Angeles–Chicago, as a contribution to the Walk; and "Chicago's own" Rachel Abraham.

Recalling their meeting almost two months past, Snyder concluded at once that a correct relationship with Rachel on so long a trek needed a proper new beginning. By phone, he asked for her in Chicago at the WISE headquarters, Marshall Field's department store, and the Abrahams' residence. He reached her in Evanston at the History Department, Northwestern University.

"I've got the new roster," he said. "Your name's on it."

"I might've called it in, but you're so formal."

"It's the way we do things."

"I've no complaints."

"You're giving up school?"

"I promised you a multitude, didn't I? Seventeen walkers is one more than sixteen. I make seventeen, actually eighteen, counting you."

"Spectators don't count."

"Oh, I'll tell you a secret, Jack. Your coming makes the point of all this much clearer for everyone."

Snyder jotted down Rachel's "secret." It was the first entry in his notebook since the assignment, and felt good, as the first bite of the season feels to the fisherman.

"I hope you won't be disappointed, Rachel," he said.

"I know we won't."

"I mean you mustn't count on me. Remember our talk!"

"Oh, Jack—we do, though!"

"You're on the stage, Ray. I'm on the aisle."

"But we're the good guys, right?"

"That's what I have to find out."

"You wouldn't bomb us? What a trick!"

Snyder answered sharply. "It'd be your bomb."

Rachel fell silent, then in a low voice or at some distance from the phone, lamented, "I get deadly sometimes."

"I can barely hear you."

"I say—I really get deadly sometimes and I was just looking at the murder weapon."

"Forget it. Everyone assumes we're on their side, otherwise journalists wouldn't get invited anywhere."

"But I should know better because of Maude and all. I respect you, like you respect a good actor playing his part. I'm sorry about the 'What a trick!' I think I should hang up now before I kill more."

"I'm still your friendly reporter from *Harrington's.*"

"I appreciate that. And I remember our talk. It's just that we want this story so badly, Jack."

"I want it, too."

"We have something to prove."

Snyder wrote down her last words.

"Me, too," he said.

2

Snyder's contribution to the "hot cities" roundup was a chore right up to the evening of May 10, the day before the Walk. At noon, there had been a quarrel over the space allotment between Rosenheim as managing editor and Ferris as project editor. Gaunt, but determined, Rosenheim won and required Snyder's revised galleys "absolutely" before midnight. Galleys in hand, Snyder had logged out with Selby and set about packing in his apartment. He stuffed rough clothes, two broad-brimmed soft hats, a toilet kit, hiking shoes, and rain gear, plus a new, lightweight mountaineer's bedroll, into his World War II green canvas duffel bag, all of which conformed to the style and bulk suggestions contained in the "Walk for Talks" walkers' advisory pamphlet issued by WISE and sent along by Rachel. The only absolute stricture was "one bag and one bedroll per person." By combining these items, Snyder gave himself permission to bring along his small, portable Olivetti typewriter. Then, at 8 P.M., Chicago time, he had landed at O'Hare with the galleys he'd edited in the air. He resisted an urge to let the clock run to midnight, and, from the terminal, called Rosenheim with his changes.

By cab in a rain squall, Snyder now headed for the Stevens Hotel, on Michigan Avenue with a view of the lake. He checked in, famished and fatigued, ate dinner in his room, and climbed into bed. The night had turned moon-bright and almost balmy, and he lay awake remembering that Chicago was the place where, besides covering Adlai Stevenson in 1956 and 1960, he had also researched a gloomy report in 1961 on the future of American cities. For him, the drawbacks of both provincial Topeka and impersonal New York coincided in Chicago, without the benefits of scale provided by either. Yet there was in its favor Lake Michigan, the Loop, and the Midwest's richest mix of sleaze and splendor that made a visit worthwhile almost anytime, and best of all in the midst of spring under a full moon—if you were not too tired or too rushed to enjoy it. Half-asleep, Snyder caught a few minutes of Irv Kupcinet on the television, and wished he might spend a day or two in Chicago for rest and rehabilitation, unassigned.

Rachel Abraham!

In the night silence, he heard Zimmerman's laughter, Zimmerman once more on the terrace, quoting J. C. Snyder, the mentor, back to J. C. Snyder himself: "All you've got to do, man, when you're on assignment, is roll the stone of celibacy over the cave of desire."

3

By cab again from the Loop, south on State Street, then east on Sixty-third Street, Snyder brought his gear early next morning to Jackson Park. It was 7:15 when he debarked, the sky already bright blue and the sun looping high over the lake. The wind was up, too, drying the park walks under the trees. Snyder held on to his hat, a flat-crowned, wrinkled khaki number with the wide brim down all around. Fluttering between two lampposts was a white bed sheet painted with neat green letters: WISE CHICAGO–WASHINGTON WALK FOR TALKS. Beyond the banner in a small plaza of brick and flagstone was a gathering of about fifty people, walkers and well-wishers, and two motorcycle policemen, now afoot, with nothing to do. Snyder took out his revised roster of walkers, notebook, ballpoint, cigarette and match, and for a moment did nothing, except watch and smoke.

Luggage, sleeping bags, twin ten-gallon gasoline cans, and a dozen large thermos jugs waited by the curb as a young man in a flannel shirt methodically worked over a checklist and another young man in bib overalls and a light Irish cap hovered above him in the bed of a

1963 Ford pickup truck. The truck's hood, sides, and tailgate were pasted over with signs: GET OUT NOW; MAKE LOVE NOT WAR; RE-MEMBER NORMAN MORRISON; and the upside-down trident that had been adopted by the anti-Vietnam War protest from the fifties' Ban the Bomb movement. Over the windshield and on the back of the cab appeared the neat green letters again, repeating the message of the bed sheet, and with a second line, MAY 11–JULY 4 ALL THE WAY, standing out like Christmas decorations against the truck's fresh, fire-engine-red paint job.

Snyder scanned the crowd looking for Rachel. A portly man with a cherubic face and thick, yellow hair guessed Snyder's identity and introduced himself. He was Nicholas Bergquist, fifty-one, a Lutheran minister from St. Paul, Minnesota. A fluttering cough afflicted him, almost immediately followed by a burst of revelation: in order to go on the Walk, he had left his congregation in the care of his wife, who was a Presbyterian. Snyder wrote down Bergquist's embarrassed confession, a reportorial act which surprised the compulsive minister, and sent him flustered into the crowd. Then Snyder carried his duffel to the loading pile and asked the checklist youth, who was an olive-skinned Negro, for a safe storage place for his typewriter.

"Name?"

"Snyder."

"*Harrington's!*" the youth exclaimed. "The name's Corrigan, George. George Corrigan. And my associate, Broyle, Arley. Arley Broyle."

Leaping from the truck bed, Arley Broyle whipped off his cap and grinned wildly. The WISE contributor's son was partly bald, a red-cheeked adolescent at thirty-one, with wide shoulders and massive forearms. Retardation had permanently inscribed perplexed wrinkles in his brow, but his eyes were round and bright and flashed with the thrill of meeting Snyder.

"Can you take care of my machine?" Snyder now asked Broyle.

"Oh, sure—Arley can, can't you, Arley?" Corrigan said.

"Under the front seat, Corry, there's a nice drawer," Broyle said, drawling sweetly.

"Amazing, *Harrington's* man, you're really here, like Sam's been saying," Corrigan said. "I read your article on Black Power."

"Not mine, but ours," Snyder said. A piece by a free-lance writer had recently made the cover predicting the demise of the civil rights movement because of declining white interest and rising Negro determination to go it alone with Black Power. Many whites and blacks wrote angry letters, accusing *Harrington's* of polarizing the races with a self-fulfilling prophecy. Within the office, Snyder himself had disputed the point, but not Erlanger's decision to feature it.

"Surprise, I liked it," Corrigan said. "Make you wonder why I'm walking, the white's Negro for peace in Vietnam, and shit like that? Want to interview me? I was one of the first to sign up. I was. Me and Petey Schumacher. Petey went down to Alabama last year with me, march on Selma, you dig, *my* white among blacks? Now I'm going to walk to Washington with him, *his* black among whites, I guess, and lay me down at the gates to the White House. All right! Petey's around somewhere. You'll want to interview Petey, as long as some things are off the record. We're best buddies and roommates, University of Indiana, Bloomington, two years, freshman, sophomore, taking our junior year abroad at home, living off the land, so to speak, okay, Mr. Snyderman?"

"Oh, yes, okay."

"Oh, yes, off the record, Mr. Snyderman. We heard about 'off the record' at the meeting last night. Sam said you're going to be with us all the way and anything we don't want to see in the magazine, we got to say 'off the record' before we say it. Simple. Is that true?"

"It's reasonably true."

"Okay, let's shake, Mr. Snyderman. The truth is, our mommas think we're in school, off the record."

"But don't tell me anything I can find out independently."

"Hey!"

"You get one free one."

"Oh, man, Mr. Snyderman!" Corrigan laughed.

Snyder laughed with him.

He left his typewriter with Broyle and circulated again, looking for Rachel. Behind him, he heard Arley Broyle snap at Corrigan: "It's not Snyderman, you Corry, it's Snyder."

On his way through the crowd, Snyder introduced himself to a man named Melvin Fishbein and his wife, Selma. It pleased them to announce that besides Sam Lucas and Sam's wife, Molly Hamilton, they were the only married folks on the Walk. They were also, according to their bios, a retired couple, from Madison, Wisconsin, where Professor Fishbein had taught philosophy of religion at the University for thirty-seven years, only interrupted by three years' service during World War II in the Army Air Corps Air Transport Command. He was sixty-eight, very strong-looking, nearly as tall as Snyder, with dark hair and skin like antique paper. To Snyder, he looked as though he could walk to Washington and back again. Mrs. Fishbein, in contrast, was small, worn, and gray at sixty-five, plainly wearied by the effort to leave Madison before dawn that morning to take the first step with the assembling walkers. Snyder checked off the Fishbeins' names on his roster.

Professor Fishbein volunteered that Sam Lucas and Molly Hamilton had gone off in a Traffic Department squad car to adjust the line of march through the South Side to the city line. Then he led Snyder to a trio of walkers, Luther Wood and Lester Kupferman, pals, both nineteen from Grinnell College, Grinnell, Iowa; and a Japanese-American girl named June Matsushida, twenty-one, from San Diego State College, who said she had hitchhiked alone with nineteen rides from California to Chicago in only four days and eight hours.

Looking up from his notebook, Snyder saw Rachel in a khaki shirt and yellow corduroys standing on the far edge of the crowd with two men, one of whom had bent over to work a recalcitrant zipper on a new duffel bag while the other spoke to her with broad gestures.

She waved as Snyder approached, but did not interrupt the monologue of her companion. The angles and planes of her striking face were muted by the shadow of her hat, a blue denim fisherman's fedora festooned with peace buttons. The man before her, partly hidden from Snyder, wore a red beret perched atop long white hair, a white linen jacket, and dark trousers clipped at the ankles above work shoes. He was an inch shorter than Rachel, but remarkably lean, so that in his baggy clothes he gave the impression of a tall scarecrow.

When Snyder came close behind, the man turned. His beak nose supported small, round dark glasses with silver rims, reinforced at the bridge with a piece of white tape. He seemed to be sniffing at the air disturbed by Snyder. There was a white cane with a worn red tip hooked on his left forearm.

With a smile, Snyder offered his hand to Rachel, who pressed it into the blind man's hand.

He was Joseph Rice, fifty-eight, a potato farmer from Riverhead, Long Island, New York. At work on his duffel bag was his son, Vachel, thirty-six, who had a long chin that jutted out and down from a broad jaw. His hair was curly and red, not the mahogany red of Snyder's mustache, but carrot color, and he wore a white linen jacket like his father's.

Joe Rice held on to Snyder's hand, ensuring his audience, but staying Snyder's pen. Snyder's memory took notes.

Joe Rice asked Snyder not to worry about him on the Walk. He had vowed to be right there, next to anyone who made it all the way to Washington, or sit down on the White House doorstep all by himself if need be. He would go to jail "again and again," because he believed in non-violent resistance in the great tradition "from Christ to Tolstoy."

He said he had been locked up for obstructing traffic in Wilmington, Delaware, on the 1962 Boston–Washington Ban the Bomb march. In the summer of 1965, he spent two days and two nights in the Tombs, New York's Manhattan jail, for chaining himself to a parking meter in front of the Federal Court Building during a demonstration against the draft.

He admitted that he could see "five percent." Vachel, his son, had accompanied him everywhere, except to jail. He insisted on doing his jail time alone, making the guards guide him around the echoing halls. Two more sons took care of business at home, one named Rupert Brooke Rice, the other Joyce Kilmer Rice. Vachel's middle name was Lindsay, after the bard of Springfield, Illinois.

He said he had given all three sons the name of second-rate poets to provide "spirituality without inferiority." His wife died in a fourth and aborted childbirth. His sight was lost in a dust explosion at a fertilizer plant in New Jersey during World War II. He'd raised his boys alone. All were Quakers.

"Whew! We welcome you to the resistance, Mr. Snyder," Joe Rice said.

His hand free at last, Snyder wrote as he thanked him.

"Can we talk?" Rachel asked.

Snyder looked up with a smile.

They walked beyond the crowd toward the lake.

"Do you always do it that way, madly scribbling everything?" Rachel asked.

"After a while, people get repetitious. Then you don't scribble so much. Sometimes, when you can't scribble, you just trust your memory, and write it down later."

"That's interesting."

"Most people don't want to know."

"I really do."

She had made Snyder smile again.

"All right," he said. Then slowly, as he reflected, having never before had to explain his method to an outsider, he said, "You take notes at random, never quite knowing the importance of anything, except that the names must be spelled right and the facts that can't be re-verified must be got right the first time. Then, when it's almost over, or when you're back in New York, you find that the notes themselves somehow contain the essential story. I mean, you've had a theme all along, but you can't hit it until the facts are fed back through your brain into the part that writes for a living. Until then, you don't know what you've got. And afterwards, it will seem as though there could have been nothing else. It is very peculiar, Rachel."

Rachel touched Snyder's arm, tentatively as though trying to resist.

"So, we're at the mercy of the writer-you, not the spectator-you?"

"Something like that. It's two different guys."

They had strolled around a narrow stand of small, lush poplar trees, back through which they could see the crowd milling, waiting for Sam Lucas. Before them, in the middle distance, was the empty, gray-gold Jackson Park beach. Waves whipped up by the lake wind smashed hard at the jetties and flung themselves across the sand almost to the walkway. Strangely, no sound reached them over the noise of traffic and the rattling poplar leaves.

"You swim?" Rachel asked.

"Some, but too many cigarettes. You?"

"All-Chicago high school marathon champ, 1955. Twelve miles to and from this very beach, six miles out and six miles back. Impressed?"

"Next time I'm drowning, I'll remember."

"Back to business," Rachel said. "This morning, we are otherwise covered by exactly two reporters, one from the Associated Press, one from a local radio station, not major."

"No dailies?"

"The dailies are taking the story off the AP. The TV wouldn't come. I tried. I called and called. I couldn't promise them enough action. Seventeen people—not enough. TV's jaded by ten years of demonstrations, thousands marching for civil rights, police dogs, tear gas—pacifism's too passive for the evening news. Besides, the Walk's in a special bind. Let's assume we could get ourselves arrested for the cameras this morning—how do we go through the police hassle and still cross over into Indiana by tomorrow night?"

Snyder memorized Rachel's complaint because transcribing it might have interrupted her flow. He also studied her hands as they struck the air, long ringless fingers emphasizing each point with a slight stroking motion, and at last coming to rest on her hips in a final, theatrical pose of exasperation and expectation. As a matter of interview technique, he knew he might commiserate or suggest solutions for her dilemma in order to provoke further response. After all, his goal was insight into the cast of characters on the Walk. But he also saw a nice opportunity to establish his own priorities.

"If you ask me," he said, "I'd say save your best efforts until Washington's in sight. Pulling off the feat is how you merit attention. The rest of it, getting started, getting there, makes copy for me but, without conflict, not much for the wire services or the local TV. You've got to decide where you want to be on the Fourth of July."

"At the White House, for sure."

"That's why I'm here, Ray."

Abruptly, Rachel stepped between Snyder and his view of the beach. Now she was smiling.

"If you'd called when you landed yesterday, it would've been easier to say what I have to say."

"I was beat, asleep at the Stevens."

"I wanted to thank you for coming."

"Not necessary."

"It is. I'm very grateful. That's personal. The other thing I wanted to say is that I understand the way things are."

"What things?"

"That you're on an assignment."

Snyder did not reply; nothing that came to mind seemed useful.

"Last time was different."

"I was on deadline."

"That's kind of you, friend. Write it down."

"What?"

"That I understand you're from *Harrington's,* and not a member of the Walk."

"I'll remember."

Rachel extended her hand and Snyder shook it, sealing the contract. Then they turned back. As they reached the edge of the crowd, Snyder consulted his list of walkers. Eight names had been checked off. He wanted to identify the rest before the Walk was underway, especially Reed Herndon.

"Over there," Rachel said.

She indicated a medium-sized young man wearing an Army field jacket over a white T-shirt who stood alone in the street about thirty feet away just beyond the truck. Snyder had noticed him earlier. His hair was an unruly blond mop that covered his ears. He wore gold-rimmed glasses. His face was narrow, almost gaunt, and he held himself, both face and body, in a kind of wary tension, as though an alarm bell were about to ring. Even at that distance, he seemed to sense Snyder's interest and turned away.

"He is the only one not thrilled by your presence," Rachel said.

"I see. Am I to know why?"

"He hasn't said."

"How do you know?"

"I only know he asked Sam whether he had to cooperate with you."

"What did Sam say?"

"He told Reed he should speak to you about being off the record."

"All the way off the record?"

"Yes—among the missing so far as *Harrington's* is concerned."

"But he's here—that's reality!"

4

Minutes before nine, the hour of announced departure, there was the sound of a siren approaching on Sixty-third Street, then silence, and in another moment a police car pulled up behind the truck. From the rear seat stepped Molly Hamilton, forty-seven, husky, dark, and almost pretty, wearing a white shirt and pink walking shorts, followed by the unloading of Sam Lucas. He was a huge, round man, weighing two hundred and sixty pounds at fifty-two, with a full, brown, gray-streaked beard, sand-colored skin, and thyroidal black eyes. His summer seersucker suit, blue business shirt, and dark tie contrasted with the hiking clothes of every other walker. He held a large three-ring notebook in one hand and a red, black, and green tam-o'-shanter in the other, both raised above his close-cropped head in greeting to the assembly. The crowd wheeled and turned as one, forming a half circle as Lucas heavily mounted the curb. A cheer rose and a vast, tooth-filled smile broke through Lucas's beard. There was another cheer as the radio reporter with a tape recorder the size of a shoe box held a small microphone to Lucas's lips. Then in a voice both loud and tense, Lucas almost sang as he read the names of the walkers, pausing after each for the obligatory "Here!"

"Oh, yes," he concluded, "and Mr. J. C. Snyder of the magazine *Harrington's Weekly World,* who's coming along for posterity."

"Here," Snyder said, just above a whisper.

"Where?" Lucas cried.

"Here!" Snyder called, chagrined, but raising his hand from deep in the crowd.

"Let me see you!" Lucas returned, shouting.

In front of Snyder, walkers and well-wishers parted until there was a clear path for Lucas's vision. Snyder saw that Lucas wore black space shoes with thick crepe soles.

"Hello!" Lucas exulted, and trotted up the gap to shake hands with Snyder.

"You're so welcome," Lucas said loudly. "We want you to be a part of us, and carry our message far beyond the reach of our own few voices. We do thank you very much for being here."

Snyder stared hard at Lucas's old eyes, almost lost in the heavy folds of the lids which bulged from the upward pressure of the cheeks below, themselves swollen by another extreme smile. He had seen those eyes before, Snyder thought, in his father's face toward the end of his life.

Lucas held on to Snyder's hand for an extra moment, as though his own warmth might prompt more than an uncomfortable smile from Snyder. Then he rolled around on one heel and returned to his original curbside rostrum, one hand raised for quiet.

Beside Snyder, Rachel said, "Bear with him, Jack. Fame is a terrible spur."

Then Lucas rose on tiptoes and raised his chins to speak.

"Greeting to you all," he said, with a toss of the tam-o'-shanter. "It's time, and this is how we will go. We will try to walk six or seven hours a day, fifteen miles on the average day, give or take a few, rain or shine, up hill and down dale, at least six days a week."

He paused as the crowd murmured and finally applauded. Then he continued.

"Our truck will always be two and a half miles ahead of the previous rest stop—precisely by the odometer—a predictable oasis and movable headquarters for each hour or so of the walk, today and every day, all the way to Washington! We will carry signs, hand out leaflets, make speeches at the slightest sign of interest, and try to avoid trouble, but not reasonable arguments. At the end of those fifteen-mile days, good people are expecting to shelter us, if not every night, mostly every night. Otherwise, we will camp out, or stay in a hotel or motel if we must. Our kitty is a little low, but we will shake a few trees and prevail, won't we?"

The crowd sighed as Lucas handed his tam-o'-shanter to Molly Hamilton, indicating it should be passed around for contributions.

"Tonight," Lucas continued, "our walk route takes us to Lynwood, Illinois, and tomorrow across the state line into Indiana, and then steady as she goes, the days and weeks ahead will take us through Indiana and Ohio, through West Virginia and a corner of Pennsylvania into Maryland and the District of Columbia, at last, full-sailed and proud as any ship at the end of a long voyage, to the portals of our President's home. [Applause.]

"What is success? We want the nation watching when, to President

Johnson, we present our call for peace talks in a petition signed by each of us who walks more than one day. Whether we present it according to law or whether we present it in an act of civil disobedience depends, to a great extent, on the actual moment in time, how we are to be received, and how the members of this walk themselves feel about a proper ending to this voluntary ordeal. That means we must be in Washington on July third, to ready ourselves for the Fourth, so be patient with me if I ask you to hurry along. [Laughter.]

"This is a seven-hundred-fifty-mile forced march—agreed? And if I can do it between May eleventh and July third, why [much laughter], so can you. But hear me, too—so far as any of us can go, more than a day or all the way, any who earns the right to sign our petition has contributed to the cause. [Applause.]

"Well, friends, may the Lord of us all bless our mission of peace. We go in peace that our people and our government will see that this war must stop now. Let none among us lose hope. And to that I will say—amen."

A half minute of quiet followed.

Snyder wrote: "No rousing rhetoric for the convinced faithful . . . No absolute pitch for money or signatures . . . No rigamarole . . . Tells them what they need to know, what they have to do . . . He gives them the feeling that the Walk can make it to Washington even if some of them fail . . . Mightn't Lucas fail? So fat!"

Moments later, the Walk began. It was ten past nine, on the sidewalk facing into Stony Island Avenue. The walkers assembled two by two, with Lucas on the grass off to one side, bawling names like a long-suffering camp director, already sweating despite the cool, sharp breeze. They were to take to the street, leaving the park through a narrow space between the truck and the squad car, cutting out the well-wishers, and thereby making life easier for the two motorcycle patrolmen who had been monitoring the crowd since early morning. One patrolman astride his machine would control traffic on the avenue until the Walk was safely into the inner lane, there to be escorted eleven miles to the city line.

Snyder stationed himself next to Lucas, imagining the excitement of the others within the frame of his own measured detachment. In front as the Walk came slowly toward him were the two Californians, Frank Dunne and June Matsushida.

"Jack, they make this little group most truly a national protest," Lucas said, as though dictating to a secretary. "We are not some fringe group, not only your usual Quakers and what have you. Dunne's a man from labor, going way back—we have to involve labor, Jack, if we're going to make waves in Washington. And June's our reminder that this war is yet another with an Asiatic nation, something like the sixth in less than a hundred years. So I chose them to lead off. See, Jack?"

Frank Dunne held high the Walk's lead-off sign, which bucked in the wind as though it had a life of its own. He was a hawk-nosed, wiry man whose skin stretched across his cheekbones like tanned leather, dressed in a flowered shirt and blue jeans and wearing a blue work cap sporting his union's logo—the initials IBSW entwined with a stylish anchor. The lead-off sign was a square piece of plywood, twenty-eight inches by twenty-eight inches, with a four-inch hole in the middle to lessen wind resistance. It was lashed and nailed to the top of a long birch pole and announced in crowded red letters: WE'RE WALKING SINCE MAY 11 CHICAGO–WASH. FOR U.S.-HANOI PEACE TALKS. Below the hole, in smaller black letters, the sign also said: MEET US AT THE WHITE HOUSE JULY 4. And along the lower rim, it said: WORLD INSTITUTE FOR SURVIVAL EDUCATION, CHICAGO. Lucas told Snyder that he had put the sign on his bathroom scale; it weighed twenty-three pounds. Snyder saw that it would always be a chore for someone to carry it, and sheer misery on a windy day.

June Matsushida, a stocky, small, dark Japanese girl with a round face and an athletic stride, carried a cardboard sign abreast of Frank Dunne. The sign was framed from behind with thin strips of plywood, painted black, and, as she held it, it covered her body from shoulders to knees. Its message was an enlarged U.S. Army photo of a Buddhist monk sitting on a street in Vietnam apparently blocking the progress of a bristling American tank. For future variety, the Walk truck carried four more such photographic signs: a grisly portrait of the immolation of Norman Morrison at the Pentagon; a jarring flash picture of a young woman at the bottom of a bomb crater, presumably dead somewhere in Vietnam; a graphic shot of an American medic running for safety with a Vietnamese child in his arms; and the blowup of a single frame of TV news film, perhaps the most influential image of Vietnam seen in America in the year since U.S. troops had arrived in force—it showed an American marine using a cigarette lighter to set fire to a hut in a village of peasants for whose loyalty the war was presumably being fought. During Lucas's speech, Arley Broyle had set out the four alternative placards, leaning them against the curbside fenders of the truck like objets d'art in a sidewalk gallery, to make a better picture for the television cameramen and photographers who never came.

Following Dunne and June Matsushida as they stepped off into the avenue were three pairs of walkers, hands free and waving to the crowd—without signs to avoid a blur of posters, as Lucas explained to Snyder: George Corrigan and Peter Schumacher, Rachel Abraham and the Reverend Nicholas Bergquist, and Joe and Vachel Rice. In the next rank, a sign appeared; it was a cross carried by Reed Herndon with "Remember Norman Morrison" lettered in blue on white on the crossbar. Beside Herndon was Dorene Quink, and behind them, without signs, were Luther Wood and Lester Kupferman, and then the Fishbeins. Finally, alone, came Molly Hamilton, carrying a trident sign, a perforated wooden disk on a long pole, lettered in red on white, reading: PEACE WALK FOR TALKS. As Molly Hamilton passed, Arley Broyle collected his gallery of photos and climbed into the truck. Lucas directed Snyder to fall in beside his wife; and he himself trotted forward to join the leaders.

Snyder heard Lucas cry, "So, we go!"

The crowd cheered and many lifted their hands in V signs. The wind rose almost immediately and buffeted the signs, forcing the sign carriers to lower their poles and press forward like knights with lances at the ready.

5

They reached the Chicago city line, eleven miles south of Jackson Park, at three o'clock that afternoon, ninety minutes behind schedule. The motorcycle patrolmen had moved them steadily through traffic, and although pedestrians along the way stopped to watch and wave or shake a fist, none interfered. The walkers took turns carrying the signs and rested only five minutes in each hour as determined by Lucas's bargain with the Traffic Department. It was Selma Fishbein's pace that had upset their timetable, Snyder noted—every calculation that was to march them into Washington on July 3 would have to be measured against the physical limitations of their weaker members. But the stronger were hardly more prepared for the demands of those first six hours on muscles and bones unaccustomed to the challenge of sustained walking, not to mention the resistance of a fifteen-mile-an-hour wind. The photographic sign proved altogether unmanageable and had to be stowed away.

They sat down to rest in an empty lot on the city line just before the township of Burnham in Cook County. Arley Broyle served sandwiches and coffee donated by Chicago friends of WISE. Their police escort shared the lunch, which passed in exhausted silence. Snyder's ankles hurt. He thought that probably none among the walkers had failed to learn already that 750 miles was a lot farther to walk than first imagined, and made a note of it.

Later, with the wind blessedly behind them, they continued south along Torrence Avenue, through a sudden stretch of farmland and a patch of woods, into Lynwood, Illinois, eighteen miles and ten and a half hours from their beginning in Jackson Park.

At dusk, they straggled up the white wooden steps of the Lynwood Free Union Episcopal Church between two lines of smiling middle-aged ladies in aprons. Cooking for them had gone on all afternoon. The minister in shirt sleeves waited at the door, pleased to announce that there would be a peace supper in the Sunday-school rooms and a place to sleep on canvas cots rented for the occasion.

Lucas, whose spirits seemed to rise with fatigue, was last to enter behind Snyder. Where Snyder had paused to observe the brightly lit white clapboard interior, Lucas tapped him on the shoulder.

"Get used to it!" Lucas exclaimed. "You'll be seeing the inside of lots of churches before we're through."

After supper, Snyder stepped out for a smoke, his notebook buttoned down in his shirt pocket. The night was cool and star-bright, but dark under the trees. On the street, the Walk truck was parked wrong way around, with the driver's side next to the curb. Arley Broyle was under the open hood tinkering with the engine. Reed Herndon held a flashlight, looking on. All day, Herndon had walked with Dorene Quink, but essentially alone. The walkers seemed to acknowledge his special position as one who had suffered most for the cause, and gave him his solitude. He carried a paperback book in each hip pocket. One was *Catch-22;* the other, *For Whom the Bell Tolls.* Snyder had noticed him reading the former in the empty lot on the Chicago city line. He had yet to speak to him. He lit up and walked toward the curb. He heard the clink of Arley's tools and the chirping of starlings in the trees overhead.

As Snyder approached, Herndon said, "It's the third plug. Can you see the ring?" His speech was slow, the way Snyder's had been before life in New York had given it more speed.

"Are you making it?" Snyder asked, peering under the hood.

"I believe," Arley replied.

"He is," Herndon said, cautiously. "Are you?"

"Okay, for the first day," Snyder said. "Tired, I guess."

Herndon accepted a cigarette from Snyder, who held a match for him.

"What are you going to be doing?"

"Just going along, Reed. Keeping a record of what happens next. Interviewing people from time to time, people on the Walk, people we meet, that sort of thing—interviewing you at some point along the road, if that's all right."

Arley Broyle changed the angle of his body over the radiator. Herndon leaned against the fender so that the flashlight beam still covered the engine. He looked back toward Snyder. One side of his face caught the glare. He had a choice of replies—Snyder could see this.

"Well, it depends," Herndon said.

"Yes?"

"On what you're going to write."

"What happens happens. I can't know till it's over."

Herndon checked on Arley, then faced Snyder again.

"Mr. Snyder—"

"It's Jack, Reed."

"Jack, well—it's this: Some of the walkers, perhaps most, are interested in civil disobedience when we get to Washington, maybe even before. There may be opportunities, and I can't be involved with them. I mean, I can't break the law while I'm on parole. I've got to stay out of trouble for seventeen months and twenty-one days, or else go back and finish that time in prison."

Herndon spoke deliberately, his prairie cadence now as familiar to Snyder as the beat of midwestern voices in his own childhood memory.

"Where?" Snyder asked, though he knew. "What for?"

"Federal penitentiary at Leavenworth, Kansas. I just finished two years and nine days of a four-year sentence for refusing to answer my draft call. My good time was exactly seven months. And I'm free exactly twelve days and I don't want to go back."

"Well, dear Christ," Snyder said, "why do this? Why take any chance at all?"

"I'm not planning to take a chance. Only I can't let them keep me from protesting, either. My parole officer thinks I'm in Washington looking for work. I'm allowed to phone in one report. That gives me sixty days from yesterday."

Snyder heard hymn singing in the church and the sound of a guitar.

"How can you win?" Snyder asked. "If I mention your name at all, your parole officer will know you lied to him."

"No, I won't have lied. I'm going to look for work. I never said how I would get to Washington."

"So you're asking for anonymity only should some of the walkers do civil disobedience, even though you yourself won't have been involved. But why, since you won't have broken the law?"

"Yes. In that situation, there may be a question of contempt, or even complicity, so I don't want to be mentioned at all. That's why I've thought it would be better not to exist, so to speak, for the purposes of your story."

"I can't make such a promise."

"Sam says I have a right to be off the record."

"We don't quite mean it that way."

"I'm asking for it that way."

"Will you leave the Walk if I say no?"

"I won't leave the Walk under any circumstances."

"Even if staying on the Walk were to mean going back to Leavenworth?"

"I won't go back, either."

"You've lost me."

"I'm sorry."

Reflexively, Snyder lit a fresh cigarette from the butt of his old one. Arley Broyle reached for the flashlight and waved Herndon toward the cab. Snyder then held the light.

"So what if I say I'll only think about it."

"We'll just go ahead and I'll ask you again. Meantime, I will try to make you my friend, Jack."

Herndon mounted the cab and slid under the wheel. Snyder stood at the open door.

"You make it hard," Snyder said.

You are on the edge of a pact, Snyder was thinking. Is it wrong to put a whole character off the record? How is it different from taking an interview that way? How many times have you agreed to protect a source in exchange for information? It is always the writer's prerogative to decide who shall be nameless. All writing is selection. Making it up is always a sin, but leaving it out—it all depends. It can be nothing or a scandal. Think—when a subject refuses to cooperate, sometimes not a word is written at all.

In the cab, Herndon switched on the ignition. Snyder leaned into the cab.

"Reed, I'll have to know, sometime."

"Not if no laws are broken."

"Okay. Not then. But is that likely?"

"It's undecided."

As the engine started, the starlings bolted from the trees. Arley stepped back, grinning with satisfaction.

Snyder waved congratulations. You have not promised anything, anonymity or otherwise, he was thinking. You have not refused, either. A subject asks for a favor, freedom from publicity. He offers friendship. You offer indecision. No rules broken, yet—just the beginning of a friendly game.

"Fixed!" Arley Broyle cried. Pliers in hand, he strained against a final engine bolt. He slammed the hood.

"Nice going, Arley," Herndon said, cutting the engine. "Let's go on inside with Jack, and hear them singing."

ELEVEN

Shoulders of Fortune

I

In the morning, it was drizzling rain. They left Lynwood sharing the Walk's ten black umbrellas, with Molly Hamilton in the lead. Snyder imagined them, as from a distance, looking like a strange, slow-moving black caterpillar with sixteen pairs of legs. Two pairs were missing, Lucas and Broyle having gone off early in the truck to arrange the evening's stopover. He had also noted that the rain shut in Lynwood, and that morning, at least, the cause of peace in Vietnam went virtually unnoticed. The waterproof paint on the signs appeared to be holding.

Minutes below the city limits, a two-lane state road took them to shelter under the canopy of a drive-in root-beer stand. Lucas arrived soon after, wearing a green canvas parka the size of a small tent. Surrounded by the walkers, like a coach pepping his team, he said he had arranged motel accommodations for the night in Merrillville, just over the Indiana border on U.S. 30. Then he briefed them on the Walk's progress, as he said he now planned to do each day at this hour when the evening's schedule had been set. A few miles ahead, U.S. 30 intersected the state road. It was the main east-west highway between Illinois and Ohio across the top of Indiana, four lanes all the way. They would follow it as far as Fort Wayne through sleep-over towns like Merrillville, Valparaiso, and Etna Green. ("Who's she?" Dorene squealed and got a laugh.) At their presumed speed, Fort Wayne would be nine days out of Chicago. On the tenth day, they would rest, with forty-five days to go. There were groans, but no questions. The drizzle had become a steady shower which drummed on the canopy. Snyder added to his notes the calculation that, in a fast car, Chicago to Fort Wayne was a three-hour drive.

Down the road another half hour, the rain abruptly stopped. Arley drove back from the next rest site to collect the umbrellas and rain gear. Then came the sun. The road quickly dried and the walkers picked up their pace.

It was not long before they climbed an access road to U.S. 30. They took to the right shoulder in reckless groups of two and three as two lanes of eastbound traffic thundered beside them. Horns in passing cars sounded, either in approval or to give warning. The shoulder was narrow, a yard or so wide at best, leaving little tolerance from pavement to guardrail for a careless driver or an absentminded walker. Lucas, carrying the lead sign and already breathing hard, bid his charges for safety's sake to move ahead single file as close as possible to the guardrails.

Snyder fell in on Lucas's left, precariously close to the highway's edge. He had been studying Arley's road map. There were alternate routes to the east, none quite so direct as U.S. 30, but none likely to be so dangerous, either.

"Do we have to go this way, Sam?"

"Yes, I'm sorry. Back roads are safer, fewer bypasses, more towns to be seen in. But none reaches Fort Wayne week from tomorrow."

Snyder waited for an explanation rather than ask for one, sensing by now that Lucas was a type, the kind of ambitious subject who hopes for justice in exchange for candor, and eagerly volunteers more for less.

"It's Friday next," Lucas went on, "and we've been invited to a Reform synagogue."

"I'll excuse you," Snyder said, unable to resist goading Lucas for one more fact. "I was raised Reform."

"The honorarium's two hundred dollars."

Snyder jotted down the dollar figure; so far as he was concerned, the subject was covered. Looking up, he saw that Lucas was watching him write.

Lucas shifted the weight of the lead sign. This gave him a free hand to mop his brow with an oversized red bandanna.

"Are you a good Jew, Jack?"

"I have my doubts. Why?"

"You brought it up."

"I meant to goad you."

"Yes, I gathered. But it's a fair question. You're going to write about us. Religion is a big part of our motivation here."

"I suppose religion's a part of mine, but practice, no."

"What about God?"

"I don't expect much—a certain logic in nature, perhaps."

"Pacifism?"

"I don't think so."

"Our cause?"

"Don't ask."

"Why not?"

"I'm working."

Lucas exhaled, winded. He shifted the lead sign again.

"Well, don't judge us, Jack. We've less than a thousand dollars in the kitty. Tonight's a good example. There's no church, no synagogue, no place free of charge in Merrillville. The motel's a must tonight. Counting you in a room with Joe and Vachel, and Arley and a volunteer in sleeping bags on the truck, we need five double rooms with six extra cots—in dollars, it comes to a hundred five. Everyone's on his own for dinner, but three or four need help, say another twenty, depending."

"Harrington's pays for me."

"So subtract ten dollars. My point is, we need the money, so I take this highway. I consider our options, figure the risks, and make a judgment. Now ask me: why can't we all camp out?"

"Question."

"It's the older people right now, the Fishbeins, Joe Rice—I have to see how they do, after a few days out."

"You see a little irony?"

"I admit it—risk-benefit analysis, the Pentagon's sort of thing."

"I wasn't judging, Sam."

"Not yet, anyway—but you can do us all a favor, Jack."

"Name it."

"Tell me when to shut up."

Snyder's answer was a quick laugh. Then he stopped to record the conversation. The file of walkers rapidly passed him in step with a march played on Luther Wood's recorder. Snyder sat on the guardrail, continuing his notes, ending with an impression of Sam Lucas:

"The fat man's a risk-benefit case himself, already breathing hard, but insists on his hour carrying the lead sign."

Then a disconnected thought occurred and was put down under his own initials:

"JCS: you know this road from past travels, but always by car. In memory, it is a ribbon of gray concrete through a forest of drive-in root-beer stands, luncheonettes, used-car lots, and gas pumps. On foot, though, you get a good look behind the blight. Look and you see fresh-plowed fields and cool green woods spread out to the horizons both north and south. These are modest beauties, but at least accessible to the walker, a compensation for these tedious hours, unmentioned by anyone thus far, but to be noted anyway.

"JCS: walking the shortest distance to Fort Wayne has nothing else to recommend it, given the renewed aches in the legs and feet that are, ouch, going to be slow getting into shape."

Holding on to his hat, Snyder ran to catch up.

On the highway, a van slowed, then sped away as a man in the seat next to the driver cried, "Go back to Russiaaaaa!"

2

At noon on the following day, they still marched single file on U.S. 30—Merrillville was behind them, farmland all around in great patches of green and brown, and Valparaiso ahead—but there had been no cooling rain. Suddenly it was not like May, but midsummer in Indiana. The sun's heat cast mirages far ahead on the highway and glinted on the concrete close at hand. There was also the heat of the traffic's blast that swept over them in staccato waves. Selma Fishbein had been struggling and now Lucas asked Arley to drive both Fishbeins to the dormitory at Valparaiso University where the Walk would be spending the night. Melvin Fishbein shook Snyder's hand from the truck window.

"So soon," he said, "for you to see that the group's divisible, even dissolvable. Bad for the old image. Or the image of the old. I hope Selma and I didn't make a mistake by coming."

Snyder did not make a note, but the professor's remark stayed with him and he wrote it down after the truck had gone.

At midafternoon, as to an oasis, the Walk came to a highway service area with four ranks of fuel tanks, a multitude of parking spaces, and a separate, air-conditioned building that housed a two-hundred-seat lunchroom, a gift shop, and lavatories. Flagged out, Lucas ordered a half hour's cool respite in the lunchroom and slumped in a booth under the solicitous eye of Molly Hamilton, who brought him an iced tea.

Arley had returned, disturbed by the fragility of Selma Fishbein, and sat in another booth with Snyder and the Reverend Nick Bergquist, who seemed able to comfort Arley with a touch of his hand on Arley's arm. Meanwhile, Peter Schumacher and George Corrigan went to the truck for a handful of WISE's five thousand "Walk fliers," still sealed in the printshop's corrugated box and stored under Arley's tarpaulin.

"Might as well make use of the time," Schumacher had said, and stationed himself at the building's revolving front door.

Corrigan worked the room. Once, at the candy counter, his offering hand was pushed away by a white man who seemed to think the subject was civil rights. Unperturbed, Corrigan had moved on and was not refused again. His cocky grin disarmed the dozen or so diners scattered on stools around the serpentine counter. A white woman in a tight T-shirt gave him a dollar. A rangy Negro wearing a cap studded with union buttons gave him his change and called him "brother."

Snyder asked Corrigan for a flier. It was a single sheet of orange paper, text on one side, a picture of havoc in a war-torn Vietnamese village on the other. Under a headline, WE'RE MARCHING FOR PEACE, the flier said:

We are citizens and working people just like you. Some of us are also veterans of World War II and Korea. But we are taking time out from our jobs and our studies to protest American intervention in Vietnam and to call for peace talks now. We agree with Martin Luther King. He said, "I'm not going to sit by and see war escalated without saying anything about it." America does not belong in Vietnam killing innocent civilians. Only the Vietnamese belong in Vietnam. Our defense is not threatened by the outcome there. It is, no matter how tragic, *their* war. It is up to them to decide their form of government, which, in any case, they must live with, not us. Some say we are in Vietnam to help build a nation and defeat the enemies of democracy. We respect such goals, but we do not believe our presence in Indochina can be other than self-defeating, and it surely threatens our ability to build our own nation and defend liberty here at home. If you want peace, if you cherish your own democratic freedoms, join us in a call upon our President for an end to the bombing, and peace talks NOW!

Snyder folded the flier and secured it in his notebook. Then he took a seat at the lunch counter next to Rachel. Her head was buried in her arms. When Snyder ordered two coffees, she looked up with a tired smile. The sun had burned her nose and cheeks and the backs of her hands.

"You should watch that," Snyder said.

"Tan's my best color," she said. Then: "I've been watching you. You're keeping busy."

"First impressions, Ray, remember?"

"Want one of mine?"

"Absolutely."

"For the record."

"Very fine." Snyder smiled and turned to a fresh page in his notebook, thinking how fine, indeed, her tan would look.

"It's how I feel about a day of walking—if that interests you—how quickly I lose track of time."

"Tell me."

"Well, I feel outside of time, in space, actually, because what counts is distance, you know what I mean? When you have fifteen miles to walk, distance is all that counts. I look ahead to a point on the horizon where the road dips down or where there's a silo or some other landmark, and I aim for that, one step at a time. It's better when Arley's truck comes into view, because I know I can rest soon. That can be an urgent matter when I'm carrying a sign. None of us talk much, have you noticed—except when you come by with your notebook? Listen, I worry about you, my friend. You tend to get lost in your notebook, and that can be dangerous if you wander off the road, don't you think? Anyway, I like it best when Luther plays his recorder and I can hum to myself. Marching songs—war songs, imagine that!—they help. Knowing you're getting a nice tan, that helps. But nothing helps all that much. When I think about walking another seven hundred miles, it's downright depressing."

"Too true!" Snyder exclaimed. Good copy excited him, and he had long since learned that to show it encouraged more later.

Pleased, Rachel smiled into her coffee cup.

"And I got you into it, Jack. End of quote."

"I'm grateful."

"Oh, yes?" She looked up soberly. "Well, we'll see."

Before leaving the service building, Snyder took himself to a stall in the lavatory, and was thus inspired to add a note for himself:

"Nice quote, above. Their hike along U.S. 30 so far is just part of a long test of this thing in reality. The Walk, day before yesterday, was only a bright idea, a dream that a group of such size and character, without training or discipline, might actually go any distance at all, might really prevail in the end, receiving the attention it seeks, not least from *Harrington's*. So far, so good—but, big BUT, might it not fail, abort itself somewhere, even right here, and leave no trace anywhere, except where it has been so far, about fifty miles east of Chicago?"

3

That night, about one hundred Valparaiso University students and a few teachers came to a Walk meeting in a campus dining hall, with Lucas and a local student alone together at a head table and the rest of the walkers scattered among the audience. Even though it was Saturday night, the turnout did not impress Snyder. The university had nearly five thousand students attending five colleges and a law school.

In the seat next to Snyder sat an undergraduate named Turner, who, upon reading the Walk flier, had whispered that the vast majority of the student body actually supported the Johnson administration's war policy or passively accepted it. On his shirt, Turner wore a large button: "Ringo Starr for President." He remained silent during stand-up speeches at their seats by Molly Hamilton and Peter Schumacher, a sympathetic response by the student chairman, and an hour's discussion. Then, toward the end of the meeting, his hand went up for a question:

"The name is Turner, sir, class of '68. Doesn't the United States have to stand up to Communism in Asia, or else repeat the mistakes of the thirties that led to Munich?"

Frank Dunne raised his hand to answer. He identified himself and his union, and said, "I'm only a carpenter and no expert in foreign affairs. But I can read and what I've read is Bernard Fall and the New York *Times* and Mr. I. F. Stone. They tell me that what we have here is the United States of America coming down on the side of one party to a civil war, a war that is being fought on the other side, so far, mostly with American-made weapons captured from our side. The issue is not Munich. The issue is us. I am one of those, although I tell you now that not everyone on this walk agrees with me—not by a long shot—I am one of those who believe that this war is powered by the capitalist dynamic in America. We have taken over the French investment in Indochina. Now we are trying to protect that investment in the name of anti-Communism. We call it containment—the Chinese are coming! But I call it imperial capitalism. What is our business in Vietnam? It is a war for markets and resources. That's what it is. We should recognize that and then ask ourselves whether we want to keep fighting for them. Maybe we will even answer 'okay,' but then, at least, we'll know what we're sending our men to kill and be killed for."

Dunne paused and seemed satisfied with the thoughtful stillness in the room. Snyder looked about, saw Reed Herndon with a funny little smile on his face shaking his head ever so slightly from side to side, saw Dorene Quink nodding, saw Joe Rice frowning, saw Melvin Fishbein thin-lipped with regret, and saw the schism among the walkers, between their own doves and hawks, respectively, liberals for whom the war was a political sin, a loss of faith, and radicals for whom it was a plot, an economic enterprise.

As though to confirm Snyder's discovery, Reverend Nick raised his hand and interjected, "Frank, are you saying we can't oppose this immoral war without opposing capitalism? How droll!"

As the meeting stirred, Dunne replied, "I'm just saying in answer to Mr. Turner's question that judgment of the one requires asking questions about the experience we've had with the other."

Turner raised his hand again. "But, sir, surely you're not a Marxist!"

Laughter exploded. Dunne's leathery face turned gray. Then even he laughed.

"Well, I read my Marx in college, yes," he said. "Socialist, yes. Six times voted for Norman Thomas, yes. But I confess—I also voted for the promises of Lyndon Johnson last time. It took Barry Goldwater on the other side to get me to do that!"

More laughter followed, threatening to waste the evening by trivializing it. Then Sam Lucas noisily pushed back from the head table, drawing attention as he seemed about to speak. At the same moment, Professor Fishbein stood tall and commanding, and took the floor. He nodded to Lucas and then, after a swift search of the audience, to Snyder, as though to say: hear me this once.

"Well, now," he began, his voice low and controlling. "I suppose you think this walk is somewhat split over its understanding of the nature of the Vietnam War? Perhaps, but rest assured we are united by our purpose. We are for peace. At home, we may be socialists, capitalists—Communists, for all I know, since FBI clearance is not required for this exercise—but we are only pacifists here, something I can explain by telling you what brings me here tonight.

"I was a desk pilot in India during World War II, an air traffic manager at an ATC base in Assam near the town of Gohoti. Boredom drew me deeper into India than most of our fliers and I gradually became a distant admirer of Gandhi and his independence movement. Now, peace returned me to Wisconsin, to my wife and my university, but only for so long as it took me to realize that on my brain was Mr. Gandhi and the Satyagraha, that is, the non-violent, or pacifist, solution to the problem of change. Then, with my wife, Selma, I returned to New Delhi to spend some time getting closer to the movement and Gandhi himself—the sort of thing you must do once in your life.

"It was a terrifying moment. There was India going free and tens of thousands of his followers gathering every day to show their support for him. You could see him on Sunday mornings, walking among them to a temple. 'Bapu,' they would say. And he would smile and wave. He was small, thin, sublime. He was seventy-six years old. He had endured and his victory was imminent and then his life would end. You wonder if he knew then how little time he had.

"One cold day in February, I was inside the temple. He had prayed and then he began talking about the atomic bomb, the meaning of the atomic bomb and whether it had destroyed his faith in non-violence. He then asked himself the question: could one believe both in truth, the truth that produced such a weapon, and in non-violence?"

Snyder stopped writing. He looked up, feeling Fishbein's eyes on him, wanting to see his words getting down, to appear next in *Harrington's Weekly Immortality*. Snyder nodded and Fishbein seemed relieved.

"The atomic bomb," Fishbein continued, "had not exploded Gandhi's faith any more than had his long years in jail. Rather it showed him that truth and non-violence were the greatest powers on earth, because they were spiritual, always progressive, resident in everybody, and unconquerable. It was a theme he returned to again and again until his death, that no more than bombs can be destroyed by counter-bombs or hatred by counter-hatred can violence be destroyed by counter-violence. Mankind, he concluded, has to get out of violence through non-violence."

Snyder saw Reed Herndon sitting in shadow behind Fishbein, eyes closed, his face tense, resisting, he supposed, the professor's oblique call to civil disobedience. The professor went on, his voice rising to a conclusion:

"And did Gandhi have anything to say about the issue raised by Mr. Turner? Well, let's put it another way. Can one be a pacifist and a real American, a believer in welfare, free markets, and democracy? The answer is yes, definitely. To Gandhi, the root of all progress, including the decision to choose non-violence, which is harder for some than others, is individuality. Excessive state power frightened him. He opposed Communism because it destroyed individuality even as it promised to reduce exploitation. Only democracy and non-violence could go together. Even the socialist ideal of the greatest good for the greatest number seemed heartless to him, because it sacrifices the interest of the forty-nine percent minority for the interest of the fifty-one percent majority. For Gandhi, the only truly human goal was the greatest good of all, which can only be achieved by self-sacrifice.

"So, do you see what brings us—me, at least—here tonight? It is my opinion, Mr. Turner, that we're on this walk to make some small sacrifice for the greatest good of all. Can you think of a better reason? Why don't you—all of you—join us?"

There was mighty applause, joined even by the skeptical Turner and the seemingly vanquished Frank Dunne, duly noted by Snyder.

Snyder also caught Professor Fishbein smiling at him and it dawned on him that they, Melvin and Selma, were now going home.

4

Lucas was going to be a stickler about shortcuts and cheating, driven by a desire to announce one day that the Walk had indeed walked every step of the way to Washington. He made Snyder aware of this next morning by having meticulously arranged for a school bus to return the walkers two miles west to the exact spot just off U.S. 30 where another bus had picked them up the night before on the way into Valparaiso.

At 8 A.M., they were back on the highway. It was Sunday and a dozen local students, including the sophomore Turner, had joined them. Molly Hamilton read a brief farewell letter from the Fishbeins, who had written that they were proud to have been first to sign the Walk's petition. The local students accompanied the Walk to the first rest site. Arley had picked a grassy spot in the shade of a billboard. The students had nearly doubled the length of the Walk's file. Now they wanted to sign the Walk's petition, but Lucas demurred, explaining the overnight rule. They stayed on to hear Lucas's briefing, seventeen miles for the day to the town of Hamlet, Indiana, population 600, and overnight at the home of a family named Scott, friends of Nick Bergquist. Then, acting as the students' spokesman, Turner meekly announced that his entire group would return to their campus. The walkers left them behind on the shoulder of U.S. 30, waving. Lucas told Snyder he was disappointed. Having lost the

Fishbeins, he was praying for at least two recruits to keep the Walk's number up to seventeen. Final exams had defeated him.

Thunderheads threatened behind them all that morning, rising but unable to take control of the sky and the dazzling sun. The Walk had blazing summer again, temperature in the nineties, as the weatherman had predicted, and no breeze except for gusts whipped off the pavement by Sunday drivers in schools of sedans with fin-shaped fenders. Once a speeding car slipped onto the shoulder, peppered the walkers with gravel, and recovered the highway. No one was injured.

At three that afternoon, nearing the end of the sixth hour's march, chance brought them to the low bridge over the narrow bed of the Kankakee River. The river looked taciturn and cool and was gray-green in that hour's light. There was a consensus for a walk below, so they crossed over the bridge and strolled downstream a hundred yards or so and around a bend to rest among some willows at the edge of a freshly plowed field. Arley Broyle had carried along the water jug and two boxes of Oreo cookies. He served everyone as they stretched out on the bank around a large rock. In a shady place apart from the others, Snyder soon dozed off.

A loud smack and a great laugh awoke him. Fifty yards farther downstream, beyond a thick clump of spruces, Peter Schumacher was in the water and George Corrigan, peeled to his skivvies, hung in the air above him, an instant before he, too, dropped with a splash. In another moment, Dorene and June followed, stripped clean, but diving so fast Snyder hardly saw them. Snyder sat up. Luther Wood and Lester Kupferman were running from the bank to the trees and were next seen flapping naked in the river. Rachel Abraham grabbed Snyder's arm, crying, "C'mon, all for a swim!"

Snyder held back, preserving his status a moment too long. Rachel skipped away, into the trees and out again, arching naked over the water in a fine swan, arms stretched out and full breasts forward like a flying manatee. She cut the water clean and bobbed up laughing almost at the far shore. Snyder waved, but would not allow himself to follow. He lit a cigarette, inhaled deeply, and watched her.

The bathers paddled and swam for half an hour, never coming too close to those by the rock. In that time, Lucas had sent Arley back to the truck for the towel supply, four towels was all, which Lucas himself carried downstream. When he called time, the boys were first out. After they had returned to the rock, the girls slipped into the spruces for their clothes. Last from the trees was Rachel, with a towel around her head, her face still damp, carrying her hiker's shoes. Snyder gave her a look intended to appear objective; it made her smile.

"You missed it," she said.

"I watched."

"You'll never be able to describe it unless you do it."

"Not so."

"You walk with us. Why not swim with us?"

Snyder knew he was barely able to disguise his interest in her. All that saves you, he was thinking, is your fear of falling.

"You have a point," he said, matter-of-factly, as though he would take it up later with a board of elders.

5

At dusk, they passed the turnoff to the village of Hamlet and continued a thousand yards along U.S. 30, then walked a mile north on a country road. Here they saw a weathered red house with a porch on three sides overlooking the humble farm of Robert Scott, his wife, and teenaged son. The Scotts worked eighty acres, mostly corn, raised a few animals, and made up their annual deficit by hiring out father and son to cut hay for the neighbors. The house seemed sturdy, but needed paint and repairs; the barn roof was askew; and the spring planting appeared to be dying of the heat. Reverend Nick, wearing his tennis hat and St. Olaf College sweatshirt, eagerly took the lead sign as the walkers went through the lower gate. Then he almost ran up his friend's farm road. Scott was waiting for him in the high grass of the front yard. They were veterans of the Korean War. Reverend Nick, a protégé of Sam Lucas, had been Major Scott's chaplain. Scott was in his late thirties, like Reverend Nick, but gaunt and dark as Nick was plump and fair. A month earlier, Scott had heard about the Walk from Reverend Nick and had invited the walkers to spend the night whenever they happened to pass by. In the farmyard, Reverend Nick dropped the Walk's sign. The two men embraced like long-lost brothers. Scott was missing his left arm to the elbow.

For supper, there was a diet meal of soup, chips, and fruit. Afterward, the single women and the Lucas-Hamiltons bedded down in three upstairs rooms, the single men sacked on the living-room floor or the porch. Except for the kitchen, the house was soon quiet. Snyder found Reverend Nick drying dishes while Barbara Scott washed and Bob Scott looked on, drinking coffee and V.O. at the table. She was a tall, weary woman who looked older than her husband by fifteen years.

"Coffee?" she asked.

Snyder knew he had intruded. He attempted to withdraw.

"I know you want to talk," he said. "How long has it been?"

Bob Scott looked up, then down and deeply into his cup. "Since me and old Nick laid eyes," he said, "it's about twelve years. Looks good, doesn't he? These Norwegians! Sure, Nick didn't like Korea, but he was in it up to his zatch. Never said much. Not a sermonizer. Just hands on, that's all. Look at those hands! Every time our company went out, Nick'd come down from Battalion and be there, and when what was left of us came back, he'd also be there, with a touch, a handshake, a pat on the back. You'll find he never says much, never. Don't even ask him. It's the hands. Eighteen months in the line, I always came back, mostly, so I figured this chaplain with the hands was my lucky man."

Reverend Nick raised both hands, towel in one, dish in the other, and grinned.

Scott threw down two ounces of V.O., bringing tears to his eyes. He swallowed coffee and coughed. Then he continued. "Well, so, my lucky man, Nick B., doesn't like Vietnam. It's only twelve years later—my, the booze that's been drunk!—and on Vietnam, we don't exactly see eye to eye. But at least I'm smart enough to know that I'm not sure of my answer. Major Scott's not one of the Joint Chiefs. But Vietnam needs some kind of a plan, any plan. We have no plan. I would hate to think this country's been on the wrong track all this time, from Korea to this moment, wouldn't you? So what's the plan? I gotta know. You, Nick, and this walk ought to be demanding a plan, a plan, that's all. Give us a plan or come home."

Reverend Nick turned from the sink, toward Snyder, the smile replaced by wet eyes and tight lips over clenched teeth.

"Hell, yes," Scott went on. "I mean, we all need a plan. Christ, I need a plan. So what's a war without a plan? It's murder. But a war with a plan, that's victory. Now, I know Nick sees no hope of that, so we can't agree. But do I care? I love Nick. I help Nick. I'd kill for Nick. So I don't have to agree with him to have him for Sunday dinner with his friends, now do I? We share what we've got."

No one answered. Upstairs, someone flushed the only toilet in the house.

"Well, bathroom's free," Snyder said, pretending he had been waiting for that all along. "Good night."

He stepped over the sleeping mounds on the living-room floor and onto the porch. The night was warm and moon-bright. Oh, the one-armed man, he thought, is in trouble.

Snyder was smoking when Reverend Nick came up beside him.

"Will you forget all that?" Reverend Nick asked.

"Scott's V.O.? Sure."

"Do you think Sam will understand?"

"What?"

"The whole picture—that my friend needs help?"

"You're signing the petition in the morning?"

"Are you surprised?"

Snyder realized he was not surprised.

6

A day's walk after leaving Reverend Nick behind with the Scotts' woes covered the distance to Etna Green, Indiana, and midafternoon of the following day found them moving apace, just above a town called Winona Lake. That moment on U.S. 30 was hazy, hot, and singularly thick with cars, trucks, and even an occasional pride of motorcycles.

With the brim of his daughter's gift-hat pulled down all around to keep the sun off his neck, Snyder trailed at the rear of the Walk side by side with Sam Lucas, who, his faith in candor undiminished, had hung back to confide in him. Their number was Lucas's great worry.

They had spent the past evening in a bull session with ten students outside the city of Plymouth at the All Souls Christian Theological Seminary and again failed to balance attrition, which seemed inevitable, with recruitment, which seemed impossible.

The proximity of mid-May to final exams, Lucas complained, as though it were not he himself who had scheduled the Walk's dates, apparently eliminated all those students not already stricken by indifference or even faith in their government. (One student had said, "You don't look like hippies!") And there was Reed Herndon, who might flee at any moment, and likewise George Corrigan, if the cause of civil rights were to beckon, taking Peter Schumacher with him. Wasn't this the greatest threat to the Walk, Lucas was asking himself, asking Snyder, that some number below fourteen would mean that neither Washington nor *Harrington's* would take them seriously, except as proof of the quixotic nature of the anti-war movement?

"Curse Nick Bergquist, anyway!" Lucas shouted.

Snyder was getting it all down in his notebook, shifting his weight away from the highway as the shoulder inexplicably narrowed, then tacking slightly as Lucas, in mid-gesture, bumped him soundly. Instinctively, Snyder was adjusting again to keep pen on paper, when a certain angle of sound and perhaps a sixth sense warned him that a car was coming up fast under the brim of his hat. He had time to think: how strange, a premonition . . . heard "Jack!" exhaled by Lucas . . . had time to think: it's the damn hat, so low, it cuts off, what do you call it, your peripheral vision . . .

Then he turned full figure to the highway and the presence of an onrushing blue sedan filled his awareness. It is right here, he was thinking, the name "Oldsmobile" neatly sited on the radiator, Illinois plates promoting "The Land of Lincoln," swerrrrving away even as it sweeeeeps toward you in a deliberate but miscalculated arc.

Snyder saw two laugh-frozen faces behind the windshield and heard the bellows of twin horns and felt the wind and the heat as the right front fender singed him along the belly and the world flipped over for him.

He knew he was down and rolling in the gravel, blessedly off the road, turning over twice more, then taking a hard knock in back, and under the arm, as he came to rest against the guardrail, with his head fortunately under the wire mesh in a patch of sweet nameless green ground cover which, in the heat, was already offering up small purple-white blossoms. He realized he still clung to his notebook.

Snyder lay still for a time, how long he could not calculate, as the walkers clucked over him, especially Sam Lucas, who seemed stricken himself, and Reed Herndon, who, a voice said, knew something about nursing, and Rachel, wearing her patented "I got you into this" look, who had recovered his hat, glasses, and pen, and Molly Hamilton, who'd had the presence of mind to jog ahead for Arley and bring back the truck with its first-aid supplies. In the far background, he heard Joe Rice and Frank Dunne fuming about hit-and-run bastards who ought to be horsewhipped. Yes, yes, Snyder was thinking, if we ever see that face in the windshield again, men, we'll horsewhip the bastard.

They did not move Snyder except the inches necessary to clear his head from under the wire mesh. Hands lifted his shirt and loosened his belt. Then various concerned faces took turns examining his wound, a welt about eight inches long at the base of the belly, just above the hip. It was the color of a ripe tomato, redder than red against his pale skin, but there was no blood, except for a slight scrape on one palm where, he decided, he must have taken the main force of his skid across the shoulder. Cool-eyed behind his glasses, Herndon took charge. He doctored the welt and the scrape and covered both with gauze pads. Then he helped Snyder to his feet. Snyder felt no serious pain.

"I'm fine, fine!" he said, euphorically, though rage rattled the cage of his mind. An intense yearning to crush the Oldsmobile into a cube of bloody tin all but overwhelmed him, then gave way in an instant to the realization that he might never again have a better moment to bring Herndon into the process of the story. Control is all, he was thinking, control, control, control.

Snyder's face was transformed by his inner exertions; from flushed red, it went to gray-pink, then almost bloodless white.

Herndon put an arm around Snyder's shoulder. "Okay, Jack?" he asked.

"Okay, but maybe an early pit stop."

Snyder had smiled with gratitude and intent to interview. Then, too, he understood his own state of shock, that it would pass in due time, and he wanted to be seated somewhere comfortable with a drink in his hand when the pain really started.

Shortly, Arley Broyle drove Snyder and Herndon over the last seven miles east to Pierceton, where the Walk was due for the night at the Baptist Brotherhood Church of God. Arley left them at the first saloon on the main drag and headed back up the highway.

It was a small place, harmless and empty, with high-backed booths, ceiling fans, and a silent jukebox. The men's room, where Snyder washed up, smelled of Airwick. The lone bar mistress was also the lone waitress. She brought Snyder a gin martini in a water glass, the drink known thereabouts as a New Yorker and Herndon a Coke in a bottle.

Snyder eased back against the booth and brought his feet up on the empty side of Herndon's bench. The shock was, indeed, wearing off, and everything hurt, especially his lower back. Just looking at the three-ounce martini, large by New York standards, made him feel better.

Herndon peeled a straw for his Coke, but did not drink. He kept his eyes lowered, as though considering the answer to a question not yet posed. The few days of sun had burned his forehead and cheeks except in the pallid hollows, where the markings of prison stubbornly resisted change.

Snyder tasted his martini, commented on its excellence, and smiled at the apprehensive bar mistress. He drank it slowly, with relief if not relish at the thought of its probable effect on his aching vertebrae. For Herndon's benefit, he criticized the red pimento in the olive, but ate it later, and waved for a second drink like the first. The gin smoothed off the sharp edges of discomfort front and backside, and also clarified his view of Herndon's problem with the article. Emboldened, he tapped his notebook on the edge of his empty glass, like an imperious conductor tapping his baton on a music stand. It was the gin speaking, on top of too much sun and adrenaline, giving an impression which Snyder caught, disavowed, and sought to correct with politeness.

"May I ask you something, Reed?"

Herndon looked up from his own thoughts. He said, "Sure, ask."

"Why you're on the Walk."

"Whose business is that?"

"People want to know—any part of it."

"Not about prison."

"Well, then, before that."

"Not unless I get to say whether you can use it."

"Okay, you get that."

They had a pact. Snyder concluded it by writing "X" at the top of a clean page. It is the only solution, he was thinking—your flourish is a bit excessive, Jack, but the young man gets the idea, "X" for "temporarily anonymous." He turned the notebook half around so Herndon could see.

"Let's shake on that," Herndon said. He reached his right hand over the top of Snyder's martini glass, letting it hang there under a half smile, signifying his own satisfaction that he was receiving more from the professional journalist, under the circumstances, than he had expected.

Snyder saw the hand waiting for his. He reckoned that Herndon must know the law, that his conviction for a federal crime had given him permanent status as a public figure and subordinated his right to privacy to the public's right to know all about him. The publicity surrounding his case would have taught him that much, and Sam Lucas would have told him that serving his sentence made no difference; certainly a parolee could not prevent anyone from writing about him. Still, a recalcitrant one could hide, to a certain extent, what might be known about himself. And by that much, Herndon was able now to force a choice on Snyder between a risky investment in more knowledge and passive acceptance of a great silence on a subject about which he felt he needed to know much more. So early in the chase, Snyder was thinking, is too early to let the man's hand dangle. He would have preferred otherwise. There was still no violation, but Snyder knew they were standing now at the top of a slippery slope.

They shook hands. Then Snyder tasted his second New Yorker and retrieved the notebook. He sat up straight, wincing as his sacroiliac protested. "Shoot," he said, and smiled his most practiced smile, the one that portrayed readiness, reasonableness, and reliability, those virtues in an interviewer most likely to disarm the most reluctant interviewee.

"I was born in Decatur, Illinois, 1943, February," Herndon said, greatly composed. "My father then was a salesman, became a partner, in a shop for pianos, musical instruments, and sheet music. The name of the shop was awful, Melody Lane. My mother's still a teacher of geography at the high school. Hobart and Adele Herndon. Both only finished junior college because of the depression, but they had poverty in common, and first-year philosophy, and a lot of feeling for one another if not what you'd call romantic love. They wouldn't belong to a church, but they belonged to a brotherhood study group, Catholics, Jews, and Protestants, and considered themselves ethical pacifists.

"My father was a conscientious objector during World War II. He said he wasn't afraid to risk his life for his country, but he wasn't going to kill another human being. He was self-made—I mean he read the New Testament and Tolstoy and A. J. Muste and Robert Graves and *All Quiet on the Western Front* and thought it through for himself. When his case came up before the draft board, they found a Quaker great-aunt in the family tree and used her to duck the moral issue. They gave my father non-combatant status on religious grounds and the Navy accepted him. They fixed it so he left home soon after I was born and saw to it that he never got a leave. They didn't want him setting an example for other boys back home.

"He spent three years in ships' services, helping manage the band at Pearl Harbor. He played clarinet, too, and never got rank above seaman first. Once my mother visited him and they had a weekend on Waikiki Beach, like in the movies, and my sister was born at the right time after that. Finally, he came home for good with a bleeding ulcer. The war was over, too. He was thirty-two years old.

"I heard more and more about that period as I grew up. My mother, especially, wanted me to know how compromised my father felt serving the Navy as he did, how he felt he'd failed to make his point, which needed a greater sacrifice to be heard during the most popular war ever fought. It was his ulcer that decided me, in my turn, to refuse any service at all. My father died in 1957.

"Well, Decatur's a fine town of seventy-five thousand and I'd never want to live anywhere else. It makes you feel as though you live in a city, but so close to the country that nature's always right there. Still, I graduated a year early from high school, loaded up a suitcase with novels, Dreiser and Hemingway and the Russians, and my father's books, and went to Chicago, a precocious kid looking for something. That was 1959.

"The job I got was cleaning bedpans in Chicago General. I was a nurse's aide, doing night shift, which was easy and perfect, because I could read. I took some English courses at the University of Chicago, but dropped out midsemester, right after I'd turned seventeen. My new friends talked politics all the time and, summer of 1960, six of us drove to Los Angeles to march around the Sports Arena for Adlai Stevenson during the Democratic national convention. We carried Ban the Bomb signs.

"Up in Jackson Hole, after Kennedy won the nomination, I made my first little decision about the military draft. I decided I'd register, but not go if I was called. Back home, my mother gave me a heart-to-heart, but she didn't disagree. She wanted me to get going with my education, maybe do medicine, so I went to Millikin University, right there in Decatur, to find out who I was and, of course, evade the draft.

"There was a little peace group on campus and, summer of 1962, outside of Richmond, Virginia, some of us joined the last week of the Boston–Washington Ban the Bomb march. At the Pentagon, we did civil disobedience and I got a night in a holding pen and my name in the records. That's where I met Joe Rice and Vachel, outside one of those D.C. neighborhood lockups.

"That winter, unofficially, I dropped out again. I just stopped going to classes and went to work for WISE in Chicago on a nuclear disarmament project. You have to understand the bomb was our issue at that time, not Vietnam. I wrote pamphlets, helped raise money, and stood in some vigils outside the Great Lakes Naval Station. Pretty soon, I sent my draft card back to the Decatur Selective Service Board with a letter applying for status as a conscientious objector. I claimed an exemption on the grounds of personal morality, not religious belief. I remember one sentence in my letter: 'A citizen ought to have the right to choose non-violence.' I got that being around Sam Lucas.

"The board took about six months to let me know how they felt—they declined my application and said they'd discuss it when my number came up. Then another six months passed before someone at

Millikin let them know I hadn't been entitled to a student deferment for almost a year.

"Forthwith, Jack, I appeared in Decatur to say I wouldn't accept induction. I wasn't for or against any specific policy, in Vietnam or anywhere else. I was taking my stand on the grounds that, as a pacifist, I had a right to choose not to serve.

"Now, one board member, a man who'd known us Herndons for years, asked my mother to get me back in school, studying medicine, so the whole matter'd be forgotten. This man even called me once in Chicago with the suggestion that I join the Merchant Marine, or something equally non-belligerent, so he wouldn't have to vote to refer my case to the federal prosecutor down in Springfield. At that moment in history, President Kennedy was just three weeks dead and his memory, this man said, was prompting him to call me. Funny, Kennedy's memory wasn't prompting him to join me in my protest. I remember him saying, 'Whaddya wanta suffah for?'

"I returned to Decatur one snowy morning in December 1963. I posted myself in front of the Macon County Courthouse wearing a sandwich board with the whole story spelled out in capital letters, saying the board had refused me c.o. status and I was refusing to report. I stood there a whole day and a night and into the next morning. I made front page in the local paper and the board gave up. They had a couple of friendly federal marshals arrest me."

Snyder could not imagine himself seeking arrest. He could, however, begin thinking that Herndon's character was really, somehow, beyond his ken and experience. He lit a cigarette for the usual craving plus gaining time to formulate a question that might shake Herndon's diffidence.

"You didn't have a girl you were going to miss? A friend or a project that needed you?"

Calmly, to the point of coldness, Herndon replied, "I had a girl at Chicago, liberated girl, age twenty, her own pad off campus, the whole bit. She said, 'Choose,' and I chose to resist. Though I was free on bail until April, she left for home in West Texas, never to be heard from again. There were people—especially my folks and Sam Lucas—who stuck by me, did their best to defend me, so she was not, finally, consequential. Her name was Bookstaver, Jean Marie Bookstaver.

"In the end, I was going to jail. There was no ground, none, for a compromise, and a Federal judge in Springfield sentenced me to four years. Of course, I expected that much, maybe even five. And the District Court agreed, in a very civilized opinion, as though they were sending me off to Boy Scout camp for two weeks. I wasn't bitter, just a moment of self-doubt, because of how strange they thought I was, going to Leavenworth at age twenty-one for something that really didn't matter, pacifism, because there wasn't any major war going on to speak of, anyway. It was April 1964, a time when President Johnson was still saying that only Asian boys should fight Asian boys in Indochina and making it seem that any escalation of the war was not just unlikely but inconceivable."

Snyder nodded sympathetically. On different turf, he would himself make much of the Administration's betrayal of public trust. "Has it mattered?" Snyder asked. "Were the judges right?"

"I served half my time, so—by that much, I guess—it mattered to the government."

"The government?"

"They could say, see, here's what happens to draft dodgers."

"Why parole you?"

"They wouldn't unless I'd applied. I wasn't going to let them use me any longer to make their point, especially since they'd escalated the war in Vietnam while I was inside."

"But what about your point?"

"In those two years, I didn't have to kill anybody for my country."

"Was that your point? You didn't have to go to jail to avoid that. You could've stayed in school. You could've left the country. The man on the draft board asked the right question: 'whaddya wanta suffah for?'"

"I had a bigger point, about my rights as a citizen. They won on that one. I didn't think they'd win. They won and I lost and now I'm making the best of it, doing the right thing within my limits toward the war in Vietnam, so they can't say they beat me completely."

"Sounds as though they taught you a lesson."

"Over the line, Jack."

"And you don't consider yourself a martyr?"

"I'm not a martyr. Norman Morrison was a martyr."

"You have to immolate yourself to be a martyr?"

"To win, I'd have to be able to take it all, my sentence less my good time, no breaks and no favors. That message would have been clear—they have the power, yes, but I have the right. I could only take about half of it, Jack, just half before I asked out. I'm not proud of that. Pacifism needs heroes and I'm only half a hero. So, you're right, all right. They taught me a lesson—how not to be a political prisoner. You lose when you ask out. You win when you endure. You asked me a question and that's the answer. I'm here on this Walk because I'd be ashamed not to be here. That's all I can tell you. Oh, shit!"

Herndon fought for control. Tears came to his eyes. His sunburned face reddened still more. He pushed up his glasses and rubbed his eyes, first with the back of his hand, then with a handkerchief.

Snyder scrambled for the banks of his own reserve as Herndon's rising emotions flowed past, a flood of grief, embarrassment, and frustration pushing Snyder himself back toward the night Zimmerman's news had arrived. And, so removed, he observed, as from high ground, both Herndon's behavior and his own reactions with a view to the professional situation, thinking, the moment has come to shut down the interview, mark it "to be continued," and lay the psychological groundwork for that time in the future when Herndon, without being asked, will put all this, and more, on the record.

"We can quit now," Snyder said.

"I guess so." Herndon drew his hands from his eyes. "How're you feeling, eh?" He cracked a sheepish grin. He seemed amused by his passing self-absorption, but disconcerted that he'd forgotten Snyder's accident. He looked into the second glass Snyder had emptied. "Your wounds all right, Jack?"

Snyder's lumbar region was just then reporting a low-grade, but steady pain. He thought, another treatment by Dr. Martini will take care of it, but—you know yourself—only at some risk of the blind staggers, loss of perfect recall, and moral tarnish in the eyes of the teetotaler. Excess gin can do all that.

"Let's say I'm recovering," Snyder said. "Another Pierceton New Yorker, martini so-called, might help, but I have to think of the old image, sober, serious, detached, and all that."

Herndon seemed grateful for the joking. "Yes, the Walk has to think of that, too, doesn't it? I mean, the image we create, whatever we really are, the thing we become in your eyes is the important thing."

"Essenes, Reed. You're all Essenes to me."

7

Snyder limped, so Herndon and he were an hour behind the Walk getting to the Brotherhood church, a small limestone box with a Victorian spire set back from the street on a rise so barren as to seem abnormal amid the greenery of Pierceton. Herndon said it was a sure sign of the blight that had ravaged Decatur and, as proof, they saw color photos in the foyer showing the church as it once was, sheltered by great, trusted old elms.

Down a flight of stairs, the latecomers discovered a well-lit pink-brick basement room with a long buffet table and their friends in line for dinner. Lucas embraced Snyder with loud praise for his recuperative powers. Other walkers crowded about, the men greeting Snyder as well as Herndon as a prodigal son, sorely missed as though for days, not merely a few hours. And there were cheek kisses for Snyder from the four women of the Walk as amiable as those bestowed upon Herndon, perhaps more so in the case of Rachel. She embraced Snyder, then turned her face up to his with a look of affectionate defiance.

"Watch out for my panache," he said, responding to the Walk's effusions with his state-of-the-art mechanism for the witty preservation of professionalism.

"Oh, yes," she replied, with mock surprise, "it's still showing."

They laughed, and continued to chat, but her look told that he had made her uneasy. His little joke probably didn't deserve her rejoinder, but it was not pointless. He had long recognized in himself a kind of journalistic neurosis, shared with the late Zimmerman and other reporters he knew, that permitted reflection on events while repressing natural affections. It was, he assumed, a specific defense against reciprocating the universal tendency of subjects, sooner or later, to identify with reporters, like victims with their executioners.

The reporter had to save himself; his trick was to preserve his independence, achieving involvement without identification, detachment despite access, and objectivity regardless of inevitable subjectivity, personal or political or both—and bring home the story. A trick, indeed! For truth, in the end, was always perceived through the eye of a mind that, one way or another, had an interest in seeing its idea become a story. You were always proving yourself. Someday, he realized, he might have to explain all this to Rachel.

When the walkers subsided, the local minister approached Snyder and Herndon. He was about thirty, tall, balding, and aggressively good-natured. He wore a blue suit with a trident peace button in his lapel. He recited his name in four distinct syllables, Heinz Pendergraft, as though the *Harrington's* man might not otherwise get it right. Then he set about introducing the church women who had prepared and were serving the food.

Of the seven church women they met, six were young to middle-aged married ladies of the Brotherhood's Sisterhood, proud of their salads, cold meats, cheeses, bread, and cakes. Each wore traditional Flemish clothes—small lace cap, scalloped blouse, quilted skirt, and high shoes. For them, the Walk's presence was "a costume event," as Pendergraft put it to Snyder. They, in turn, bragged to Snyder that the dashing Mr. Pendergraft had energized their church, turned it to world concerns, and, hopefully (ha-ha), would repopulate it if they could find a wife for him in Pierceton.

The seventh woman was Pendergraft's sister, Amelia, and "only nineteen." As the dispenser of fruit punch in four-ounce cut-glass cups, she also wore a costume, but her familial distinction was made clear by the deference of the others. She was a study for Vermeer, fair-haired and sturdy with small breasts and slim hips. Her skin was vivid, with natural color high on the cheeks. She had the naïve, yet avid look of a fan, as though she were about to ask the two celebrities for autographs.

As Herndon tasted the punch, Snyder saw the color suddenly rise to Amelia's temples accompanied by a tight smile filled with nervous little white teeth. When Herndon held out his cup for a refill, she said, with great relief, "Sit, we deliver." And later, she did, standing close to Herndon's chair until he drank and complimented her again.

After dinner, the Walk appeared upstairs in the whitewashed

chapel, seated on the stage with Lucas at the pulpit and their lead sign displayed in a space behind. They had attracted a small, but chatty crowd of local people, older couples mostly, with a lively interest in foreign affairs. Questions and answers kept the discussion going after Pendergraft's 9 P.M. deadline. In the rear pew, well separated from the crowd, Snyder felt his aches returning as the effects of alcohol wore off. Amelia Pendergraft came up from the basement by a rear stair, spotted him, and took the seat beside him.

"You're not on the stage," she said.

"I'm fine."

"I'm sorry you were hurt. A nasty thing to happen in Indiana."

"It was an Illinois car."

"Well, that's something for our side."

Amelia moved her eyes toward the pulpit, where Herndon had begun to apply the judgments of Nuremberg to American policy in Vietnam. "I believe our sins in Vietnam are more than sins," he said. "They are war crimes." Zimmerman, thought Snyder, would have liked that line. Amelia listened with half-closed eyes giving her innocent face a look of utmost concentration. As Herndon sat down, she turned to Snyder.

"I wish I could join you," she said.

"The Walk welcomes the blind, the halt, and the lame, like me."

"My brother won't let me, I'm afraid."

"Don't tell him."

Amelia laughed, the suggestion was so absurd.

Afterwards, the crowd mingled with the walkers and Snyder saw Amelia shaking hands with Herndon. When the crowd had departed, she distributed towels and thin bars of soap and helped the women of the Walk get ready for bed among the pews. It was almost eleven when Snyder came upon her again, outside under the church lantern at the top of the steps, with Reed Herndon. The air was cooler but still heavy. Snyder lit his cigarette.

"We've been talking," Herndon said. "Amelia wants to come with us."

Amelia shook her head.

"She spoke to her brother," Herndon said.

"No good?" Snyder asked. The reverend, he was thinking, is a type.

"He said no," Amelia replied. "Heinz and I, we're from Terre Haute, orphans for eight years. He's taken care of me all that time, since he entered the seminary. Of course, I've taken care of him, too."

"He's a lucky man."

"He feels it's not right, no chaperones, that sort of thing."

"But we're here," Herndon said, as if complaining to the brother. "He invited us here."

"He's got limits," Amelia said.

Snyder asked the obvious question: "How old are you?"

"I know, nineteen. I can vote, but he's a parson. This is his first mission. How would it look?"

Behind them, the door opened and Pendergraft himself joined them on the steps. Leaving for the night, he carried his jacket, briefcase, and a rolled umbrella. If he had overheard, it was not apparent. He was smiling with easy satisfaction.

"It was a fine evening," he said. "Are you well, Mr. Snyder?"

"Recovered."

Offering his hand to Herndon, he said, "You spoke well."

"Thank you," Herndon said. "Listen—"

"No, please," Amelia said.

Herndon went mum, folding his hands at his waist.

"What is it?" Pendergraft asked, readily understanding.

"Nothing—just time to go home, Heinz," Amelia said.

"Yes, it is," Pendergraft sighed.

At the crack of dawn, Amelia Pendergraft was back in the Brotherhood basement preparing a country breakfast for the Walk, assisted only by the church caretaker, a round-shouldered old man named Mollenhoff. Seemingly obsessed, with a striped apron over a yellow bib dress, she whirled and dashed among the tables, serving all fifteen meals before 7 A.M. Mollenhoff was fast, too, in charge of cleanup.

Within the hour in front of the church as the Walk said goodbye, Amelia stood sad-eyed with Mollenhoff on the steps while her brother went among the walkers with blessings and handshakes. Once she turned away and old Mollenhoff patted her shoulder.

The day's march passed and the night was spent at the Red Wagon

Motel outside the town of Coesse. Lucas briefed them next morning in a red-and-white Texaco station on U.S. 30. He was exultant. Here it was Friday and, as planned, they were eighteen miles from downtown Fort Wayne. "That is 31,860 paces," he said, succeeding with a bellowing laugh. Snyder's right foot, punished the day before by his injured gait, tingled in anticipation of the great blister it seemed certain to acquire that day. Snyder refused Rachel's suggestion that he ride with Arley, but was pleased that she'd thought of it.

After lunch, with about half the day's distance still ahead, a high wind came down upon the Walk. The clouds rolled together and turned black. Rain fell, heavy and hard, and the traffic on U.S. 30 slowed to a watery crawl. A few sheltering willows drooping at roadside protected the walkers momentarily. Arley arrived with umbrellas and rain gear. Then, to lower the risk from lightning, Lucas moved them into an open space between two fields of early corn. They were huddled here twenty minutes later when a battered green Plymouth coupe pulled off the road onto the shoulder behind Arley.

From the passenger side came Amelia Pendergraft, wearing a blue poncho and carrying a rolled sleeping bag. She spoke to Arley in the truck and climbed into his cab. In the next moment, Mollenhoff, the church caretaker, alighted from the driver's side into the wet. The old man bent under the trunk lid and transferred a yellow suitcase to the back of the truck under the tarp. Then he returned to his car.

Herndon had been sharing an umbrella with June Matsushida. "It's her!" he cried, as if the walkers should have expected no one else. Herndon looked for Snyder, who was just behind with Luther Wood and Dorene. "I told her to argue he could always say he'd said no," he said, and Snyder waved to indicate comprehension. Herndon then rose and ran heavily through the mud of a long furrow toward the highway. The walkers moved together as close as their umbrellas would allow, and many cheered. There was a moment when it seemed that Mollenhoff was waiting for Herndon, but then he waved and slowly drove off. Herndon reached the truck on the driver's side. He threw open the door, and reaching across Arley, appeared to manage an awkward handshake for the new walker. Now everyone cheered, even Snyder.

TWELVE
The Saints Come Marching

I

That afternoon, they walked eleven miles, all but the last two in a misty drizzle. Wet shoes brought on many blisters; and the slow, steady upslope of the highway, on its way east toward the hills of Ohio, forced June Matsushida into the truck with shin splints. But they kept up the pace until, in good time, Fort Wayne lay just ahead, drying itself in a late burst of sunlight.

They left behind a final dreary stretch of garages and bungalow motels on U.S. 30, and followed Goshen Avenue into the city. They took State Boulevard over the St. Joseph River and Anthony Boulevard over the Maumee River. A traffic cop held a light for them, shaking his head in sad disbelief as their bedraggled file passed him by.

Then, on a quiet street not far from the city center, they arrived at a youth hostel run by a local social agency in an ordinary one-family brick house with twin dormers over a porch roof. They claimed six reserved rooms, four on the second floor and two in the attic, plus extra cots, respectively assigned by Lucas to himself and his wife; the Rices and Frank Dunne; June and Dorene; Rachel and Amelia; the four college boys; and Herndon, Arley Broyle, and Snyder. As they trooped upstairs, hearing their names and room numbers read off by a young woman wearing an ID badge ("Hello, I'm Ruth Givitowski," it said), there was a palpable sense of relief among them: The hostel wasn't too bad for their first rest day. They weren't too late to collect their honorarium for that evening. And Reverend Pendergraft with a fleet of state patrol cars had not descended on the Walk to rescue his sister. "We're pushing our luck," Frank Dunne said, and Snyder put it in his book.

Near nine that evening, bathed and fed, and without Walk signs, they rode a city bus past the darkened mall on Calhoun Street and beyond the city center to B'nai Jacob, an ornate, green-domed synagogue for Reform Jews. In the foyer, they met a lone teenaged boy wearing a suit and tie. He advised them that Rabbi Arthur Wolfe had concluded Sabbath services early that night to accommodate their program. Then he led them through a long passageway into a modern building attached to one side of the old temple. About two hundred people awaited them, packed into a small auditorium. The walkers went forward to join the rabbi on the stage, while Snyder took his preferred seat against the back wall.

Snyder crossed his right leg over his left knee to ease his blistered right foot, opened his notebook on his lap, and transcribed another first impression. "Our third church in a week," he wrote, "but it is not the scene—it's the setting that makes the place so familiar. A Sunday-school assembly room with kids' drawings of Old Testament stories pasted on the walls and windows, and a rabbi in a black robe waiting at the rostrum . . . like your old childhood-in-Topeka, hometown-style Reform Judaism, the religion you rarely feel, absent insult, except as here, with other Jews." A Jew you are, he almost added, but are you Jewish? Didn't you exchange Judaism for journalism? That was a thought he would just as soon not be found when his notes went to the checking department.

For forty minutes, as the Walk presented its standard program, with Lucas as chairman and Herndon, Joe Rice, and Dorene as speakers, Snyder recorded no notes and even let himself doze toward the end. He awoke to gauge the applause ("lukewarm," he put it), but became fully alert only when Rabbi Wolfe, a tall, gray man wearing black-rimmed half-glasses, stood to pose the first question for the Walk. He was seated on the stage next to Lucas. He asked, "Can Israel count on America if Vietnam can't?" Elaborating, the rabbi conceded that the Israel-Vietnam connection was not obvious. "Israel, after all," he said, "has not asked and won't ask for American troops to defend it from aggression." But he argued that the question was about the value of America's word among nations. "If you assume our government makes commitments in good faith with us, the people of the United States, then don't national interest and integrity require us, the people, to remember those commitments and make the sacrifices necessary to keep them sacred? If we forget, if we deny, do we not only tear the web of alliances upon which our defense depends but also dishonor the domestic contract upon which our survival as a nation depends?''

Snyder recognized the ponderous question as a version of the standard Administration defense of Vietnam policy—but it gave voice to a political link so far avoided in the hawk-dove debate and a fear among anti-war American Jews who also cared about Israel that they might have to answer for a broken connection. Snyder underlined the rabbi's quintessentially Jewish question; he knew he himself could not have conceived it. Then he looked up as Lucas silently turned to Rachel, calling upon her to speak for the first time on the Walk. She's the best choice, Snyder was thinking, better than young Kupferman, the other Jewish walker, because he is not clever enough, and better than the rest of the walkers, well, because they are not Jewish. He caught himself pulling for her.

Rachel stood at her chair. She looked bosomy in a white dress that Snyder had not seen before. Whispers whether she was or was not a Jew rushed through the audience until, with her first words—"I'm Rachel Abraham, from Chicago, a master's candidate at Northwestern University in American history, Indochina relations"—the mention of her name let them know that she was.

"Israel and Vietnam," Rachel said, her tone instructive, "are linked in our minds at the peril of both, and America, too. Israel rightly fears a war of aggression against it. But the North-South war in Vietnam cannot accurately be called a war of aggression. It is a civil war within a country of very ancient origin over many issues, some of which are as old as memory. This is history. And so is this: we have become involved, essentially, because one side is avowedly Communist and it is our government's policy to contain Communism everywhere in the world. And this: I am here because I disagree with that policy and want to see it changed insofar as it involves military intervention in the internal affairs of sovereign nations."

Rachel paused. The audience waited expectantly; Snyder, too, and at the same time, registered her steadiness as one positive effect, at least, of her failed acting career.

"I disagree with that policy in Vietnam because military intervention is as wrong for America as it is wrong for the Soviet Union in Eastern Europe and China in Tibet. It is morally wrong and self-defeating. We can gain nothing but shame from it and, in the process, we are destroying not only enemies but friends. So, we must stop now. Believe me, stopping is no threat to Israel. We support Israel, not to contain Communism, but because we support the right of independent nations to exist. That commitment is not contingent upon whether or not we acknowledge our mistake in Vietnam. It is separate and distinct, based on an understanding of our proper role in the world. Vietnam and Israel—the two are not one. It seems to me that world peace depends on seeing the difference and making our commitments accordingly."

As Rachel sat down, the audience applauded, but not beyond decent respect; her logic had not persuaded them that an American withdrawal from Vietnam, followed by a predictable Communist victory, would not be bad for anti-war Jews when they next spoke out for Israel.

The rabbi stood again, a hand raised for attention. "This is our sixth open forum on the war," he said. "A month ago, Vice President Humphrey was here, and like our guests tonight, very persuasive." Appreciative applause greeted Humphrey's name. "I just wish I had Miss Abraham's confidence. I mean, should North Vietnam overwhelm the south, when and if America leaves, won't that signal Israel's enemies that, in fact, we won't stand by our commitments?" The rabbi smiled. He seemed to believe his question had only one answer.

Rachel studied her palms, then looked slowly over the audience, seemingly to the very back row, where Snyder sat, chin up, listening. "On the contrary," she said firmly. "I believe our withdrawal now would give us greater moral influence in the world than we have ever had. Perhaps that is what we need to bring about a settlement between Israel and its enemies."

Rabbi Wolfe leapt on her assumption. "But failing that, don't you believe Israel must have the ability to defend itself?"

"I don't know the answer to that, Rabbi. I believe in non-violence —not non-resistance, but non-violence. I am sure that I would resist non-violently were America threatened, but I hesitate to prescribe for anyone else."

"Israel doesn't have the luxury, Miss Abraham. Neither does South Vietnam. Without our men, there's little doubt which side will win. Do you care what will happen to those people who have resisted, the violent and non-violent alike?"

Rachel hesitated warily. "I care," she said, "that they settle their dispute among themselves."

The rabbi seemed to think he had made a kill. For the first time, he raised his voice above a monotone. "By taking neither side, we actually favor one side, the stronger side. And you, who believe in non-violent resistance, end up where I'm sure you don't want to be—in the camp of 'might makes right.' "

"No, Rabbi," Rachel replied adamantly. "Not at all. I'm in the camp of those who believe this country is wrong to intervene in that war."

"But at least you can see why Vietnam worries some of us as it relates to Israel. Someday, Israel may face a stronger enemy and then it will mean a great deal whether Americans care which side wins."

"But you're speaking of an outside enemy."

"I assure you, Miss Abraham, once you accept non-intervention as a principle, that is a distinction without a difference, not in the real world."

"But what is the real world, Rabbi, but what we make of it?"

"That's what I'm afraid of," the rabbi said, with great bitterness.

For a moment, they faced each other in silence. Then, as if by agreement, both sat down and the audience stirred, murmured, and finally applauded.

Snyder eased back in his chair. Neither won, he was thinking, or could on the ground they chose. They know might makes both right and wrong, don't they, depending on your war? But A-plus for performance, Rachel. Would you like a coffee?

2

"Well, he beat me," Rachel said.

"No. It was a draw," Snyder said.

"TKO," she said. "No converts tonight."

They were alone on Calhoun Street and walking north toward a late-night coffee shop in the far corner of the mall. Over the final hundred yards, Snyder limped with new grief from his blister. At the door, he needed Rachel's arm. "It's not been my week," he said.

"Can you make it?"

"I wanted to talk to you."

"Why don't we take something back home? You need Mother Ray's first aid."

She handled the order, hamburgers-a-pair and coffee, and called a cab. But at the hostel, since Arley Broyle had locked the truck and gone to bed, there was no first-aid kit. Rachel found Ruth Givitowski watching television in the parlor room and gained access to the hostel's medicine chest. She also got permission to use the kitchen. It was a small room with a high-top gas range, porcelain sink, and a picnic-style redwood table with attached benches on two sides. The refrigerator was locked. Rachel put a pan of water on the stove and ordered Snyder to sit on the table under the ceiling light. She straddled the bench below him with his right foot bared in her lap.

The blister was the size of a walnut, still closed, just below the big toe on the ball of the foot. Rachel soaked it with a gauze pad dipped in hot water. After two such treatments, she turned the foot this way and that, giving it a close inspection as though with X-ray eyes and, through the circle of her mouth, repeating, "Oh-oh-oh-oh." When she was ready, at last, she said, "This will hurt you more than it hurts me," and asked, "Any last words from Shakespeare, or other?"

"Hurry," Snyder said, "before the native hue of resolution is sicklied o'er with the pale cast of thought."

Liking that, Rachel sterilized a needle with a kitchen match, then wiped the needle and the blister with alcohol. The needle pierced the blister.

The operation stung, but not so much that he did not otherwise enjoy it.

Rachel painted the raw spot with iodine. "Oh-oh-oh-oh," she said. Then she covered the ball of the foot with crossed Band-Aids.

Beyond the kitchen, other walkers returned from the synagogue, low voices in the parlor, footsteps on the stairs, sounds upstairs.

"Dear Hamlet, you will walk again," Rachel proclaimed, lowering his foot from her lap.

"I was afraid of that, but thanks, anyway."

Rachel stood, leaned across the bench, and quickly but firmly kissed his lips.

"All better," she said.

Her face remained close. A long second passed as Snyder rummaged through his arsenal of defenses, found none not absurd, and kissed her lightly in return.

"Thank you, Mother Ray," he said. "Now we should eat."

Snyder moved himself off the table, coming down on the heel of his wounded foot, then brought up a chair to avoid climbing awkwardly over the bench to sit at the table.

Rachel opened the sandwich bag, unwrapped the hamburgers and removed the lids from the coffee containers. She sat on the bench close to Snyder and leaned toward him dubiously. "Are you going to interview me at this hour?"

"I was."

"Let me interview you."

Snyder reached for his hamburger. "That's fine, too," he said.

"The other day, why wouldn't you swim with us?"

"I made notes."

"And now?"

"Just now?"

"Answer."

"What's the question?"

"How can you ever know anything we may be feeling from inside that journalist's cocoon of yours?"

"You're getting serious."

"Yes."

"I ask questions." He had put his own spin on her meaning. You mustn't concede you can't know her feelings, he told himself, or that you can't control your own. He thought of an example. "Like, tell me," he asked, "how did you feel tonight with the rabbi?"

"The truth? I was thinking of you. I saw you way in the back."

"What about me?"

"I wanted you to be proud of me."

"I see."

"You don't see."

"What?" She's right, he thought, you don't.

"You don't see any of us, what your presence means to us, how you concern us, how we care about you. How can you? You won't let any of us get closer than your notebook."

"It's the business, Ray."

"Oh, I'm hip, and we're your goods. What's new? I only wonder whether you know yourself."

Snyder ducked with a smile, but the remark caught him in the throat. He examined the last of his hamburger and decided not to finish it. He dropped the final bite into the sandwich bag and replaced the lid on his coffee. A limit had been reached. The use of self-revelation to encourage others to reveal themselves was one of the tools of his trade, but self-defense meant knowing when to stop.

"I'm sorry, Ray," he said. "Maybe it's time to pack it in for the night."

Rachel peered into him rather than at him, her hair shading her eyes so that her gaze seemed all the more penetrating. Her lips parted, then formed a circle. His blister had inspired the same expression. It was the way she looked at wounds.

"Oh-oh-oh-oh, yes, time out," she said, touching his hand. "Next comes morality."

"As between you and the rabbi?"

"That's cryptic, Jack."

"Like you both said, morality is knowing when to stop."

"I never said that. Neither did Rabbi Wolfe."

Snyder ignored the denial to make his point. "Self-defense is the same thing, one and the same subject, knowing when to stop."

Rachel shook her head, laughing in resignation. "How then," she asked, "do babies get born?"

"Very funny," he said, covering her hand with his.

"Think we'll make it?"

"The Walk?"

"Us, as is."

"Good chance, Ray."

"Because you've always made it, right?"

"Something like that, I guess."

"Oh, boy."

Snyder saw Rachel leaning toward him across their hands. As she paused, then came forward again, numerous farcical visions of escape flashed on his mind screen, but none more ludicrous than the reality of his actual situation. Upstairs, he heard laughter. They kissed for a very long minute, hands tight, but still at right angles and separated by the table. Snyder felt her release his hand. For a moment, her breast was there. Then she pulled back, thoughtful and unsmiling.

"Henceforth, on good behavior," she said.

"It was something in the hamburger," he said.

"Walk comes first, Jack, and the Walk's story."

"Right, but I feel a coward."

"Thinking does that—I believe you were just rendering that line. Let me help thee upstairs."

"Thank you, no problem. Look, no limp."

Snyder lit a cigarette, walked well around the kitchen, and then tested himself with a simple time step. It was almost painless.

"No Astaire, but a miracle!" Rachel exclaimed.

"It's sainthood for you."

"That makes two of us."

She burst with laughter and, after a moment nursing his own tweaked pride, he laughed, too.

Later, as Broyle and Herndon slept, Snyder lay on his back on his cot under a curtainless window in the space below one of the attic dormers. Sometimes he mainly watched the clearing blue-black sky. Sometimes he mostly discoursed with himself on the soul of the celibate journalist, the "prim" in "primitive." But as long as he remained awake, some part of his mind was thoroughly preoccupied by considerations of the variousness of Rachel's intelligence and the long muscles of her swimmer's body and her arching dive into the sparkling river.

3

Late next morning, with his laundry in a pillowcase, Snyder came downstairs, limping again. He learned from Ruth Givitowski that the walkers had scattered early to refill prescriptions, repair shoes, wash clothes, shop. Then she gave him breakfast in the kitchen. She hardly spoke to him, but he knew that someone had arranged special treatment for him.

On the porch, Snyder donned his khaki hat. The sun was high and white in a fresh-minted pale sky. Arley Broyle, sitting in the truck at the curb, waved to him.

"I'm to ride you if you're going anywhere," Arley said.

"Who said?"

"Rachel said you had a bad foot."

Arley offered the morning newspaper and the latest *Time* magazine.

As they drove five minutes to the laundromat, Snyder made notes on the news: a general strike in Saigon; anti-draft sit-in at the University of Wisconsin; statement by Defense Secretary McNamara supporting a two-year national service program, military or civilian, for every draft-age American; a "no substitute for victory" speech by a West Coast publisher. At the same time, someone's grandmother with a tin ear had a hit on the rock-and-roll charts. Her name was Elva Miller and her song was "Downtown." Rex Reed, a movie critic, said Marlon Brando's new movie, *The Chase,* was "the worst thing that has happened to movies since Lassie played a war veteran with amnesia." And the so-called Now generation had a new fad— psychedelic tennis shoes.

"These are contentious times, Arley," Snyder said, "contentious times."

"Oh, yes, Jack. Yes, indeed," Arley said.

The laundromat was in a narrow storefront next to a neighborhood supermarket. Inside, with his notebook put away, Snyder found Herndon, Amelia, and Luther Wood sitting together on a wooden bench facing a churning laundry dryer. A woman was emptying a second dryer. There were two washers, waiting for use. "Come join us," Herndon said. Snyder deposited his laundry in a washer, added soap, and switched on the cycle with two quarters. Then he took a seat on the bench next to Wood and busied himself with a cigarette.

Herndon asked about Snyder's foot. Wood wondered about his night's sleep. Especially without his notebook in hand, Snyder was considered one of their own. They could go on with their conversation.

"Well, Reed, could I?" Wood asked.

"Handle it?"

"Arrest, trial, jail?"

"Depends on what for and how long."

"I can't imagine it."

"Don't try."

"I've tried. It comes up like the movies."

Snyder leaned forward, now facing the three walkers as an aid to memory, reporting without the inhibiting presence of his notebook. Not quite fair, he thought, but at least they can see you listening. Then he caught a conditional look from Herndon, who, for one, had seen.

"I'd never known anyone who'd been in jail," Herndon said. "I didn't know any more about it than what they tell you at the draft board, trying to talk you out of it. 'Four years of your life, think about that,' they kept saying. So, when I thought of it—I mean, when I thought about not spending four years of my life in jail, I decided I could do it. I mean I had no idea what those years would be like, only that anything else'd be immoral.

"Prison isn't imaginable, Luther. You think about it before they put you away and you have no image of it, except from the movies, and you think you can take that, and more, because you don't have any real idea, not even the rancid smell of it. When I think back, I remember that I felt ready for it. I imagined myself doing the time and not missing those years outside too much. Reed Herndon is up to it, I told myself. I even had an idea I wouldn't cooperate with them if a bad situation arose. If there was a chance to take a stand inside, and if there were other draft resisters with me, we'd take a stand together. I'd lead them.

"Only it was not that way, Luther. When I got to Leavenworth, there was only one other political prisoner like me in the whole place. There were only five when I left. The government spread us around the whole system. None of us took a stand for very long. All we did was our time. That's all. We did our time as fast as we could.

"After the publicity, it meant nothing. Zero. I'm here on this walk to make it mean a little something more, but when you're inside, it seems as meaningless as the war. Oh, I would advise anyone against it, Luther."

Herndon looked up with a start as the laundry dryer lurched to a stop. "I know you're thinking of Thoreau and all the rest, but don't try it," he said. "Think of being a zero."

"Zero," Wood repeated solemnly. "I feel I'm a zero, hiding out in college."

"You can do nothing in jail. You'll be among the missing, that's all."

"It's a statement."

"Yes, a one-day news story."

Wood sighed. He seemed to grieve. Herndon looked past him to Snyder.

"I really wanted to do something terrific inside," he said. "But you learn that the only thing that means anything is an escape—the one option closed to me. I mean, if you go to jail deliberately, you can't turn around and escape, can you?"

"No," Snyder said, finding himself unwillingly involved. He realized that Herndon and Wood had been talking within two distinctly different time frames, the short one for civil disobedience, the long one for draft resistance in wartime.

"No, you can't," Herndon agreed with himself. "You can only serve your time. Protect your rear. And think how you'll never choose prison again."

Wood giggled and sighed again, louder. Then he crossed over to the dryer and began unloading the clothes, making two piles, one for Herndon, one for himself. Amelia rose to help him. Snyder realized she had not spoken. Herndon stood, too, but facing Snyder. He seemed to feel he had talked too much.

"We still have a deal, Jack?"

"Oh, yes."

Alone in the laundromat, Snyder copied the conversation from memory into his notes. And once more, he saw his story angling toward Herndon's crisis, depending on Herndon, who, rather than jeopardize his parole, might not even let him tell it.

Later, carrying his clean laundry, Snyder returned to the hostel. He found June Matsushida sitting alone on the porch. She was fashioning her own flag to carry on the Walk. With heavy red thread, she had stitched together two large squares of white silk; a mop handle served as a pole. She showed Snyder one side stenciled in red ink, reading: STOP WAR; the other side: GO PEACE.

"It's almost finished," she said with satisfaction.

"It's a fine flag, June."

"The Japanese like flags."

"What are you going to do with it?"

"I want you to see me plant it on the White House lawn."

"You think the guards'll let you?"

"If they believe in free speech."

"How do you feel about civil disobedience?"

"You mean jail?"

"Yes."

"I feel all right. I was born in one."

"Would you tell me about that?"

"Oh, yes. It was early 1945, three months before the government released my mother and father from the detention camp at Tule Lake, California, I entered this world."

"They were American-born?"

"No, but they were U.S. citizens. They'd lived in Sacramento for fifteen years before Pearl Harbor. They were good Catholics. They ran a grocery store. Now they have the only Japanese restaurant in San Diego. It's very tiny and there aren't enough Japanese to make it grow, but they could not go back to Sacramento. Their store was stolen."

Snyder nodded as he wrote. He said, "That's unbelievable."

June misunderstood. "It's true, Jack," she said. "It's all in the legal papers, the case of *Matsushida* v. *U.S. Government.* It's all in my father's diary. I was their first child. My mother suffered very much when I was born. The medical facilities at Tule Lake were very poor. A scandal, really. Many died in those three years of hardship. Have you heard about it, Jack?"

"Some."

"About the panic after Pearl Harbor and how Mr. Roosevelt ordered the internment within weeks after declaring war? It was shameful."

"I know."

"Tule Lake was Siberia with all the trimmings—barbed wire, dogs, armed guards. My father's diary is partly a scrapbook. I've seen many pictures. You should do a story."

"You could be right."

"You know, it wasn't the first time—during the depression, the government rounded up thousands of migrant workers and deported them to Mexico. Lots of them were citizens, too. I worry, Jack."

"Yes?"

"Now there are Negro riots in the cities, and the anti-war movement is rising. What couldn't happen?"

"How does that bring you to the Walk?"

"How? I have another year at San Diego State. I'm studying Latin American history and the Portuguese language. I'm going to do my graduate work in Brazil. There's a very large Japanese community in Brazil. I may not come back. I don't know. I'm on the Walk to make my statement, to plant my flag. On July Fourth, I want President Johnson to know that the daughter of Mr. and Mrs. Fumimaro Matsushida was there and wasn't silent like the people in Sacramento in 1942."

"So you hitchhiked to Chicago?"

"A boy from my class intended to drive me in his jeep. His family knows Sam Lucas. Then he failed calculus and decided to stay. So I came along, anyway."

"You weren't afraid?"

"Oh, yes, but my very first ride came from a young priest, a young Jesuit priest. Nice? He left me in Barstow with a blessing. He told me that God would certainly see to it that I would stand face to face with President Johnson."

"You believe that?"

"I can hardly wait."

"All the way to jail?"

"You'll see. I want you to see."

Snyder forced a smile. The story he had to tell was barely a week old. At the end of the next day, they would just be entering Ohio. They were almost three weeks away from the halfway mark, June 6, a date to be celebrated presumably in Wheeling, West Virginia, with another long month beyond to make Baltimore, and then Washington, if they could. Yet, he was thinking, there's an ill-defined, but still notable pressure already building toward a particular denouement. Should June Matsushida opt for civil disobedience, to be seen by you, no less, she can only make it that much harder for Luther Wood and perhaps many others to do otherwise. Perhaps even Herndon.

THIRTEEN

A Shadow in the Valleys

I

Eleven more days passed and they had walked on U.S. 30 across the Ohio state line to the gateway town of Delphos, then by lesser roads east and a little south into green-rolling farm country, through the small western Ohio cities of Lima and Marion to Mount Gilead, north of Columbus, northwest of Mount Vernon. It had not been a fertile time for Snyder's story. The Walk had neither gained nor lost a member, and there had been no great internal revelations or external surprises.

Occasionally, working farmers, men and women, would come down from their fields for a closer look at the Walk's procession. They would offer a cold drink or a piece of fruit and encourage their children to follow the Walk to the next horizon. Townspeople, on the other hand, would be more likely to take a step back, as though the walkers were too close already, and they would more often talk among themselves than to the strangers in their midst. Still, at night in the cities, the Walk's meetings had not failed to fill their public rooms.

Some days, in the Ohio hills, there would be long stretches of cool, dark forest above the farthest acres of tilled soil and, now and again, as the road led them through a particularly sweet wood, they would be able to enjoy nature for as long as two hours without seeing a billboard or any other sign of commerce. A group of four or five walkers might even leave the road altogether, striking a path at the edge of a nondescript bridge over a stream still full and swift with the rains of April, exploring down below until they found a crossing, and rising on the far side within the trees to walk a cheery mile hidden from the tedium of the highway. Luther Wood had been a regular on these side trips, accompanying the walkers' respite with his recorder, and they had sung the songs he knew. His favorite seemed to be "If you get to heaven before I do, just dig a hole and pull me through."

There had also been the consequences of a stretch of bad weather. A cloudburst in Lima had washed out their evening's rally in the town square along with the first TV coverage set for the Walk. Then, after two successive days of heavy rains, flooding near Marion had forced them to shelter in a Salvation Army dormitory for an un-scheduled day off. It was not a total loss. Lucas had promoted an interview for himself with the Marion *Daily Clarion,* which, next morning, had published a report on the Walk so detailed that even Snyder and his mission for *Harrington's Weekly World* were men-tioned. On the other hand, the schedule adjustment had meant can-celing the next rest day, for which Lucas had long planned a walkers' side trip to see the bright lights of Columbus.

Finally, in Mount Gilead, Luther Wood's friend, Lester Kupfer-man, a tall, well-built boy with an equine face and dark mane, had almost been lost to the Walk. He had slogged through those first rainy days with the sole of one shoe missing, and left Marion with a slight cold, a subnormal temperature, and diarrhea. He had insisted on continuing with the Walk but, virtually on the hour, sought long-distance medical advice from his mother in Des Moines. Then, at the Mount Gilead View-Right Motel, Sam Lucas had taken a call from Mrs. Kupferman, asking that Lester go home or, at least, back to Grinnell College. She had relented only when her son called yet again, vowing both to take his Pepto-Bismol and to repair his shoes.

At dinner that evening, Kupferman had told of his escape from humiliation as a Jewish-mother joke on himself, concluding with a short self-deprecating laugh. "Folks, all hazards are not on the high-way."

The walkers had laughed and Luther Wood had patted his friend on the head. Snyder had not joined in; it seemed reasonably clear to him that Lester Kupferman was a very angry boy.

Of such were Snyder's notes in that time, as the Walk traversed half the width of Ohio.

Later that night in Mount Gilead, on checking the schedule with Lucas, Snyder learned that, by coincidence, there had been another parental intervention during the day. Dorene Quink's father had called WISE in Chicago to locate his daughter and arrange a meeting with her at the closest airport.

Next morning, before breakfast, Arley Broyle dropped Dorene at Port Columbus.

By nightfall, the Walk made a campsite halfway between Mount Gilead and Mount Vernon and Broyle drove back to Port Columbus for Dorene. They were still at the campfire when Dorene returned. She was a husky, athletic young woman with coarse dark hair and blue eyes, wide-set and normally merry. She looked worn out and distressed, and went straight to bed in the tent that she shared with June Matsushida. From Broyle, later, Snyder learned that Dorene's father had flown in and out of Columbus's airport to tell her of his separation from her mother.

Next afternoon, on a gray day, as they walked above a scattering of fishermen along the Kokosing River on the state road to Mount Vernon, Snyder fell in beside Dorene and June, fifty yards off the pace at the rear of the Walk. Dorene did not seem to object and even grinned, as though she herself felt she had already spent too much time in a funk.

"You don't mind?" Snyder asked.

"I don't mind, Jack, talking to you. You won't use it anyway."

June Matsushida skipped ahead. "Later, D'reenie," she said.

"I won't," Snyder said.

"You were divorced, weren't you?"

"Yes, it's been some time now."

"What did your kids think about it?"

"My two never quite said, but they showed a lot—I lost."

"Did you do it?"

"She did."

"Were you at fault?"

"That's another question."

"Oh." Dorene frowned. "In my case, it's my father. He's so liberated!"

"I suspect, usually, both parents go wrong, with one perhaps going wronger than the other."

"I suppose so. It is just that I never suspected, because he talks such a game. Happy, happy, happy. My mother, too. Now he tells me it wasn't right for a long time. How do you figure that?"

"Never a hint?"

"Maybe I wasn't paying attention. He was so liberated! So liberal! He was almost like one of us. I hate liberals."

"What does he do, your father?"

"My father's in advertising. Ever hear of Quink and Baybridge?"

"The butterfly in the oatmeal?"

"That's my pop! He wrote the line '. . . with a touch of sunlight.' It's the second most famous slogan in the world, after 'Love thy neighbor as thyself.' "

"Mother?"

"My mother's a board woman. Not 'bored,' but 'board,' as in the New York City Center, Vassar, and the Cosmopolitan Club. She's also a Wickersham, liberal wing of the family."

"Wickersham grain elevators?"

"That's where the oatmeal comes from."

"I see."

"Oh, it's no big deal. Quink and Baybridge won't lose the Wickersham Oats account, no way, Jack. It just makes me so god-awful sad, all the time you put into a family and now, no family. You see?"

"I do see."

"The Quinks've always been such optimists."

"A big family?"

"I'm the youngest of five."

"Optimism makes big families."

"Somewhere it was phony, Jack. Do you detect a certain phoniness in liberated liberals?"

"I haven't looked yet."

"Don't be afraid. Look."

"Dorene, are you staying with the Walk?"

"Are you kidding? Me? But to the death."

"I thought so."

"To the death."

"It shouldn't come to that."

"It shouldn't, not this year. Do you want to know about me?"

"I know a little. Hunter College and SDS."

"Not very interesting."

"The Quink and Wickersham connection makes it interesting."

"I chose Hunter College because my brothers and sisters chose Harvard and Radcliffe. Populism ran in other rich families, but not mine, not until I came along. I was in Port Huron for the original SDS convention four years ago. I went to every convention since. Remember the fellow who said, 'The women made peanut butter, waited on table, cleaned up, and got laid'? He was talking about me. I got pregnant, even—in a good cause, of course—followed by a god-awful abortion. Are we still off the record?"

"That part surely is."

"That's the only part I meant. I want you to say I am here on the Walk because, for one reason, I'm not there. I mean I'm not active in SDS anymore. I am against the war, Jack, heart and soul. The system? It stinks. But my body—that's mine from now on. And long after SDS has disintegrated."

"Is that how it ends?"

"I don't know. I don't care. Internal contradictions. Problems. Irreconcilable differences. Sounds like a bad marriage, doesn't it? I really think, were the war to end tomorrow, so would SDS. On the other hand, let Mr. Johnson end the college draft deferment, I suppose SDS might lead us in a real nifty revolution."

"Is that for my notes?"

"Oh, God, Jack, please quote me, yes! Use it all! I want my folks to read every word."

According to the schedule, that day being May 31, the walkers were to reach Mount Vernon, in central Ohio, 315 miles from Chicago, at nightfall. And with it all, they did, there boarding a commuter bus to spend the night in the nearby village of Gambier as guests of student activists at Kenyon College for men.

For Snyder, riding on a bench seat beside Rachel Abraham among the same fifteen walkers with whom he had left Fort Wayne, their precise arrival in Mount Vernon was having an unexpected feel of climax. The month of May was over. Three weeks on the road had ended. Virtue prevailed. Their progress was its testament and, by last light, not unaware that Rachel might be reading over his shoulder, he made a note about it.

"Everyone's up tonight, even Dorene, feisty, almost giddy. You'd think it was the millennium, not just the end of the month. Still, it's something to be right on time after twenty-one days on the road. It makes you feel God's on your side. It almost makes me feel God is on *their* side! Virtue is rewarded. The same faith carries them to the rest stop at the end of an hour, on to the day's distance, achieves the third week's planned destination, gives reason to believe in Wheeling, Baltimore, and the finale in Washington—plus one more thing, of course, the story in *Harrington's*. The longer I'm here, the more they expect from me, now more than ever, with my piece in the 'hot cities' round-up out today, and my name on the cover.

"Here's George Corrigan, followed by Peter Schumacher, swearing he won't shave until it's over, waiting for me to write it down and believing that a note is sure to appear in a published paragraph . . . June Matsushida wants it said that the flag she plants on the White House lawn was carried by her and her alone . . . Frank Dunne tells me he will do civil disobedience no matter what and to spell his name right in the magazine (an *e* at the end of Dunne) for the union folks who sent him . . . This afternoon, Sam Lucas asked me, 'How's our story?' 'Fine,' I said. He waved today's *Harrington's* at me and sighed, so deeply, as though only the promise of publicity could keep his mountain of flesh moving toward Mecca . . . Another thing: the walkers are male and female, on the highway together, day after day, often closing ranks, chatting and singing and horsing around, teasing, like ordinary people on a day's outing—but 'nothing' seems to come of it . . . Sometimes the younger ones chase each other in the fields, boys after girls, girls after boys, yet (so far as I can determine) that obvious sexual energy is rigorously contained at night . . . Even Herndon and Amelia, almost always together doing the daily distance, seem to abide in celibacy, or in a discretion so complete that no shred of contrary evidence has appeared in fact or gossip . . . Excepting Sam and Molly, a strict buddy system prevails: June and Dorene, Rachel and Amelia, Dunne and Herndon, Kupferman and Wood, Corrigan and Schumacher, the Rices—father and son—and Arley and me . . . This seems to be the code of the Walk: do nothing on the road in May that you wouldn't want to read about in six million copies of *Harrington's* come August. If not faith in virtue's reward, what is that?"

Snyder closed his notebook. Rachel stirred, then sat back, lighting a cigarette. The bus was groaning up a steep hill through a dense purple-black wood. He lit his cigarette off Rachel's.

"Can't see the page," he said.

"Let me hold us a match, here."

"We were done writing."

Rachel touched his hand in contrition.

"Okay, you caught me reading over your shoulder. But listen, no one is immune to publicity."

"No one."

"And the longer you're here, true, the more we expect of you."

Snyder listened to the wrench of gears and the creaking of springs; the bus was cresting another hill.

"I'd rather ride this hill than walk it."

"Wait till the Alleghenies."

"I can wait."

"Listen, Jack—one more thing," Rachel whispered earnestly. "Most people will only see us through your eyes. Your name is on the cover of *Harrington's*. It makes you God."

"No, thanks."

"That's no answer."

"There's no God."

"Okay, Jack—I made my point."

"I got it. I'll do my best."

It was past nine when the bus, followed by Arley in the truck, climbed the last slope to the Kenyon campus, which virtually encompassed the hilltop village of Gambier. Moonlit silhouettes of school buildings loomed above the trees along a central boulevard. There was a guest house for the women, rooms in a dormitory for the men. Without Sam Lucas, who was tired, and Molly, who worried over him, the Walk reassembled for a late-night "No-Speeches Beer Fest and Foot Rest Mixer" in its honor. They were greeted at the door of the campus tavern by the organizer and advertiser of the mixer, one Richard Dobbs, class of '66, chairman of the Kenyon Student Peace Action Committee. Dobbs was a husky boy already balding with a compensating black goatee. He wore a peace trident on a chain around his neck and a button on his lapel: "Suppose They Gave a War and Nobody Came." In April 1965, he had met Sam Lucas in the crowd of 15,000 at the White House during the anti-war demonstration organized by SDS. Dorene Quink explained to him that Lucas had retired for the night.

"Reed Herndon?" Dobbs asked.

"Here," Herndon said.

Dobbs smiled with relief.

"Sam promised you," he said. "We've raised fifty-seven dollars for the Walk and all you have to do is mingle. Not bad, eh? Come on in."

Dobbs led them to a lounge behind the main dining room. A crowd of about thirty young men with a dozen or so young women from a neighboring school awaited them. There was a stand-up bar beside the entrance, serving only 3.2 beer and soft drinks, and a few tables already covered with empty bottles. From oak beams overhead drooped rainbows of confetti from some long-ago celebration. Peace signs handmade by Dobbs's committee covered the walls. In lonely contrast near the back exit stood a tall, expressionless youth, wearing green surplus Army fatigues, holding up a large cardboard sign with white letters on a black background. His message was: "Victory through Air Power: Nuke the North!" Snyder asked Dobbs about him.

"That's Mark Brideaux," Dobbs said. "Birdy comes to our peace parties, we go to his war parties. The expenses even out. And college rules prohibit exclusion. There'd be more hawks like Birdy here tonight, but I said it'd be too late for speeches. Most of them won't come if they can't heckle. But Birdy's a hard case. Some say a nut case. He's nasty, but not really a problem. Our side's got some of the same. So, all's fair, you know."

Snyder chatted for a while with Dobbs, then drifted over to Brideaux, who held his sign chin high with one hand while shaking Snyder's hand with the other. The bones in Brideaux's face seemed too large for his skin and gave his looks an unnerving edge of taut disdain.

"Birdy Brideaux never misses a dove affair," he said.

"They let you in free?"

"I buy my own ticket, Mr. Snyder. Somebody has to stand up for Christianity."

"They do?"

"How many Jews on the Walk?"

"I haven't counted."

"In your article, be sure to say I asked. Oh, yes, and that I've enlisted."

Rankled, Snyder moved away, then precisely recalled Brideaux's words for the record. He was not immune. The fuck's victory, he was thinking, is you having to say he's enlisted. Brideaux knows that. It's as Rachel says: no one is immune to publicity, not anymore.

In time, the party grew louder and warmer, formed and re-formed by groups from Kenyon centering on one or two walkers, Herndon and Amelia attracting more than the others, with Frank Dunne, who was wearing a Stetson cowboy hat he'd picked up in Lima, a close second.

Snyder saw a laughing, red-faced student open the exit door, followed outside by Lester Kupferman. They returned moments later, with Kupferman grinning over a beer bottle, looking for someone else. Quickly, Kupferman went out again, this time with Luther Wood, and both came back giggling. Then Kupferman doggedly cleared a space at one table. Wood sat on it, cross-legged, and played "Summertime" on his recorder.

Curiosity soon placed Snyder at the exit door, where Kupferman swayed with the music. There were boys outside spiking their beer. Snyder declined Kupferman's offer to fetch him a drink.

"I understand," Kupferman said. "Always working, eh, Jack? But just listen to my friend Luther—looks like a snake charmer, and I'd say he's playing much better! Hey! All it takes is a little depth charge of bonded bourbon."

There was applause and some cheers for Wood's solo and then, again, a shifting of groups, bringing Herndon and Amelia together with Rachel and the Rices in one circle, June and Dorene with Frank Dunne and Peter Schumacher in another. Now at the bar with Arley Broyle and George Corrigan, as Luther Wood played on, Snyder saw Kupferman alone circling the room, stopping at last in the farthest corner where the vigil of Mark Brideaux continued. It was almost midnight, curfew time.

"Well, Jack, man," Corrigan was saying, "best thing tonight about us is an excuse for a party, yes? But wouldn't you say we needed a break, like every workingman does? I figure Sam and Molly went to bed so as we could enjoy it. What do you think? When are you? I mean, taking a break? Well, it's a nice party for our third week's anniversary, hey? Any excuse for a party. And fifty-seven bucks for the poke. That's all right! Now, see there—you see Lester Kupferman? Lester's drunk, man. Oh, he needs to go back to the dormitory, quick-ly! Lucas'd have a fit. Hard liquor's a no-no. Look at Lester! Arley, don't you rat on him, either! But a definite no-no, man. Oh, Lester is getting deep with that sign boy. What's up? Just look at Lester!''

Snyder had a sudden clear glimpse over Arley's head through the crowd toward the corner where Kupferman was gesturing toward heaven with his bottle while peering down into Brideaux's aroused face.

"My, my"—Corrigan was laughing—"hasn't Lester got the call this evening!''

Abruptly, Brideaux's sign came up to Kupferman's eye level, as though answering him with its slogan: "Victory through Air Power: Nuke the North!''

Snyder thought he saw Kupferman smile. Then Brideaux appeared to add a word and Kupferman hit the boy's bony face with a left jab above the right eye near the temple. The blow made a popping noise, sharp enough to be heard over the din. With a look of sadness, Brideaux showed the whites of his eyes and dropped below Snyder's line of vision. Abruptly Kupferman sank from sight, too.

Someone shouted, "Fight!'' The crowd gasped and rocked, then separated into two rapt groups, instinctively opening a path for the authoritative view of the bartender, a grizzled man in his fifties, to the floor where Brideaux sat akimbo staring at the kneeling Kupferman.

In the sudden silence, each peered at the other, the vanquished hawk confounded, the one-punch victorious dove dumbfounded. In his right hand, Kupferman still held his bottle and, rising again, seemed anxious not to spill it. He looked up as Luther Wood came toward him, then Richard Dobbs. Kupferman straightened, turned once around as though a spin would clear his head, and dashed through the exit door into the campus night. His friend Wood followed him, with a wave of his recorder, a sign read by the crowd that he should be allowed to pursue Kupferman by himself. Arley Broyle trailed them anyway.

Then a great cheer arose. Kupferman had thrown a popular punch.

Richard Dobbs, swiftly joined by the bartender, with Snyder close behind, was first to tend to the friendless Brideaux. Dobbs helped Brideaux to his feet and examined the damage. There was a small, almost bloodless cut in the tight flesh above Brideaux's right eyebrow. With his left eye staring hard at Dobbs, his jaws clenched tight, his teeth showing, Brideaux seemed about to cry. Behind him, the separated bodies of the crowd had noisily reunited, then mostly turned away, allowing a certain privacy for ministering to his wounds, if not his ego.

"Right, okay, I was right," Brideaux said.

"Hey, sssshhh!" Dobbs sighed. He placed a handkerchief against Brideaux's temple.

"A Jew."

"Shut up, man. Just shut up! For the college, man!"

Brideaux, losing control of his tears, exhaled and began to sob.

Dobbs turned haplessly to Snyder.

"You won't print that?"

Snyder shook his head, a double negative.

"Kenyon's part of the story, eh?"

"Yes."

"So much for the old school's image, Mr. Snyder."

Snyder shook his head again, thinking Lester Kupferman hadn't done much for the old Walk's image, either; what he'd done for the story was another thing—enough for one night already, but perhaps more at the inevitable morning's confrontation with Sam Lucas. As a human being, Snyder could sympathize with both men. As a journalist, he could only hope to be present at the execution.

After the party, Snyder found Arley Broyle waiting up for him in their room. Broyle was still dressed and wore a Kenyon beanie that Dobbs had given him. He blinked and fidgeted, groping for speech. In bits and pieces, Snyder learned that Broyle had reported the drinking and the fight to Sam Lucas—after he had seen Luther Wood help Kupferman with his gear into a campus taxi. It had happened very fast, all before midnight.

"Lester's gone, Jack," Broyle said.

"What about Luther?"

"Gone, but his gear's still here."

"It's not your fault, Arley."

"Sam should've done something."

"How?"

"Oh, I guess—go to the Mount Vernon bus station."

"What's there?"

"Them. I heard them talking."

"Well, it's not your fault, that's for sure, Arley."

"Sam said, ah, if Lester's gone, he's saved me the trouble."

"But not that about Luther?"

"Nothing about Luther."

"What do you make of it, Arley?"

"Me?"

"Sure, you."

"I dunno, Jack. Only that Sam was really upset Lester hit some-body. I mean Sam's face turned all red, almost blue."

It turned out that Kupferman had spent the night with Wood in the Mount Vernon bus station and, alone, took the 6 A.M. commuter bus to Columbus.

Two hours later, when the Walk's bus arrived in Mount Vernon, a note from Kupferman waited with Wood, who, sleepless and bedrag-gled, seemed openly anxious to stay with the Walk. In a quiet corner of the station, Lucas read the note to the walkers. "Dear Everyone," Kupferman had written, "I'm very sorry. I guess I wasn't up for non-violence. Good luck today and all the way. Love, Lester."

With one hand on his beard, Lucas waited, then looked at each walker, one by one, seeking eye contact. June and Dorene were misty-eyed. George Corrigan and Peter Schumacher exchanged guilty looks. Frank Dunne found a point of interest on the tiled ceiling. The others solemnly returned the leader's stare. Snyder thought Lucas was seeing his company's first moment of real self-doubt, as though Kupferman's note was an omen of their own uncer-tainties. "Lester's mother got him back safely," Frank Dunne said, but no one laughed.

Then Sam Lucas said, "I know you people understand the issue as well as Lester did. If violence must come, let it come to us, not from us. That's why moral politics takes more than courage. It takes self-control. And for that, we avoid the booze. Am I clear? I'll say no more on this subject. Shall we go?"

It was prime material, Snyder thought, and as useful in its way as the scene Kupferman had made. Beyond virtue, he was thinking, the Walk has a certain rigor in Sam Lucas.

2

That day, walking east from Mount Vernon on U.S. 36, they had sun and clear skies. The Ohio countryside rolled in earnest, with tilled land in the valleys and hazy green woods on the ridgelines above. From time to time, they passed a slow-working oil pump, standing alone in an open field like a huge, rusty praying mantis. In the afternoon, near the cemetery at the town of New Castle, a funeral procession came their way, led by an orange patrol car from the office of the county sheriff of Coshocton, in the county seat by the same name some twenty miles east. The walkers politely stopped and lowered their signs as the cortege approached. The officer, driving with his elbow on the windowsill, gave them an equally polite, if noncommittal, wave.

Further along, they looked down from the top of a ridge from which the road fell off into a long glide to the village of Nellie. At the bottom, the Mohawk Dam captured the streamlike Walhonding River flowing from the west. Nellie was off to one side, a few dozen houses, a general store, and a gas station. Below the dam, the road climbed again, long and steep. Here the fields were dark and sprinkled with new grass. Their campsite was precisely at the top of that further hill, sheltered on three sides by thick woods with a long, lovely view east down the river.

As they started downhill, Herndon took the lead and Amelia Pendergraft moved back to walk with Joe and Vachel Rice. Snyder, as it happened, was just behind.

"It won't be long, Joe," she said.

"I'm doing fine. How are you?"

"I'm all right—a little sunburn."

"Are you wearing a hat?"

"No hat."

"You should wear a hat, Amelia."

"Tomorrow I'll get one at the next shop we pass."

"Are you glad you've come along?"

"I am glad."

"What about the Reverend Pendergraft?"

"He's all right, Joe. I've called him twice. Sam spoke to him, too."

"He understands?"

"No, but Sam told him I've got lots of chaperones."

"What did he say?"

"He wants to trust me."

"What did Sam say?"

" 'You can trust her and Reed Herndon, too.' "

"He said that?"

"Word for word."

"Good for Sam."

"He calmed Heinz a lot."

"Yes, but what are you going to do when this is over?"

"I don't know—go to New York with Reed, I hope."

"Is that so?"

"If it's all right with Reed, Joe."

"Is it?"

"He doesn't say."

"Did you ask him?"

"No. I can wait."

"You're a strange girl, Amelia."

"Seems that way, doesn't it?"

"Good, though."

"Thanks, Joe."

"Vachel says you're pretty, too."

"Well, thanks, Vachel."

Vachel blushed, but said nothing. Then they walked on in silence. The sun was dropping fast. Snyder tried to hang on to that exchange. He had made no notes. The dialogue had taken him by surprise. He realized he had lost all but the sense of it. Amelia rarely spoke, so far as he had known, except in smiles and whispers to Herndon. She seemed to have no politics, except pure love, and no present interest, other than Herndon's presence. And for Herndon, she seemed to be a thing exclusive of the Walk, a small, pretty, fair-haired link with another way of being, that of an ordinary human being, perhaps, to be considered and valued only after the issues of the Walk and the war itself were resolved. How, if at all, she might relate to that resolution, Snyder told himself, is a hard question. God, indeed!

Half an hour later, the Walk trudged to the top of the hill and, in the last light, got busy making a camp at the edge of the woods, clearly marked "No Trespassing." Lucas's local contact had been a World War I conscientious objector named Dr. Josef Miller, who lived in Warsaw, the next town, four miles east of Nellie. Along with Arley Broyle, Lucas had visited Dr. Miller that morning for accommodations. Dr. Miller proposed the hilltop and located its owner through the general store at Nellie. Camping for one night was no problem.

Dr. Miller came early for dinner, bearing three apple pies and a gallon of vanilla ice cream. He was a slight, freckled man, a veterinarian in his late sixties, with ageless blue eyes and a halo of white-blond hair around the top of his skull. The chest pocket of his green tweed jacket bulged with several cigars, two gold pens, a yellow pencil, and a pair of reading glasses. He sat close to the neat, careful fire and, for dessert, served the pie à la mode himself. Then he offered to share his cigars. Snyder accepted when no one else would. Dr. Miller said he smoked one a day and did not worry about lung cancer. "I do like the Dunhill cigar," he said, accenting "do like der Dunhill" with a trace of someplace in Germany. Dr. Miller said it was his father's place, Cologne, and that he himself had been born and raised in Cincinnati, moved up to Coshocton County in 1922 at age twenty-five, and never left. With that, and having adroitly lit his cigar, the old man puffed with pleasure. "Good," he said, "but I liked them better when they were Cuban. Embargo's a silly business."

Long before the sun went down, there were shadows in the valley, so that nightfall came from below as well as above. By then, in a close circle around the modest fire, it felt like a family reunion, with many stories to be told to Dr. Miller. The Walk had lasted long enough to enjoy the pleasure of its own reminiscences and he was a good listener.

Yet, sitting furthest from Dr. Miller, Snyder thought that he would not be the only one wanting to hear the old man's story (there has to be a story, he was thinking). It was just that no one seemed to have the chutzpah, innate in journalists, to ask for it. The fine point, to him, was whether he should, so arbitrarily, induce the pregnancy. He decided to try before Luther Wood, who was falling asleep, prompted the rest to call it an evening. He did not raise his voice, taking care that he should not seem to be what he was, a reporter asking a question.

"Tell us about your town, Dr. Miller," Snyder said, "about Ohio and Vietnam."

"The war? Oh, no, it's not quite here—not yet," Dr. Miller said. "Maybe soon, with more boys going."

"But no protests?"

"A few around these parts. Only a few, actually. No stars in the windows. No blue stars. No gold stars. It's not yet like any other war. It may never be. So, you will pass through Coshocton County like some strange beast carrying signs that we won't quite understand."

"What does that mean?"

"Yes, exactly! Here's the heartland. It always makes the difference. Once many of us refused to fight. Many would not go, not to World War I—but even then, there were not enough of us, not in the heartland, dying to keep the country out of a bad war. So it went on."

"You yourself refused the draft?"

"Sure, refused. Spent six months at Crane Creek—a prison camp up north, on Lake Erie. A cold winter, but a long time past—that was 1918. You wouldn't want to hear about it."

A hand went up to Dr. Miller's left. It was June Matsushida. Dr. Miller waved at her with his long-dead cigar. The very thought of that time in his life seemed to amuse him.

"Hello?"

"I'd like to hear," June said. "Why did you do it?"

"Yes, young lady, for my father. He, my father, left Cologne in 1891 to avoid the Army himself, the wars of the Prussians. He was very religious. A man of conscience. A Lutheran and a socialist and a pacifist. So he came to Cincinnati. He was a machinist. And when the United States declared war on Germany, he spoke out against it. He went to meetings, reminding people that President Wilson was elected to keep America out of that war.

"They came one night, in the fall of 1917, stoned our house. Windows broken. You know Ibsen? A scene right out of Ibsen, except that my father threw a rock back at the rock throwers. They put his picture in the newspapers. One week later, they took away his job —sympathizing with the enemy. Was he pro-German? I suspect, yes, he was pro-German. But more than that, he hated Mr. Wilson's war that was taking the boys away. My father sued to get his job back but, somehow, his case never came before a judge. The court kept losing his papers.

"That was the winter my own call came. I was twenty-one years old. But I was not going to go, not until someone found my father's papers. So they took me away. There was no trial, just a hearing, like in traffic court, and they sent me to Crane Creek to wait for a decision about due process and perhaps a term in a real prison with stone walls. How do you like that?

"Anyway, I have to thank them. I had been working in an auto body shop. Never thought about college. Six months on the lake inspired me to take up medicine, which my father liked because it meant you don't have to go to jail to avoid war. With just a slight correction, into veterinary medicine, dear old Cornell University sent me sailing through. But, do you see, I had no deep belief? No, it was to spite them on account of my father. Actually, I served in World War II. And my father was right. I did not have to fight. I only took care of horses for the Third Army."

Dr. Miller smiled apologetically, adding, "Truth? Crane Creek is so long ago, I hardly remember how I felt."

"You mean about resisting?" June asked.

"I mean about all what I myself did. Nothing heroic, or even romantic. Not to exaggerate—it was bad, but not too long, and not too cruel—mainly, I think, because we were all the same. We were draft resisters, malingerers, conscientious objectors, and everyday cowards with one issue, every man the same, taking his stand against compulsory military service. So, we did not run away—climbing the wire fence would've been easy—but we could not be pushed around, either. We were a company of boys, you might say. We did nothing except tend to our necessities and the guards did nothing except keep order among us. And they were boys, too. Crane Creek, after all, was not Andersonville or even Alcatraz. It was certainly not Dachau. I visited Dachau in 1946. Dachau was not Crane Creek.

"Well, I am trying to remember in an orderly fashion. I really am trying. You see, it was very cold up on the Creek and influenza came. Everyone had it and about thirty of our five hundred died and two of our twenty guards. Still, it's the weather I remember. Going around the whole winter's day wrapped in a quilt my grandmother'd made. I collected wood. I believe we collected wood all day, every day. We must have cleared two hundred acres for our stoves. The smell of wet clothes drying on a pinewood fire comes back to me.

"One night, there was a real fire. My tent burned and the tent next to us burned. Two men died. The rest of us, eighteen of us without clothes or bedding—I did save my quilt—got out. That was my worst night because one of the dead men was my friend. But it was a good night in this sense—everyone pulled together to save the camp. How can I say this to you? My time in that camp was, in many ways, the best of my times, and the friends I made, the best of my friends to this day.

"Yes, well, in the Lord's good time, there was talk of shutting down the camp. I don't know why. Perhaps the Army life and our camp life were too much alike. If the two were one, then what was our punishment? Or perhaps the camp was closed by mistake. Anyway, with the war still on, they sent me home on probation. Maybe they knew that would be the hardest part. People in Cincinnati hated me so! Even my old neighborhood turned away. Our mailman, I remember, took the greatest pleasure in delivering unsigned death threats sealed with a skull and crossbones. I very nearly almost changed my name—my father's name was Josef Miller, too. To this minute, I am ashamed that I even thought of it."

Snyder looked up from his notebook to see Amelia Pendergraft frowning. Dr. Miller seemed to have piqued her, the matter being, Snyder guessed, his alarming inability to forgive himself, even after nearly fifty years.

"Would that have been such a crime?" Amelia asked.

"No crime, but a denial. To have shared so much with so many men and then to deny it—that would have been terrible."

"Not even to save your life?"

"You know the answer to that, young lady."

The walkers stirred uneasily. Amelia glanced at Herndon, as though she could not continue without his permission.

"She means me, Dr. Miller," Herndon said, his voice sharp. "My name is Reed Herndon. I am a draft resister, too." Whether or not he wanted the old man's answer in that context, with Snyder and the walkers listening, it was clear that he intended to have it in the only context available.

"I know of you," Dr. Miller said, "from the news."

"That's my curse."

"No—it's news that makes prison worthwhile."

"Then I have to envy you."

Dr. Miller clicked his teeth with a little grimace of self-derision. "For what? Where is the difference?"

Herndon turned his face to Amelia. Her steady look seemed to reassure him, and he turned back to Dr. Miller.

"In this," Herndon said, "that you were hated outside, and I was hated inside, and that makes a big difference, personally and politically. Being hated outside builds a movement. I never expected anything else, okay? It was the other, the inside, that nothing, no literature, no history, no movie prepared me for.

"In prison, my joint, Leavenworth, for conscription crimes, there were ten or twelve Jehovah's Witnesses, a couple of Black Muslims —all religious prisoners who'd been denied CO status. There were a handful of old-fashioned draft dodgers who hadn't dodged fast enough. But in my time, besides me, there was only one other in my block, his name was Walter J. O'Rourke, and just five others in the whole prison, who were moral cases, or politicals, or whatever you want to call us, who had refused the draft on ethical grounds.

"Even O'Rourke was kept on a separate level. He's a Catholic from Alton, Illinois, who grew up near a military academy, and used to say that explains everything. He's doing five years for draft refusal, not four, and won't be out until 1968, with no hope of parole, for reasons I don't want to speak of. We are friends, all right, being the only two in our block without an excuse for being there, except 'Hey, guys, me and Walt are here because we believe we have the right to refuse to go to war'.

"But there is the difference—that we were only two, and you were five hundred. Funny, until tonight, it never occurred to me that it could have been another way—that prisoners of conscience might at least take their punishment together, make a community in the clink, and feel part of something bigger than themselves.

"Being a minority of two made us easy to hate. We were despised traitors, Communist cowards who would not defend America only because we didn't want to. To the rednecks and the hard-ball felons, we weren't even religious objectors or malingerers—we were damned activists! All those boys who'd robbed a bank, or shot up a post office, or stole a car in one state only to get caught in another, they quarantined us. They bragged a lot—yes, oh, of course, they'd gladly trade a year in Vietnam for a week off from the joint—you can be sure some of them even believed that. And in any case, they were not weird political prisoners, not a breed of moral freaks. They saw themselves simply as people who had messed up. They'd been caught, that's all. They were not even mad at the state. They were mad at the enemies of the state—it was safer—so Walter and me, we were worse in their eyes than the guards.

"It came to this: there are no atheists in foxholes—and no anti-war heroes in the lash-up. I could have done civil disobedience right there, hunger strikes, letters to the warden, protests of all kinds. I had those choices, but I did nothing because I was alone and hated or disdained by everyone except O'Rourke, who was in the same boat. We did our time in a kind of public solitary, in a state of irrelevance, and shared ideas about how to commit suicide painlessly. The publicity part was long past, Dr. Miller. Now do you see the difference? And when I got a chance at parole, I grabbed it, yes, and here I am, afraid to be on the Walk and ashamed to be anywhere else."

Herndon paused and the only sound was the sizzle of sap in the short, green logs that Arley Broyle had kept burning. Amelia embraced herself, her eyes fixed on the fire and glistening.

"Swell," she said bitterly.

"He can't change the past," Dr. Miller said, picking up on her one-word comment, as though Herndon were suddenly invisible. "Looking back, no one has any choices."

The invisible man returned. "Yes, but I had choices," Herndon said. "I think of Gandhi's hunger strike—I think of those who've refused to cooperate. They're not hard to find in history."

"Mr. Herndon, the very act of going to prison is enough," Dr. Miller said. "You've got no further obligation. The obligation lies with those who never went. They should remember and give meaning to your sacrifice. It's over, Mr. Herndon. Believe me—and just as I can't help that I'm not Jonas Salk, you can't help that you're not Jesus Christ."

"No, I lost."

"Where is your defeat?"

"In that I feel nothing is worth enduring prison again."

"You did endure. What more is to tell?"

"That's not the point. I'm here now."

"You are a hero of the peace movement," Dr. Miller said somberly. "That I never was. So I envy you."

There were murmurs of agreement around the fire. Herndon shook his head, but did not reply. Dr. Miller had had no clue for him after all. "Respect is a better word," Sam Lucas said, his voice obscured by gaseous noises whistling from an underaged log. Snyder ended his notes with a final credit for Amelia. Her candor had enabled Herndon to share more of his burden with the walkers; each time Herndon told the story more was exposed. Snyder felt certain that no interview could have elicited such an account—duly noting that it seemed to just miss the weight of the whole truth.

Dorene began to sing and, for the hour or so it took the last logs to burn, everyone remained by the fire, following her lead into "I Dreamed I Saw Joe Hill Last Night" and all the old labor songs she'd learned at summer camp. Even Snyder sang from time to time, but he rarely took his eyes off Herndon. Again and again, as Dr. Miller's final question—"What more is to tell?"—turned over in his mind, he played with Herndon's answer—"That's not the point."

It was only when Snyder had begun to doze off in his sleeping bag that an answer of his own came up to his consciousness: Herndon's prison tale had a beginning and an end, yes, and a large hole in the middle.

3

Next morning, ever so briefly, they saw Dr. Miller again. The weather was warm and bright, bringing out the old man to walk an arthritic mile with them. He seemed subdued as though the evening of campfire tales had left him overexposed in sunlight. Making an exception to the overnight rule, Sam Lucas asked him to sign their petition.

Toward noon, they were on the march less than ten miles from Coshocton, the county seat, expecting two Coshocton ladies from the River Valley Methodist Church to arrive soon with a picnic lunch. They crossed a narrow brook, down which they could see the remains of a nineteenth-century sawmill, its roof gone and one side caved in, beside a fieldstone dam. Two white boys and an elderly Negro fished below the dam. They did not look up. Then the road curved sharply behind a high cliff and surprised them with an oversized trailer truck stalled in the westbound lane. Yellow flares burned on the divider and, without police help, traffic in both directions moved slowly through the eastbound lane. The Walk took to higher ground on the safe side of a drainage ditch, and so proceeded in single file above the truck. Just then, from behind, came roaring two motorcycles. The riders in black leather had squeezed onto the shoulder and now gunned between the line of eastbound vehicles and the ditch. A blast of air and gravel struck the walkers and blew down both Dorene, who was carrying the lead sign, and Joe Rice, whose cane skidded away from him as he fell. Vachel Rice quickly lifted his father. Herndon, Lucas, and George Corrigan scrambled to help Dorene. Joe Rice angrily insisted he had not been hurt. Dorene, stunned, gave up the lead sign, but refused to ride the last mile to the rest stop. The motorcyclists, meanwhile, had made their getaway, vanishing within seconds around a sharp curve. Snyder caught the number on one license plate and recognized both machines, respectively, a Harley-Davidson and a Honda.

On the shoulder again, the walkers passed through a scrub forest into a vast green-and-black checkerboard plain as beautiful as any they had seen. Bright cloudless sky suddenly extended in a great arc to the east and south and over low brown hills to the north. At hailing distance, they could see Arley Broyle's truck and the Coshocton ladies' Peugeot sedan aptly positioned off-road on the frail blue line of the Walhonding River where it slipped through a narrow ford crossing north to south under U.S. 36.

They gathered by the river for their Methodist feast. With Broyle's help, the Coshocton ladies, a round and kindly pair, had set a buffet table on the sandy bank at the base of the road bridge. On the menu were cold potato soup, fried chicken, tomatoes laced with raw onions, potato salad sprinkled with bacon, hot buttered rolls, oranges, brownies, and ice tea. The walkers served themselves and most of them waded through the ankle-deep water to lunch and lounge in the soft grass on an island just off the east bank of the river.

Snyder and Rachel Abraham stayed behind, sitting on a blanket in the sand near the buffet table with Sam Lucas, Molly Hamilton, and the hostesses, Mrs. Thelma Becker, president of the River Valley Methodist Ladies' Auxiliary, and Mrs. Bettina Durbin, the minister's wife. From across the ford, they heard Dorene cry, "There's Methodism in our madness!" Snyder jotted down the laugh-line; then his notebook remained open in his lap. The prospect of immortality so close at hand prompted Mrs. Becker to tell Snyder about her late husband's early years in the steel business over in Youngstown. Mrs. Durbin was more serious, concerned about just and unjust wars according to the Methodist canon, but the roaring flatulence of two motorcycles speeding west over the bridge ended her disquisition almost before it was fairly begun. At his angle below the bridge, Snyder caught a bare glimpse of the commotion but, with fair certainty, assumed the passing motorcycles had already been seen on the road that morning—one Harley-Davidson, one Honda, driven by men in black leather jackets and jackboots, the impatient riders who had earlier blown two walkers down. Rachel put down her paper plate. She had seen them, too.

In seconds, the motorcycle pair again screamed across the bridge, going east toward Coshocton; turned once more with controlled skids; and, like giant crows, landed on the bridge at the safety railing above the picnic. The Honda's rider was frail and the Harley's burly, but to Snyder, their sameness was more remarkable. As they dropped their kickstands and dismounted, they puffed up, presumably to appear equally indomitable. Each was a shaggy, unkempt man in his mid-twenties. Each hid his eyes behind pilot's shades; bore the name "Holy Smokes" and the face of a red devil on his jacket; trimmed his body with silver buckles, bracelets, chains, and studs; and projected an image in direct descent from Marlon Brando in *The Wild One* plus a decade of publicity for the Hell's Angels of California—in *Harrington's,* as elsewhere. Their motorcycle-gang slouch, swagger, and sleaze might even seem farcical, Snyder was thinking, were its intention entertainment rather than intimidation.

With a sour smile, the Harley rider lumbered down the path toward the buffet table. At the same time, Sam Lucas rose awkwardly to represent the Walk. Rachel whistled softly. The Harley rider came to a stop about five yards below the table at the edge of the blanket, behind Mrs. Durbin. Lucas wavered and slipped, sending paper plates skidding onto the sand. Then he righted himself and lifted his bearded jaw toward the rider. "Yes?" he asked, without apparent fear, expressing courtesy as well as curiosity. The rider remained silent. He seemed to study Lucas's girth. He even winked down at Snyder and Rachel, as though Lucas were a mere spectacle, a whale or an elephant outside of captivity, not to be missed. Snyder glanced toward the east bank. The other walkers were standing now, contained by the thin slice of river that had become an unwelcome moat, and straining to hear. Protectively, Snyder closed his notebook on Mrs. Durbin's page and moved it from his lap to his shirt pocket. That gesture caught the rider's attention—and drew him behind Lucas to a towering halt above all those seated on the blanket. Snyder looked up from under the brim of his Azores-hat.

"Are you proud of something?" the rider asked.

"No," Snyder said.

"What is this?"

"Notebook."

During the exchange, the rider had partially lifted the notebook from Snyder's pocket. When the title "Walk Notes: VII," in Snyder's script, appeared, he let it drop back again. Then he turned to survey the walkers on the far side of the river ford. Seemingly satisfied by his strategic position, he gazed up toward the Honda rider on the bridge. "Right, Timbo!" he called out in self-congratulation. "These people don't like their country, carry signs, carry flags, mess up traffic, and still get a big story in the Marion *Daily* damn *Clarion."* He looked down on Snyder. "More—they have here a man's going to tell their story nationwide for *Harrington's* magazine. We read about you, didn't we?"

The disadvantage of his sitting position gave Snyder no choice, but he rationalized it anyway: for the sake of the Walk, especially since the Kupferman incident, you can't provoke a man who has, presumably, more friends than just Timbo in the neighborhood. Furthermore, the situation is not quite covered by the First Amendment. Should you identify yourself, at least you might limit the abuse, though suffering humiliation; and should you not, a kick in the head will turn up the press card in your wallet just the same, while worse may come of it for the others.

"Yes, you did," Snyder said.

"You see, Timbo!" the Harley rider exulted. "I told you, hey. It had to be them."

"No, boy, I told you," Timbo objected. He leaned far over the rail, spit into the sand, and defied the burly man with a sharp lift of his chin.

"Oh, suck, Timbo," the Harley rider said. "J. J. Cockburn don't lie."

Sudden exasperation spun Timbo away from the railing, then returned him with both hands outstretched. "Christ, J.J.," he lamented, "you give them your whole name!"

"Can't get your name in the magazine unless you give it," Cockburn said. "Timothy Beauregard Wayne, that's you, hey, Timbo?" Cockburn looked again to Snyder. "J for James, J for Jerome," he said, "I forget yours."

"Aw, J.J., you're nuts," Timbo said.

"No, I remember," Cockburn said. "I remember, Something Snyder. Well, here, you can write down that we've twenty-two of us out of Columbus with thirteen cycles, four each by Harley and Honda, two BMWs, two Kawasakis, and one all-out goddamn Moto Guzzi, who mean to be in your story."

As Snyder reached for his notebook, Sam Lucas took a step back, a telltale flush of anger rising above his beard toward the temples. He touched Cockburn's studded wristband.

"This is a peace march," Lucas said. "All we need is a small piece of the highway. The rest is yours."

"Don't get unfriendly, uncle," Cockburn said. "We just want to see you safely out of the state of Ohio."

On the bridge, Timbo clapped his hands. "Tell him, J.J., and let's get on."

Across the narrow neck of water between the riverbank and the island, no one was sitting anymore. The island people had come to the very edge of their shore. Only twenty yards of shallow water separated them from the confrontation below the bridge. Snyder saw Corrigan and Dunne step down into the stream.

Cockburn moved toward the edge of the west bank and mounted a stone. Puffing up, he said, "We took a vote. My friend Timbo and me, when we saw you back down the road, we took a vote for the Holy Smokes. It's unanimous—you have to leave hereabouts tonight —by bus, train, horse cart, we don't care—just so you don't march around here, not anymore, like it says in the Marion *Daily* damn *Clarion*. Let's make it, say, anyway, no roads from here to Wheeling, I mean on our side of the Ohio River anymore. How's that?"

Sam Lucas's face had swelled. Now it turned bluish red.

"We can't," he said bravely. "We're walking all that way."

Cockburn sighed, letting his jaw drop in mock amazement. Then he stepped down from the rock and moved quickly around the buffet table to the foot of the path. He stopped, seemed about to turn, then continued up to the highway. Snyder, Rachel, and Molly scrambled to their feet. Behind them, the walkers splashed toward the west bank.

Above, at the railing, Cockburn stared down at Lucas.

"No joke," he said, and backed from view.

J. J. Cockburn was next seen on his Harley-Davidson, noisily revving his engine. On the Honda, Timbo Wayne punctuated with deliberate backfires. By the time the walkers had come together, the pair of Holy Smokes were moving off, side by side, accelerating east toward Coshocton. Snyder squeezed Rachel's hand. He let his anger rise, but remorse rose with it. He had been both victim and perpetrator; they violated his independence, but he did not defend himself. Fat Sam Lucas had the bigger balls. Snyder removed his hat and wiped the moisture from the sweatband. The air was cool on his forehead. Then suddenly, he realized, everyone around him was talking at once, as people will do after a bad accident.

"Typical fascists," Frank Dunne said.

"I want to take another look at non-violence," Dorene said.

"Total bastards," Joe Rice said.

"We ought to be able to walk through the state of Ohio," Sam Lucas said, indulging his outrage.

Then Lucas shuddered and shook. His face turned pale.

"Sit down, Sam," Molly said.

She chafed his hands as Arley Broyle bounded across the sand for the picnic blanket, which he draped around Lucas's shoulders. Lucas refused to sit.

"I'm quite okay," he said. "It was Jack they threatened."

Snyder forced a smile.

"Clark Kent without a phone booth," he said, "is only Clark Kent."

"Fine, just fine," Rachel said.

"They should be arrested," Mrs. Durbin said. She made two plump, angry fists. "The sheriff in Coshocton, McClelland Alexander, he's a decent man. A Presbyterian."

"We're mortified," Mrs. Becker said. "Sheriff Alexander won't stand for it, especially in an election year."

"Oh, no, my God," Lucas said, "no police! Think of the delay. Let's clean up."

In the grass off-road beside Mrs. Durbin's sedan, the walkers formed a half circle with Mrs. Becker and Mrs. Durbin in the middle to receive their thanks. The wind was picking up and the dust on the shoulder scattered in little gray puffs. Snyder saw Mrs. Durbin's eyes roll first to Mrs. Becker, then heavenward, as though her next intention needed special help. Finally, her eyes looped down, fastening on Lucas.

"I know about police and courts and judges, Mr. Lucas," she said. "To press charges or ask for a police escort could, I've no doubt, delay you—"

Interrupting, Lucas said, "More than delay—a police escort denies our very purpose, Mrs. Durbin. Non-violence is our best argument. Armed guards defeat it."

"But there's this: Mrs. Becker and I feel morally bound to make a report to Sheriff Alexander. We're sorry, but then the sheriff may take these steps himself."

Somberly, as though polling the group, Lucas looked from face to face among the walkers until he found Reed Herndon's. It was Herndon who had the most to lose.

"High risk," Lucas said.

"Why don't you make the report, Sam?" Herndon replied.

Well done, Snyder thought. The agreement among the walkers had saved face for Mrs. Durbin and Mrs. Becker while giving both ladies a new role to play, secondary, but still righteous.

Gratefully, Mrs. Durbin proposed to drive Lucas, Molly Hamilton, and Snyder in the Peugeot with Mrs. Becker to the sheriff's headquarters in Coshocton. Meanwhile, Herndon assembled the walkers, Frank Dunne in the lead, Rachel Abraham at the rear. She waved to Snyder, who replied with a V sign.

Looking back, as the Peugeot pulled away, Snyder saw a mirage on the highway. The walkers seemed to be ankle deep in water again. With only twelve of them afoot, the whole effort seemed very small to him, and no longer certain to endure.

4

Coshocton was only twenty minutes down the road, home for 12,000 people, past a sign advertising the local motorcycle and stock-car racetrack, over another Walhonding River crossing, beside a factory making rubber gloves, and into the business district, where, out of sheer local pride, Mrs. Durbin proposed to drive twice around the town square so that the visitors could see it all. In appropriate isolation, the old county courthouse sat alone on the square surrounded by blooming elms and a neat lawn. It had a grand baroque five-story central tower and twin courtroom wings, all in red brick with white-trimmed windows. Some renovation work had been undertaken, but not so as to ruin the look of the place, so far. And there was a monument on one side, a purple shaft with a globe on top commemorating the county's war dead, pre-Vietnam. Mrs. Durbin recited the motto for Snyder's notes: "Let none forget they gave their all, and faltered not when came the call."

"I suppose someday we'll feel that way about the boys in Vietnam," she said, "but first we have to get them home."

"Exactly," Lucas said.

Second time around the square, Mrs. Becker pointed out the landmarks facing the courthouse: the Park Hotel, a Carnegie library, the Presbyterian church, and the Salvation Army home with a sign up proclaiming: "God is Love."

It was midafternoon when Mrs. Durbin stopped on a short street off the square where, in separate wings, a one-story modern security building housed the county jail and the sheriff's headquarters. Inside was a small public room manned by a desk clerk. Behind a gate across the room was a glassed-in office for the sheriff with his name, McClelland Alexander, stenciled on the door.

After a moment, Alexander emerged. He was about sixty, taller than Snyder, white-haired, and thin as a board. His old Scot's face was very long and careworn, yet relieved by a witty white beard cut straight across the chin. And though he affected a western style, wearing cowboy boots with a business suit and, instead of a necktie, a lanyard fastened by a silver Zuñi clasp, he wore no badge and seemed unarmed. With diffident correctness, he first greeted the minister's wife, then her friend, and then the visitors, the director of WISE and his wife, and the writer for *Harrington's* magazine, as though their like were of the sort who dropped in at his headquarters every day. In his office, he sat them in a line of chairs facing him across a blue metal desk, behind which was a large road map of the state of Ohio; then he reached around for a yellow Stetson five-gallon hat and put it on, low over his eyebrows. "Shoot, sir," he said.

Lucas sat forward. "I want to make it clear," he said, "that we do not wish to make a complaint at this time—we wish to report a disturbing incident and ask your cooperation, essentially, in doing nothing."

"Tell me," the sheriff said, as though he had heard that request every day, too.

Lucas's narration lasted fifteen minutes. Every so often, the sheriff would say, "I see—I see," and make a note on a legal pad. Once, when Lucas could not remember Timbo's full name, Snyder filled in the blank. At the end, the sheriff tipped back in his chair until the back brim of his Stetson touched the map on the wall.

"To make a long story short, sir," he said, "you allege two members of a motorcycle gang have threatened to violate your civil rights. And you say you did not provoke them—"

"At our picnic, Mac!" Mrs. Durbin exclaimed. "Thelma Becker and I were right there."

"Thank you, Mrs. Durbin," the sheriff said. "And you, Mr. Lucas, want only to report it, but not complain about it. Will you tell me why?"

"I will, yes. My point is 'the law's delay' and we must keep walking. As I say, we have thirty-two days and no leeway."

"Well, would you complain just a little, so this office can officially warn them against perpetrating a crime against you in Coshocton County?"

"Only if it can be done without pressing charges, yes."

"I understand. Well, let me take another angle. You say the Marion *Daily Clarion* published your route. Can you change it?"

"People are waiting for us along the way. Our accommodations have been prearranged. The distances are set."

"And where do you go from here?"

"Tomorrow on Route 751 to Newcomerstown—"

"Excuse me, sir—only fourteen miles?"

"Yes, our average—six hours, maybe eight depending on the hills, maybe ten if the weather's bad."

"I see—you know, by then, you'll have crossed my county line?"

"Yes, and going on, of course, over to the Ohio River. The map—"

"It's all right. You're coming through very clear, sir. Amazing events are taking place in the country, but I understand you. And we do know the Holy Smokes. Not the worst motorcycle gang in the state. They race here at the Coshocton Speedway. One problem is that they also race to and from the Speedway. And they've been in trouble, some drugs, mostly around Columbus. By chance, Mr. Lucas, did they offer drugs to your group?"

"No, none."

"You're sure?"

"Yes, and as I said, it's publicity they seem to want."

"From this man," the sheriff said, shifting toward Snyder. "You believe that?"

"Yes, because it's national publicity," Snyder replied.

"Something's happening to this country," the sheriff said. He turned for a straight-on view of the big road map. Then he removed his Stetson and used it for a pointer. "End of tomorrow's walk puts you here, across the line into Tuscarawas County. From Tuscarawas, here, you're in Harrison County. And next thing you know, you're in Belmont County, over on the big river itself." The sheriff put on his hat and faced his guests again. "Now, let me explain about our coverage. We patrol Coshocton County with three cars, maximum. One of my officers says he passed you this morning—did you notice? He was leading a funeral motorcade. Well, so, we are spread very thin when you figure how those bike riders can get around. They know it, too. But it's about average. It's the state highway patrol that has more flexibility. Maybe that's your best bet. Only, ah, to get them to cover you'd have to complain through Columbus."

Lucas tapped the desk top for emphasis. "Sheriff Alexander," he said, "we wish to continue at our own risk. If the cyclists stop us, we will try reason. And failing that, non-resistance. We're up against a time factor, do you see?"

"I can't order you, sir," the sheriff said, then paused to lift a leather-covered diary from his desk drawer. "But I can make calls for you to Columbus and some other places. If these men can be found, I can have them warned. I hope so. Otherwise, it's my job to try to see to it that no harm comes to you in Coshocton County."

"But not an escort," Lucas insisted.

"We will escort you to our county line."

"Respectfully, we decline."

"You can't decline, sir."

Lucas straightened. Molly placed a hand on his arm. The sheriff clasped his hands on top of the diary.

"If you seek martyrdom, Mr. Lucas," the sheriff said, "don't do it on my turf."

"It's not that at all," Lucas said, "but we do decline."

"I call it a draw, sir. It comes to this: you people will be on Route 751 tomorrow and one of our cars will be on the same road at the same time. If nothing happens, no one will ever know. If something happens, well, perhaps one of you could stay behind to deal with the law's delay. It's the best I can do." The sheriff stood, offering his hand. "What else?" he asked himself. "What else? Day after tomorrow and the day after that? I will just say we have a fine sheriff in Tuscarawas, in Harrison, and so on. We keep in touch."

Lucas rose from his seat, doing his best to seem undaunted.

"I can't beg you, so I think we're through here," he said. "Thank you very much."

Lucas and the sheriff shook hands.

"I have my duty," the sheriff said. It was a statement, not an apology.

"We have our rights," Lucas said, with a touch of bravado.

The sheriff removed his Stetson, turned toward the women, then turned back to Lucas as though with an afterthought. "I'm doing that," he said, "respecting them, sir. You might even be surprised to learn that not all the rednecks around here are as thrilled about the war in Vietnam as you might think. Where we differ with you people is support for our fighting men, first and foremost, is all."

"We support them, too, Sheriff."

"Well, then, we share that, Mr. Lucas."

The sheriff shook hands with his other guests, Snyder last.

"Useful information?" he asked.

"Oh, yes," Snyder said.

"I'll look forward to reading all about us."

FOURTEEN

A Crisis of Identity

I

Sheriff Alexander had kept his word, assigning a radio patrol car and a deputy named Armand Magid for the next day to escort the Walk to the county line near Newcomerstown. After 10 A.M., Magid would maintain minimum visual surveillance and avoid physical intervention, pending superior orders. The sheriff also informally discussed the Walk's plight with the sheriffs of the three neighboring counties and with the commandant of the state police, but asked for no commitments.

That night at the Methodist church, the Walk heard about all this from Mrs. Durbin; out of deference for Lucas's scruples, the sheriff had briefed her, not Lucas. "Your friend goes with clean hands, Betty," the sheriff said, "or clean feet, as the case may be." Among the walkers, only Lucas failed to laugh. Red-faced, he cut short the merriment and expounded on the importance of avoiding collaboration with the police. There were murmurings of agreement, and no disagreements. But that failure of humor by the admirable Lucas made Snyder wonder what it was really like living with a faith in goodness so great that even self-defense was disallowed. Knowing that he might never find out, Snyder made note of the question and answered it for his man: "It's no fun."

In the morning, the escort appeared at ten sharp; with the temperature suddenly pushing eighty-five degrees under a blue-white sky, and the Walk about four miles east of Coshocton on a rolling stretch of Route 751 between two fields of fresh-turned black earth, a voice had sung out: "Look behind! Look behind!" It was Vachel Rice, marching at the rear with his father, who carried the sign of the peace trident. Then Joe Rice called, "Sheriff's come! He's here, hey!"—pointing accurately, as he so often did, without seeing.

All heads turned. Three hundred yards back at the top of the last rise, Deputy Magid in an orange patrol car was just then braking, having pulled over onto the right shoulder. He flashed his headlights twice and waited in place. He would have a view to the next curve about a quarter of a mile down the road. Uncertainly, the walkers shuffled on. Soon that curve blocked Magid from their sight; and once again he appeared. The walkers saw him parking at a discreet distance, this time on the upside of the highway where his range would probably cover most of a mile to the top of the next rise. Magid waved with his left hand, palm up, seeming to signify his inability to do other than follow orders. Peter Schumacher, who had been sharing the lead for that hour with Sam Lucas, pumped the WISE sign as if to say, "We understand. The pattern is clear. Hello!" Sam Lucas brusquely raised a hand to cool Schumacher's enthusiasm; it was a testy reminder that his discipline prevailed and that no one was to approach the patrol car.

That noon hour, they stopped for lunch at an Amish café in the town of West Lafayette; the thermometer on the screen door read ninety-two degrees. The window looked out on an empty street and across to a service station, where Magid parked and debarked to use the facilities. He had not been seen standing before. He wore a yellow Stetson like the sheriff's and a khaki uniform with a low-slung gun belt. The back of his shirt was dark with sweat. He returned mopping his brow with a paper towel. Then he drank a Coke, ate a candy bar, and apparently told a funny joke to the attendant. Snyder realized Armand Magid was probably younger than Reed Herndon.

Midafternoon, a light rain began to fall and a cloud dropped low over a vast quiltlike expanse of farmland. Magid began to fade into the fog. Then he moved his car closer to the Walk and, at the next rest stop, parked only about a hundred fifty yards behind Arley Broyle's truck. Both vehicles faced east on the south side of the highway and triangulated a giant billboard on the north side; the sign doggedly advertised a warning against forest fires and, simultaneously, blocked much of the view of the only substantial wooded area on either side of the road for five hundred yards in any direction.

Nature called Magid again. Snyder watched him hurry through the rain wearing an ankle-length yellow slicker, across the rushing highway and behind the billboard into a thick glade of evergreens. A moment later and, along with the walkers, Magid would have seen two Harley-Davidson motorcycles flying west toward Coshocton. The riders wore their jackets tied by the sleeves around their waists, concealing their trademark; their rain-soaked shirts billowed out like parachutes. They soon vanished behind a curve, reappeared on a hill, and then dropped from view about a mile back. They had left the walkers under their umbrellas at the roadside gaping at the horizon, their unanimous silence telling Snyder they knew they had been scouted.

After another moment, with the walkers ready to move on, the insouciant Magid strolled innocently out of the woods toward his car. Lucas's rule against fraternization meant that no walker would run to him with the news. But Snyder was not bound by it. Suppose, he was thinking, you tell the escort about the Holy Smokes' fly-by; Magid's reaction could not be insignificant. But still—do you intervene in a way that must alter the situation, or do you shut up, letting the Walk happen as though you aren't here and accountable? There is no absolute rule, but mostly you shut up.

Magid climbed into his car with another wave, as if to say, "I'm ready." Snyder joined the Walk beside Rachel Abraham, letting it be.

The rain stopped, the humidity rose with the heat, and then it started to drizzle on the day's last distance. Ahead of Magid by nearly half a mile, the Walk descended into a long green valley just west of Newcomerstown. A farm prospering at the bottom boasted three blue silos and a long white barn. A man and a boy under one umbrella stood by the barn to watch the Walk go by. Dorene Quink gave the man a leaflet. He smiled shyly and handed the leaflet to the boy. Then he sent the boy running with the umbrella for a proper number of apples. The man shook hands with George Corrigan. He said they were standing smack on the Tuscarawas-Coshocton county line; someone had stolen the sign at Halloween. Corrigan borrowed June's flag to wave at Magid. High on the hill behind, the patrol car's lights blinked. Walkers waved all the signs, lead, trident, and the REMEMBER NORMAN MORRISON cross. Magid crossed the highway and drove off toward Coshocton. Snyder noted the time and joined Lucas at the head of the march.

"You think I'm wrong?" Lucas asked, at work on a red apple.

"I don't know. What might have happened without Magid?"

"Hopefully, nothing."

"Maybe he helped, Sam. When those bikers saw us, they saw his car."

"It was luck Magid didn't see them. He might have called headquarters. He might have called the state patrol. Who knows what he might have done? We could all be back in Coshocton by now, talking to the judge. Tomorrow, we'll know more."

"You've noticed there's no Tuscarawas escort here to meet us?"

"The less cops, the better our chances, believe me, Jack."

Snyder thought to reply, "You don't need my belief, Sam—you've got all you'll ever need." Instead, he merely nodded. The comment would have been misunderstood anyway.

That night, the Walk made an appearance at the Newcomerstown volunteer firehouse and bedded down just east of town at the Cy Young Motor Inn. There was no word of an escort.

Next day, they walked sixteen miles in ninety-degree heat to a campsite on the eastern edge of Tuscarawas County. Four times, twice in the morning, twice in the afternoon, a white patrol car had cruised by, but did not stop or acknowledge them. There were motorcyclists, too, single riders, pairs, and once a roaring herd of twenty-three on fourteen bikes wearing jackets with the name "Unholy Rollers," which was close enough for a scare, but not the same.

2

In the early afternoon of the third day out of Coshocton, on a high, flat, windless stretch of old highway, they crossed into Harrison County. Again there was no escort, and no incident, either. Perhaps, Snyder was thinking, it is just too hot for the law as well as the outlaws. The temperature was past ninety degrees. Arley Broyle had heard on the truck radio that it was a record for the day for the second day in a row, and altogether unusual for early June. The pavement patches bubbled under the sun. Even on the straight and level, the walking was hard.

They came bushed to the top of Piedmont Lake, which filled a narrow valley south of the highway. The lake was about eight miles long, shaped like a lost piece from a jigsaw puzzle. Arley Broyle had been scouting on his own. He reported a small public beach and log-cabin general store on the lakefront four miles up a gravel road. They had two hours, Sam Lucas agreed, for a swim. Broyle drove them in on the truck, seven each in two trips.

They found a calm, gray lake which seemed to absorb the sun into its mirror surface and reflect a pale green Impressionist light on the woods all around it. A few fishing boats loafed in the shade along the eastern shore. Close by, a dozen or so young swimmers splashed about watched by a sunburned boy in a purple dinghy. A diving raft floated about fifty yards from shore. Snyder learned that he was the only one who had failed to pack a swimming suit, except Joe Rice, who did not swim.

Snyder sat on a shady knoll with the blind man, who wanted him to describe the walkers—Sam Lucas drifting like a floating whale with the dolphin, Molly, paddling nearby; Dorene and June making waves with Corrigan, Schumacher, and Wood; Frank Dunne and Rachel, both serious swimmers, she in a blue tank suit, gracefully circling the raft; Vachel Rice and Broyle already in and out, dozing on the shore; Herndon and Amelia swimming lazily together beyond the raft toward a roped row of red bobbins marking the outer limits of the bathing area.

Joe Rice lay back, an arm across his eyes. Shaving his chin that morning had left him with a cut and a patch of white hairs like winter frost.

"Go ahead in, Jack," he said.

"It's all right."

"Can't swim?"

"Passable—Camp Cherokee, Kansas, junior lifesaver, but no swimsuit."

"Your skivvies, man. Go in your skivvies!"

Snyder found swim trunks in his size at the general store. He swam alone from shore to the rope boundary and back again, twice, about three hundred fifty yards in all. The effort was less tiring than he would have expected. The Walk, he realized, had done something for his legs. He set off on another round trip but, this time, stopped at the rope, out of breath. As he rested, holding on to a red bobbin, Rachel swam up beside him, then around and behind him with seemingly effortless grace. She ducked under and resurfaced at his side, pushing back her wet hair with both hands. The gesture lifted her chest from the water, her breasts tight against her suit.

Snyder said, "You are a fish, aren't you?" Her closeness made him ache. "Where's Frank?"

"We've been watching you," she said. "He's had enough."

"I did my laps. Enough for me, too."

"You're a good swimmer."

"Many too many cigarettes."

"We've got thirty minutes. Are you okay?"

"Yes, but resting."

"Then let's go to the raft."

They swam the forty yards slowly. Snyder hated to admit he was winded, but he knew he wanted the raft for a rest stop on the way to shore. Even the effort to climb the ladder told him that he had had his major exercise for the day.

For a time on the raft, they had to sit on the edge, sharing the narrow space behind the diving board with another couple, a boy and girl from the town of Piedmont. Then, as the couple set off for shore, Rachel stretched out, lying flat on her stomach as Snyder turned to face her, sitting cross-legged with his back to the sun. He wished for his shirt. But it was, as he recalled, a rare thing on the Walk to be as alone with her as at that moment on the raft in broad daylight.

"You okay?" he asked, resisting a desire to touch her wet hair.

"Yes, and you?" Rachel squinted up, adding, "I mean, in general."

"Yes, very fine. It's all in the feet, Ray. If the feet are fine, the body is fine. How're your feet?"

Before answering, Rachel wryly examined the soles of Snyder's feet. His blister had long since healed.

"My feet?" she asked. "My feet are fine."

"We'll be in Wheeling soon."

"Oh, yes. It's just that we don't know who will be waiting for us around the next turn."

"Maybe no one, Ray. J. J. Cockburn could realize that he's already got his wish. He's in the story. He doesn't have to come again."

"You know that. I know that. But do the Holy Smokes know that?"

Snyder shrugged at the question; it was otherwise unanswerable.

"What a name!" Rachel cried. "When the Unholy Rollers went by, I liked the sound of theirs better, safer, like a pharmaceutical association. But Holy Smokes—what does that mean?"

"In Ohio, I don't know. In Japan, the shrines burn chips or punk in a kind of stove so you can brush yourself with smoke for good luck. Touch it to your head, it prevents baldness; to your heart, heart disease; scrub your hands, goodbye arthritis. That's holy smoke."

"My," Rachel exclaimed, "what knowledge don't you have!"

"I'm a storehouse of irrelevancy," he said. "Didn't you read last year J. C. Snyder's 'Hiroshima Plus Twenty' in *Harrington's Weekly World?*"

"Afraid I missed it. Sam Lucas is our expert on that subject."

"No wonder I get no respect."

Rachel pushed up, bringing her knees forward and sitting back on her heels. "You can tell me about Hiroshima," she said.

"Condensed version?"

"One-page summary, so I'll know whether to subscribe."

"Hiroshima's like this twenty years later: The dead are buried and homesteaders have arrived from everywhere, especially overseas Japanese from the lost colonies, Korea, Manchuria. They've restored the port, built a baseball stadium adjacent to ground zero, put up skyscrapers, factories, new housing. The city's alive. The physical signs of its trouble are gone or going. The memory is kept in the holocaust museum and in the stories of the survivors who are still around telling people what happened. The newcomers tend to shun them, the hibakusha, and you get the feeling that when the last of them has died off, the city won't mind if the museum disappears, too."

"You wrote that?"

"Something like that in four thousand words."

"I wouldn't want to make you mad."

"Well, you take this job to get even."

"With whom?"

"People who make you mad."

Rachel frowned. "Is that anybody?"

Snyder realized he had opened himself, bringing her inside looking out at his job, for the sake of which no subject, not even the suffering city of Hiroshima, was immune to objectivity. He had not meant to do that.

"Yes and no," he said. "First you get the story. Then you do it."

"And that's where we are—still begetting for you?"

"Still."

"How will you do us—in?"

Snyder felt trapped; the story had a long way to go.

"I don't do people in, Ray. People do themselves in and I write about them."

"You never quite said that before."

"You never quite asked."

"Well, what about us? Aren't we the good guys?"

"It seems so."

"Isn't that your theme?"

"No, that's your theme. Mine is endurance." Snyder lifted his hands, palms up. "People want to know how good the opposition to the war really is."

"That makes us a metaphor when, dammit, we're only a tiny fraction of the effort. You're not being fair."

"No, I guess not."

"We could fail and the movement still turns the country around."

"That's true."

"Or we could be glorious in Washington, and the war just goes on as always."

"That could be true, but you don't believe it, do you? Divided countries don't win wars."

"That's not fair, either. We're not trying to divide this country."

"I didn't mean that."

"You make me nervous when you're being the man from *Harrington's.*"

"I didn't mean that. I mean you're part of a momentum in this country, going one way or another, making a difference, maybe, or maybe not."

"I give you that."

"You make me nervous, too," Snyder added, remembering to smile.

"We almost talked about this once before."

"You mean the night we met."

"Click's Bar, when you said two wars and a depression made you a journalist."

"Something like that."

"I didn't quite understand."

"It's about detachment, Ray."

"Explain."

"I have a theory for everything."

"Please. I'm serious."

"Okay, the Theory of Detachment goes like this. First, disaster makes you a realist. Second, realism teaches you to watch out. Third, caution makes you careful about the obvious. Ergo, it all adds up to a certain detachment—a habit of detachment. When you've got that, one profession or another chooses you for a life. In my case, it was journalism."

"But you're involved. I know you. If ever there was an engaged journalist—"

"All right, engaged—but with a professional caveat."

"Ah, the thing we hear so much about—objectivity. Is there any such thing?"

"You're making fun of me."

"No, no—I'm just asking. What happens to the real thing. How do you avoid real involvement?"

"We're getting way off the trail, Ray."

"I want to know. What happens to the things you care about? People? How about intimacy?"

"Well, how about it?"

"You're not this person you call 'professional' twenty-four hours a day."

"No, I'm not."

"Are you then capable of intimacy?"

"My then wife used to complain about that."

"Living with a caveat man?"

"I brought it home, okay? I admit it. My habit. It's like smoking in bed. You can't quit just because it's risky."

"How sad."

"I don't know. Maybe it is. Maybe it's a challenge."

"You'd be a challenge, Mr. Tschacbasov."

"You, too." Snyder smiled. "Ray, you, too."

"Well, I'm glad of that."

"Yes. That's why I like swimming with you."

Snyder was relieved to hear her laugh. The quarrelsome look in her eyes vanished. He saw her hands rising to his face. Her touch was precise, almost witty. She half opened her mouth as though a word was on the tip of her tongue. He felt an ache again, more specific than before, which he did not care to examine. Without her help, he knew he could fail as White Knight before another month passed.

Rachel kissed him lightly and pulled back before he could respond.

"So much for intimacy," she said.

"You do everything well," he replied.

She shifted herself toward the edge of the raft.

"You sit like that, Jack," she said. "Watch me dive for pearls."

3

A night and another hot day passed; they had walked eleven hours that day, seven miles beyond a scheduled campsite to Bannock, Ohio, a wide place on Route 331, with floor space for sleeping at the local Grange Hall. From here, an inexhaustible few led by George Corrigan drove off to *Spartacus,* the Kirk Douglas movie playing in St. Clairsville. The rest, including Snyder, opted for a nearby diner. *Spartacus* was advertised as the epic story of a gladiator who falls in love with a Christian slave girl and joins her cause. Snyder did not particularly want to sit through that.

It was about ten when the movie safari returned, with Peter Schumacher solemnly carrying a copy of the final edition of the Wheeling evening newspaper. A white gunman on a highway in Mississippi had made headlines that afternoon, wounding the black activist James Meredith en route from Memphis to Jackson on a Walk-style civil rights march. George Corrigan went to the bathroom as Lucas read the story aloud. Then, fully clothed, Corrigan climbed into his sleeping bag and covered his head.

At dawn, a break came in the spring heat wave; cool air pushed down from Canada, accompanied by heavy fog, like smoke. The sudden chill woke Snyder.

He sat up with a cigarette, thinking of James Meredith, and then their own, his own day ahead. He could not believe that they were quit of the Holy Smokes. Yet no patrols and no scouts had been seen since Tuscarawas County. Here was June 7, a day presumed to end with sanctuary across the Ohio River in Wheeling, via St. Clairsville, Bridgeport, and the vehicular bridge on Interstate 70. It could vindicate Lucas, who had undertaken yesterday's longest walk to position them in Bannock for a final, six-hour dash to the river. But suppose J. J. Cockburn still wants his name in *Harrington's*. Then what? Somewhere along the road, something happens.

Before breakfast, acting on more than curiosity but nothing he might have described as a premonition, Snyder borrowed the Walk truck to advance the day's route for himself. He drove slowly, wipers beating at the mist, through St. Clairsville, onto Interstate 70, and along the service lane to the last exit before the bridge. The driving time was sixteen minutes; the distance eleven miles, or about five hours' walk. Ahead, but only on faith, was the bridge and the West Virginia shore, both hidden in the fog. Snyder passed under Interstate 70, then followed a parallel Ohio state road past the gray stone pillars of the spidery old walking bridge between Bridgeport and Wheeling. Strangely, the walking bridge was visible to the end, only to lead nowhere; the old river city lay beyond in an impenetrable gray cloud. Snyder stopped in an emergency repair zone to write:

"Superhighway and the vehicle bridge seem both the shorter and the more public way, certainly the obvious route over the river. But for that very reason, the parallel road and the walking bridge, given more exits and slower traffic, may be safer. General Lucas has little choice; neither route offers a place to hide."

Returning, Snyder left Interstate 70 for the blacktop to St. Clairsville. He turned on the radio. A man named Dacey was discussing his book *How to Avoid Probate*, the current non-fiction best-seller in America. Looking up, Snyder saw George Corrigan, wearing his white yachtsman's cap and green slicker, hitchhiking back toward Bannock. Corrigan said he'd been to Bridgeport sending a condolence wire to James Meredith. As they drove off, Snyder turned off the radio.

"Bad news, no, George?"

"Oh, yes. What brings you out, old Jack?"

"Secret of success. Looking ahead."

"Yes, I bet. You're looking for the thugs on the bicycles."

"Not exactly, George."

"I mean, hoping they're not here."

"How about you?"

"Well, I'm hoping, Jack, likewise. To tell you the truth, I'd all but forgotten about the Holy Smokes until Sam started our marathon yesterday. Now, well, maybe he's got it figured. The way to go is with God, sort of. He knows, God does, there was plenty of Mississippi fuzz watching over James Meredith, and look what happened. I worry our women will get hurt."

"Worries me, too."

"Especially Rachel, hey, Jack?"

"What, hey?"

"Oh, man—everyone saw you on the raft!"

"Well, man!"

Corrigan grinned.

"No one wants to tease you, Jack—they want this story good."

"Tell me."

"Nothing to tell, Jack. We like you."

Corrigan sat back, quietly.

Snyder stopped at the St. Clairsville Interstate Café for two takeout containers of coffee. Then they drove off again toward Bannock.

"Well, too bad, about Jim Meredith's leg," Corrigan said. "Meredith's a real main man. You ever know him?"

"No, but Medgar Evers."

"They're trying to kill all of us."

"I interviewed Evers in Jackson a month before he died."

"What was he like?"

"A quiet man, surprised to be in the limelight, a little like Martin King ten years ago."

"King is my main, main man."

"He is special."

"Medgar didn't watch out for himself."

"Big lesson, George—watching out for yourself."

"You know, if it wasn't for Martin Luther King, I wouldn't have let Peter talk me into this walk. Martin's into peace now. My first issue's still down South, Jack, not this going East, you know what I mean, on a peace trip? My issue is rights, man. Let us have us some real rights, as Stokely Carmichael's been saying. I don't even believe in peace, Jack. I mean, I am about fed up with non-violence, except like Dick Gregory says, it's the Man that has the Army. You see my meaning?"

"I see it, George."

"I'm here because of Martin, and then Peter, for sure. Hardly anyone better than my boy Peter. He's shy, oh, my, but a real something! He was in Selma with me, remember, I told you? He impressed some black bitches, too, let me tell you. I mean, *impressed!* Okay, but here, it's four weeks gone by, you notice how few Negroes you see in our nice churches, in the schools, the Grange Halls? Hey, Jack, my skin's the color of brown olives, dark brown olives. See, I mean, peace is a white man's issue, Jack, and I sometimes think we ought to let them, the whites, fight it out, except now they're using dark brown olive troops, so that's a good reason to stop the killing for the time being."

Snyder had angled the truck into a muddy patch at the rear of the Grange Hall. A sign on the corner indicated a Farm Bureau office in the hall basement. He had coffee to finish. Corrigan faced him with a smile and removed his yachtsman's cap. In the past week of walking, as he had let his beard grow, George had also begun to affect a red bandanna, with a small knot tied in each corner, worn like a skullcap. Snyder's eyes rolled up to the bandanna and made Corrigan squirm.

"I'm wearing it, Jack. They call me 'handkerchief head,' anyway, so I might as well wear something to keep my head cool." Corrigan swallowed his bitterness and laughed. "Hey, man, you should try it! You might like it!"

With a smile that he hoped did not seem patronizing, Snyder

climbed from the truck. The handkerchief was no more ridiculous than a yarmulke, and far more practical, yet he had stared, putting Corrigan on the defensive. The stare did not match his politics, but there it was. He could have kicked himself.

4

Down from Bannock to St. Clairsville, the prospect of fog and heavy traffic on Interstate 70 pointed the Walk east on the parallel road to the Bridgeport walking bridge. The fog persisted. By midafternoon, they had not yet been able to see ahead farther than a quarter mile and, finally, not even a hundred yards to the top of the next rise. They were about two miles beyond the village of Blaine on a stretch of straight road with blossoming woods on both sides. Patches of sky above the ash-colored fog had the sullen glow of tarnished silver. The air felt heavy and smelled of wet earth. There were muffled sounds, dogs barking in the distance, an ax chopping wood nearby. The moment seemed strange to Snyder, a portentous passage that he knew he would not forget.

It was a little after three when they left the woods, scattering a flock of noisy crows which had been working in the furrows of a freshly turned field. Ahead, the highway dipped sharply across a stream and rose again to meet the fog; on the horizon, not fifty yards off, a weathered stone-and-stucco garage at the northeast corner of a crossroad came into view. From a scaffold on the garage roof hung a red-on-yellow sign, fogbound but readable, announcing "Buckeye Motors."

Snyder counted ten motorcycles and drivers on the garage ramp, all mounted and some with a second rider, crowding the space around the gas pumps and the driveway down to the edge of the road. He reckoned first that they would have assembled here by way of the crossroad in the half hour since Arley Broyle had passed; otherwise, for sure, Arley would have returned to the Walk with a warning. Then again, he thought, they might have somehow tricked poor Arley. In any case, he realized he had been expecting the Holy Smokes all along. Later he would discover that a reflex had then removed his precious notebook, "Walk Notes: VIII," from his jacket to the wallet pocket of his trousers and buttoned the flap.

As one, the walkers slowed at the first sight of their trouble, but no one stopped. Molly was in the lead beside Lucas, with the lead sign she had been carrying since lunchtime. Snyder himself came next, and with a glance registered the order of those behind him. June was at his heels, her flag hoisted. After her, four or five paces apart, respectively, came three pairs, Herndon and Amelia, Corrigan and Schumacher, Wood and Dunne. Rachel followed alone, shouldering the REMEMBER NORMAN MORRISON cross. And about twenty-five yards off the pace marched Dorene and Vachel Rice, escorting Joe Rice, who held aloft the peace trident on its long pole. Snyder cursed the luck of his position that placed all but two walkers in back of him.

"Hey, Jesus," Molly said, skyward, "here we are!"

With a hand on Molly's arm to guide him, Lucas turned to walk backwards. His knees, distended from overweight, worked stiffly in reverse and seemed likely to bring him down at any second. As his face colored, he called out, "Close it up! Don't stop, and don't speak!"

Lucas walked forward again. He seemed to strain toward the crossroad, willing the others to follow him.

Snyder stepped aside, then fell into the line of walk beside Rachel. She held her sign only chest high and welcomed him with a melancholy smile.

"Can you run with that cross?" he asked.

"No."

"Let me carry it."

"No, I have to."

"You sure?"

"I'll remember you asked."

The wind picked up suddenly. It pressed them from behind and helped, Snyder was thinking, like an unseen hand at your back, moving you along in spite of the weakness in your own knees.

From Buckeye Motors, there was as yet no sound.

Lucas again faced to the rear. By then, about twenty yards and the width of the highway separated the walkers from the Holy Smokes.

"Don't stare," Lucas said, in a whisper that somehow carried against the wind. "Don't stop walking unless I do. Don't resist."

Snyder stared anyway. J. J. Cockburn on his Harley-Davidson and Timbo Wayne on his Honda, both riding single, were parked in front of the band of motorcycles, their front wheels touching the road. Behind them was one of the shirt-sleeved cyclists who had scouted the Walk in the rain near Coshocton while Deputy Armand Magid was answering the call. One riding couple seemed familiar (although, under the circumstances and in that gray light, Snyder could not be sure), suggesting that an occasional passing motorcycle in recent days, even that day, had been keeping tabs on the Walk's progress.

Now, almost abreast of Buckeye Motors, Snyder again counted the waiting riders and machines. There were actually eleven motorcycles, a young man driving each, six with young women behind. The men wore an assortment of costumes, basic black leather jackets over olive-drab British Army surplus sweaters, T-shirts, or bare chests; various colorful helmets, caps, and sweatbands; and boots or tennis shoes—no two pairs alike. But the six back-riders all wore red headbands, white leather jackets, and blue dungarees stuffed in boots; they had their own chic.

For an instant, Snyder was mesmerized. The look of them carried him out of himself into their midst, the sense of his own danger virtually dispelled by fascination with their arbitrary power to commit violence against the Walk and himself.

Then he caught his body in a flinch at the sharp, grinding sound of a single kick by Cockburn firing the Harley-Davidson's engine. It was then, too, that a wrinkled old Chevrolet sedan passed in the eastbound lane between the two groups. Blue exhaust smoke billowed around Cockburn. The boy driving the Chevy slowed to rubberneck, turned, and accelerated north at the crossroad—while help, if any, lay east in Bridgeport.

Snyder would have sworn Cockburn was watching him, personally, though the man's eyes were illegible under a pair of oversized slate-colored sunglasses. And as once before, on the bank of the Walhonding River, Cockburn seemed to play on the edge of farce. Broadly, he lifted a black-gloved hand, motioning first as a greeting and second as an order, waving the Walk through the intersection. You, Snyder, he seemed to say, let the comedy begin.

And for a third time, as though remembering one more thing,

Lucas turned toward the ranks of the Walk. He pointed toward Dunne, asking, "Will you take Joe's trident, Frank?"

"Not on your life," Joe Rice croaked from the rear.

"Let me," Dunne said over his shoulder.

"Goddamn, not now!" Joe Rice replied. "I'm coming front with it!"

On his son's arm, Joe Rice skirted Snyder and shuffled ahead quickly. He braced the trident's pole on his belt and sustained it with both fists like a kendo sword in readiness. His knuckles were white. He surged beyond Molly and, with Vachel, led the Walk into the intersection.

Last across with Rachel and Dorene, Snyder thought they might be going safely, that without some provocation, the Holy Smokes were finding sufficient pleasure in the walkers' obedience to let the scene close that way. Cockburn had to know that his show of force was enough for a paragraph in the magazine.

Engine noise dispelled that fantasy. Back and to his left, Snyder saw Cockburn wheel into the intersection. Timbo and the others waited, still draped over their silent machines. Cockburn sputtered forward on the far shoulder, pulling even with Joe and Vachel Rice, then throttled down to walking speed. A moment later, he angled over to the Walk's side of the road and stopped ten yards above the oncoming Rices. His feet came down to the gravel and his chest puffed.

Unless the walkers were to move into the traffic on the highway, the only path around Cockburn's machine was a shallow drainage ditch off to their right. A barbed-wire fence above the ditch separated them from an open field, ending in a wall of fog. The field still wore its winter cover of chopped straw. Behind the Rices, Lucas and Molly stepped decisively into the ditch. Vachel led his father down. Joe Rice grunted and stumbled. Vachel caught his arm and the trident pole slipped away at an angle, bracing both men before they could fall. They found a foothold in the mud and Joe Rice raised the trident again. The other walkers followed, with Snyder trailing Dorene and Rachel into the ditch. Mud sucked up around their shoes. Snyder stared straight ahead as he went by, not six feet from Cockburn.

"You're still here," Cockburn said.

Cockburn's grin seemed almost obsequious. *Harrington's* makes you indispensable, it said to Snyder, protects you, and shields you from the reality you'd like to share with the Walk. The trick will be to fake it truly, when you write it.

Go fuck, you clown, Snyder thought.

Engines exploded on the garage ramp. Blue smoke erupted among the motorcycles. All ten machines teetered and slowly rolled across the road, forming a single line on the shoulder. They came abreast of the walkers struggling in the muck. Cockburn moved to accompany Lucas and Molly, his place just above and beside Snyder taken by another Harley-Davidson. The rider had a beak nose and a tiny ball for a chin. He wore black goggles, and carried an angular blond girl behind. For balance, he kept one toe on the ground, but tilted ominously as he sought to steer precisely along the lip of the ditch. Snyder looked for an advantage should the rider fall. Hidden by weeds, there was a narrow space between the inner lip of the ditch and the fence. Snyder helped Rachel up and walked behind her. The tilting rider did not comment on their move. His birdlike face was at rest, even pacific, as though tranquilized by the noise and the advantage of his heavy equipment.

From the path with his height, Snyder could see ahead as the parallel lines of riders and walkers moved forward together like members of a single unit. There was even the illusion of Lucas extending himself in order to keep up with Cockburn. Lucas was actually slogging heavily in the mud while Cockburn kept pace. But at a distance, as from a speeding car, who would know the difference between duress and determination? Insofar as a passerby might surmise, the Walk and the Holy Smokes were as one. Help, Snyder realized, would not be coming.

Looking ahead another hundred yards, Snyder saw a very large billboard advertising a motel and restaurant in Bridgeport. Just beyond, the road curved away to the left. At the near turn of the curve, a small brass marker was affixed to a metal post beside the beginnings of a guardrail. He could not read the marker at that distance, but the guardrail suggested an approaching hazard, a creek or a drainage culvert, probably well known to Cockburn, which could force the walkers into the highway.

Some minutes later, the curious procession entered the curve. The marker came up on Snyder's left. It said French explorers in the Ohio winter of 1683 had camped by the creek just ahead.

Fifty paces on, about halfway through the curve, the ditch ended at a concrete buffer. The land fell away sharply into a slow, clear stream about eight feet below the highway. On the far side, where the ditch resumed, an old oak tree with wide, strong branches sheltered a picnic table. Behind the tree, the barbed-wire fence resumed and another field lay alongside, its farther boundaries hidden in the fog. Snyder had seen the end of the ditch from his vantage point, but Lucas, in a sudden surge past the Rices, seemed to stumble onto it. The fat man fell forward, turned, and abruptly rested on the buffer with his legs and feet still down in the ditch. Above the beard, his face was the color of boiled beets. Then Vachel and Joe Rice sat down beside him on the inner edge of the ditch. Attended by the motorcycles, the other walkers took to the path in front of Rachel and Snyder and assembled behind the Rices. Facing them, the Holy Smokes gathered in parallel pairs. A woman in a Volkswagen slowed on the highway behind the machines, smiled, and drove away.

As they were joining the others, Snyder felt Rachel sag. He took her hand at his side and received a discouraged grimace.

Over the engine roar, she said, "Maybe that woman thinks we're getting our picture taken."

"Sure, happens all the time."

"How can she look and just go?"

Snyder did not have to answer. A hand raised by J. J. Cockburn silenced every engine. Snyder's ears rang in the sudden quiet.

Cockburn climbed down from his machine. He seemed hugely satisfied. He had forced the Walk into the mud. He controlled the road. Now he seemed about to make a grand speech. With exaggerated care, he folded his sunglasses into a beaded leather case and handed the case to Timbo Wayne, beside him on the Honda. The walkers behind the Rices sat down on the path in two rows. Herndon, Amelia, Rachel, and Snyder had their backs against barbed wire. Rachel held REMEMBER NORMAN MORRISON against her knees. The lead sign remained aloft in Molly's hands. June's flag fluttered beside it. With help from his son, Joe Rice dug the trident pole into the mud and took a fresh grip. Sam Lucas stood up with a

hopeless glance behind into the creek bed. There was no place to
run. Cockburn waited until Lucas looked into his face.

"You went to the sheriff," he said.

"Yes, I did," Lucas replied.

Cockburn turned to his people. He seemed to have a plan, to be
executed as far as possible from Coshocton County. "The signs!" he
shouted.

A lone rider removed his jacket and dismounted. His arms and
chest were bare under a yellow cotton vest and marvelously deco-
rated with blue tattoos. By straddling the ditch, he was able to lift the
lead sign from Molly's hands without getting mud on his boots.

"This is a lesson in non-violence," Cockburn said.

Snyder looked past Rachel to Reed Herndon, who had crossed his
arms over his knees, his chin on his arms.

"So much for free speech," Herndon said.

"You shut up," the tattooed rider said.

The tattooed rider pried the lead sign from its pole. Then with the
sign under one arm, he snapped the pole and threw the pieces over
the walkers into the field.

June lowered her flag. None of the Holy Smokes seemed to notice.

The tattooed rider returned to his machine. He was keeping the
sign.

Now Timbo Wayne left his seat. He pointed to REMEMBER NOR-
MAN MORRISON.

"Give me that," he said.

"Please," Cockburn said.

"Please," Timbo said.

Rachel hesitated.

"Norman Morrison," Timbo said. "Must be a great guy. Give me
the cross, please, ma'am."

"He was a great guy," Rachel said.

Rachel passed the sign to Peter Schumacher, who crossed himself,
and passed the sign to Timbo Wayne. Briskly, Wayne pried the sign
from its pole. Then he shoved the sign into a rear saddlebag. Rachel
leaned against Snyder, defeated.

Now Cockburn himself stepped across the ditch for the trident
sign in Joe Rice's hands.

"He's so bad," Timbo Wayne said.

Cockburn placed his hands on the trident pole just below the circle of wood, left hand crossed awkwardly above the right like a novice ballplayer who hadn't learned to hold a bat. Snyder thought the blind man did not yet know what was happening. Cockburn slowly pulled the sign forward and down. Joe Rice seemed to be listening, like a fisherman to his invisible game, and yanked back smartly, off-setting Cockburn's strength with the leverage of his seated position. Joe Rice's back stiffened. The pole bent his way, surprising Cockburn and drawing him forward, off balance, toward the space between Rice and his son. Vachel Rice bent low for a two-handed purchase on the pole and all three tugged hard. Then Joe Rice lost his grip. His beret blew off. And the release of tension brought Cockburn down, bellowing, virtually horizontal, with his feet lifting high behind.

Vachel Rice still held the pole, uncontrollably whipping the trident sign through the air and against his father's forehead and right cheek. Wood-on-bone made a sickening crack and drove Joe Rice to the right and flat across Lucas's knees. There were cries of anguish from the walkers, but no one of them was yet moving to the rescue. The sudden passion of Joe Rice pained Snyder as well, but he knew he must not move.

Snyder watched. The job is to watch, he would have explained. Besides, *you* do not do violence for people whose cause is non-violence.

Joe Rice recoiled and clawed at Cockburn's jacket. He found the lapel and bared his teeth with the effort to hang on. There was a smear of blood like dark rouge on his right cheek. Then a long, still moment unfolded, with Cockburn in suspense, almost horizontal, struggling against gravity, yet inexorably falling down. Cockburn's gloved hand slid forward on a puff of grass. His body twisted slowly. Joe Rice let go of his lapel. Then Cockburn landed. He fell hard on the flat of his back below the Rices and Lucas in the mud at the bottom of the ditch. He struggled clownishly. He rolled sideways and over, one full turn, making a sopping mess of himself. Hoots and shrieks of laughter burst from the ranks of the Holy Smokes.

Seconds passed. The hapless Cockburn lay fuming, legs flapping like the tail of a beached whale, with one fist overhead shaking at Joe Rice. The walkers scrambled to their feet, as though their inaction had been rendered inexcusable by Cockburn's absurdity. Snyder saw Herndon tearing at his glasses, and Amelia stepping around him with a hand outstretched, that Herndon might let someone else take the first lunge to protect Joe Rice from Cockburn's revenge.

Mud-soaked back and front, Cockburn came to his knees at the feet of Joe Rice, torturing his face with an apparently gargantuan effort to transform mortification into indignation. Vachel Rice threw the trident into the ditch and pulled his father to his chest.

Snyder heard a shout: "Blind! He's blind!" It was Lucas standing in the muck to beseech Cockburn.

The cry mixed with new whoops from his own friends seemed to block Cockburn, holding him motionless in the ditch. And that gave courage to Timbo Wayne, who suddenly laughed and sounded his horn in unmistakable, taunting derision. "Jim's a mudder!" Timbo screeched, with his eyes rolling left and right as he savored the misery of his leader. "Mudder fucker, haw!" The Holy Smokes laughed unanimously, riotously.

The rebellion brought Cockburn swaying to his feet, then purposefully down on his knees again to dig out the trident pole. He pointed the butt end at Sam Lucas as though covering a retreat. "Just stay put," he said. He climbed stiffly from the ditch and set off alone on a bowlegged mission along the shoulder toward the guardrail over the creek.

Vachel and Lucas, now with Molly and Herndon, were hoisting Joe Rice into a sitting position on the high ground. Frank Dunne turned to the remaining walkers, quickly scrutinizing each face with a pale eye and a wordless question seemingly about the limits of their faith in non-violence. Dunne's last look came to Rachel, who shook her head bitterly. Turning again to check Cockburn's progress, Dunne left Snyder to answer to himself as the outsider he was. Responsibility leads to chagrin, Snyder thought, the common lot of witnesses and professionals—you get to know it so well in journalism. Are you chagrined, too, Frank? What about Solidarity Forever?

Cockburn had reached the guardrail. Standing spread-legged in the faint mist at the edge of visibility, he began pounding the trident sign on the sharp edge of the support pillar. The sign split on the fifth blow and the two halves of the disk dropped into the creek. Cockburn braced the pole against the rail and snapped it with two kicks into three pieces. He tested and weighed each piece, chose one about four feet long, and, cross-handed, swung it like a bat. Then he returned in a straight line aimed at Timbo Wayne astride his Honda. He stopped at Wayne's rear and puckered his mouth into a fierce little round pout. Wayne ducked forward against his handlebars.

Cockburn swung his bat against the Honda. The rear reflector shattered. He poked inside until the bulb broke, too. "Aww," Timbo moaned. Cockburn swung the bat across four feet of open space, whacking Wayne himself across the small of the back. Wayne coughed and rolled off his machine against the Moto Guzzi, next in line. Cockburn swung at the Honda again, striking the seat, and swung again, crushing the spotlight. After a flurry of blows to the front fender, he shoved the motorcycle on top of Wayne. Groaning, Wayne caught it with his feet. Cockburn now grasped the bat at each end, balanced himself, and leaped forward, boot heels first, onto the engine housing. "Die, you fuck!" he screamed.

Wayne's rear wheel turned slowly in the air. Cockburn aimed a golf swing under the wheel, catching something with an ugly thud. Wayne coughed again. Cockburn stumbled. And as he caught himself, he discovered REMEMBER NORMAN MORRISON jutting from Timbo's saddlebag. He broke the sign into three pieces and sailed each, one at a time, across the highway. The pieces flew like Frisbees and landed out of sight below the shoulder.

Cockburn seemed released. He felt his pockets. Sunglasses? He stooped over Timbo, jabbed with the blunt end of the bat, and came up with his beaded case. Once behind his shades, he mounted his Harley-Davidson. He appeared his old arrogant self again, almost restored to power. Just across the ditch, Joe Rice sat braced against Vachel as Molly and Herndon worked from the first-aid kit on Molly's belt. Joe Rice had three visible wounds, a dark cut from the cheekbone down to the jaw on the right side, a muddy welt the size of a Ping-Pong ball over the right eye, and a hairline abrasion trickling blood from the scalp over the right temple and into the white hair above the ear.

"That wasn't my fault," Cockburn complained, as though in answer to a criticism that no one had dared.

Molly was pressing a gauze pad to Rice's cheek.

"Why don't you go away?" she said.

Cockburn seemed to consider a reply, then shrugged, dusting dried mud from his gloves and sleeves. "I stay in the state of Ohio, lady," he said. "You go." He flexed and swelled, released his kick-stand, and fired his engine. He hoisted the front wheel, turning him-self and the machine on the back wheel. With a wave, he rolled around his people toward the Buckeye Motors garage, as though he should not be regarded as such a bad sort after all.

Warily, the walkers waited in place for the other bikers to follow. The tattooed rider lifted the Honda from Timbo Wayne. Battered, but grinning despite a split and already swelling lip, Timbo success-fully tested his machine. He wheeled into second position. The Holy Smokes fired their engines and formed obedient ranks behind their leaders. Blue exhaust rolled across the ditch and over the walkers, as Cockburn circled back yet again.

Cockburn stopped on the shoulder at a point closest to Snyder. The mud was turning gray as it dried on his black leather. Little gray spitballs of mud had congealed in his sideburns and there was a large, molelike clot above the left corner of his mouth.

"Read all about it, yes?" Cockburn said, as though in private, mocking a defeated enemy.

"No," Snyder lied.

"I know the business," Cockburn said with scorn. "I win."

"Like hell."

"Need another scene?"

Snyder knew they were on the edge of a very deep hole—the Walk could end in this place. Besides, he was thinking, Cockburn has it right about his place in any history of the Walk. You must give him a mention.

"No," Snyder said, hating the sound of his own expedience.

"All right, Mr. Harrington—just say how we're so bad, okay?"

Cockburn rotated his machine and ecstatically gunned the engine before shifting. At the peak of acceleration, a ragged pop blasted man and motorcycle as from a chute through the intersection and into the fog. The Holy Smokes chased after him, like hounds after a bitch in heat, heading west toward Coshocton.

Snyder glanced up the line of walkers strung out along the fence. They were staring west in dismayed silence, as though Cockburn might reappear at any moment. Above them, the sky had turned from gray to melancholy yellow as the lowering sun came through. Joe Rice looked half dead in that light. Herndon was bent over him, showing Molly how to close his cheek wound with thin strips of adhesive tape. Rachel looked back at Snyder as tears began to move down her cheeks. She knew Joe Rice was finished on the Walk. Everyone can see that, Snyder thought, which means Vachel will not go on, either.

A few minutes later, Arley Broyle arrived with the truck, in high dudgeon over the Walk's delay and just after Schumacher and Wood had set out on the highway to fetch him. Herndon and Dunne prepared to lift Joe Rice into the truck bed. And Snyder took a deliberate step back to observe the evacuation.

First, Vachel and Molly squeezed Joe Rice between themselves among the sleeping bags and luggage in the back of the truck. Next, too agitated to trust another navigator, Sam Lucas climbed into the cab beside Arley Broyle. He carried a town map of Wheeling to guide them to a hospital that Molly knew. It was called the All Souls Sacred Heart Infirmary. Then Lucas shook hands across the windowsill with Herndon, in effect acknowledging that, temporarily, the torch had passed. Herndon was to lead the remaining walkers and Snyder across the river and into downtown Wheeling, where two nights had been booked at the Griffin Hotel on Chapline Street. Meanwhile, Rachel had retrieved the fragments of REMEMBER NORMAN MORRISON and committed them to Arley Broyle for safekeeping.

Finally, as Arley started his engine, Herndon reached over the tailgate to press Joe Rice's hand.

"We'll see you, Joe," he said.

Rice turned his patched face sideways. With his right eye swollen shut, he seemed to want to look at Reed and the others behind the truck with his good blind eye.

"I made a mistake, Reed," he said. His voice was muffled and slow, with an extra beat between each word. "Lost the trident and Sam's going to be sore."

"He's not sore," Molly said. "Don't speak."

"I can speak."

"We'll replace all the signs tomorrow," Herndon added.

"Still, my mistake."

"Maybe we were wrong, Joe."

"No, because you will cross the river in a few hours without me."

"You're crossing."

"Driving doesn't count. You know how Sam feels."

"One of us counts for all. Sam said that, too."

"I didn't keep the faith."

"Joe, you're the last—"

"Just tell Jack Snyder to say I said that."

"He's right here."

"Well, okay. I'll tell him."

"He's here."

"Okay, be sure you quote me, Jack."

"I will," Snyder said.

"It's the trouble with this country, see?"

5

The remnant needed nearly three hours to make the distance to the Ohio River. They had walked more slowly than usual, and more often one by one, in silence, without offering one another the usual encouragements. Snyder thought the difference was not only the letdown after a trauma but also the peculiar focus of Cockburn's raid itself. Suddenly, they were naked, walking without their peace signs or even their postered truck. For all that the world knew, they were a local gang themselves, a nondescript batch of birdwatchers or migrant hippies, in transit, going nowhere in particular, with one Oriental in their midst carrying a curious, ragtag, unreadable flag. And so what that Herndon had promised that every lost sign would be replaced by the end of the rest day in Wheeling? Or that Rachel swore to restore REMEMBER NORMAN MORRISON that very night? Right then, on the highway, they were nobodies. "No signs, no signify," Snyder wrote in Bridgeport. "Cockburn wins the day."

At half past six, they passed between two tall, blue-rusty steel suspension pillars and set off on the walking bridge across the river. An early-evening breeze had begun to lift the fog, and let them see across to downtown Wheeling, flush against the east bank. The bleak, towerless skyline reminded Snyder of Hoboken, but there was one memorable image, a dandy work of inadvertent Pop Art, a brown-and-yellow poster painted over the entire brick backside of a huge waterfront warehouse. It advertised Wheeling's hometown brand of cheap cigars and instantly sold Snyder on the idea of sending a box to himself (at first, he had thought: to Phil Zimmerman) to compete at the office with Erlanger's pipe.

Moments later, they were at midstream. The pewter-gray river flowed high and fast below the bridge, while in the near distance, colorless barges strained against the current to make crossings delayed by the day's fog. It was the Walk's halfway point; back twenty-eight days was Chicago, ahead twenty-seven was Washington. Herndon announced it, but none of the walkers seemed to savor it. They remained cheerless, stepping down on West Virginia soil as though they had left something behind in Ohio that might never be retrieved. Their malaise touched Snyder. And though he himself had had to stand by more than once on an assignment as terrible things took place before his professional eyes, he shared it. At least, he felt dispirited to the extent that he yearned for a respite, Christ, a night off in contemplation of pleasures other than peace in Vietnam—say, a decent meal on the expense account. It would do them all good to get drunk that night, he thought, knowing that none would.

At last, on Chapline Street several blocks from the bridge, the Griffin Hotel beckoned them with a "Transients Welcome" sign in green neon. It was a four-story building of white brick, with a spooky griffin carved under the roof line and a red fire escape down the front. At the hotel curbside, the walkers came upon the Walk truck, already unloaded. And immediately inside, they found Sam Lucas, Molly Hamilton, and Arley Broyle waiting for them, seated off the lobby in one corner of a narrow, windowless parlor. The only light came from a large globe connected to a ceiling fan. Wooden chairs and aluminum ashtray stands lined the walls. Like strangers, the newcomers filed in and virtually filled the room. Snyder sat between Arley Broyle and Amelia Pendergraft. She gave his hand a squeeze and a chins-up, perhaps-the-worst-is-over smile. Snyder thought that might have been the first time since the incident at Buckeye Motors that she had taken her eyes off Herndon. Then he felt Arley Broyle's elbow gently in his ribs. Broyle rolled his eyes from Snyder to Lucas.

"Notes for you coming up, Jack," Arley whispered, indicating the Walk logbook open on Lucas's lap.

"All the news isn't bad," Lucas said. "Joe Rice is in 'fair' condition, stable, alert, and complaining. The infirmary is treating him well. They've given him and Vachel two beds, side by side, in a nice ward. I simply told the registrar he'd taken a nasty spill crossing a street in Bridgeport. By some miracle, a plastic surgeon was immediately on hand to sew up Joe's cheek. He showed us X rays, a hairline fracture of the upper right jaw, to be wired in a day or so, when the swelling subsides, but no broader damage to the skull. A slight concussion seems likely, less worrisome because all other tests are normal for an older man. Walking's been good for Joe. Now he must have several days for observation and rest, with no visitors except Vachel, plus a train ride when ready—no planes—back home. There's no reason to expect him to rejoin us by the Fourth. Joe's sorry. He's really sorry. Vachel's sorry, and I'm sorry, too."

"How did you leave him?" Frank Dunne asked with an edge of anger in his voice.

"We left him sitting up in bed, listening to TV, with an ice bag on his head," Lucas replied, looking up for the first time. "He has a bad headache and the shock is wearing off, making it worse."

"I wish it was J. J. Cockburn's headache," Dunne said bitterly.

"Vachel's spending the night in the next bed," Lucas said.

"But that's two lost and gone!" Dunne exclaimed. "It's so rotten, Sam."

Lucas ducked his head as though a blow had fallen. His chin spread out in triplicate below his bearded jaw. The Walk needed Dunne, without whose help in Washington it would be all the more difficult to call on labor unions for local demonstrators in support of the final march on July Fourth. Doggedly, Lucas turned to his next page.

"That's why I called Sheriff Alexander in Coshocton, Frank, yes," he said. "He came right on the phone, which meant he hadn't forgotten us. I told him our story and he said I must file a complaint in person. 'That's the law in Ohio,' he said. So I said I was calling from West Virginia, not to complain but to report. He was furious. He said, 'You can't put politics above justice.' Oh, that hurt! I said I'd write a letter for his files, 'after July Fourth.' He ranted about means and ends, but we both knew that I was doing the best I could under the circumstances. Finally, he gave up. He even wished us luck. And that's how we left it."

"I know cops," Dunne said. "He could have done something about the Cockburn group—he still can, if he wants to."

"We couldn't have had it both ways, Frank."

Dunne was sitting close enough to give Lucas's knee a cautionary touch with two leathery fingers. "You don't have to tell us that now, Sam," he said. Then he pulled back. He shot a glance at Snyder, as though surprised to find himself on the brink of rebellion and, simultaneously, going into Snyder's ever-present record. He shifted his mood openly, his dark face offering quick deference to Lucas.

"Okay, I retract," he said. "I apologize. You got us this far, Sam—and you'll get us the other half. I know it, for sure. I'm just not naturally a non-violent person, that's all. I'm sorry. Do you understand?"

Lucas seemed disoriented. "Yes, I do," he said.

"So, why don't we go on to new business?"

Lucas blinked rapidly, as though he'd been given an eleventh-hour reprieve. To Snyder, he seemed deeply fatigued, weary down through all that fat into the marrow of his bones. A day's rest is going to do wonders for that man, Snyder was thinking, or else.

"We are free until noon tomorrow," Lucas said, "when we should make new signs. Okay? Then there's one meeting, at the Wheeling YMCA, sharp at six. Day after, we walk to Moundsville, the last little stop in West Virginia, then to a camp at Ryerson State Park in Pennsylvania. In a week's time, we do the southwest corner of the state and into Maryland at a town called Keysers Ridge. Then, it'll be a bit more than two weeks getting down the mountains and through Baltimore to Washington." A smile broke through Lucas's beard. "We will get there," he said.

Snyder wrote this last with a nod. There was no story in a failed peace walk.

It was just then, across Amelia's lap, that Herndon reached out with one hand to stay Snyder's pen. When Snyder looked up, Herndon was staring hard at him, both determined and solicitous. "I want to say something freely," Herndon said, "and have others feel free to say something, not for the record. You understand, Jack? Are we off?"

"All right," Snyder said, closing his notebook. He lit a cigarette, and settled himself for a siege of memory; if not directly usable, off the record was by no means useless.

"Thank you," Herndon said. "I know everyone would like to get this meeting over with, but I'd like a minute to go back over Sam's phone call with Sheriff Alexander. I think we have to try to answer the sheriff's question, whether politics is more important to us than justice, because that's the essence of everything that lies ahead—the rest of the Walk, the ritual at the White House, the question of civil disobedience, the future of our protest against the war, and, above all, how we protest next year, and the year after that, if the war continues. We have to consider what Joe did this afternoon because, if you see my point, he did put justice above politics."

"Did he?" Lucas asked warily.

Snyder thought the fat man could not be blamed if he felt he had had enough for one day.

"He drew a line for himself," Herndon said. "So, yes—he did."

"He did—you know for sure?" Lucas asked, still cautious but sharper.

"I think he did. He came to a point of physical resistance. He's a blind man, but he saw—in every sense of that word—that he had come to that point and he put justice above politics. I think we should consider what that means."

"He might not have resisted at all," Lucas said, his voice rolling again, like an old heavyweight who had somehow tapped a forgotten reserve in the late rounds. "I mean, Reed, if Joe were a sighted person like the rest of us, he might well have handed over the sign. It was instinct that moved him, I believe. Pure instinct, meaning he had no choice."

"Do we know that it was instinct—mere self-defense? All we know is that he really did resist. He fought, but not only in self-defense. He fought to protect our trident from a thug. Isn't that true, Sam?"

"The truth is that Joe Rice has dedicated his life to non-violence. He's a blind man. His sign was suddenly ripped from his hands. He hung on, that's all."

Herndon gave his head a hard shake. "No," he said. "I saw Joe's face. I saw his look. He was making a choice. And now I feel ashamed that I was not beside him, like Vachel. I'm sick that I didn't help him."

"That would have been the end of the Walk."

"It might have been. I'm trying to discuss that with you. I may be the wrong person to raise the question, but it's a question all the same. Is there a limit to non-resistance? Do we have a limit?"

Lucas shifted his bulk forward, balancing precariously on the edge of his chair. "If we respond to violence with violence," he said, "the Walk is over."

Luther Wood laughed nervously. He said, "Not to mention our broken heads."

"That's no joke," Molly said.

"It depends," Peter Schumacher said. "If the war goes on long enough, who says there won't be other tactics, even fighting?"

"Exactly," George Corrigan said. "They've shot James Meredith, haven't they?"

"One thing I know is that non-violence is not a tactic," Lucas said. "It isn't an expedient. It's the WISE principle. The whole point is to settle political disputes without war, overseas or in this country. Besides, we have five women here."

Dorene stirred. "I don't like the sound of that, Sam."

"I don't either," June said. "Because we're women is not the reason we're non-violent."

"A woman can fight," Rachel said. "We don't, I don't, because you happen to make the right point, Sam. We think non-violence is an end in itself, and I'd like Jack Snyder to have that on the record."

"But I agree, too," Herndon said. "I say ends and means are the same in non-violent theory. I just wish it was easier to accept in reality. I have to admit to you that it wasn't only ideology or the fate of the Walk that held me back this afternoon. It was several kinds of fear. Fear of getting hurt. Fear of others getting hurt in a general brawl. Fear the police might come and delay or defeat the Walk. And fear, okay, that I'd be arrested, discovered, and sent back to the joint. All those fears—not ideals or politics, but fears worked on me. I admit it—and now I've got a bad conscience. Like Molly says, it's no joke."

With her hands on her cheeks, Molly said, "We were all frightened to death this afternoon—even Jack Snyder, I'll bet."

"Oh, yes, especially Jack Snyder," Snyder said.

"Not my point," Herndon said humorlessly, and shaking his head again. "Okay, Molly," he said, "the issue is not fear, but the choice each of us makes from fear. There is the problem. Even if Joe Rice had no choice—as you say, Sam—still, I did. I did and I chose, and I'm not proud of it. And what if we're raided again, or attacked some other way? I don't know. What will I do? What's the limit? When, in conscience, do you strike back?"

Listening to this last, Lucas sat back, seemingly more exhausted than ever. Yet he raised a hand apparently to signal one last try. "We all respect and respond to you, Reed," he said. "None of us has been through your experience. None of us brings your background to the Walk. But in all brotherhood, I have to say that the Walk has a life and it won't survive unless we protect that life at all costs. I think we all feel a certain shame for our behavior this afternoon. All right, that's part of the price that this Walk life extracts from us. It's personal. It can be very painful. It is not pleasant to act against one's strongest moral feelings for the sake of any organization, even this one, which exists in response to another moral feeling. It is the same question that arises when we consider civil disobedience. We will consider that, but rest assured, we will ask no one to participate who does not believe he can remain civil, that is, non-violent. Isn't this our message from Joe Rice? Didn't he say we have to keep faith—or the Walk is over? The militarists and the violent anti-Communists will have won. And would that not be a greater shame? I mean, how else are we going to ever stop the killing in Vietnam?"

"All right, yes," Herndon replied, impatiently. He seemed torn, perhaps less impatient with Lucas's piety, Snyder thought, than with his own vulnerability to it. In the same tone, Herndon added, "All right, Sam, of course. But how can we know how we'll feel tomorrow?"

"One day at a time," Lucas said, "is all I ask."

Herndon was down, but not pinned. He shoved a hand up under his glasses and squeezed both eyes shut, sighing with tension. Then he squinted at Snyder.

"Tell us what you thought this afternoon, Jack," he said.

"About what—you? Sam? Cockburn?" Knowing the answer, Snyder bought time with the careful squashing of a cigarette butt. In that process, he also caught an inspirational stare from Rachel.

"About yourself as a member of the Walk," Herndon said, "tell us what you thought."

"Not as a member," Snyder replied. "Let's be strict. But as a reporter—"

"As a reporter, Jack."

Now Snyder hesitated. He wished he had declined straight out. Now it was too late. "Same as everyone else, Reed," he said, "not too proud, but comforted by good excuses. The odds were bad, for one thing. And my job restrains me from excess personal morality, for another. But, no matter, I felt bad."

"Would any reporter?" Herndon asked.

"Any? I don't know about 'any,' but perhaps many. Reporters stand around a lot in a lifetime while other people fight. It may be we like fighting less than holding coats. Or maybe we think we also serve who only watch and write. Whatever, we choose our compromises when we choose our jobs. We may want good conscience, but we mean to get our story."

"And no apologies?"

"None," Snyder said, deciding in that instant to let them know where he stood, once and for all. "I'm saying, as a rule, reporters hate getting personally tangled up in the story they're writing. If one uses 'I' in something he writes, it's an impersonal 'I,' or it had better be. It's always the story that counts. That's our principle. Believe it or not, some of us actually think our job is the truth, and that means the view from arm's length—even if, sometimes, we don't look so good to ourselves in the morning, as, I daresay, I won't tomorrow, in the mirror, shaving, and thinking about old blind Joe Rice taking that pole in the face and poor Vachel knowing the pole was in his own hands when it broke his father's jaw and myself watching, doing my job, like you, Reed. Do you see?"

"That's the problem, for sure, when morality is impractical."

"For sure."

"But you, at least, still have access to a large public, your famous magazine. You can console yourself that a story might help change things."

"We do have that, don't we? And, in a way, so do you. It's your story."

"You can say that. But we can't count on it."

"No you can't, not really. No story is guaranteed."

Herndon turned to Lucas.

"That's the risk, isn't it, Sam?" he said.

"There's always that risk," Lucas said bleakly.

Snyder felt as though he had let down the side. But perfect assurance of publicity was the one thing he could not give the Walk.

6

There were six double rooms assigned to the Walk and a single for Snyder, all in a row on the third floor. By eight, Snyder had bathed and shaved. He put on his orange windbreaker over a shirt and tie. Then from the hotel guide, he picked out a restaurant, Foyle's Riverside Grill, for a solitary dinner on the embankment. He was ready to leave when Rachel Abraham called him from the room she shared with Amelia.

"You were fine," she said. "A nice dose of reality. Just what the doctor ordered."

"I talked too much," Snyder replied.

"I really love you, Straight Arrow."

"I shouldn't have said anything. Something's happened to me. Bruce Erlanger would cut my throat getting between Sam and Reed."

"No, you were just right."

"Thank you."

"Now, let yourself take me fast to dinner. I've still got to fix REMEMBER NORMAN MORRISON."

"I've a date."

"You lie."

"Yes."

"Who is she?"

"No one. Can I tell you, Straight Arrow needs out for a few hours?"

"No, but when you're back, knock twice for blisters, coffee, gossip
—the usual intimacies."

"I love you, too."

"So what?"

"See you in the morning."

"Anyway, you were fine."

Snyder took a cab to Foyle's Riverside Grill. It was a candlelit
steak house in a converted warehouse with a romantic view of the
night river between the two dark bridges. Of two rooms, one was
big and noisy with dining tables, the other smaller with a horseshoe
bar, a nine-by-twelve dance floor, and a plugged-up jukebox committed to slow, quiet elevator music. The dining room had no small
tables available; besides, the men wore jackets. Snyder approached
the bar. On the far side, two couples were laughing with the cashier.
On the near side, two lone women sat with backs to Snyder, a blonde
talking to the bartender, a brunette quietly drinking. Snyder chose a
barstool beside the brunette and felt lucky. She was well scrubbed
and pretty and wore no rings. Her dress was white linen and her red
leather belt matched her pumps. Her hair was braided and tied into a
bun with an ivory comb in back. She was about thirty.

Snyder ordered a gin martini. At first, the woman told him she was
waiting for her escort, but she let Snyder buy her a drink second time
around. She liked vodka and quinine water. They talked for a while.
Her name was Lubie Glover, she said, and her role in life was secretarial. She said her boss was a vice president of the Mail Pouch
Tobacco Company. She claimed that she hardly knew a soul in
Wheeling, having accompanied her husband from Pittsburgh within
the year only to be widowed by a bus accident. It happened on
another day of heavy fog. That's why she had come out this night.
She'd been thinking about Eddie Glover all day. Actually, there was
no escort, only a girlfriend who had offered to help.

When, by nine, the girlfriend had not appeared, Snyder borrowed
an ill-fitting sport jacket from the bartender and escorted Lubie to
the dining room. Counting high heels, she was nearly six feet tall.
They ordered another round of drinks, Chianti, and steak dinners.
Snyder liked her better after the wine. He found her interesting and
intelligent with no hard edges. She had an assortment of blues, and
no desire to talk about them. Instead, she gave him a full briefing on

the chewing-tobacco business, which had fallen on hard times. Snyder told her about the Walk and *Harrington's*. Lubie said she did not understand people with so much passion, but she was against the war.

After dinner, they returned to the bar. Lubie had another vodka and quinine. Snyder switched to Scotch. The bartender unplugged the jukebox and played a slow rock song by the late Buddy Holly. Snyder played it twice more and danced with Lubie. Then they drove in her car south of the city to the Howard Johnson's motel on Route 2. Snyder registered them as Mr. and Mrs. Bruce Erlanger.

In their room, Lubie took her hair down. It fell to her waist. They took a shower together. Her small dark-tipped breasts and narrow hips were not the stuff of Snyder's fantasies, but she overcame all that. They made love on a pink towel on top of the bathroom rug. Lubie made a great whooping noise at the climax and dug her fingers into his scalp. He did not quite believe in her, but her eyes were shining. She reminded him of Bliss Carpenter.

They smoked in bed. Pretty soon, Lubie dozed off. Then Snyder slept.

At dawn, he awoke. Lubie was making love to him. When she realized he had been watching her, she blushed and laughed. They made it last longer than the first time, and her final whoop, Snyder thought, probably woke the third floor at the Griffin Hotel. They slept until the wake-up call and had breakfast at a coffee shop near the walking bridge on Chapline Street. The day was clear and the temperature rising. Back at the hotel, Snyder wrote Lubie a note, thanked her for his good luck, and mailed it to her before he lost his nerve.

FIFTEEN

Conflicts of Interest

I

That afternoon, they had transformed a luggage room in the hotel basement into a Walk sign shop. Herndon and Amelia reproduced the WISE lead sign—WE'RE WALKING SINCE MAY 11 CHICAGO-WASH. FOR U.S.-HANOI PEACE TALKS—using a smaller piece of plywood so that the sign, while harder to read, might be easier to carry. Molly and Dorene created a triangle-shaped sign with the trident in blue above the words PEACE NOW. Rachel restored REMEMBER NORMAN MORRISON with Elmer's glue, wood strips, and carpet tacks. And in red letters on a pine slat about a yard long and six inches wide, Dunne contributed a new slogan: CHRIST SAYS GET OUT. He nailed the painted slat to a two-by-four, then held his handiwork aloft. "Not bad for a godless socialist," he said.

Peter Schumacher, a Catholic, gave Dunne the finger. Snyder and the others looked for Lucas's reaction.

Lucas blinked hard at Dunne and whistled through his teeth. "Really, Frank—" he said, as though that was all he could possibly say. "That makes two crosses."

"Let me carry it," Dunne insisted. "I might become a believer."

"And alienate every other believer."

"Freedom, Sam."

"Bullshit, Frank."

"Tell me not to carry it and I won't."

Lucas replied with silence and an irritated shrug that seemed to mean "offended I am, but a dictator I'm not."

Dunne lowered his cross to his shoulder and left the room without a decision.

Lucas started to follow, then seemed to think better of it. He slumped against a storage bin, looked heavenward, and sighed in contemplation of the mountain that had so suddenly risen from a molehill.

Snyder thought Lucas had won with restraint, at least temporarily. It was not freedom of speech that had prompted him, he reckoned, but Dunne's freedom to leave. Likewise, it was not deference to the leader that limited Dunne's response, but the specter of reporting failure back home. In the balance was the Walk's premise: get there in time and intact. The weight of it seemed to have come down on Lucas's side.

Next morning, in the hotel lobby after breakfast, Dunne took Snyder aside. "I dismantled it," he said, "and packed the crosspiece in my bag for a souvenir. Okay?"

"Want to say why?" Snyder asked.

"Vulnerable, maybe, I guess. One cross is enough."

He laughed as if to say he should have known. He patted Snyder's notebook and moved away, toward June. Her flag had been upgraded with a ceramic dove glued to the top of its pole.

Bitter, bitter, Snyder was thinking, the man wants to do his own thing and hates that he isn't. He also wants a record, in case he must.

Instinctively, Snyder began taking stock.

It is June 9, the Walk's thirtieth day, with twenty-five days to go. There are eleven walkers, Arley Broyle in the truck, and yourself. The route to Washington, D.C., points virtually due east via U.S. 40, the old, crooked, and mostly two-lane road that runs all the way from Wheeling through the Alleghenies to the coast. En route, it slips across the northern sliver of West Virginia, then over the southwestern corner of Pennsylvania to Uniontown, then by way of Cumberland through the panhandle of western Maryland to Hagerstown, and then into Baltimore. To make it that far by the end of June asks the walkers to maintain their Indiana-Ohio pace despite bumpier terrain—not an impossible request, difficult but doable, assuming a certain solidarity. "The whether," he wrote, "does not depend upon the weather."

and a paperback book by Frederick Lucas: The Trial of His

2

In three days, they made Washington, Pennsylvania.

As it happened, this placed Snyder less than ten miles south of Canonsburg, Phil Zimmerman's hometown. Were Zimmerman alive, Snyder thought, Arley Broyle could have driven him up. A postcard from Canonsburg would have tickled little Phil, like the one Zimmerman had once sent from Topeka, as he remembered verbatim: "Here's your correspondent visiting the turf of Jacob Snyder and Alf Landon. Clearly, not enough room here for the both of you. Still, go for glory—send your clippings and all will be forgiven!" Instead, there were only Zimmerman's next of kin in Canonsburg, the ones with "Von" in their names, and the Walk gave Snyder an excuse for not mourning again. He told himself he couldn't take a chance on missing anything.

3

On June 14, in Uniontown, Pennsylvania, they conducted an evening rally, billed as a teach-in, from the stage of the auditorium at Roosevelt Community College. From the wings, Snyder witnessed the audience of about two hundred students giving the Walk its most enthusiastic reception since Chicago. Most of the boys had been letting their hair grow and most of the girls wore blue jeans. Snyder knew the date must be helping—the college semester would end on the morrow—but he could not otherwise account for the chemistry of that meeting. The students often stood to applaud the walkers' answers to their questions and, though predominantly white, actually cheered George Corrigan after his standard three-minute speech. The linkage of "the waste of folks' resources in Vietnam" to "you dig, poverty back home" hit a home run in Uniontown.

Afterwards, about thirty students stayed for a reception on the stage. And in time, Snyder saw one boy among them tentatively approach Lucas. He was a Negro, rangy and handsome, with fine features and close-cropped hair, carrying a small Japanese camera and a paperback book by Herbert Marcuse. The front of his sweat-shirt bore the initials SCLC stenciled in red letters. Snyder heard Lucas explode: "Join the Walk! By all means, join! It's so important!"

With that, and an arm about the boy, Lucas lumbered from the stage to seats in the front row. Snyder took a seat behind them.

"Don't mind him, son," Lucas said, "he's our scribe."

It was a petty insult, to be charged to anxiety and discounted, but not graced with a laugh.

The potential walker dismissed it anyway, half turning in his seat so that he spoke to Snyder as well as Lucas. His name, he said, was Ellroy Kendall. He was nineteen, in pre-engineering, the son of a Uniontown mailman, and wanted to join the Walk because George Corrigan's anti-war speech was the first of its kind he'd ever heard by a Negro.

Lucas glowed. Yet he glanced at Snyder as though to question his own enthusiasm: will this boy help?

Snyder nodded *of course* in that curious, humorless manner of pro-fessional journalists responding to questions asked of them.

"James Meredith's been shot, you know," Kendall said, "and there's a big march for him going on right now through Mississippi, heading for Jackson. I'd planned to do something about that after finals—when along comes one of my own people, my own age, do-ing something about the war. Well, then, I knew I'd have to do my something along with him, no matter that his issue is not desegrega-tion, because, you know, I'm not only a Negro but a human being."

Snyder, writing, took pleasure in the quote, more expressive, he was thinking, than any possible rumination of your own on the scar-city of Negroes in the anti-war movement. Whether or not Kendall will help the Walk, he's already helped the story.

Only moments later, there were two white girls standing above Lucas and Kendall, asking questions about joining the Walk. They were friends and classmates, age twenty, named Sylvia Vecchio and Martha Bishop. Sylvia, in child psychology, with frizzy black hair, a mouselike little body, and a defensive gold cross at her throat, ap-peared chronically uneasy, excessively shy, and fragile to the point of brittleness. Martha Bishop, in anthropology, was blond and bovine, wore a macramé necklace, and seemed to be Sylvia's precise oppo-site, imperious, controlling, and athletic-looking. Martha did most of the talking. She said both were daughters of working families "that never went anywhere." Joining the Walk, she said in effect, gave them a chance not only to take a stand against the war but also to fulfill their wanderlust as well. "We have a pact," Martha said stoutly. "We intend to see the world, together if possible, separately if necessary."

Glowing again, Lucas turned to Snyder. "Put me down, Jack," he said. "The Uniontown threesome lets us forget about Ohio."

Snyder saluted with his pen and copied the line. The unlikeliness of Sylvia Vecchio made him think Lucas was only two-thirds right; but still, given the Walk's best night in quite a while, he felt good about Uniontown, too.

4

Next afternoon on U.S. 40 east of Uniontown, they lost Martha, not Sylvia, as Snyder would have expected. In tears, Martha had been forced off the road by severe shin splints and could not continue. Arley Broyle drove both girls back to Uniontown, but before the day's last rest stop, Sylvia returned with Broyle.

Lucas embraced her and told her he had prayed for her return.

Then Snyder walked with Sylvia to find out why she was continuing without her friend. "To finish," Sylvia said, with a light in her face by which, Snyder thought, you could read the cardinal rule against journalistic arrogance: never assume a goddamn thing.

5

Two days passed in a strange and sudden zone of forlorn landscapes, broken-down farmhouses and forfeited lands, where the last depression had yet to end. There were scarred ridges and deep ravines littered with stripped cars, burned-out stoves, empty oil drums, and piles of rusting junk, and finally a long, dark valley where in the weary emptiness of a redundant coal town, Snyder noted, with Kendall carrying the lead sign, nobody gave them a wave. Men in overalls on the porch of the general store eyed them suspiciously.

Snyder knew there would be little change before Cumberland. So that night, when Lucas volunteered Dorene, Dunne, and Kendall, with Arley Broyle driving, to leaflet a mineworkers' 3 P.M. shift break next afternoon, Snyder thought him naïve or dauntless.

The mission had begun on schedule and, at the end of six miles off on a shale road northeast of U.S. 40 above Addison, Pennsylvania, a mountain of anthracite slag rose up where the odometer said it ought to be. But Lucas's advance information had been incorrect. Instead of hundreds of men, only twelve had worked the mine on the shift just ended. The walkers found them lounging in the shadow of a worn-out shaft held up by a scaffolding that itself seemed about to collapse. Surprised in their sweat and exhaustion, the miners were darkly indifferent, then casually impolite, and finally barely able to conceal their dislike for the Walk's cause in general, and Ellroy Kendall in particular. Judiciously, Kendall stepped back, but never looked down. He also made himself last to climb back into the truck bed, even behind Snyder.

"Absolutely fearless," Dunne said as they drove off.

"They had to respect you, Ellroy," Dorene said.

Kendall shook his head; he knew better.

"How do you feel?" Snyder asked.

Kendall looked up at the sun just dropping below a jagged peak. "Misplaced," he said.

6

Came June 20, they left Frostburg, Maryland, for a day's walk to Cumberland. They had a 6 P.M. date with an activist named Cynthia Foote, chairman of the Cumberland Peace Action Committee, who was to bus them from a downtown corner to her home for a meal, a meeting, and the night's lodging. In the late morning, the sky turned aluminum blue and a rainless northwest gale came up that blew against them to the top of the last mean hill, then died rather than follow them on the long downslope to the valley of the Potomac and the old gateway city. By phone at 5 P.M., Lucas had put back the Cumberland schedule by three hours. And at 9 P.M., after nightfall, while they rested under a streetlamp beside an overlook on the north bank of the river, he sent Arley Broyle ahead with a word for Miss Foote. "Please wait. We're an honest hour away."

Seated on the overlook wall, Snyder made a note: thirteen hours, the longest day of the Walk. He was also acutely aware of the effort he himself had made. His calves ached, and the sweat drying in his shirt made him shiver. He imagined others felt the same. There was Kendall above him, with the lead sign drooping over his shoulder like a weary scythe. The black youth had lifted their morale by lugging the sign for the last three hours, but now he looked spent. He was apparently too tired even to sit down.

As the final leg began, it was Lucas who reached for the lead sign. "Let me carry it, Ellroy," he said. "Cynthia Foote is an old friend. I want to greet her with it. My vanity, don't you see?"

"I can do it," Kendall said.

"I know, but you don't have to prove it."

"Prove what?"

"You don't have to prove anything."

Kendall passed the sign. "We all look alike after dark anyway," he said.

Snyder saw Lucas wince, as though the bite of Kendall's quip had drawn blood. So far as he knew, it was Lucas's first inkling of the uncertainty that Kendall had revealed for an instant to those in the truck after the incident at the coal mine.

"Is that a joke?" Lucas asked.

"Yes," Kendall replied, as though confessing evil.

"You belong here, you and George. I told you it's important."

"Oh, I know."

"I, vaingloriously, want to be carrying the sign when we meet Cynthia Foote, is all."

"It's okay, Sam," Kendall said. "You've got it."

In less than an hour, they reached a broad avenue near the river about fifteen minutes' walk from downtown. Lucas again sent Arley Broyle to reassure Cynthia Foote. Then he motioned the Walk through a small riverside park that lay between the walkers and the appointed corner.

There was an old house in the park. A plaque, barely legible in the darkness, said George Washington in this place had made his first headquarters twenty years before the Revolution. It aroused interest in Ellroy Kendall and Peter Schumacher, and in Snyder because it had interested Kendall. Detaching from the Walk with Snyder close behind, Kendall and Schumacher rapidly skirted the house. They peered together through a rear window into the only lighted room. It was merely a caretaker's office, with a desk, files, and a cot stripped to its mattress. Snyder laughed.

"George Washington slept there, Jack," Schumacher said.

"No, only his slave, Jack," Kendall said dryly, just as a Negro in a blue uniform was entering the office from an inner door.

They continued around to the front of the house. Up ahead, silhouetted against the city lights, the Walk was leaving the park. Snyder could make out Corrigan, beckoning them to hurry along. They waved back. Then Schumacher let his arm fall across Kendall's shoulder. "What does make you say things, Ellroy?"

"Say which, Peter?"

"About the slave."

"What did I say?"

"It was the way you said it."

"Like what?"

"I don't know."

"Forget it."

"Like, you don't belong, quite."

"I don't, man, quite."

"Who says?"

"Like, forget it, I said."

"It's Sam?"

"At least, you're awake."

"He said just the opposite."

"Well, maybe I misunderstood."

"Oh—I knew he got to you back there about proving something—"

"He wants his old friend seeing him carry the sign."

"—saying you belong."

"He thinks me and George, we're important because we've desegregated his Walk, that's all."

"Is that bad?"

"I for sure didn't join up to do that—can't I be against the war without being black?"

"You can, but still, you *are.*"

"Lucas's nigger—"

"For Christ's sake, Ellroy!"

"That's how he makes me feel, important because I'm black, not because I'm Ellroy Kendall. You get that, don't you?"

"You'll kill Sam if you say that."

"Oh, shit, Peter."

"Oh, shit?"

"Oh, shit is right, man."

Kendall broke from them and ran ahead. Schumacher froze beside Snyder.

"What happened, Jack?"

"Everyone's tired. Ellroy's got his limit."

"But what did I do?"

"Sam did it. You only forgot to agree with Ellroy."

"Oh, Jesus!"

Schumacher darted forward. Kendall had caught up with the others. Snyder watched as Schumacher came up beside Kendall, again throwing an arm around Kendall's shoulder. They were both tall and, in silhouette, reminded Snyder of a tree with two trunks. Kendall seemed to tolerate Schumacher, then veered away.

Snyder did not hurry. Around him, as he left the park, late-evening traffic moved slowly away from the Cumberland city center. He paused to light his cigarette. Kendall's complaint, he was thinking: neither Kendall nor Schumacher is likely to speak about it to Lucas or any third person, meaning Lucas won't know to intervene unless he hears about it from *Harrington's* man, or God.

Snyder felt something new, a pinprick of cynicism, which he decided to excuse as professional self-defense. He smoked and told himself to take care of business.

Moments later, there was Lucas with Miss Foote, a pleasantly round-faced blonde, about sixty, bundled up in a mannish spring coat with an elegant silk scarf around her head, shepherding the Walk into four waiting sedans on the corner of Baltimore and Greene streets. Lucas introduced Snyder, then pointed him toward Arley Broyle in the truck, behind which was the last car, Miss Foote's limousine.

"Only five miles, Jack," Lucas said. "It's a wonderful old mansion."

Snyder hesitated as the temptation to speak to Lucas about Kendall rose and fell. At last, he turned away; it was not the place or the moment, with Miss Foote among them, and everyone anxious to get on with the evening. He took the seat next to Broyle. "Only five miles," Lucas repeated, laughing as they drove off.

Snyder searched for news on the truck radio. He found a mid-hour wrap. The Soviet Union had rolled out the red carpet for General de Gaulle. A congressional anti-war caucus criticized the President's alleged obsession with the Pentagon's daily body count in Vietnam. Negro unrest increased in the Cleveland ghetto. And two thousand demonstrators, including Martin Luther King, were expected as the march for James Meredith proceeded along a Mississippi highway just days from Jackson.

Arley Broyle whistled at the number.

"That's the competition," Snyder said.

"We're so lucky to have George and Ellroy," Broyle said.

Snyder said nothing.

The cavalcade crossed a stream called Evitts Creek and turned onto the well-lit grounds of Miss Foote's estate, where a handsome Tudor house stood at the end of a paved circular drive. Snyder guessed twenty-five rooms.

Inside, there was a large living room with a grand display of English antiques. The seating and the floor easily accommodated the forty or so well-dressed local guests for whom dinner had already been served. A reheated meal of fried chicken and grits awaited the Walk. And now, as they ate, Lucas, sitting Buddha-like on the floor in the center of the room, began a discussion on the goals of WISE. Snyder made a few notes, but both the walkers and their audience were repeating opinions he had heard many times before. So he was barely listening when Miss Foote, standing by a marble angel on a pedestal, asked a rhetorical question: "Why, with so many Negroes fighting in Vietnam, are there just two in this room? I personally invited several to come here tonight. They promised they would come. They have not come and that troubles me."

Lucas looked around the room, past Corrigan, until he spied Kendall, seated in a high-backed chair by the fireplace.

"Want to answer that, Ellroy?" he asked.

Kendall gave Lucas a bleak look and shrugged. "I don't know," he said.

"Try," Lucas persisted.

Kendall turned in his chair to face Miss Foote. He said, "Maybe they don't feel they can come here any other time as individuals, so tonight they didn't want to come as Negroes."

Miss Foote reddened from her chin to the roots of her yellow hair. The room shifted uncomfortably, people moving legs, crossing arms, looking for invisible objects on the Turkish rug. Kendall, jaw clenched, seemed to be waiting for a blow. Snyder glanced to the corner where Corrigan and Schumacher sat together with a young couple from town. Both boys were smiling.

"Why do you assume that?" Miss Foote asked, her voice cracking on "that."

Kendall compressed his lips and inhaled deeply, as though he might cry.

"Well, a lot of us do," Kendall said. "That's why so many are marching tonight in Mississippi."

"But it's not true on Evitts Creek," Miss Foote protested. "Eight years ago, the Allegheny Civil Rights League was organized in this very room. The people I invited tonight consider me a friend. They are my Negro friends."

At this, Kendall sat back, suddenly limp, as if to say *"It's hopeless."*

"George Corrigan?" Lucas called, undaunted.

Corrigan raised his hand, then lowered it. His smile had faded. Almost imperceptibly, he shook his head, negative, as though he knew the diplomatic things to say, but did not care to say them.

"Well—maybe I could just comment," Lucas said, seemingly immune to shock. He climbed to his feet with the air of a patient fireman, and said, "I think, at heart, Ellroy and George are concerned that the peace movement, being so overwhelmingly white and middle-class, may actually replace liberal white commitment to the goal of racial justice in this country. On the one hand, they see liberal whites leaving the civil rights movement with hurt feelings because more and more Negroes are proclaiming Black Power. On the other hand, they know activist Negroes who are reluctant to join the peace movement because they expect to be left behind by those same whites, once the war has ended. That's what makes Ellroy and George important to this Walk. They answer that concern by keeping faith in a great American coalition against both war and racism. Isn't that about right?"

With a look, Lucas addressed the question to Kendall and Corrigan. Snyder watched Kendall, whose own dream of colorlessness—at which Corrigan would have hooted—had been left out of Lucas's attempt to explain and to save the evening.

"About right, Sam," Kendall said, without conviction.

"You got most of it, Sam," Corrigan said, almost inaudibly.

"Exactly!" Lucas exclaimed. "We're all trying. We all want it to happen. Let's take a moment of silence to see if we can't get some help in making it happen."

There was silence. As they prayed, Snyder scanned the room. Miss Foote seemed intent on Kendall. She needed more, perhaps a word of truce, Snyder thought, or—at the very least—simple recognition, which she wasn't going to get. Kendall looked down at his hands. Schumacher stared at the eighteen-candle chandelier. Corrigan met Snyder's eyes with a wink.

"Okay," Lucas said.

The couple with Corrigan and Schumacher began to applaud. The room applauded—everyone applauded, Snyder saw, even Corrigan, all except Kendall.

By the time the guests had left and the walkers dispersed to rooms on the second floor, it was almost midnight. Snyder remained in the living room hearing Lucas's final word with Miss Foote. Lucas told her he was sorry and hoped she understood. Miss Foote said she understood and that it was no matter. She withdrew to her room, somewhere above. Then a maid aimed the two men down a long gallery hung with photographs of Miss Foote and horses.

"What's left over from horse feed," Lucas said, "goes to WISE."

The gallery ended at a small library with a bar. Snyder fixed them each a light Scotch and stood by the open window. Lucas sagged into an overstuffed chair.

"Was it all right, Jack?" he asked.

"Your speech was good enough, not your best," Snyder answered, too tired, he felt, to lie very much. He was thinking, perhaps, you should even tell Lucas about Kendall's beef after all.

"It didn't feel right, Jack. Imagine how Cynthia feels."

"I can imagine."

"The woman pays our rent in Chicago. Never married. Horses and liberal causes only. I've known her thirty years. Did Ellroy end all that?"

"Did he?"

"No, but I'm asking you."

"Sam, do you worry about losing Ellroy?" That, Snyder was thinking, was the question.

"Should I? To whom—Mississippi?"

"Just asking."

"We need him. He needs us. I think he chose us because he sensed how important he'd be to us. One more Negro on the road to Jackson—what's that?"

"You've got it wrong, Sam. He's an idealist."

"Aren't we all?"

"Some are more so. Ellroy's like Jews I used to know before the Holocaust became news, wanting to be accepted as human beings in a world that never looks up your ancestry. They're right, but the world pays no attention."

"Meaning what?"

"I mean, Sam, Ellroy wants acceptance from the Walk."

Lucas set down his glass and ran the fingers of both hands upwards through his beard, scratching along the way.

"You know something I don't?"

"No," Snyder lied. "Divine inspiration."

"I see. Well, tomorrow, when we're on the road, I'll talk with him."

"May I listen?"

"It's your story, Jack, so by all means," Lucas said. "But 'fat and aging Sam Lucas,' you won't say that about me, will you?"

"No, I promise," Snyder said.

7

Next morning at seven sharp, along with breakfast on Miss Foote's screened-in porch, there was television's Tuesday morning edition of

the *Today Show* with Hugh Downs. At the top of the news was a
special report on the night's rioting in the Cleveland ghetto. Blocks
of tenements smoked and burned. Hundreds of Negroes pelted police with rocks and garbage. Police backed by National Guardsmen
gassed and clubbed the Negroes.

The walkers seemed to share similar responses to the pictures,
looks of amazement combined with a tendency to lean against one
another. Snyder noted that the violence intrigued the females no less
than the males, the whites no less than the blacks, and Dunne, who
had seen so much in his life, no less than Amelia, who had seen so
little. It was violence in search of attention, justified by the same
morality they'd heard from Barry Goldwater addressing the 1964
Republican national convention: "I would remind you that extrem-
ism in the defense of liberty is no vice! And let me remind you also
that moderation in the pursuit of justice is no virtue!" Violence,
Snyder was thinking, has become the universal attention getter.
What, then, can the Walk expect without, at least, civil disobedience?

Snyder saw Kendall, in jeans and a clean white T-shirt, turning
away from the group as they were listening to Hugh Downs's news
bridge from the Cleveland riots to the march for James Meredith.
The next footage showed Negroes walking on a Mississippi highway,
an anonymous voice-over saying, "The encampment outside Jackson
and the tension inside grows hourly for Sunday's climactic rally at the
state capitol."

Kendall stopped at the screen door to Miss Foote's sunlit English
garden. Snyder looked beyond, down the row of stones that made a
path through the garden, past a stone wellhead, and over a stretch of
lawn to the parking area, where Arley Broyle was loading the truck.
As was his custom, Broyle had skipped breakfast in order to collect
the Walk's baggage on schedule. With a half turn, Kendall glanced
back, his gaze sweeping the group until his eyes locked on Snyder's.
His expression was blank, or unreadable, as though the effort within
had summoned every atom of personality for a final analysis. He
began chafing his bare forearms though the air was warm and humid.
He consulted his watch, twice. Then he stiffened, as though a set of
springs in his body had been suddenly pulled tight. He pushed open
the screen door.

To Snyder's surprise, Lucas moved his bulk out of the breakfast area into immediate pursuit, soon with Corrigan and Schumacher following him. And when Snyder tried to approach, Lucas stopped him out of earshot with a wave of his hand.

Now Lucas and Kendall faced one another about thirty yards from the outer edge of the garden. Corrigan and Schumacher waited in the middle distance near the wellhead. And Snyder stood on a pebbled plaza at the foot of the porch stairs, straining to hear. The sun was already angling up and to the south and beginning to flatten the colors in the flower beds.

At first, Kendall did the talking, his hands up, palms out, explaining things to Lucas, who nodded repeatedly. Schumacher and Corrigan carried on a whispered conversation of their own. Behind Snyder on the porch, the other walkers and Miss Foote looked out in silence. Minutes later, they sighed with hope as Lucas put an arm around Kendall's shoulder and turned himself and the boy away from all spectators. To Snyder, Lucas's move seemed desperate.

The climax was Kendall and Lucas walking together across the lawn to the Walk truck. With Broyle's help, Kendall retrieved his duffel bag. Apparently, he would not say goodbye back at the house.

Schumacher turned and strode quickly toward Snyder and the porch steps. Going by, he announced, "Ellroy's hitchhiking to Mississippi," and held the screen for Corrigan. In passing, Corrigan shook hands with Snyder. With a grin, he said, "We're going with Ellroy!" Then the two boys flung themselves onto the porch and into the arms of the walkers, embracing, kissing, shouting farewells.

After a few minutes, Corrigan and Schumacher urgently disengaged, retreating back down the steps and into the garden. With a wave to Snyder, they began to trot along the path. The walkers left the porch and gathered around Snyder in the garden. Kendall had not come back to them, and no one seemed able to approach him uninvited. They could see the three boys shaking hands with Lucas. The boys shouldered their bags. Dorene wept and Amelia buried her face in Herndon's shoulder. Corrigan and Schumacher waved to the group again, then followed Kendall, who was already nearing the vanishing point at the top of Evitts Creek Road. Molly ran forward to Lucas where he stood with Broyle. As she reached him, Lucas slapped the truck fender and sagged against it. Other walkers and Miss Foote began moving toward the truck, all except Rachel, who waited for Snyder.

"Sad," she said. "We were fourteen, and now, all of a sudden, we're eleven again."

"It is sad," Snyder said, lighting a cigarette.

"How many did Christ have, anyway?"

"Ask a Christian. Twelve."

"We're going to have to count you."

"Yes, I'll play Judas."

"What does that mean?"

"I had something for Lucas and didn't give to him. It didn't seem right to."

"What?"

"That Ellroy really hated being his Negro for peace."

"He told you?"

"Some, and I knew. Sam just missed it for worrying about Miss Foote."

"You don't care that I might tell him that?"

"No."

"I wouldn't."

"You can. I did the right thing, Ray. I'm not here to change history."

"Did you hear me criticize?" Rachel asked sharply, tempered by a look of surprise at her own irritation.

"Reporters trade information with their subjects all the time," Snyder said. "It's just some who don't believe in it."

"Are there more like you back home?"

"More than you'd expect."

"So it won't help us to put in for your transfer?"

Snyder laughed. "No, about now, the rest would be feeling bad, too." She'd made him laugh; it is the difference, he was thinking, between her and almost everybody.

"Feeling bad is not bad," she said. "None of us should get too smug about doing good. Maybe that's why Ellroy left us."

SIXTEEN
Majority Rule

I

"I'm ready, if you're ready," Snyder said, turning his hat brim down all around.

"I think we're ready," Lucas said. He wore a green eyeshade and held the lead sign. "I'm ready."

The Walk was downtown in Cumberland, again at Baltimore and Greene streets. Twenty or so curious passersby had gathered around them, but the walkers were withdrawn and were not working the crowd with leaflets, or even conversation. To Snyder, only Lucas seemed "ready," the rest without spirit, barely set to go nearly two hours after they'd lost the three boys. Lucas was wise in Snyder's notebook: "He knows not to make a speech. Rather, he sets an example. Tears, followed by outrage, followed by getting up again. He's got himself up: despite beet-faced flushes and borderline hyperventilation, he bounced well. Now he will have to resuscitate the others."

Momentarily pressed against the crowd, Snyder registered the day and date and proposed distance for the Walk: it was Tuesday, the first day of summer, to do twelve miles/eight hours from Cumberland along the northern edge of the Green Ridge Forest to the town of Flintstone, home of a community of Mennonites, four days from Hagerstown. On the way to town, Reed Herndon had helped Snyder fill in on the Mennonites: Protestant evangelicals, spiritual kin to the Amish, Quakers, and Shakers; lived in Pennsylvania and neighboring states since before the American Revolution; descended followers of Menno Simons, a sixteenth-century Dutch reformer; advocate private simplicity and public humanitarianism; maintain strictures against infant baptism, intermarriage with non-believers, and military service. The source was a Mennonite bank robber whom Herndon had known at Leavenworth.

As Snyder now wrote this last, he heard an odd, croaking voice behind his ear, asking, "Are you a reporter, bud?"

Snyder looked eye to eye into the worn, flat face of a white-haired passerby whose body tilted right, supported by an aluminum cane.

"Yes, sir," Snyder said.

"These people don't want to stop the Communists, do they?"

"They want to stop the war, yes."

"But not the enemy."

"They wouldn't mind stopping the enemy."

"They have a way?"

"Talk."

"Talk?"

"Korea-type talk."

"This is a guerrilla war. Talk is defeat."

"Maybe we can't do better."

"All right, then send for Big Boy."

"What's your name, sir?"

"Age seventy-one, Thomas Mayberry, with two *r*'s. Silver Star, 1st Marines, Belleau Wood, 1918. What's your paper?"

"*Harrington's Weekly World.*"

"My, I'm a reader! What's your name?"

"J. C. Snyder."

The old man nodded.

"Detroit last?"

"Yes."

"So you cover this sort of thing—riots, protests."

Snyder was writing: ". . . send for Big Boy." He said, "Sometimes."

The old man breathed a whisper into Snyder's ear. He said, "Aren't you ashamed of yourself, Mr. J. C. Snyder? I mean, publicizing these people?"

Astonished, Snyder looked up to see anger crease Thomas Mayberry's brow, extend downward into his eyes, and finally bare his long yellow teeth. Snyder turned sideways and backed toward the

walkers. He hoped a dismayed grin would keep the man at bay.
Never reply, he was thinking. The last thing you need is the last
word—you just hate to be reminded of it.

So they began again, all but Lucas down if not out. And as the
Walk's day wore on, bringing a mass of southern air and cooking it to
ninety degrees, perhaps one hundred degrees at Rocky Gap, Lucas
seemed bent on physical therapy for the walkers' blues. In the lead,
he picked up the pace; in the ranks, he urged the leader to go faster.
He delayed and then shortened rest periods. By midafternoon, he
had them groaning as he greeted each new sun-broiled hilltop with a
defiant shout, as though resistance to heat and gravity was, finally,
the answer, not just to forgetting the loss of the three walkers, but to
arousing the remnant's self-respect.

Then there was the final hour on U.S. 40, and Snyder judged the
therapy was working by its effect on himself. You know it, he was
thinking, when in the vacuum after each new blast of blistering air
from the trucks highballing on U.S. 40, in that moment without the
woosh of traffic, you yourself actually enjoy a kind of highway delir-
ium, as though you really belong with these people, waltzing together under a great, inverted burning glass bowl, accompanied by a
concerto of determined grunts and wheezes. Lucas has you soldier-
ing like everyone else because he understands the psychology of
survivors, the nature of teams, to wit, solidarity is shared struggle,
and community virtually irresistible under trying circumstances,
panic excepted. "Solidarity is shared struggle," Snyder wrote. A trite
line, he thought, but probably true, sometimes.

At seven that evening, the Walk having left U.S. 40 and begun the
last mile into Flintstone, he added: "It's true enough. Fat and aging,
Sam Lucas wins the day! Though exhausted, he's in the lead again
and we are whistling the theme song from *The Bridge on the River
Kwai.*"

Near dusk, between Flintstone's main street and the open fields,
they came with their signs to a red-brick and yellow-stone Mennonite
church at the center of a well-kept neighborhood of two-story houses
and half-acre vegetable gardens. There were horse carts, well-pre-
served jalopies, and some late-model cars parked in front, but evi-
dently every last congregant had gone inside. The look of the church
was both squat and stalwart, without a touch of elegance other than

the figured iron railings on the steps leading to the doors, and some-body had painted even these battleship gray. The only contrast to such determined austerity was a stand of lithe blue-green poplar trees behind the church and tall yellow flowers asleep in large beds across the façade and on either side of the steps.

Following Lucas, the walkers bypassed the main entrance and, in a rear yard, actually a one-net basketball court, with the hoop mounted on the church's back wall, met their host, Minister Felix Hoffman. He was a tall, muscular, fiftyish Dutchman, defying the heat in a plain gray gabardine suit with all his jacket buttons fastened. They followed him, and met en masse half a dozen perspiring ladies pre-paring dinner in the church basement. One of the ladies provided soap and towels so they could wash themselves. During that time, Herndon wrote on a sheet of notepaper asked from Snyder. Then again Hoffman led them, this time up an inner stair to the chapel rostrum looking down on a congregation of about a hundred fifty sweltering men, women, and children in a severe white room. From the pulpit, an unadorned reading stand, the minister introduced Lu-cas, who doggedly spoke for twenty minutes. Then Lucas introduced Reed Herndon, who, Snyder noticed, held the notepaper in his hand as he stepped to the pulpit.

"I've asked to speak," Herndon said, "very briefly because it's a hot night, but still, to speak because I've had occasion in recent years to learn something about the Mennonite way. I can tell you, in short, that we are a small group of men and women who take much inspira-tion from your faith in equality, in togetherness, in the simple life.

"Moreover, given our cause, which is to stop the killing in Viet-nam—this, for the sake of our own freedom—we are not only in-spired but sustained by the Mennonites' stand against participating in war on the eve of the American Revolution."

Herndon took a deep breath, like a diver on the high board for the first time, and consulted his note.

He continued: "The Mennonites' message, if I may read it as I remember it, to the State Assembly of Pennsylvania, 1775: 'It is our principle to feed the hungry and give the thirsty drink; we have dedicated ourselves to serve all men in everything that can be helpful to the preservation of men's lives, but we find no freedom in giving, or doing, or assisting in anything by which men's lives are destroyed or hurt.' "

The congregation murmured, and many older heads nodded approval. Herndon smiled, relieved, his memory having survived the plunge. "That stand is my guide in life," he said. "I think I can say all of us want it for America today. I, at least, know of none that comes closer to defining the means to freedom and, as such, the effort we are making to change the policy of our government in Vietnam. Thank you for it."

The walkers joined in the congregation's applause. They seemed to Snyder to have received a final lift, all the more welcome because it was purposeful after a day of physical challenge from Lucas. And a few moments later, there was one thing more. The minister's appeal for the Walk kitty raised $181, a one-night record.

2

After a cheerful dinner under colored lights in the rear churchyard, the walkers returned to the chapel by the inner stairs to see a transformation. Some women of the Mennonite congregation had chosen twelve pews for a Walk dormitory, six on each side of the aisle with a wall of blankets hung from a string in between, and neatly arranged cushions, sheets, and pillows, making a comfortable, if narrow, bed for each walker and Snyder. The walkers applauded the women, and Lucas embraced Minister Hoffman, who shyly fled to the front door followed by the entire Walk. Outside, at the top of the steps, the minister shook each walker's hand, then Snyder's, and, at last, returned Lucas's embrace with a bear hug of his own. Hoffman gave Lucas a look of such intense benevolence that Snyder thought Lucas might weep for the second time that day.

Instead, Lucas fell.

As he fell, he twisted sideways just beyond Snyder's grasp. At first, in a burst of simultaneous impressions, Lucas seemed to Snyder to have caught his heel starting down the steps with the minister, perhaps having decided to escort their host below, or even to his car. Then, more likely, it seemed he had lost his balance simply trying to extricate himself from the minister's embrace, and might even recover before the bottom step. Finally, perhaps this was it, he might have just slipped, suddenly a man too fat and too old not to fall down after that day on U.S. 40. He was falling, however, somehow falling, and Snyder saw that from the top step he could not do a thing about it. Lucas skidded first on his backside, then on his knees down seven steps, and rolled sideways into a terrible heap on a bed of flowers. Minister Hoffman lurched toward him, then tipped back. For a moment, he was also off balance, imminently in danger of falling over the railing. The closest hands were Molly's and Dunne's; they caught the minister. Moving to their right, Snyder slipped beside them and down the steps to Lucas. Simultaneously, Herndon landed beside him with a leap from the opposite railing. Herndon cried, "Sam!" so sharply that Lucas sat up, florid and wincing, looking dazed, with an instant reply: "Is *he* all right?"

On even keel again, the minister skipped a step and lurched between Herndon and Snyder to take charge of Lucas. He had reached that stage of alarm when prodigious feats became possible.

"I'm all right, thanks, Sam," the minister said. "You should be thinking of yourself."

"Too embarrassing," Lucas said. "Look at your flowers!"

"A spill, Sam, just a spill."

Unassisted, Minister Hoffman hefted Lucas to his feet and braced his great bulk while Lucas let Molly lift his torn trouser legs to examine his knees. Both knees were scraped raw, but with little bleeding. Molly sent Arley Broyle to the truck, where she had left her first-aid kit. On second thought, she ran ahead of him to fetch it. Then with Hoffman and Herndon helping, Lucas boosted himself up the steps; at the top, he let them half carry him into the chapel. By some miracle, Snyder was thinking, he does not seem seriously injured—saved by his padding.

It was almost midnight by the time Molly had washed and bandaged Lucas. Meanwhile, the minister and the Mennonite ladies had gone. Outside on the steps, Snyder and Rachel smoked in the dark.

"It could've been worse," Rachel said.

"Much."

"He's so ashamed."

"People fall," Snyder said, taking her hand. "He's going to hurt for a few days."

"What happened, Jack? You think he wore himself out?"

"Why do people fall? It's a mystery. I think he just fell," Snyder said. "And so quick, no one could save him."

"I saw you trying."

"I tried and missed."

"It proves you don't always just watch."

"Oh, yes?"

"Yes, it's nice to know."

3

Next morning, like a gallery of student interns, the walkers watched as a Cumberland doctor brought to the church by Minister Hoffman examined and rebandaged Lucas's knees. The doctor also probed a bruise on Lucas's left calf, without comment. His advice was clean bandages morning and night, leg up, and no walking for a day or two. Snyder thought Lucas looked relieved, as though he might otherwise have had to tough it out that day to maintain the old image of Dauntless Sam. Arley Broyle and Molly fixed a bed of soft luggage for Lucas in the back of the truck and Rachel found a notions store nearby that sold her a lady's pink umbrella, lighter and more manageable than the Walk's standard-issue black bumbershoots, to help keep the sun off Lucas in the afternoon. Lucas insisted on hobbling to the truck under his own steam, but needed help from Dunne and Broyle climbing in. "I feel like Grandma Joad," he joked, but didn't even try to disguise that he was hurting.

Lucas rode that way, umbrella down in the morning, up in the afternoon, so obviously uncomfortable, but every time the walkers caught up with him at the end of an hour, letting them know one way or another that he was feeling better than they were. That night, though, the truth was that he needed help from Dunne and Molly getting over rough ground into their scheduled campsite in the Green Ridge Forest near Piney Grove, and from Dunne alone getting through the trees to urinate.

He was still pained in the morning, probably worse than the day before, Snyder thought. So again he rode all day, at noon moving into the truck cab with Arley Broyle to avoid being seen sitting in the sun under Rachel's pink umbrella.

They made the distance late in the afternoon. It took them just past the village of Hancock to Camp Victory, a private coed summer camp for about sixty younger teenagers from Richmond, Virginia. A rail fence surrounded the property, with bunkhouses scattered inside below a dining hall set on a wooded hill with a fine sunset view over the upper Potomac. The camp director was an enthusiastic little man named Noah Keppler, who had contributed twenty dollars to WISE after the 1965 peace demonstration in New York. He assigned the women among several girls' cabins, the men to one empty cabin, and all to various dining tables, at which, he emphasized, they could talk with the campers in lieu of a meeting. His inflection told Snyder something about the subtleties of camp culture: a political meeting would risk parental criticism while an educational dinner conversation would not. Keppler also invited them to the evening's activity, barn dancing to recorded music in the dining hall.

The dance began early, as soon as the dinner dishes were cleared and the dining tables folded away. Snyder intended to watch, period. The caller was a pretty yellow-haired girl in bib overalls. Keppler placed an armchair beside her so that Lucas could sit comfortably and share the fun. "You have to dance," Lucas goaded Snyder, so Snyder danced two reels. When a third reel was called, Lucas himself got to his feet and entered the march. His movements amazed Snyder. They were remarkably fluid, balanced, and witty. Above all, they made the fat man seem well. The walkers and campers alike gave Lucas a big hand. And Snyder saw Lucas blush with pleasure—he was not letting down the side.

In the morning, Snyder's cabin awoke to reveille piped in through a squawk box. It was six-thirty. The men had slept on canvas cots, all in a row facing a narrow aisle, with Lucas's cot next to the door. They got dressed and packed and were awaiting breakfast call when Molly arrived to doctor Lucas's knees. She was wearing a white T-shirt and her hair was pulled back and tied with a white ribbon. She carried her ever-present first-aid kit and a bottle of rubbing alcohol. Lucas lay down on his cot with his back against a pillow and let her pull off his trousers. He looked like a giant turtle, belly-up on a beach, shedding part of his skin.

Snyder, as well as the others—Arley Broyle, Dunne, Herndon, and Wood—moved closer to watch Molly perform. She peeled off the bandages and bathed the scrape wounds with alcohol. Then she applied an antibiotic ointment and taped fresh bandages. Lucas shifted position and winced; his fingertips went not to his knee but to the left calf. Molly eased the leg over to catch the light. Herndon came forward to assist. Lucas's calf displayed a mean blue-red spot the size of a silver dollar amid a network of puffed blue-black veins streaking through butter-colored, hairless skin. A bad mosquito bite might have caused the same kind of inflammation. Snyder's medical knowledge did not cover the case.

"The spot's warm," Molly said, looking up at Herndon.

Herndon tested it with his palm.

"Was it warm yesterday, Sam?" he asked.

"Yes, it felt so," Lucas said. He stared toward the rafters.

"Camp doctor should see that," Herndon said.

"No camp doctors, please," Lucas said.

"Arley can have you in Hagerstown in an hour."

"No Hagerstown doctors, either—all it needs is exercise!" Lucas pointed Molly toward his trousers.

"It may want ice," Herndon said. "Anyone would put ice on a bruise like that."

"I can't walk with ice."

"He's hopeless," Molly said.

Lucas flung his legs over the side of the cot, hoisted his trousers, and stood up unassisted. He seemed a little shaky to Snyder, but not about to fall. Dunne came up on Lucas's shoulder.

"Ride shotgun one more day, Sam," he said.

Lucas shook his head and stepped into the aisle between the rows of cots. End to end, the cabin was about twelve paces long.

"Watch me," Lucas said.

He swung briskly up the aisle, touched the far wall, and returned. He did not limp, but his face showed the effort. It turned the old familiar crimson. Everyone could see his hurting, and the slower pain of his chagrin.

"You take another day of rest, Sam," Dunne said, "and use ice." His voice was good-natured, but firm, and carried the authority of their mutual seniority and the antagonistic bond between them. "Then you can dance again."

So, all that day, an ice bag donated by Noah Keppler rode in the truck with Lucas. Arley Broyle kept it full and, in the town of Indian Springs for the penultimate rest stop, he took Snyder aside to brag that Lucas was actually using it.

The day's final distance, as it happened, was a challenge as difficult, given the heat and the hour, as anything U.S. 40 had offered, a mile-and-a-half climb on the back of a sheer peak just below Fairview Mountain, elevation: 1,690 feet. At the top, they stood facing away from one another in every direction as though the exhaustion of each in triumph was endurable only in private. At the same time, the euphoria of the climb seemed to Snyder to unite them as perhaps never before. A tremor of regret surprised Snyder: poor Lucas had missed it.

A while later, some three hundred yards below the crest and around a bend, they found the Fairview Inn. It was a faded Victorian tourist hotel advertising a view of the Alleghenies from every room, at motel prices. Lucas was alone on the front porch, displaying a kind of arch bravado, unnaturally chesty, rather too anxious, Snyder thought, to show that one day of the rest-with-ice treatment had worked for him. In the lobby, he signed the register with an extra-bold flourish, ordered too grandly one table for twelve in the restaurant, and revealed too proudly that he and Arley Broyle had been to Hagerstown to buy three bottles of Chianti for the Walk's dinner. And later, as they ate in a quiet, nearly empty room with orange wallpaper and strawberry-colored tablecloths, he was overly himself, overeating more than usual, and enjoying his own company—only too much. Now he is really unattractive in the grotesque way only a fat man can be, Snyder was thinking, because the fall has upset the equilibrium that normally exists between his anxiety and his obesity, and he makes it worse, overreaching to make it better.

At nine that evening, with the restaurant empty, save for the Walk, Lucas stood at his seat, Luther Wood piping him to his feet with a ripple on his recorder. "I do intend to walk tomorrow," Lucas said. He was inexplicably defiant, as though an inner voice had called upon him to answer whether any fears about his health could force him to ride another day.

There was an embarrassing pause, since no one at the table had asked the question. Dorene and June looked as though they might applaud, then merely smiled after an exchange of uneasy looks among the others. Disappointment and determination competed for control of Lucas's expression, but both passed in an instant. Lucas lifted his hand toward Molly. "Ask her," he said, chuckling with the confidence of advance information.

At the center of attention, Molly stared into her coffee cup, smoking her nightly cigarette. Her bind seemed to Snyder to allow no escape; she could hardly pronounce her own husband unfit without also proclaiming him compulsive and self-destructive.

"I've had a look at Sam tonight," she said. "Whatever was happening this morning isn't now. The redness seems almost gone. I know Sam might fake it, but his leg wouldn't. Certainly the inflammation is down, and he says it no longer hurts."

"It was the ice," Lucas said, "thanks to Dr. Herndon."

"Are you sure?" Dunne asked.

"Why not ride one more day?" Rachel asked.

"We'll be in Hagerstown tomorrow," Herndon said.

"We need you in Washington," June said.

Lucas listened, head down as though looking for a speck on his shirt. He rocked forward and back several times, and once glanced at Snyder's open notebook. Snyder smiled up at him, and felt unaccountably depressed. He would have liked to join in the walkers' appeal.

"I'm grateful," Lucas said, "but as a personal matter, I think you'll agree that a decision whether to walk or ride tomorrow is mine to make. And the decision to walk has nothing to do with whether the Walk needs me tomorrow, or anytime. It does not. In fact, one survivor of this Walk is all we need—someone to carry our names to the White House. I'll go even farther. We don't need any survivors, so long as Ishmael here tells the tale. We're more than a walk now. We're Jack's story of a walk—so why I am walking tomorrow? It's to show that, for the long run, we have the character necessary to build a peace movement. That's our role, don't you see? And if we show it, Jack will tell it. That I myself feel well enough tonight to walk tomorrow makes walking a matter of character—so it's out of my hands, isn't it? Tomorrow must be a walking day for me."

Lucas sat down heavily. The walkers remained silent. Snyder wrote rapidly, Lucas's self-accounting and their non-response. As he wrote, he heard the tinkling of spoons against wineglasses and, looking up, found them applauding, accompanied by a reprise from Wood's recorder of the theme song from *The Bridge on the River Kwai,* which started Dorene laughing. It is not, Snyder realized, so much that they are pleased as that they love the ponderous, pompous man and can only support him when, as now, they can do nothing to stop him. And while some still laughed, others began to sing "We Shall Overcome," which started Sylvia Vecchio crying.

Then they took one another's hands around the table, June and Rachel taking Snyder's hands, to repeat "We Shall Overcome," still more seriously. Snyder sang, too, his participation receiving prompt criticism from the internal monitor of his life, caveat emptor, so to speak, to which he protested, you can't help getting involved with people who are so goddamned helpless.

On the final note, Snyder finished off a glass of Chianti. It's only later, he told himself, that you must discount yourself and leave out the part about your story as part of their story. Of such is the form, knowing that you are leaving out part of the truth.

4

During the night, the weather broke. A storm front moved down over the mountains, fog rose up from the valley virtually to the foundations of the Fairview Inn, and a soft rain began at dawn. At six-thirty, in a gray drizzle, the truck was loaded from the front steps. Lucas supervised, back to normal, fretting over rain gear, logistics, time and mileage, but carrying and lifting more as though the walkers required additional proof of his wellness. He signaled the kind of day he would make it by changing the order of the first hour. He was leading off and Arley Broyle would drive Herndon to Hagerstown to arrange the Walk's Saturday-night meal and Sunday-morning meeting with the Society of Friends. The truck led them to the highway and, within seconds, gave them the strange experience of seeing Broyle and Herndon abruptly vanish in the fog. Lucas hoisted the lead sign, and seemed to touch off a cloudburst. Rain pelted the line of walkers. Bringing up the rear, Snyder was soon wet and miserable, an umbrella notwithstanding. He wondered who was the bigger fool, Lucas out front with the lead sign or himself, working at all on such a day. Where is it written?

Heavy traffic and minimum visibility increased the usual risks of walking two-lane highways. For safety's sake, once inside the fog, they left the shoulder and crossed the drainage ditch to a slight ridge of tall grass and shale. Their feet slipped and their ankles bent. It was like walking on ice skates. They passed a Maryland state patrol car waiting out the fog. The officer leaned out of his window and gave each a wave. "Don't get lost," he said to Snyder. Snyder laughed. He could not see Lucas forty yards ahead and half expected to come across him tumbled in a ditch.

For the second hour, the lead sign went to Dunne, but Lucas walked ahead of it anyway. He took it back for the third hour, as though he owned it. The rain stopped and the fog turned to a warm mist. Arley Broyle collected their rain gear. Everyone was ripe with sweat.

Toward noon, the sun appeared, working behind low clouds like white gold. They picnicked off the back of the truck below the town of Clear Spring. Then, as they readied themselves again, the clouds parted, revealing Fairview Mountain once more, and summer returned. Snyder saw Lucas holding on to the lead sign, apparently reserving it for the next hour, to be his fourth carry in five hours on the day. That, gentlemen, is zeal oozing from Sam's pores, Snyder was thinking. He knew that Lucas could not feel less discomfort than his own in damp clothes and sodden shoes. And he could guess that Lucas's obsession with the lead sign was a torture after three days of inaction. Why let him go on with it? Snyder was verging on a suggestion to Molly that someone else should take a turn, when Molly herself put an arm around Lucas, laughed at something Lucas said, and carried off the lead sign for herself.

Midafternoon, the weather warm and muggy-bright, they came down on easier terrain into a suburb of Hagerstown called Cedar Lawn. The lead sign had passed to Herndon. They walked slowly and carefully along a crowded main street among many who were curious and a few who smiled. Then Arley Broyle magically appeared on foot to guide them into the vast parking lot of an A & P supermarket jammed with Saturday shoppers. Broyle's magic had also opened a convenient space for the truck beside a pedestrian island near the highway. The walkers could rest sitting on the curb in the partial shade of the truck.

Dorene and Sylvia took a stack of WISE leaflets into the supermarket. The other walkers lounged quietly, drinking Coke and staring back at passing shoppers, not one of whom had yet dared speak to any one of them—fat man wearing a green eyeshade, beautiful girl under a white umbrella, spindly boy playing a recorder, and the like. The suburban peace movement needs work, Sam, Snyder was thinking. Character is not enough.

"The leg, how's it?" Dunne asked Lucas.

"Okay, I guess," Lucas said.

"Have you looked?"

"He was just going to," Molly said.

There had been no warning that Lucas might be in trouble again. Yet, hearing Dunne's question, no one seemed surprised. Obediently, Lucas rolled up his left trouser leg. As he rolled higher, the task apparently became more delicate. He stopped below the knee. Molly turned the leg slightly, showing a pink area on the calf now almost as big as a man's hand. Inflamed streaks extended behind the knee and below the calf muscle. The blue-red center was darker than before, the skin stretched tighter over the puffed veins. Molly covered the area with her palm. She motioned Herndon to kneel beside her. Herndon probed the pinkness with his fingertips.

"Don't," Lucas said.

"Has it been hurting?" Molly asked. "It's hot again."

"I take the Fifth."

"No lies, Sam."

Lucas glanced mildly at Molly. He had no fight. "We need the name of a doctor," he said.

"The Friends gave me a name this morning," Herndon said. "An internist, Dennis Malcolm, clinic on Virginia Avenue."

Lucas gave Herndon a little pat on the shoulder, as if to say he was grateful but not amazed, Herndon being Herndon.

"Thank you," he said.

Unassisted, Lucas got to his feet. "Damn, shit," he said as he straightened first one knee and then the other, both of which remained bandaged. Then he shrugged off a hand from Arley Broyle and lifted himself into the truck. "Molly's driving me, Arley," he said.

Snyder walked with Molly behind the truck to the driver's side. When she was behind the wheel, he closed the door for her. He had never seen her look so fiercely married.

She frowned. "Another casualty, eh, Jack?"

"He'll be okay."

"Can't fight a war without casualties, can we?"

"May I come with you?"

"Can you be denied?"

In barely ten minutes, they had pulled up at the Malcolm Clinic on Virginia Avenue. Its home was an ancient two-story clapboard building, renovated and painted white with green trim. Snyder jumped down from his seat atop the luggage and, as Molly went ahead, helped Lucas manage the sidewalk and three porch steps. Inside, they directly entered a small waiting room full of children and children's toys and comic books. Dr. Malcolm shared his building with a pediatrician. He did not appear; instead, a friendly nurse came for Lucas, alone.

"Somebody has to watch the truck," Lucas said.

"I will," Snyder said.

"And somebody has to wait for me."

"Fingers crossed, Sam," Molly said.

Lucas smiled, vaguely, as though at a fleeting memory. "Secret of a great leader," he said, "is give everyone something to do."

Snyder returned to the truck. He smoked and dozed and listened to the Beach Boys on the local rock station and tried not to make any assumptions. Once, for a few seconds, he crossed the index and middle fingers of both hands. Then he discovered Lucas's log and the Walk's road maps under Arley Broyle's raincoat on the shelf behind the bench seat. He occupied himself with a note listing the schedule of the Walk's final ten days:

"June 25–29, U.S. 40, Hagerstown to Baltimore, crossing U.S. 29 about ten miles east of Baltimore, back to U.S. 29 later. It runs south, thirty miles to Washington.

"June 30–July 1, Baltimore, guest of Johns Hopkins University Summer '66 Peace Council, day of 'peace action,' day of rest.

"July 2–3, return to intersection of U.S. 40–U.S. 29, two days'
walk to Washington.

"July 4, petition White House."

With Lucas sick, Snyder knew, the notes themselves were assumptions, at best.

At 6 P.M., he was awakened, disoriented, by a distant "Hey!"
Malcolm's nurse was waving from the front door. Had he missed
something? Had the others reached the Friends? He scrambled up
the walk and through the waiting room, following the nurse into a
small office. An air-conditioning unit throbbed in the only window.
Molly was alone on a two-seat vinyl couch in front of a cluttered
walnut desk. "Doctor's coming, Jack," she said, and indicated a
plaque on the wall. "He's a Harvard man."

Dr. Malcolm entered through a pocket door behind the desk. As
the door slid shut, Snyder caught a glimpse of Lucas, eyes closed but
apparently not asleep, perched on a high stool and stripped to his
skivvies. An elastic bandage wrapped his left leg from knee to ankle.
The doctor shook hands with Molly, then Snyder. He was a sapling-
thin, gray-cold man in his fifties, wearing a white coat and the manda-
tory stethoscope. At his desk, he opened a drawer and fished for
cigarettes.

"Mr. Lucas is meditating, I believe," he said.

"Is he all right?" Molly asked.

"Yes, of course. I wanted to talk to you first, anyway. Am I correct
about your name?"

"Hamilton, yes, but I am Mrs. Lucas. Mr. Snyder is not a relative,
but a friend-journalist. We're always on the record with him."

"Mr. Lucas told me. I understand I may speak freely."

Snyder placed his notebook in his lap.

Dr. Malcolm sighed and looked down at his notes.

"Well, I'm sorry, it is something, not nothing. Mr. Lucas is suffering one of the many ailments of obesity. He is obese, in his bare feet,
two hundred sixty-eight pounds."

Molly grinned sheepishly. "I'd forgotten," she said.

"And obesity has given him hellish swollen veins, 'varicose'
veins."

"I know."

"And when stressed, those veins, or 'phlebo,' are susceptible to inflammation, 'itis,' hence 'phlebitis.' More severe stress, namely, the contusion from his fall, will cause a clot, 'thrombus,' in the vein. Thus 'thrombophlebitis' names the problem Mr. Lucas has today. Is it life-threatening? Not now. But, perhaps, yes, should the clot move to the heart or lung. Treatment? Absolutely. Bed rest, anticoagulants, blood thinners, hot packs—for starters."

"We did ice," Molly said. "It made the spot go away."

"I can hardly believe the risk he's taken in the past few days. But now we need heat for circulation."

"How long?"

"Best case? Two to three weeks of hospital care, another month of rest, three months on anticoagulants, then back to the hospital to have some of those veins stripped out."

"Oh, my—socks!"

"Mr. Lucas said pretty much the same thing."

"Then what did he say?"

"Your husband is a realist."

"Since when?"

"I mean, he understands the situation. He must go to the hospital, ours or yours. The possibility of a miracle makes him want to think about staying here in Hagerstown. He's a religious man, I know. But the thing about a miracle is its impossibility. And its otherness. It always happens to the other fellow. He wants you to think it over before he sees you. Hagerstown or Chicago? The miracle or Doc Malcolm? He says he knows there are daily flights to Chicago from Washington until after midnight. The drive to Washington National is two hours. If he were my relative, then we'd both be practical, and I would have him back home with his regular doctor at his favorite hospital tonight in time for the *Late Late Show*."

"Flying is not a risk?"

"Not risk-free, since a loss of cabin pressure might add stress. But the benefit of getting him home right away is the better bet to me. I've wrapped the leg. I've given him a cane. He's mobile."

"So let's look at the wounded man," Molly said. "He knows he has my proxy."

Dr. Malcolm tapped on the pocket door. After a moment, Lucas appeared, wearing his trousers and shirt, but no shoes. His face hung like a melted mask. He limped on the doctor's cane. Snyder gave up his place beside Molly, and Lucas sat down, draping his left leg over Molly's lap and onto the arm of the couch.

"What a mess, yes, Jack?" he said dourly. "Doctor says the leg must be elevated. Now, he knows you can't walk with an elevated leg. Only one thing an elevated leg is good for, and this is the wrong leg."

Molly grinned.

"The best-laid schemes," Snyder said.

Lucas's spirit flagged. "And we never know the purpose of a damn thing," he said, "just that there's a purpose."

"Do we go home, Sam?" Molly asked. "Say yes."

Lucas nodded bleakly. "We've lost so many people," he said. "How will that read, Jack?"

Snyder hesitated. He did not want Lucas's morale on his conscience. "Sam," he said, "certain cheeses get better as they get worse."

Lucas smiled, then seemed unhappier than ever.

"Frankly, it's a success story I want. The lost patrol with no survivors is not going to build a movement any time soon. Understand?"

"Nine walkers left is a story, Sam."

"Assuming nine last. Herndon is key, if he's willing. They'd follow him, and he's a member of WISE. Rachel's a member, too, but Frank Dunne would never accept a woman in charge."

Molly said, "You can't ask Reed, Sam—he'd have no choice."

"I wouldn't ask him," Lucas said wearily. "The others must. And Reed knows it's coming. He's the only one who thought to find Dr. Malcolm—you think, Jack?"

"I think he hopes you'll spare him. And there's always Frank Dunne on deck."

"But that means Reed won't refuse. He'll be all right if he's careful. I feel like we're plotting against him."

"It's the best we can do," Molly said.

"Maybe I should stay—ride in the truck."

"No, Sam," Molly said firmly. "Chicago."

By seven, between them, Molly and Snyder had arranged everything on Dr. Malcolm's phones: a late flight from Washington National, a large car at Chicago O'Hare, a semi-private room at South Side General Hospital, and a specialist on call. Then Molly called the

Friends' meeting house to explain the situation to Herndon for the Walk. Lucas and she were passing by to unload the truck, say so long, and exchange Snyder for Arley Broyle so that Broyle could bring the truck back from Washington that night. Snyder noted that she had said nothing about choosing a new leader for the Walk.

The meeting house was a long, low red-brick bungalow on a quiet street of old homes with deep lawns not far from the clinic. The truck turned into the street at dusk and Snyder saw the walkers waiting at the curb. Up a long walk at the door stood a man and two women, aproned members of the inevitable dinner committee, watching. As the truck braked to a stop, Snyder swung down on the street side to help Molly debark. They rounded the hood together. Lucas was staying in the cab with the window open and, for a moment, sat still, staring straight ahead, as though unable to look out. The walkers took their cue from Lucas, waiting cautiously.

Lucas turned toward the group, deadpan. He said, "It looks like I miss dinner." A friendly moan arose and, as they converged on him, he reached out his hand to touch them all. Dorene and June climbed the running board to kiss him. The others shook his hand, questioned him, and called to him for a speech. Lucas wept and laughed. He turned away to blow his nose and then turned back, with the Walk log in his hand, held up like the grail. The Walk's processes were all there, the schedules, contacts, expense records, lists, and daily reports, so well organized that anyone could have followed them and continued managing the Walk's affairs. Lucas turned to the back page, on which, as everyone knew, were the names of all those who had walked a day and spent a night with the Walk and were to be listed on the final version of the Walk petition. The walkers stood almost at attention.

"Reed Herndon, Amelia Pendergraft, Sylvia Vecchio, Dorene Quink, Luther Wood, June Matsushida, Frank Dunne, Rachel Abraham, and Arley Broyle," Lucas said, reading slowly as he picked out the survivors. "And Jack Snyder. All present and accounted for." He looked over the faces below him. "That's the list of my best friends. And moments ago, I was asking myself what do I say to them in two minutes when I have to leave in a hurry, and Jack Snyder is here getting it all down for posterity."

"No hurry, Sam," Dunne said, sentimentally.

"Well, yes, Frank, some hurry. Anyway, I'm not a very original man, so I have remembered something Gandhi said. 'The true thing for any human being on earth is not justice based on violence but justice based on sacrifice of self.' Now that is something to get you all to Washington. And you can imagine, it makes me feel bad that I have to go home to Chicago to save myself. Some hero, eh? But not too bad. Or not bad for long, because I know you will go on and do that true thing and that makes me feel fine."

Lucas paused, and scanned the walkers' tanned and somber faces.

"That's almost it," he continued. "Only two housekeeping items. One, you will have to choose a leader. I suppose I have the authority to choose, but since I would follow any of you, you must choose. And, second, you will have to decide individually and together about civil disobedience. I cannot tell you to lie down in the street unless I am there to lie down with you. But I know you will do what you feel you must do and each will understand the other. In the meantime, watch out for the cars—especially you, Jack!"

The walkers laughed and applauded, but not long and with little pleasure. Their smiles faded and eyes filled.

"Now, I think that's all," Lucas said. "Free night tonight—Quaker meeting tomorrow morning, and fourteen miles to Myersville, all downhill."

Lucas leaned from the window and handed the papers to Herndon.

"When is dinner, by the way?" he asked.

"Half hour. Showers after."

"Sorry, we can't wait. Ha-ha."

The walkers crowded in on Lucas once more. Lucas shook hands with the men, and the women kissed him. When Snyder came forward, Lucas shook his hand and held on. Lucas was crying just enough to wet the laugh lines at the corners of his bloodshot eyes.

"Okay, Jack?"

Snyder nodded. "Take good care of yourself," he replied. He hoped Lucas knew that he liked him and that he was sorry to see him go.

Molly said her goodbyes with an embrace for every walker, but a handshake and a kiss on the cheek for Snyder, to the end respecting his remove from the others. At eight-fifteen, she returned to the driver's seat, worried about the time. Broyle and Wood unloaded the Walk's luggage. Then Lucas remembered the kitty. He removed a wad of bills from his shirt pocket and counted $287 into Herndon's hand. Seconds later, with Broyle sitting up on a gas can in the rear, the truck pulled away. Broyle waved and the walkers waved back. They stood on the curb amid their bags and duffels until the truck had turned into a cross street and the Friends' meeting house blocked their view. Rachel smiled at Snyder. He nodded in reply; yes, it was a touching exit.

Leaderless, they seemed momentarily immobilized. One group, Dunne, Wood, Dorene, and June, milled about on the meeting-house lawn like a foursome looking for a lost golf ball; Sylvia and Rachel remained with Snyder at the curb, as though the truck might be returning at any minute. Herndon, with the Walk's money and papers, stood alone on the front sidewalk, Amelia a step behind him, her look apprehensive. Then slowly, as if by instinct, there was movement to form a circle around Herndon.

"Everyone wants you," Wood said.

"We've talked about it behind your back," Sylvia said, pleased by her own boldness.

"I know we want you," Dorene said, indicating herself and June.

Though Herndon had not agreed to serve, one more voice, Rachel or Dunne, would have accounted for a majority. Amelia inhaled audibly and clasped her hands at her chest. Snyder could see sweat glistening on her forehead. "Please," she said, "no."

Her glance darted furtively from Herndon to Dorene. Amelia seemed dismayed by herself. For Snyder, there followed at once the need to admit he hardly knew her, because, to be honest with himself, many of the others had interested him more. He could say she was probably the Walk's most placid member, a romantic rather than an activist, relating only to Herndon, affectionate toward him, but subdued even in that consuming relationship, which, Snyder thought, remained celibate as prescribed by Herndon's reticence as well as Lucas's word to Amelia's brother. She walked the distances, carried signs, passed leaflets, and submitted to the Walk's discipline regarding chores and room assignments, all without complaint. Herndon had taught her the Walk's rhetoric, and a look from him, not to mention a smile, on those occasions when she had cleanly fielded a question, turned the tan of her face to sunburn. Beyond this, she was part of the background, as, on any endurance story about a group so large, most people had to be—like all things, Snyder was thinking, subject to change.

Amelia inhaled again. "I know I'm not one of you," she said. "You're fighting against the war for all the good reasons and, if you see what I mean, I'm fighting against it just to be with you. That makes me selfish and a little silly, but I'm so serious now—please, choose someone else, anyone but Reed, so he won't have to go back to jail."

A faint smile from Herndon rewarded her and let her know, Snyder thought, that a case would have to be made.

Across the uneasy little circle, Dunne began cracking his knuckles. Then he pulled on the peak of his work cap as though getting ready to hammer some nails.

"Reed, can we talk it out?" he asked.

"I want to."

"Well, are you available?"

"If you want a leader who won't do civil disobedience, yes."

"So you are available?"

Herndon looked down at Sam Lucas's legacy, the Walk papers and the money. "Yes," he said, "if you understand my limits. This is not news to any of you, or to Jack Snyder, or to those in prison who sacrificed a whole lot more than I did. For me, my life is about prison and freedom, with my conscience in between. When they had me in the joint, I could have carried on my protest—fasted, refused, fought back in a thousand ways, but I did not—you know this and I'm ashamed to repeat it. I don't have to go into all the gory details. Just be sure—listen, I worked the system, saved up Brownie points, racked up all the good time I could get, and got out in about half the time, about half free. You understand? I'll never go back, Frank, but I've come this far on the Walk to prove they can't say they made me completely afraid. You understand? We are here, ten days to go, and you want me to lead, and I'm saying, okay, but only up to my limit. That is, no more jail. Knowing that, you may not want to follow."

Rachel said, evenly, "No one is asking you to do more than you can do."

"But it may not be enough for Frank," Herndon said. "I want to be clear with Frank."

Dunne removed his union cap and wiped the inner brim with a handkerchief. There was a white stripe on his forehead, above his deep tan and below the hairline.

"I'm going to answer with a question from left field," he said. "Would this walk be different without Jack Snyder? I mean, publicity is what we're all about. We're fighting against a war, and Jack's our secret weapon. You know what I'm saying? I come from a generation who lost out to Senator Joe McCarthy in the newspapers ten-twelve-fifteen years ago. The least I can do is name the game for the next generation. The game is publicity, Reed, and the issue now is what makes the best story for our cause. We've lost Sam and Molly. That's a pain and a sadness. But, Reed, you may be an opportunity for us—the Walk may be a better story if our new leader is a draft resister who has come from jail to oppose this war a second time. In the end, who cares whether he will or won't go back to jail again? He's taken some heavy risks. I'm doing civil disobedience, Reed, and all I want you to do is lead me to that point. Please."

Herndon grimaced, then nodded several times. He took Amelia's hand.

"All right," he said.

Pertly, the victor popped his cap back on his head.

"Move the question," Dunne said. "All in favor?"

There was a chorus of aye-sayers around Herndon, only lacking, Snyder noted, Amelia's contralto. Dunne was then first to step across the circle to shake Herndon's hand. Snyder felt used. Dunne persuades Herndon with the promise of your story, he was thinking, and Herndon takes the risks of higher visibility for the sake of a story you have yet to write. Herndon should know stories can die.

"Well, Jack," Herndon said, "now you're my only worry."

Snyder shook hands with Herndon as they turned toward the meeting house for dinner. Herndon looked older in the twilight, already burdened by his responsibility.

"Don't worry about me," Snyder said.

"I didn't want you to write that I wouldn't take the lead."

"I know."

"You're upset, Jack."

"Hell, yes, I'm upset. I'm not supposed to make a difference on a story, until I write it."

"You do, though. You have to accept that."

"Where did you get that idea!" Snyder exclaimed.

At 7 A.M., Arley Broyle woke Snyder on his cot at the meeting house. Lucas and Molly had caught the Chicago plane. Now Broyle wanted Snyder to be first to see the front page of the early Sunday edition of the Washington *Post*. There was a telescopic photo of scores of people fleeing from club-swinging policemen and clouds of tear gas. The caption said it showed Saturday's consequences for non-violent demonstrators on the Meredith march near Jackson, Mississippi.

At eight, Snyder called Selby at home to check through Ferris, Esther, and any other staff member for the names of Kendall, Schumacher, and Corrigan on Mississippi's casualty list. When he had hung up, he realized how like Erlanger she was. On the road, you are on the road. There is no interest in the progress of your story or even your health. You are a true professional, expected to bring home the bacon. So long, Jack.

HERNDON

SEVENTEEN
Command and Control

I

Without Moses, they continued on toward Canaan. After the Quaker Sunday meeting, Herndon had asked Arley Broyle to ferry them back west about two miles to a diner on U.S. 40 at the western edge of Hagerstown. It was Saturday's turnoff spot. One trip returned them all—three walkers beside Broyle crowded into the cab and five plus Snyder on top of the luggage in the rear. It also enabled Herndon, as Joshua, to reassert the supreme law of the Walk: thou shalt not skip a step.

Outside the diner at noon, as the sun peaked and melted asphalt, they assembled on the exit drive for the scheduled distance, seventeen miles to the village of Myersville. Broyle unloaded June's flag and the usual signs—the lead to Herndon, the trident to Dunne, and REMEMBER NORMAN MORRISON to Rachel. Then he climbed into the truck to drive Herndon to Myersville in the first hour. Snyder was wondering why Herndon had accepted the lead sign; now it became clear. As the new head of a group virtually without hierarchy, Herndon needed someone to fill his own former position as heir presumptive and sometime surrogate leader. The power of patronage came with his new office. He expressed it by offering the sign to Rachel. "You be exec, Ray," he said. Rachel passed REMEMBER NORMAN MORRISON to Luther Wood and took the lead sign—and, as no one seemed to object, accepted her promotion to second-in-command.

Frank Dunne was not ready just yet to start walking. Snyder saw him directly behind Herndon with the trident. Dunne weighed the sign like a hitter testing a new baseball bat, his look benighted as he seemed to consider its bulk. The muscles in his forearms strained against his oak-colored skin. Herndon turned to him.

"All set, Frank?"

"Sign's heavy."

"At least the mountains are behind us."

Dunne checked his swing. "Less walkers," he said, "with the same number of Walk signs, makes more work for everyone."

"Yes?"

"You could ask Arley to carry signs."

Herndon glanced toward Broyle, who was just then leaning from the truck cab. "Arley just drives," Herndon said.

"Make it easier on the women."

"He drives," Herndon insisted.

"Any of us drives," Dunne said.

"I don't want it easier," Sylvia said.

"Speak for yourself, Frank," Dorene said.

"You forget, dear Dunnski," Rachel said. "It's Arley's truck."

Snyder marked the faces of the key players: Broyle's squeezed tight, pinched between outrage and despair; Dunne's bemused and mocking; Herndon's somber, humorless, responsible.

"Let's leave it to Arley," Herndon said.

Broyle called out eagerly. "I'm the driver. You know that, Reed."

"Fine with me," Herndon said. "Fine with you, Frank?"

"No," Dunne said, "but it was only a suggestion."

Dunne seemed undefeated. Behind Herndon's glasses, there was a momentary flicker of anger that Snyder saw. Or thought he saw. Then Herndon joined Broyle and they drove off for Myersville.

In another minute, the walkers took to the highway, Dunne in the rear carrying the trident, with Snyder beside him.

"What did that mean?" Snyder asked.

"Nothing," Dunne replied. "A little test for the new management, is all."

"Arley's feelings got hurt."

"He'll live."

"What's the point?"

"I'll let you know."

"Are you sore about Rachel?"

"Definitely not."

"So?"

"So Reed's got the Walk in his hands."

"You didn't oppose that."

"Off the record?"

"Okay."

"Okay. I can tell you, Jack, I've been around idealists a long time. They've one great weakness—they don't understand about giving orders. Down the road, something has to make Reed lead this walk to a proper ending. Signs and petitions are not enough."

"Not so bad—"

"We're past that phase in this movement. Reed's got to see to it that every last mother's child among us gets down on the pavement at the White House and goes to jail."

"He won't unless he does it himself."

"You can't be sure."

"He won't go back to jail."

"I don't wish that, not for a minute. But he can't be neutral on civil disobedience for the Walk. It won't happen if he is."

"That's tricky, Frank."

"Funny word, tricky. Still off the record?"

"Until you say otherwise."

"I'm going to fix it somehow. It'll make your story."

"I'm getting a story. Can't you tell?"

Dunne laughed. "That Reed, he is the story, man," he said.

Snyder didn't laugh. He concentrated on memory, to be able to write up Dunne's conversation later, not to publish, but not to forget, either.

The Walk reached Myersville at twilight. Two neighboring households of Jehovah's Witnesses took them in, men in one house, women in the other. About nine, under a string of Christmas lights in the yard between, there was a reception, thirty guests in Sunday clothes. There was no alcohol, and no one smoked. Only Herndon spoke for the Walk. Snyder took one note: "In prison, he tells them, he admired, above all, a Witness, sentenced for draft resistance, who won parole after fasting for eighteen days in solitary confinement." He doubted that Dunne realized how angry Herndon was with himself, how tricky to push him.

Later, Snyder saw Rachel talking to one of the hosts. He caught her eye and they met at the edge of the yard in front of a long, narrow greenhouse. The Christmas lights reflected against the glass like multicolored stars.

"I need a cigarette," he said.

"I can help you," she said.

They walked the length of the greenhouse on a flagstone path. In the faint light at the rear, they found a bench half occupied by a box of empty flowerpots. Snyder set the box on the ground and they sat down. Rachel gave him her last cigarette. They shared it.

"This is how I started smoking," Snyder said. "At night, in the backyard, my mother's Chesterfields. I was nine."

"My secret place was the attic—Lucky Strikes and Charlotte Brontë."

"You've saved my life."

"Is that all?"

"This cigarette? No, there's Frank Dunne."

"Frank's not very subtle, is he? He has his own agenda."

"He wants to finish with a bang, period."

"And cares less about Reed, yes."

Snyder sat forward, elbows on his knees, and entered his journalistic mode.

"What will you do about it, Ray?" he asked. "You're the exec."

"Is that an official question?"

"A shot in the dark, so to speak."

"Do you know something I don't know?"

"It depends upon what you don't know, but I don't think I do."

"Would you tell me if there was more?"

"It depends."

"What rule is that, my friend?"

"Comes under the section on Fine Distinctions. Involvement is okay, but not interference. I can be your friend, but not your lover. In this case, Frank Dunne spoke to me off the record. That's privileged, but, in fact, you know what he said, so I can ask you about it."

"You are a man possessed."

"What's the answer?"

"I don't know, Jack. The answer about Reed is Reed—he's in charge. I wish Sam were here."

"Life would be easier."

"A lot easier."

"It would also be easier if I weren't here."

In the near-darkness, Snyder sensed Rachel turning toward him. He turned, too. Her eyes caught a point of light refracted through a greenhouse window.

Rachel said, "Frankly, I wouldn't care for that solution."

Snyder smiled, but wanted to persist. "Without me," he said, "Reed could opt out at any time, and no one would be the wiser."

"That would never be easy for Reed, the way things stand. But the reality—you're the realist, remember?—the reality is, you're here."

"My role, Ray—I never said I always enjoy playing it."

Snyder heard a footstep on the flagstone beside the greenhouse. Rachel stood up. Hastily, Snyder ground out the stub of their forbidden cigarette.

"I'd give a lot," Rachel said, "after the Walk, of course, to see you playing yourself for more than one evening."

"Are you angry?"

"I'm not angry. Just name the place—New York City. But not Click's Bar. Somewhere, just for curiosity, of course—the real Jacob Charles Snyder."

"I'm always on assignment, Ray."

"Yes, but not this assignment, dear man. That's my point."

"So, maybe we can arrange it."

Snyder took Rachel's hand as Arley Broyle rounded the greenhouse corner.

Giggling, Broyle said, "Hey, you guys, people are saying good night."

2

For two more days, they walked. The distances were mostly downhill, as Sam Lucas had predicted, and seemed incidental to Snyder, given the adventure that lay just ahead. He made few notes, with a promise to himself to get back to work in Baltimore.

Monday had passed moving quietly into the city of Frederick, once around the courthouse square, and out again to a Boy Scout campsite a few miles east. "Disappointing day," Snyder wrote. "Teatime appearance before the local League of Women Voters missed by a scheduling error, not Herndon's, but Lucas's first. According to the chairman of the League, Walk has arrived three days early! Also, a humbling day. Arley B. relayed a radio report: 15,000 people—fifteen thousand!—for the Meredith rally yesterday in Jackson. Dorene Q. asks, 'What will they say about us, all nine of us?' Reed H. answers, 'Numbers aren't everything,' and the way he says it makes them laugh a little. They laugh because numbers do count and they fear the indifference of the press."

And Tuesday had brought them to the Redwing Motel in the town of Lisbon. "A dump," Snyder wrote, "featuring noisy plumbing and torn window screens, but phones work. Neither New York *Times* (Selby) nor Ferris reported Corrigan, Kendall, or Schumacher injured at Jackson. Chicago hospital (Molly) confirmed Dr. Malcolm's diagnosis. Poor Sam Lucas, pain but no danger, minor surgery next week to remove a small piece of the offending vein. It's June 28, 1966—the Walk's last week began today, but no one celebrated. Herndon turns out to be a hard-nosed boss whose demeanor simply discourages high jinks. Lucas, for sure, would have sprung for wine one more time."

Then it was Wednesday, at the end of the second hour, waiting for Herndon and Broyle to return from Johns Hopkins University. The walkers had stopped east of Lisbon below U.S. 40 on Route 144. The sun was high and bright. Beside them was a slow-rising meadow filled with clover, with a stand of poplars beyond. Amelia volunteered to remain by the road as lookout for the truck. Snyder decided to stay with her as the others climbed over the barbed-wire fence to rest in the shade of the poplars. With Amelia, he sat on a grassy embankment, high enough to avoid gravel flying from the road, and idled himself weaving a chain of clovers. The sun felt hot on his neck, so he turned his hat brim down all around.

"You never got your hat, Amelia," Snyder said.

"I'm tanning instead."

"Yes, you look healthy."

"I like walking in the sun without a hat."

"You've come to the right place, lady."

"I told Reed—I said I think we ought to go walking sometime for its own sake, in Nova Scotia, or someplace like that, you know?"

"I may never walk anywhere again."

"No, I mean it. Reed told me he'd dreamed some nights in prison that he was walking in a forest and I told him I'd had the same dream, that the forest is in Nova Scotia."

"When were you there?"

"Only in freshman geography. Well, no, Reed said, his forest is not in Nova Scotia. It is someplace else. Not exactly in any country, just a certain place, he said, where you are alone, but not alone, what with green life all around and birds, thousands of birds, he said, but no animals to speak of. There were animals in my forest, harmless ones, squirrels and deer and the like. But I know we'd both like Nova Scotia. Have you ever been there?"

"Yes, on a farm story, years ago."

"Did you like it?"

"Very much."

Snyder presented his clover chain to Amelia. She reminded him of Eve. Hoot, Daddy!

"Thank you," Amelia said, and looped the chain twice around her wrist, forming a bracelet. "You know, Jack, you've been awfully nice about me."

"I have?"

"I mean, no questions about the war in Vietnam to show my ignorance, or about Reed and me, either. When I realized you were a reporter, I was afraid of your questions. I mean, I'm not an expert on anything, especially the war. And about us, Reed and me, well, Heinz always used to say that reporters only care about gossip, and you haven't asked, not that there is any. There isn't, but I was afraid you'd ask. Or make it up. My brother would be terribly hurt by any —you know—you know?"

"I like to read gossip. Most of us are like that. You read about the movie stars, don't you?"

"Oh, yes."

"Novels?"

"Yes, I read novels."

"The best novels are gossip."

"You know what I mean, Jack."

"A few times, when an article about a personality won't make sense without gossip, I've written it, but I think we can get along without it this time."

Amelia grinned and seemed to relax toward him.

"Reed assured me about you," she said. "Besides, there just isn't any gossip about us."

"But you did come along on the Walk all of a sudden."

"Want to know why?"

"Sure."

"I don't know what you'll think. So. Well, it was watching Reed speak on the pulpit, you know? My brother's pulpit! I mean to say, it was not listening to Reed—it was watching him. It was like he had an aura, not a real aura, because I don't believe in that, but an aura of—I told this to Heinz—it was grace, Jack, you know?"

"I think so."

"Heinz slapped me when I said that. Not hard. He's slapped me many times harder."

"I see."

"Do you see? About grace? It's a bit sacrilegious but, well, it's there. I can't explain about Reed even to myself. He has grace. I told him so. I told him I didn't know anything about the war, but I told him I'd come on the Walk if he'd ask me, just to be with him. No more than that. I knew my brother couldn't stop me, not really, just because people at home would talk—you know what I mean? He could always say I've gone away for a while, that's all. Do you know?"

"I do now."

"And Reed said—listen to what he said, Jack—he said, Amelia, you'd be a gift. You can imagine how that made me feel. Reed has grace and still, I'd be a gift! Oh, so, I wanted to come and still I was afraid actually to tell Heinz, so I told Mr. Mollenhoff—you remember that dear old man? And Mr. Mollenhoff told me he understood and he helped me. I needed help, too. Do you know, Jack, I've never, I mean never, been away from my brother in eight years, since I was eleven and our parents died. Heinz took care of me always. He took care of me—like a third parent. You could say that Reed's the first person who ever wanted me to take care of him, sort of. Do you see?"

"I understand."

"Everyone has to take care of someone, you know. Even Reed—especially Reed, after what he's been through. I guess that's my gift to him, all in that spirit, do you see that, too?"

Snyder nodded.

Amelia said, "I've been thinking about talking to you, Jack, because I wanted you to know that Reed hasn't done anything with me that he should be punished for in your magazine, or anything that would give God the idea that he should be sent back to prison, because he hasn't and I haven't done anything, except hold each other. There's nothing we've done that could upset anyone, not even my brother. Can you believe that, Jack? Let alone God."

"I'm sure it's true."

"It is true and I want God to hear me saying it to a reporter."

"You've said it, Amelia."

"Thank you."

"Does he talk about it, Amelia?"

"What?"

"Nova Scotia—I mean, how the Walk will end? Can you tell me that?"

"Only this, Jack. I know, I know he's not going back to prison."

"Yes, he's told me, too."

"Well, I really know it."

Snyder saw her lips tighten, as though willing her hope into life. He realized that she did not know for sure.

Moments later, the truck appeared on the horizon. Amelia leaped to the shoulder, her skirt billowing in a sudden wind, and signaled the truck with both hands upstretched—almost, Snyder thought, ecstatic.

"Meeting time," Herndon said, holding an armload of papers and new maps, enough for everyone.

He spread one map on the meadow grass beyond the fence and hunched over it as the walkers seated themselves before him. When they had found the Walk's position on their maps, Herndon began. "Here we are," he said, "on Route 144, about fifteen miles above U.S. 29. You see, there's U.S. 29 running south, thirty miles, maybe thirty-two, to Washington, entering the District of Columbia just below Silver Spring."

"Hallelujah!" Dorene cried.

"Amen, yes," Herndon said, all concentration. "Now, according to Sam's plan, we walk to U.S. 29 today, then we drive north the ten miles to Baltimore, then drive back to U.S. 29 on Saturday, and walk to Washington on Saturday and Sunday. You follow? That's so we've walked it all, Chicago to Washington."

"Walked it all, folks!" Wood exclaimed.

Herndon wasn't stopping. "In between," he said, "we're guests of the Peace Council on the campus of Johns Hopkins. Saturday, we camp out here, above Silver Spring, and Sunday night, July third, we make Washington, guests of a WISE member, here, he lives on Military Road, a lawyer named Milton Katz."

"Our lawyer?" Dunne asked.

"Yes, I called him," Herndon said. He did not look up. "We shape up our petition at his house on Sunday night. Then here, morning of July Fourth, we walk to the White House."

"Alone?" Rachel asked.

"I hope not—Katz expects some Washington peace groups. How many live bodies, who knows? He's arranging things for high noon, Sam's orders, a good time for television coverage when you want to get on the nightly news. And Katz will now be notifying the White House gate that we're coming to see the President."

Wood played ta-da on his recorder.

"LBJ gets my flag," June said.

"I do believe we've made it," Sylvia said.

Herndon allowed himself a smile for Sylvia. Lately, she had been troubled by the sun and wore zinc oxide ointment on her nose and forearms.

"Not quite," Herndon said. "We've got some decisions to make about Johns Hopkins. It's summer break. Campus is almost empty. No rally tonight. A planning committee of six to greet us is all. The Peace Council's big deal is tomorrow, a coalition demonstration against the war at the Baltimore regional office, Federal Civil Defense Commission. The coalition is something rounded up for summer protest—unions, local students, civil rights workers, the usual suspects. They want us to bring our signs and join them, beef up their ranks, picket through the lunch hour, make a minute for the local TV. No c.d.''

"No c.d.?'' Dunne asked with a sigh. "Boring.''

"No c.d.,'' Herndon said. "That's number one. Number two is Friday. They want to give us a picnic on the ocean at Slaughter Beach, Delaware. I think the second is kind of payola for the first. We can do the first or both, but I don't think the second without the first.''

"Oh, both!'' Broyle cheered.

Broyle's delight made the walkers laugh. Snyder grinned but, tied to his note taking, failed to catch the spirit. He was scribbling when Dorene reached over and tickled his ribs, then lost both pad and pen as June and Sylvia climbed over him. They rolled him over in the clover, sent his hat flying, and worked his sides until he roared.

"Tell us you love us, Snyder!'' Dorene cried.

"I love you! I love you!'' he shouted into their gales of laughter.

3

They were all day getting to Baltimore. It was after six when they reached the junction of Route 144 and U.S. 29. Then they crowded into the truck with Broyle and followed a stream of thickening traffic into the city. Blocks and blocks of tidy old row houses passed by and, after a questionable loop, downtown rose up around them. Snyder remembered two visits to Baltimore, one a long time ago, married, during Preakness week, the other on a *Harrington's* assignment in 1962 to interview the Colts' Johnny Unitas for "What Is a Quarterback?'' The city layout came back to him, the University on Charles Street near Thirty-third. At the loop, he now realized, Broyle had made a wrong turn. Snyder pounded on the truck roof and pointed Broyle north; a corrective U-turn followed, and they headed up East Baltimore Street.

They passed a bookshop advertising *Lady Chatterley's Lover* and *Fanny Hill;* and the Clover Burlesque; and the Two O'Clock Club, featuring "The Queen of Exotica,'' Blaze Starr. The hour was early for nighttown, but people were already cruising the block. At a stoplight, a Negro dude waved and Dunne handed him a leaflet over the tailgate. "All right," the dude said, "bring the war home," and flashed a V sign as they drove on.

After a while, they found Madison Street, and Madison put them on Charles, going north, with a lavender-and-orange sunset on their left, and suddenly the campus, dense with trees, bloomed ahead. They drove through the gates past a Georgian manor into the smaller of two adjacent quadrangles. Over the entrance to the central dormitory building hung a painted bed sheet: JHU SUMMER '66 PEACE COUNCIL in blue; WELCOME WISE WALK & REST YOUR FEET IN PEACE in red. And on the wide steps below, a double-edged scene: Snyder counted twenty-three students applauding them, a group larger than promised, but nothing to stop the heart. The Peace Council, he thought, might better have met the Walk with its six-man planning committee, as expected, than dramatize its inability between semesters to attract a larger crowd. Still, as Broyle repeatedly sounded his horn—da-da-da-dit—and the students, shouting hellos, surged toward the truck, Snyder felt, unmistakably, joy. He watched the walkers jump from the truck to merge with their well-wishers. One after another, they embraced the students and the students embraced the walkers. Snyder took the long step down from the tailgate into the arms of a tall girl wearing braces on her teeth. She kissed him on the mouth, twice. "Don't be a stranger!" she cried. Snyder embraced her, and let her know, for a moment, there was no strangeness between them.

That night, the Walk was staying on campus. After the welcome, they were left with the planning committee, two boys and three girls, led by the chairman of the Peace Council, a gangling, fair-haired, hawk-nosed undergraduate from Baltimore named Ezra Little. The committee moved them into a dormitory wing on the main floor where, for the first time since Chicago, privacy had no premium; there were eight more rooms than walkers. Herndon assigned one to each and set up two shifts for the showers. When they reassembled in the common room, most notable to Snyder was Rachel's hair, still damp from washing and tied back by a yellow scarf.

For dinner, they feasted on "Ma Little's" cold buffet, fried chicken, potato salad, fruit, and oatmeal cookies, all literally prepared by Ezra Little's mother, and Cokes from the resident machine. Then they stayed on, telling road stories to their new friends, until silenced at nine, in a tight half circle of chairs and floor spaces, for *Gunga Din* on television. Snyder relaxed on the floor and went to India with the others, pausing only to caution himself that he'd hardly made a note, three days in a row.

They were watching the part about the snakepit when the station interrupted with a news bulletin from Washington. Over a graphic news logo, a voice said, "From combined news sources, we have reliable unofficial reports that American bombers struck today for the first time at docks, fuel dumps, and railyards near Hanoi and Haiphong. If confirmed, the raids are seen here as a major escalation of the war in Vietnam. A White House announcement is expected by morning."

There were gasps and whispers and someone quietly said, "No." Then the movie resumed and Herndon turned off the television. A white light on the tube closed down to a pinpoint and went out, as though signaling a moment for complete silence.

Two insect-repelling bulbs in a ceiling fixture caught Snyder's attention. He found that he could stare into their yellow light without blinking. He closed his eyes. The scar under his mustache tingled as memory connected him to its source. Noiseless yellow lights flared up and flickered out on his inner screen, the way bomb bursts flash on and off at night, he was thinking, making yellow light on certain targets, and not white, as you might expect. "You lied, Mr. President," he said to himself, "and now you've lost it." By "it," he guessed he meant both faith and trust.

Sound and motion broke in on Snyder. One of the two boys on the planning committee with Ezra Little was standing, excusing himself, self-obligated to spread the word across the near-empty campus. The other boy, so red with rage that he seemed feverish, twice pounded a pillow in a pillow sham made of red, white, and blue stripes. And two of the three committee girls wept. Ezra Little put a comforting arm around the third girl. The walkers impressed Snyder. They had remained calm, almost professional, as though the latest betrayal in Vietnam had long since been discounted by experience. The thought struck Snyder that he himself might be altogether more innocent than they. He turned up a blank page in his notebook and wrote at the top: "Haiphong/Baltimore." As always, he liked to begin work with a clean slate.

Snyder asked, "Are you surprised, Reed?"

"Disgusted, but not surprised."

Dunne smiled. "Wouldn't you guess, Jack," he asked, "the closer we get to Washington, the wider they'd make the war?"

"Maybe they heard we were coming," Rachel said.

"I wish tomorrow were the Fourth," Dunne said. "There'd be a crowd at the White House."

Dorene banged her knee with a fist. "Why are they doing it?"

"Our side is losing, that's why," June said.

"You'd think they'd stop," Sylvia said.

Ezra Little turned toward Herndon. "They won't stop," he said. "It's our new national motto—'Escalation Forever.' They're putting it on all the coins."

Arley Broyle laughed.

"It makes you wonder what good *we* can do," Dorene said.

"We have to do more, I can tell you, to do any good at all," Dunne replied. "Two big marches last year, umpteen hundred teach-ins—"

"Remember Norman Morrison," Rachel said, answering Dunne.

"Remember! And now, draft-card burning, more marching, and see what happens? They bomb Hanoi. And what do we do? We show up at the White House in a few days with another petition, signed by a few nobodies."

"I'm somebody, Frank," Rachel said.

Dunne grinned, then reached a hand to pat the television tube.

"What counts, friends," he said, "is what shows up here. And the stuff in Jack Snyder's notebook. If our picture's not on TV the night of July Fourth—if we look sorry in *Harrington's* magazine—we've been irrelevant. We won't count. That's what bombing Hanoi means. The war's gotten beyond us."

"Hope—must have hope, Frank," Rachel said, cajoling him.

Ezra Little said carefully, "Now I suspect lots more demonstrations will end in jail. Like ours."

Herndon looked startled. "Say that again?" he asked.

"We talk about it all the time on the Peace Council, but no action. Now, after tonight, I think you'll see. There'll be some civil disobedience tomorrow."

"Hey! Hey!" Dunne exclaimed just above a whisper.

"We've discussed it, too," Herndon said.

"For tomorrow?" Little asked. "With us? We picket until one, then maybe we try to enter the building, or maybe we only try symbolically. That's the moment of truth."

"No, Washington only. We're set on Washington."

"No substitutions," Rachel said.

"Ezra's action may be a better shot," Dunne said, again in his diffident mood. "I mean, he's got some numbers."

"About fifty. It's why we need you."

"Beats us, my man, by a mile!"

Rachel jeered. "Just another suggestion, eh, Frank?"

"Listen, Ray," Dunne said. "I've got one creaking body for which I reserve the choice of disposal."

Rachel let her look dissolve into a too sweet smile, stinging Dunne a second time. "Frank-old-Frank," she said, "surely Ezra and our summer coalition friends will understand if you save your old bones for a few more days to Washington?"

Herndon nodded. "The Walk is to the White House," he said. "We decide what to do at the White House in Washington. That's the agreement."

"Did I say otherwise?"

Rachel made a fist. "Listen," she said coldly, "you make it damn hard for those who might want to decline civil disobedience when we get there."

"Hard? You're right," Dunne said. "I'm trying to do just that. I think we are coming to the end of the road for this country as well as this walk. I go back to World War II, a rifleman, no Audie Murphy, but I fought in a good war. I don't worship non-violence like you do. I can't. But I say now we've got to get into civil disobedience, not just for civil rights, but to change the system that's given us this war and the bombing of Haiphong and all that goes with it. I think of Joe Rice and Vachel. And Sam and Molly, and Nick Bergquist. Even George and Peter, if they hadn't run off with Ellroy. I think I know how they'd be feeling here tonight. Remember the black man downtown this afternoon? He said, 'Bring the war home.' He knows, Ray. He knows, Reed."

"You're off the mark, Frank," Herndon said.

"No, right on it."

"What do you gain if the system is violence and you change it with violence? What are you?"

"You're George Washington."

"No, you're just another system of violence."

"You're arguing, Reed. I'm talking facts."

Ezra Little became anxious. "We're still set for tomorrow?"

"All flags flying," Herndon said.

"I think I go to bed now," Dunne said. "I've upset enough people for one evening."

"Good night, Frank," Rachel said.

"Night, Ray dear," Dunne said.

"Have dreams," she said, "dreams of glory."

Dunne grinned. "Put it in the notebook, Jack—a low blow, but I'll sleep anyway."

With Dunne gone, Snyder tried to read the faces of Dorene, June, Sylvia, and Wood, those for whom he thought civil disobedience might have most appeal. They were the youngest and, except for Sylvia, who would always be a newcomer, they had been with the Walk from the start. Now they seemed subdued, perhaps embarrassed by Dunne's rough ways, even guilty, as though the burden of carrying the torch for, especially, Joe Rice and, less certainly, Sam Lucas and Molly Hamilton was too much for them at that moment. Dunne is right, Snyder was thinking, the outcome is in the leader's hands. And Herndon must know that to delay the decision as long as possible gives him the best chance to avoid a further split among them. That would explain his rueful stance now in front of the television, his back to the room, discouraging any more talk. At last, Herndon switched on *Gunga Din* at the moment Sam Jaffe began to blow his last bugle call. Perfect, Snyder thought.

Snyder felt a tap on his shoulder. It was Rachel from behind Ezra Little touching him with a rolled-up copy of the Baltimore *Sun*, attempting to say good night without disturbing the viewers. Snyder caught up with her in the dormitory corridor.

"Walk you home?" he asked. "I'm taking a poll for the *Sun*."

She sighed. "The end of *Gunga Din* is too tough for me."

Rachel's room was ten steps down the corridor. They stopped at her door. "I'd invite you in," she said, smiling, "but the place is a mess."

"Talk to me about Frank."

"I like you better when you're laughing."

"Say something funny."

" 'The place is a mess' was funny."

"Yes, it was. What do you make of Frank?"

"He doesn't confide in me, Jack."

"Speculate."

"You really want to talk? You buy the Cokes while I tidy up."

4

Rachel's room had no bedding, no rugs, and no curtains. There was a narrow bed and mattress, desk and chair, and two ancient floor lamps. A pennant from Duke University hung on the closet door. Rachel's sleeping bag lay rolled at the head of the bed, her duffel bag underneath, with a laundry bag beside it. When Snyder returned with the Cokes, Rachel was perched on the desk with her feet on the chair. She had removed the yellow scarf and was slowly brushing her hair. Snyder sat on the bed, notebook on his knee. Her brush strokes were lovely to watch.

"Of course, you're right," she said. "Frank wants and needs to be arrested."

"Do you think he's sincere?"

"I think he wants to look brave back home, sure, but yes. Look at the rest of us. Goodness is all we need. Why not Frank?"

"If he were a Communist, what would you say?"

"He might have his 'bring the war home' scenario, more repression here makes good propaganda over there. But then he wouldn't want a non-violent, ordinary, liberal, reformist, pacifist like St. Reed to be your hero, that's for sure. I think Frank's so inconsistent that he's straight, if you see what I mean."

"How does Sam know him?"

"What did Sam say?"

"I never asked Sam. Frank didn't seem all that important until now."

"Sam's known Frank maybe thirty years. They did the late thirties together. Sam would tell you Frank was as radical as the next socialist, maybe left of that, but not a member of the Party. Could he hide that? I doubt it, not through the McCarthy period. His union would know. Sam would know."

Rachel paused, switching her hairbrush from one hand to the other.

Writing, Snyder said, "I need a motive."

Rachel raised her fist to her chin. "A motive for Mr. Holmes, Watson," she said. "You're looking for a motive? I make the motive Frank's union. It's his only home, three or four wives later. The union is California liberal, but it's lost touch with the Beatles generation. I mean, the members eat lettuce, okay? I suspect Frank's union sent us one of its toughest, oldest, leatheriest sea dogs to polish up the political image among young recruits. With everybody working, they've got to get on moral issues, yes? Frank Dunne's got a real stake in that union. That's why Reed's conflict drives him over the edge. I don't know. You said speculate, so I'm speculating. If Sam Lucas were here, he'd tell you that he himself likes the word 'progressive' for his own politics, equality in freedom, that sort of thing —he'll use that if you corner him some night about something other than the damn war. And since you've asked, dear man, I'd place Frank Dunne in Sam's camp, minus God, plus the union, and driven quite nuts by the war. Any progressive would be, don't you see, because he's got to ask himself, in shock: what kind of people are we?"

"You're doing so well, Ray—"

"I like to listen to myself talk to you."

"What about Frank tomorrow?"

"My opinion? Frank can't do civil disobedience with Ezra Little. He'd miss Washington. How would he explain that to the union?"

Snyder raised his pen like a torch. "Unless he's so fired up, goodness and all, he wants the bird in his hand. What would he tell California should the Walk bomb in Washington?"

"I can't answer that."

"He's spoken to me about that, too."

"Saying what?"

"Saying off the record."

"Oh."

"Tends to put the fate of the Walk on TV and me."

Rachel slipped down from the desk to the chair.

"Can you tell Reed you've got your story no matter what happens?"

"He knows that."

"That he doesn't have to risk more than he's planned?"

"He knows it makes no difference to me."

"Only you must write it as it happens?"

"I have to."

"Reed's trouble is facts, isn't it?"

"I can't lie."

"That's the scary part. You've spooked all of us."

"Why, Ray?"

"Just because you're so good. We're afraid you're going to diminish us. We've all read your stuff, the way it reveals people. And we know all about images. Portray us as frustrated intellectuals, draft dodgers, and religious freaks who haven't got the courage of our convictions, and you ruin us. Portray us as rational citizens with facts and purpose and a certain valiance and *Harrington's* becomes the first mainstream publication to endorse us. You're big stuff, dear man."

"We don't endorse, Ray."

Rachel sat beside Snyder on the bed and purposefully closed his notebook. Snyder lit a cigarette.

"I'm sorry, Jack," she said. "I'm pressuring you."

"Not true."

"I keep wishing you were one of us."

"I worry that I am."

"Five more days, Jack, then we're all someone else."

Snyder turned to her. She's only half right, he was thinking—only *her* life will change next week. Rachel was studying the backs of her hands, her hair flowing over her shoulders. Snyder kissed her cheek. Then her lips. She returned the kiss. He felt her lips part, so that the empathy he had intended became a confusion of desire and restraint. Her hand touched his cheek. They kissed for a long moment. Then the cigarette between his fingers required attention.

"I'm about to burn myself," he said. He kissed her briefly and moved off the bed for the wastebasket.

"Are you all right?" she asked.

"No, but it's go-or-stay time."

"We have our understanding, don't we?"

"Yes, but the damn flesh is weak."

"I'll sit here. Do you want the local newspaper?"

"Yes, thank you, Ray. Good night."

5

Herndon looked up from his desk as Snyder passed by in the corridor. The light was on over the desk, so that Herndon could not make out Snyder's expression. Did Snyder want to come in or move on? Herndon lifted a tablet of foolscap with one hand and his pen with the other to show that he was writing a letter. Snyder waved his newspaper, and said, "See you in the morning." Herndon signed his name to the letter and reread it.

"Dear Mom: Sorry I haven't been writing these past few weeks, but so much has happened since Wheeling. We've lost a third of the Walk, including Sam Lucas himself, so here we are in Baltimore with only nine, counting Arley Broyle (the truck driver, remember?), plus J. Snyder from *Harrington's* mag. Moreover, the Walk has elected me to lead into Washington and I'm happy to do it, so long as I don't end up back in the joint. That exception, of course, creates a p.r. problem, which I'm trying to deal with as best I can. I don't want Snyder to write that prison beat me down, but I don't want to have to prove to him it didn't, either. So we're tiptoeing along here. Snyder understands I'm trying to do the right thing, like he is, if only we knew what it was. Just you rest assured, I'm not going back to L'worth. Love, as ever, Reedy."

EIGHTEEN
Right of Salvage

I

The yellow school bus chartered by the Peace Council came by for them and their signs at ten Thursday morning. Ezra Little and about forty students had boarded at an earlier rendezvous and now readily shared seats with the walkers. Snyder noticed Frank Dunne choosing to sit alone by the exit. Dunne stared out the open window at the brilliant blue day as though it was raining.

They drove slowly, south on Charles, west on Pratt past Babe Ruth's birthplace, beyond the old Mount Clare railroad station. Here, they were joined in train by three more buses and continued south again to a small wooded park that appeared abruptly at the end of a shopping street. Above them, off by itself on a hill in the park, they could see the Federal Civil Defense Commission building. It was all green glass and khaki-colored aluminum, two stories high and about fifty yards long, with an entrance plaza facing a broad lawn. There was a flagpole on the lawn taller than the building, its flag fluttering without much enthusiasm. As they moved closer, Snyder counted twenty-five Federal Security guards in blue uniforms and blue caps with black visors, some strolling on the lawn, others standing easily on the plaza with both batons and pistols holstered on their belts; four were posted in the shade against the double front doors. And scanning the crowded parking lot behind the building, he also picked out a gray Baltimore Police Department security van for transporting prisoners.

In a reserved space just behind the parking lot, the four buses debarked 120 demonstrators, many with identical new signs, STOP

THE BOMBING, and all dressed for a summer's outing. Two three-man television crews, two local newspaper reporters, and a wire service still photographer, each wearing a red plastic police card, moved amiably among them, asking a name here, filming a snippet there. They focused as one when Ezra Little mounted the front bumper of the Council bus and tooted a penny whistle for attention. Around his forehead, Little wore the words BOMBS AWAY in red on a white sweatband. He seemed to Snyder, who stood below him with the walkers, to be transformed by elevation; with the band above his hawk nose, the addition of loft gave him the face of an Indian, the look of a leader, and the immanence of self-confidence. All shyness had left him. Little, Snyder thought, was born for what he was then all about.

"This is no drill!" Little shouted. "Our non-violent demonstration against the bombing of Hanoi and Haiphong—consists of two hours' picket—at the prescribed distance of the flagpole to the doors! Then we will request rightful entry—entering this public building to continue our protest! Failing that, volunteers—volunteers to express our indignation by the only means left to us—passive resistance! We will not be moved! We will accept arrest!" Little paused.

"Overnight," Snyder wrote, "civil disobedience has become part of the day's program. The demonstrators shout yes, wave V signs and fists, and jiggle their signs."

"One more thing!" Little cried. "We have moral support today from Chicago! Some folks who've walked here all the way from Chicago—for peace in Vietnam! They are on their way to Washington to see the President—right here, by me, these nine people!"

An appreciative cheer swept over the Walk, Snyder realizing that Little's phrase "moral support" nicely exempted them from any pressure to volunteer.

"These marathon walkers will be leading a march on the White House at noon come July Fourth," Little said, adding with a laugh, "So, if you're not in jail, join 'em!"

To another noisy surge of goodwill, this one with foot stamping and rebel yells added, Little dropped to the pavement. He gathered the walkers around himself like an honor guard and led the demonstration onto the lawn. Up ahead, the leader of the security detail, a small blue-black Negro, about forty, with no sideburns showing beneath his cap, came forward from the flagpole. He wore a name tag over his left chest pocket: Captain J. G. Berry.

"Good morning, Mr. Little," Berry said.

Little waved airily. "Good morning, Captain. We're here, sir."

"Over a hundred. Twice more than you said."

"Bombing Haiphong did it."

"We thought. And so interesting. More black in the guard than in the guarded."

Little did not look to make a count. Snyder found a dozen Negro faces among the demonstrators, ten in the guard; the captain was wrong, but not by much.

"Any last word, Captain?" Little asked.

"Behave yourselves and no one will be hurt."

"I hope."

"Any arrests will be remanded to the Baltimore city police jurisdiction."

"I understand."

"This isn't Jackson, Mississippi, Mr. Little."

"I hope not, Captain."

For nearly two hours, the demonstrators circled around the flagpole under the eyes of the guards, the journalists, and the civil defense workers at their office windows. They chanted slogans and sang and created nothing for the evening news. Meanwhile, the sun rose directly over the flagpole, the last ripple of a breeze died, and the flag dangled from its ropes. At noon, demonstration monitors began bringing up Cokes and cold milk from the shopping street below the park. Then Ezra Little became first, frugally and neatly, to deposit an empty can on the concrete slab at the base of the flagpole; in no time at all, the demonstrators accumulated a large, well-behaved pile of returnable trash below their country's limp flag.

In the circle, as the demonstrators wheeled round and round, and the hour moved toward one o'clock, tension rose in anticipation of the coming confrontation. There was more talking and less chanting, more distracted stumbling and bumping instead of smooth marching, a tendency of one rank to check out the expressions on the faces in the ranks behind. The guards and reporters seemed more excited, too. The bearing of the guards stiffened and reporters' eyes appeared less remote. At 12:55 P.M., the television crewmen lifted their gear and got themselves saddled up. The word was passed that Ezra Little would call for a halt after the next circuit. Conversations died. Birdcalls sounded in the trees at the foot of the lawn and traffic on Pratt Street sent up honks and screeches. Frank Dunne dropped back between Rachel and Snyder. He asked Snyder to hold the trident for a moment. With his free hands, he tied a red bandanna around his forehead, then replaced his cap. "You look good," Rachel said. Dunne showed them his strong white teeth in a manic smile. Dark visage and all, his age notwithstanding, Dunne looked dashing and knew it, Snyder thought.

"Can't tell, Jack," he said. "The revolution may yet get on television."

At the top of the circuit, the demonstration was swinging wider, in a rising cloud of dust, coming closer to the entrance plaza. Simultaneously, just below the plaza, a technician, carrying a camera on a body frame and wearing headphones and a square backpack the size of an outboard motor, played out a wire for his TV reporter, who held a microphone in one hand while assembling the loop of wire with the other. The two men were roped together like pack mule and prospector. The TV reporter abruptly thrust out the microphone between Rachel and Snyder into Dunne's photogenic face. "Say something, man," the reporter demanded, "it's only a test."

Dunne scowled and shook his head. The technician grinned encouragingly. The reporter moved again toward Dunne. The microphone jabbed forward and punched lightly, accidentally but inexcusably, into Dunne's upper chest. "I'm sorry," the reporter said.

Dunne was already bringing up his right arm, pushing hard at the microphone. The contact apparently made a loud thump in the technician's ears.

Wincing, the technician stepped around the reporter and snarled at Dunne. He said, "Hey, hey, hey, Mac!" Tall as Dunne, but burdened with his load of equipment, he did not look all that anxious to fight.

Dunne shoved the technician with the fingertips of his left hand, just hard enough to stop the man's forward momentum.

The guard next to Captain Berry quickly moved between Dunne and the technician. He was a square-built young white with no obvious rank. Sweat ran down both of his cheeks from under his blue cap. His name was Earl C. Edwards. "Easy, easy," he said.

Dunne and the technician glared at one another over the guard's shoulder.

"Creep," the technician said.

"Stuff it," Dunne said.

Rachel took Dunne's arm, whispering, "Moving on, Frank."

"Provocation, Ray," Dunne said. "Provocation, dammit!"

"Non-violence, Frank," Rachel hissed, paused, and repeated: "Non-violence."

By then, a ripple of alarm from the scene had summoned Herndon, carrying the lead sign, with Little right behind.

Dunne was not waiting. He sloughed off Rachel's hand and ducked into the open center of the demonstration. He came to a halt beside the pile of trash at the base of the flagpole. His bandanna had fallen over one eye. Then, as Herndon approached him, he turned his back toward the plaza. He seemed to listen to Herndon's entreaties, but he did not return with Herndon to the Walk's position in the march. He remained at the flagpole, facing away with his hands on his hips, a portrait of exasperation.

The toot-toot of Little's whistle drew all attention to the entrance plaza, where Little with his arms raised high stood beside Captain Berry. "One o'clock!" Little shouted. The demonstrators merged into a collective mass, two or three persons deep, stretched almost the full length of the building. The space between the front rank and the plaza was about ten feet across. The walkers, without Frank Dunne, stood close together in the rear rank but centered on Little and Berry and only a few paces from the three parallel lines of four guards each protecting the front doors. There were government workers at every window. The sun was above and slightly behind the building, angling its rays almost directly into the demonstrators' eyes. The TV crews and the reporters had stationed themselves beside the door against the building for the best view of the demonstrators' anticipated moves.

Another blast from Little's whistle brought forward eighteen civil disobedience volunteers, twelve men and six women, without signs, who quietly took a stand in a section of the narrow space between the plaza and the line of demonstrators. A look back by Captain

Berry signaled the guards to unholster their black rubber batons.
Snyder noted that eleven out of twelve guards held their batons with
the right hand, suggesting that one should, under attack, run to one's
left. Then the volunteers took a coordinated step forward, placing
themselves upon the entrance plaza itself. Little joined them at dead
center and faced Captain Berry.

In a voice thick, unsteady, and barely audible, Little said, "Captain
Berry, sir, we have a legal right to enter this public building."

A small chorus of demonstrators facing the building between the
plaza and the parking lot began humming "We Shall Overcome."

Captain Berry held himself at attention. "I am asking you, Mr.
Little, to desist," he said courteously.

There was no reply from Little, not even a gesture. Berry's military bearing, formal civility, and threatened violence all seemed to
Snyder to be so professional, so impersonal, and so dangerous that
Little might well be pinioned, at least momentarily, by the weight of
second thoughts.

As if for a moment of relief, or to take stock, Little looked around
and over the heads of the volunteers, to a distant point behind the
rows of demonstrators, and up toward the flag, which was just then
beginning to descend, some seven hours before sundown. The flag
caught Snyder's eye, then the attention of Berry and the guards, and
then almost everyone as Frank Dunne, amid the pile of cans and
bottles, slowly played out the ropes bringing down Old Glory.

Dunne kept his back to the crowd and his head up, measuring the
flag's descent by the inch. Sweat soaked through the back of his khaki
shirt and his cap rode askew on the side of his head. Herndon set off
at a walk for Dunne, with Rachel and Snyder close behind. But
Berry, shouting "No way!" and waving his hands, led four guards on
the run to prevent the theft or, worse, defilement of the flag by the
overaged hippie who had already had a near-fight with a TV technician.

First to reach Dunne was the guard named Earl C. Edwards. With
a mighty shove, he pushed Dunne about six feet from the flagpole.
Pushing back like a wrestler, Dunne slipped and fell face down
among the trash. Edwards flung himself on Dunne's legs. Dunne
easily rolled away and bounced up with a can in each hand. The
bandanna had slipped over one eye again. He might have looked

crazy to Edwards, but Snyder recognized behind the feverish stare the awareness of a calculated risk. It was Dunne giving his impression of a mad scene, of behavior so aberrant that nothing he might do would reflect on the Walk's non-violent charter.

Dunne pulled himself to his full height and peppered Captain Berry with two in the strike zone, one of which Berry batted with his baton, catching the other harmlessly on his belt buckle. The third and the fourth pitches kept Edwards ducking on the ground; and the fifth and the sixth seemed to drive off Berry. Dunne rubbed up two more cans, unaware until the last split second that Berry's move had been a feint. Turning, he faced three guards with batons coming to the plate at the same time. The guards were close enough to attack and far enough away to duck the next throw. They held their batons at the ready, but pointing from the thigh toward the ground with less than maximum prejudice. The demonstrators, after all, outnumbered the guards at least four to one.

Suddenly, Dunne seemed ready for arrest. He dropped his cans and reached a helping hand for the fallen guard. Something jarred him. He slipped slapstick style, at last falling on top of Edwards, and they rolled together in the tinkling trash.

A guard read Dunne's last moves as an attack, bringing one sharp flash of his baton with a short right-handed swat to the back of Dunne's skull before Berry could intervene. "Stop!" Berry shouted, and dove into the tangle of Dunne and Edwards, taking the next blow on his own shoulder.

The melee drew the demonstrators tentatively down from the plaza, more in curiosity and surprise, Snyder thought, than with ready outrage. So much had happened so quickly, and the worst of it in a fog of dust and confusion. Snyder felt few could have seen the guard's attack on Dunne, while many more might have witnessed with some satisfaction the same guard's accidental rap on Berry. Then hardly a moment was lost before Berry regained his balance, enlisted another guard to help him lift Dunne to his feet, leaving the humiliated Edwards prostrate, and half walked, half carried Dunne further down the lawn below the flagpole and away from the crowd. A rear guard prevented Herndon and Rachel from following, though the lone still photographer slipped through. Emerging from a park road at the tree line was the prisoners' van, last seen in the parking lot.

From where he stood, Snyder spotted a blue-brown ribbon of blood in Dunne's hair at the back rim of his cap. Dunne's stride was, at best, a stagger. But at the van, Dunne turned and, smiling drunkenly, raised a groggy hand clenched in a tight fist to salute the crowd. The van's side door slid open behind him and the inside man, a Baltimore patrolman, lifted him by the armpits. Dunne did not resist. The TV, Snyder realized, had missed it all.

A groan of sympathy and angry murmurs sounded together among the demonstrators, suddenly pierced by Little's whistle, calling the eighteen volunteers to occupy the space on the entrance plaza vacated by the diverted guards. The Dunne show, stills only, was over. With the crowd, Snyder turned to see Little curling himself into the fetal position on the plaza's concrete apron. Then, in slow sequence, each of the volunteers chose a place to emulate Little, virtually filling the plaza to the line of guards positioned immediately at the front doors. There was a new murmur of anticipation, underscored by the noisy gears of the prisoners' van as the driver steered up the lawn toward the building, paced by Berry and his guards.

Snyder ran to a corner of the plaza as Berry ordered the arrests. Pairs of sweating guards carried the volunteers one after another to join Dunne in the van. They were fast, efficient, and polite. An occasional insult did not faze them. At last, they deposited Little and shut the van door. Behind the green windows, the office workers were applauding. The new prisoners called out, "Conway Street police station!" And they inspired the ninety or so remaining demonstrators to join hands and sing "We Shall Overcome." The TV cameras panned the demonstrators' mournful faces.

Soon, the van backed away, turned, and departed by the park road below the flagpole. The singing stopped and the demonstrators began drifting toward their buses. Two men in green overalls were already cleaning up the litter. Berry and his guards repositioned themselves on the entrance plaza for a last decorous word with the TV crews and the reporters. Then Snyder rejoined the Walk. They were now eight, and he made nine. Amelia carried Dunne's cap and Luther Wood slyly played the Marine Corps hymn on his recorder.

The demonstration was over, Snyder noted, and it was not yet one-thirty in the afternoon.

"Where is Conway Street?" Sylvia asked.

"We'll find it," Rachel said.

"Do we pay the bail or bust him out?" Dorene asked.

"The kitty's got three hundred dollars," Arley Broyle said, alarmed.

"Don't mind her," June said.

"Well, sure." Dorene smiled. "Either way, I need to talk to Frank."

"We all do," Rachel said.

Dorene gave a thought to her next sentence. She said, "Like, maybe Haiphong pushed him over the edge."

"Maybe that was it," Rachel said.

"Yes, or that he didn't trust us about Washington."

"Maybe."

"Or maybe, Ray, he'd had enough of moral support."

"Right on, Dorene!" Wood exclaimed. "The trouble with moral support is you feel so bad after it's over if you're not in jail."

"Say that again," Dorene said.

"That's for sure, Luther," Herndon said, his face turning red.

2

Herndon was the Walk's only representative allowed inside the grim, gray station house on Conway Street. From midafternoon to almost nine that evening, a line of police barricades set up nearly a block away confined the walkers and the scores of relatives and friends awaiting the fate of the demonstration's heroes. The foot patrol changed shifts at four and an off-duty patrolman advised the crowd that there would be no word before eight. Then Rachel asked Arley Broyle to provide a shuttle service to a nearby restaurant district and a selection of gas stations with bathrooms. It was an order of little significance, but it reminded Snyder of something he had forgotten, that even the present Walk leader was not indispensable.

About ten minutes to nine, a sunset afterglow in the sky, there was a new light in the street as the high door at the top of the station-house steps swung open. The freed prisoners came out, and the crowd surged to greet them in the street. Snyder spotted Herndon and Ezra Little almost at once and knew from Herndon's melancholy silhouette that Frank Dunne had not been released.

With some of Little's friends, the walkers met Herndon and Little in the half-light at the side of the truck.

"Well, as you can see," Herndon said, "we've got Ezra and no Frank."

"Is he all right?" Dorene asked.

"He's staying till Tuesday with six stitches, and a bandage that he loves."

"Refused bail," Little said. "All of fifty dollars. He's one of four."

"I don't believe it," Dorene said. "How'm I going to talk to him?"

"He's refused, even though he didn't have to," Herndon said. "We sat around for hours before we could see him. The coalition lawyer was there and a few group representatives, like me. Every now and then, the guards would bring someone alone from the detention pen, walk him across the public room, and into an office for fingerprints and all the rest. Then they'd take him for interviews and make sure he knew he'd made a police record—or added an item to an old one. Twenty arrested, two cops on the detail, takes a long time.

"Frank was absolutely dead last because, it turned out, they'd whisked him off three blocks to an emergency room to patch his head. Luckily, he took part of the blow on his cap and the rest on the thickest part of his skull. But it was a nasty scalp wound.

"Finally, looking like the American Revolution, Frank waves at me going in for his paperwork and I don't see him again for two more hours. Several times, the coalition lawyer talked to the sergeant and the lieutenant, and it seems we were waiting for an assistant district attorney to come up from downtown.

"Well, the man arrived about seven and started moving things. I found out, if you can believe this, they had waited till they saw the evening TV news. 'Nothing untoward,' the a.d.a. says, meaning nothing to embarrass the justice system. Next, it turns out, everyone, even Frank, gets off with disorderly conduct. Because of the Fourth of July weekend, there are no judges around till Tuesday. But you can leave on your own recognizance if you've got a Baltimore address, or pay fifty dollars if you're from out of town.

"That meant Frank and three other out-of-town demonstrators could walk for a token, and all four of them refused. What did Frank say to me? He said, 'I never told them I was with the Walk, just the union and a peacenik from California.' And I asked him, 'But why, Frank? I mean, why in the first place?' And he said, 'I wanted to be sure I had my moment.' And then Ezra asked him, 'What about the picnic tomorrow on Slaughter Beach?' And Frank said, 'I don't really enjoy ocean swimming.'"

3

They had watched the eleven o'clock world and local television nightly news in the dormitory common room, with Arley Broyle switching back and forth between Channels 2 and 5. Channel 2 ran a forty-second feature on the demonstration starring Ezra Little and Captain Berry within a two-minute roundup of nationwide reactions to the bombing of Hanoi and Haiphong. Channel 5 presented a fifteen-second montage including a still photo of Frank Dunne's arrest over a reporter's voice describing him as a California union leader, arrested for disorderly conduct. "Frank would love that," Dorene said. Last came Captain Berry's interview, crediting his men for a swift end to the protest without serious injury on either side. Berry tilted the subject, transformed it, actually, from civil disobedience to an exercise in crowd control. The walkers jeered but, Snyder was thinking, the man had been quite clever, managing the news for his own purposes. At best, for both sides, the demonstration was a wash.

After the news, Snyder turned in. He found that day's Baltimore *Sun* in the bathroom and took it back to his room. He sat on the bed in his skivvies reading the baseball scores, the comics, and the editorial hand-wringing over the bombing. Then he fished in his duffel bag for his new swimsuit, sun-block oil, and a pair of sneakers to wear on the beach. He was lighting a last cigarette when he heard a soft knock on his door and Herndon calling his name. Snyder said, "It's open," and Herndon entered, shutting the door behind.

Herndon wore a T-shirt and khakis and carried his toilet kit and an orange towel. He squinted over his glasses and smiled uncertainly.

"Do you believe I smelled your cigarette?" Herndon asked.

"That's quite a nose."

"You mind? It's midnight."

"Sit."

Herndon sat in the metal chair by the desk. He noticed the newspaper on the bed.

"Do you think they'll cover today's demonstration, Jack?"

"Tomorrow's *Sun?* A decent burial, is all."

"Seems like a great effort for so little attention."

"But better than nothing. What are you doing up?"

"Talking to Luther about Washington."

"Scared?"

"He wants to do civil disobedience. He says he owes it now to Frank. Isn't that interesting? Of course, he's afraid, too."

"What'd you tell him?"

"I told him I understood. People do get hurt. They do go to jail. But then, there's the cause. So a choice has to be made."

"What did he say?"

"He asked what I was going to do."

"And you told him?"

"Off the record?"

"All the good things are."

"First, I told him that I myself did not want to risk going back to prison. I told him I guessed Frank knew that and wanted to make certain for himself."

"Did he understand?"

"He admires Frank for that, yes. I guess I do, too. Then I told him I have had a little problem, because *Harrington's* magazine is here."

"I see."

"We left it at that."

"With a load on me."

"Well, there you are."

Snyder stalled for reflection. "The best I can do is say the leader of the Walk did not want his real name used," he said and, as he said it, could tell he had disappointed Herndon. Snyder knew his own position had not changed since somewhere back in Indiana when he could hardly imagine the Herndon issue coming down to this. "I can do that, Reed, change a name to protect the innocent as long as I mention it. It's awkward, using a made-up name, but I've done it and it's permissible. I've got some discretion."

"Then I'd be a coward with a made-up name."

"Who's going to cast the first stone, Reed? Fifteen seconds on television against a year in prison. The hell with it."

"It's more than television. You'd have to write that this John Doe, the leader of the great Walk, chose to stand aside while others went to jail."

"Maybe not those exact words. You're awfully rough on yourself, Reed. I won't lie for you, but the truth doesn't have to be vicious."

"So, I'd be twice cursed. Once for standing aside and once for asking you to protect my name."

"Nobody's cursing you."

"I need help, Jack."

"Ask me to protect your name, Reed, and I will. But I can't leave you out."

"I'm not going to ask."

"Don't be so righteous, Reed."

"I'm not. It's up to you, Jack."

"We both have a little problem with the good."

Herndon took one of Snyder's cigarettes and lit it amateurishly.

"Listen, Jack, I want you to know something," he said. "I mean, why I'm not going back to the joint, okay? Will you listen, and not write anything? . . . All right. Thank you. Well, here: it never seemed fair to me, you understand, but it was a fact of life inside that a regular thug who'd stolen from people, or beat on people, or killed people stood a better chance of getting through prison than the few like me who never did anything to anybody. I mean, for most prisoners there's a system of constituencies organized to take advantage of any opportunity that comes along so they can do their time a little easier. But for me, there was only one way I could have played in the system, especially when I first got to the joint, and I wasn't going to do that.

"So it happened that for a while I was kind of a celebrity, a draft resister who'd had his name in the papers a few times, and nobody bothered me. And despite some horror stories I'd heard before I'd ever dreamed I'd be a prisoner someday, I began to think I was going to make it through, maybe even with God to protect me.

"Until a friend, the Jehovah's Witness you know about, told me one day that he'd heard some dudes joking about my walk.

"And it wasn't long before four of them escorted me out of the kitchen one morning—after breakfast, mind you!—and down to the furniture shop and invited me into their club in exchange for my rear end. I said no, and they began to beat on me, and I scrambled around the shop, tearing up the place. I couldn't escape, so they got me down to a pair of ripped shorts and got me half buried in mattress ticking where they were going to force me to do one thing or another. I got hit very hard on the side of my face, so hard that I just lashed out with the first thing that came to hand, a chair leg that caught one con in the throat and sent him running from the shop. In a minute or two, there were three guards in there ordering the cons to their stations, and I collapsed in tears back into the ticking. One of the guards held me like a baby, while the other two stood there getting hot, and before long, they had me spread-eagled and all three of them did it to me. There was blood and shit all over the place and they didn't seem to care.

"I was in the hospital for ten days and, when I was well enough, I asked to see the assistant warden to tell him what had happened. He tried to persuade me that I had been in no state to positively identify the four dudes or the three guards. I told the story twice, and then he let me know that he wasn't persuaded. But he asked me how I'd like to be assigned to nursing duty in the prison hospital and live on the ward, where it's safe. And I realized that was the best I could do. So that's how I became a nurse, Jack, and learned something in the joint besides dishwashing."

An unprofessional impulse to say how sorry he felt very nearly overwhelmed Snyder. He crossed his arms over his chest and kept it to himself.

"Then one day in the ward," Herndon said, "about ten months into my term, my friend, the Jehovah's Witness, comes in dehydrated and half dead from a hunger strike in solitary confinement that absolutely no one had reported. He survived—he would do it again, about a year later, and get paroled. But after that first time, I wrote a letter to the warden protesting the way his hunger strike'd been ignored and took the precaution of getting a copy mailed outside to my father, who sent it to the head of the Federal Bureau of Prisons. I couldn't let my family know what had happened to me, but they gathered things weren't too smooth.

"There was a small miracle—one guard was actually transferred from solitary to another job. But something else happened, too. They sent me back to my old cell block and to work again in the kitchen.

"Nothing had changed, either, except the joint had a new draft resister. His name was Wesley Sullivan. He was about your height, Jack, only he weighed about two hundred fifty pounds, and had a brown belt in karate. So, after a while, there were five of us, and we made our own little constituency with Wesley to protect us, and the joint actually became tolerable. In fact, Wesley and I got permission to share a cell and I sent for some books he'd wanted to read and he sent for some records I wanted to hear, and I felt I'd made a friend for life.

"Until the night when he came on to me and I, Christ, would not let him. He tried every night for a month, and I talked him out of it each time, and he never seemed to be angry. But at the end of that terrible month, on a Sunday afternoon, he was showing me how to do karate, and deliberately put me in the hospital with a cracked collarbone. He cried and I cried and I decided, friendship or no, I had to get out of our cell.

"And, of course, I knew, asking the guards for a transfer was like telling them what was going on and they'd see to it I spent the rest of my time with Wesley. Oh, it was the perfect punishment! So, hell, Jack, I decided to get out altogether, and get even, too. I was in a corner of the ward, with a wall next to me on one side and an empty bed on the other. I hurt a lot, and I knew how to get some Demerol and I mixed it with some aspirin, until I was about to float away. And then I tied my sling around my neck and over the bedstead, and just rolled off the bed into the corner. I hung there, gagging for a few seconds, until I went to black.

"It almost worked. I was pretty close to dead when Wesley came by to apologize and to promise he'd let up, and he found me purple in the face. Another nurse revived me, and I never had to go back to the cell block again. They reassigned me to the hospital and the nursing, and I accepted that and kept my nose clean until they paroled me. You see, Jack? How it all became a mess? More than anything, I wanted to be safe, so they won."

Snyder's eye fell on his notebook, the slim, tan rectangle hinged by a spiral of metal, his trusty shield closed and out of reach on the bed. "They didn't win, Reed," he said. "They didn't."

"Shit, Jack," Herndon said. "They did."

"You're on the Walk."

"But they can take away my freedom."

"That's reality, Reed. Be realistic. Think of Amelia. Wait out your parole."

"With you here?"

"We've been over that. What about Amelia?"

"I can't let her in, Jack."

"You don't let anyone in."

"Yes, well, I hoped knowing why I don't want to go back might make a difference with you."

"You're asking me now to leave you out?"

Herndon stood up and collected his towel and toilet kit.

"I have no right to ask. But I told you the truth. Good night, Jack."

Snyder watched Herndon step to the door. He knew that "No" was again the answer he would have given. "Good night, Reed," he said.

Herndon looked back from the corridor. He said, "We all have more vanity than common sense, don't we?"

"Yes, we do," Snyder said, and was reminded, for an instant, of Phil Zimmerman.

4

In his room, Herndon sat down at the desk and started a letter.

"Dear Mom [he wrote]:

"We might have skipped the demonstration today, but we went along for the ride and, dumb! we lost another walker, our oldest survivor, a union man from California, named Frank Dunne. His example has increased the feeling for civil disobedience among the rest of us. On the other hand, now that we're eight, we can't take a chance on losing any more before the White House. Fortunately, we have little opportunity to stop traffic between Balt. and Wash.

"As for me, I find it harder and harder to think about asking others to do civil disobedience without leading them. Yet I can't conceive going back to prison, either. I guess I have been wrong not to realize that there is no such thing as free publicity. Jack Snyder, the *Harrington's* man, has a code of his own that I have to respect, although I've told him some very personal things (off the record) in the hope that he might make an exception. We all seem to be tangled up in codes. But there's time, before the Fourth. And where there's time, there's hope. I'll keep you posted.

"Too bad I have not written more. You'd have a record of the famous Walk. Now we have to depend upon Jack Snyder. Well, I am looking forward to our outing tomorrow at Slaughter Beach with our local hosts. And, hopefully, all will work out for the best.

"Love, as ever, Reedy."

5

The weather held. Midmorning was clear and hot as they joined Ezra Little, his committee, and fifteen now familiar members of the Peace Council on the yellow school bus. Little was in high spirits, hawking the Friday-morning newspaper; the demonstration story played on page three with ten paragraphs and a two-column photo showing Little's own arrest as supervised by Captain Berry. The headline read: ARREST 20 AT VIET PROTEST. Snyder asked for a copy of the paper and clipped the story for his notes. The demonstration had received better treatment than he would have expected. It challenged the Walk.

They rode steadily for nearly three hours, rolling out of Baltimore, through Annapolis, and across Chesapeake Bay to the Delaware state line at Burrsville, then east about thirty-five miles to the Atlantic Coast and, finally, south along the sparkling gray-blue sea to a point just below Delaware Bay. At one o'clock, they passed through the summer village of Slaughter Beach. Then they came up on a low range of scruffy green dunes at the end of which was a weather-worn shore hotel and, beyond, a scattering of modest shingled houses. Thereafter began a great, flat, buff-colored expanse of sun-baked sand, stretching for miles and seemingly capped at the end by white clouds. The bus stopped about a mile further on where an ambitious stone jetty formed an ideal picnic cove amid dazzling breakers. Civilization was represented by a dilapidated red sign advising all comers that they swam at their own risk, mustn't litter, ought to look out for riptides, and had to be off the beach by sunset. But except for two small, bronzed boys, neither older than ten or eleven, running in and out of the feisty surf, the walkers and their friends had the beach, the ocean, and the view across to Cape May to themselves.

The group undressed and dressed, women on the bus, men behind the bus, and spread their picnic on blankets and beach towels. In his hat, T-shirt, and swimsuit, Snyder went down to the surf with Dorene and Sylvia, who immediately sprinted seaward on the jetty with the two little boys. He watched Herndon and Amelia playing at the first line of breakers, and suddenly saw Rachel close by, abruptly rising from a dip, laughing at his surprise. "It's warm!" she cried, lifting the flaps of her white cap.

Snyder took a step into the surf, and found himself wondering how he was going to feel on, say, Tuesday in New York, not to see Rachel again, and not to be remembered by her as other than he had been for so long. The word is grim, he was thinking, made grimmer by the sudden proximity of her good, long, healthy body in a blue bathing suit. To be alone with her just then, somewhere, in the Atlantic Ocean, seemed urgent to him.

"Ray," he said, "let's swim before lunch."

Rachel smiled up at him and toward the jetty, where Dorene and Sylvia were diving and the two little boys were testing themselves against the undertow, now with June Matsushida close by. In the cove, Arley Broyle was helping with the food and Wood practiced his recorder with a student who had brought his accordion. All eight surviving walkers were accounted for.

"Think we can make Cape May?" Rachel asked.

"At least," Snyder said. "Five hundred yards out, five hundred yards back. Slow."

"I'm game," Rachel said.

Snyder tossed his hat and shirt above the tide line and followed Rachel into the deeper surf. He paused, admiring her ability to flatten onto the cushion of an oncoming swell, her arms cutting the foam, and then pushed himself forward in awkward, but nervy, emulation.

He went through the next wave, and down, touching the hard sand with his fingertips and letting the undertow carry him forward beneath the second line of breakers. When he surfaced, he saw Rachel only a few yards away, her face bobbing above the calm water. She laughed and swam on, over a third stretch of breakers, turning again to wait for him. They met in the depression between two swelling dunelike waves with all land suddenly gone from sight. Rachel embraced him and they clung together, legs lazily paddling. They kissed easily and the sea held them, gently lifting and dropping them like bobbins, and almost imperceptibly carried them back toward shore. The tide was coming in.

"Did you plan this?" She laughed.

"I did."

"So did I."

They kissed, separated, and began swimming east again, slowly, without strain or rush. Snyder's legs felt strong. But he recognized his limitations, and soon turned over on his back, paddling only fast enough to stay in place, and conserving his wind. A wave lifted him. He saw that they had swum perhaps two hundred yards from shore, a distance that looked longer than it felt. The swimmers they had left behind were unrecognizable except for the two little boys, who had climbed onto a high rock at the very eastern end of the jetty and stood in silhouette against the sun, poised to dive.

While he rested, Snyder noticed that Rachel had changed to an easygoing breaststroke and was moving off from him parallel to the shore. He swam after her in a kind of bastard crawl. He calculated that they had passed about fifty yards beyond the end of the jetty and were moving out to sea at a moderate angle. He saw a sail for the first time, and beyond the sail, the clouds on the horizon over Cape May seemed to be rising. The water grew calm and felt warmer. He waved to Rachel and was thinking about turning back.

He was twenty yards behind her and swimming to join her when he felt lifted from below by a rapid, cold swell. He began to move east through the water faster than he was swimming. Ahead, he saw Rachel buoyed upward, apparently on the same swell. She had extended her arms and brought her palms together, making a point. She seemed to be racing seaward without effort. The ocean rolled under him as though a great bubble had burst and, against the normal, incoming tide, something was sweeping him ahead farther and faster than he would have dared go.

It was over in a few seconds. The strange current passed, leaving a confusion of crisscrossing waves. Snyder swam to the top of a breaker, looking for Rachel. Two incoming whitecaps converged, then separated. Between the waves, he saw her, still beyond about twenty yards on a high-rolling swell. He saw her turning to find him and smiling.

"Are you all right, Jack?" she shouted.

"What was that!"

Rachel plunged into the swell, disappeared, then came up behind Snyder, holding his sides so that he could hang in the water without swimming. He knew he looked frightened.

"Lord! Riptide!" she said.

They rose up on a fresh swell. On shore, Snyder saw in miniature the tops of the dunes, the roofs of beach houses, and that was all. The riptide, he guessed, had carried them about one thousand yards from the beach.

"That's a swim, Ray," Snyder said.

"Don't worry," Rachel said. "Relax—swim on your side—easy floating in salt water—you know that?"

"Oh, yes," Snyder lied. You can swim, he was thinking, but not in her league.

"We'll go slowly," she said. "I'll stay close, love."

So, Snyder told himself, she knows.

They rode up on another expanding wave. This time, Snyder caught sight of the yellow bus on the lower beach, a tiny thing, toy-sized, with black dots around it for people. The sun above the dunes had dropped below two o'clock.

"The picnic's started," Snyder said, meaning they might soon be missed.

"Stay close, Jack," Rachel said, and tossed herself sideways into a slow stroke-and-scissor toward the beach.

Snyder had a moment of panic. His arms hung weightless in the gray water, independent of his will and reluctant to begin. Seconds passed as he told himself that salvation is possible in salt water with the tide's help if you don't get excited, oh, yes. The game is to think hard about making a yard at a time, steady, steady movement with the sun in your eyes. And to kick. You have always tended to swim with your arms alone, he was thinking, and this will not do. The game is winnable, you can swim a thousand yards in the Atlantic Ocean, if you swim easy on your side, and kick. You have a job to do. Do your job.

Snyder stretched forward and, at last, his arms began to move, then his legs, and he felt his body transported through the thick water. He swam deliberately and thought about the tale he and Rachel would have to tell back on the beach. Riptide—an undersea barrier breaks, and an instant ebbtide rushes into the deep, with you on its back.

In another moment, a wave lifted Snyder, carried him over its crest and boiled out from under him to climb the back of the next wave ahead. Rachel was swimming nearby in the wake of yet another wave. The two waves converged, turning the swimmers together at an angle between the sun and the tip of the jetty, which now appeared on Snyder's right almost as far off as the shore. Snyder reckoned that the riptide had swept them out to sea at a forty-five-degree angle from the picnic cove and the normal tide was carrying them south and west away from their friends.

The two little bronzed boys, first seen on the beach and again on the jetty, now bobbed up quite near them.

Snyder saw first one, then the other in the valley behind the last wave, about fifty feet to his right. He heard the word "Mister!" urgent beyond despair.

The boys waved and flailed at the water.

Snyder looked for Rachel and discovered he had lost her again. He shouted, "Ray!" And a boy answered, "Mister!"

Snyder swam forward. He had consciously regressed to his arms-only crawl, his best for speed, the instinct to save his strength losing to a habit momentarily more profound. After a few strokes, he adjusted his direction, aiming at a point some yards ahead and to the left of the floundering boys, thereby gaining the advantage of the

right-to-left movement of the waves. Here, the ocean helpfully ran
flat and brought Rachel into view, to his right.

By some blessing, she had changed to a backstroke, so that she saw
both Snyder and the boys at the same moment. She tumbled over,
dove down, and surfaced again, slashing across the trough between
them.

They reached the boys from opposite directions at virtually the
same moment. The smaller of the two boys lunged for Snyder's back.
Rachel swept up the larger boy. Snyder went under, twisted, and
came up with the boy in his arms. He crossed his left arm over the
boy's chest. The boy retched and struggled, but Snyder held on until
the boy began to float.

"Oh, Christ, Ray," Snyder said, in amazement at such bad luck.

Rachel held her boy by the armpits. The boy faced her, chest deep
in the water. His face was the color of putty. Rachel shouted at him,
"How far can you swim?" The boy's mouth hung open. There was a
large space between his front teeth and his tongue showed through.
He said, "Not far—jetty."

Snyder took that to mean that they had been swimming close to
the jetty, which was eight hundred yards or more from where they
now struggled. A heavy swell lifted them. The boy in Snyder's arms
said, "Hold me."

Snyder spoke close into the boy's ear, "Do you swim?"

"I will."

Rachel took a deep breath. She said, "All right, Jack, we must go
in."

"All right." Snyder nodded, pinching his nose and pushing air
against his eardrums. He forced himself to relax. "Ray," he asked,
"why not the jetty?"

"We might never find it," she said. "Are you good for the beach?"

"Follow the sun," Snyder said. "See you there."

Snyder saw that Rachel knew precisely what to do. She had transferred the boy to her back. Now she placed his hands on her shoulders and positioned herself for a breaststroke. The boy seemed to
understand that he was to help with a kick of his own. Together, they
began to move, heading across a wide space of calm water. Snyder
attempted the same adjustment with his boy, but once on Snyder's
back, the boy tightened both arms around Snyder's neck and, to-

gether, they sank. Snyder tore at the boy's wrists. When they returned to the surface, he crossed his left arm over the boy's chest again. "Don't fight me," he said. "It's the only hold I have."

Snyder and the boy rode down a long roller, then came up high on a swell that gave them a view of the horizon. Snyder saw Rachel swimming steadily far to his left. Inspired, he began to swim, holding the boy, pulling with his right arm, kicking one leg at a time. "We're going to make it," Snyder said, and felt the boy shudder.

They picked up the current and made progress, perhaps a hundred yards, then another fifty yards, until Snyder's right biceps began to ache. The pain forced him to change his hold and try pulling with his left arm.

Not as much there, he was thinking, not enough, so little—you can drown without rest.

"Try my back," Snyder shouted to the boy, thinking again that you drown if you don't rest.

The boy paddled around behind, digging his fingers into the nobs of Snyder's shoulders, trying to help with a feeble kick. He hung from Snyder like an anchor.

"Kick! Kick! Kick!" Snyder chanted.

"I can't, mister!"

They went under again. Snyder felt the boy's grip sliding off to his right. He groped for the boy, missed, then sensed the boy's body surging upward. The boy broke the surface, screaming. Snyder seized him by the hair. He shouted, "Listen, you little son of a bitch. Help me! You can swim!"

"Don't leave me, mister!"

"Then swim, you bastard—we can't make it unless you swim!"

Snyder pushed the boy forward and let go. The boy fought the water until something overcame him—perhaps mortal terror, Snyder thought—and his thin little arms began to make strokes. He splashed ahead, down one trough, up another wave, then down the other side. He could swim. Snyder cheered, "You're swimming!" He stayed close beside the boy, pulling with his left arm, dangling the right while alert to an easing of the pain in his right biceps.

Snyder believed they had gained another hundred yards. Then the boy floundered. Gasping, the boy seized Snyder's face. Snyder swam under him and paddled so the boy could rest holding on to Snyder's waist. The boy began swimming again, little foot flutters between pathetic arm strokes, but he labored forward, over the next wave and the next. The boy was trying. Snyder loved him.

Then, without a word, the boy fell still and quickly drifted away, like a stick. He rolled over. Snyder saw his face, pale and sick, the eyes straining from the sockets. Snyder lunged through the water, seized the boy's hair again, and yanked unmercifully. The boy seemed to wake from a dream, wailing, his tongue protruding. Snyder caught the boy under the ears with both hands and lifted as a new wave came by. They hung suspended. Snyder could not see the beach below the sun, only sea and sky. And yet, far ahead, there was Rachel on a wave of her own, swimming on her right side with her boy under her left arm. Snyder knew where he wanted to be. He called, "Ray!" The wave broke under him and when he surfaced again, Rachel had vanished.

Almost immediately, a special wave rolled by, as though a speedboat had stirred contrary folds in the creases of the swells. Snyder shoved the boy to the top, then dove down as the boy slid into the trough. They came up together, a miracle for sure, and floated forward on a waveless plateau. Thirty yards in one sweep! Now, Snyder was thinking, if he will swim, even a little, we can make some headway.

Snyder spoke softly into the boy's ear, "You've got to swim now, I'm getting tired." They swam, made some headway, until a giant wave smashed them from the side, sweeping the boy to Snyder's left and away. The boy flailed upward and gagged horribly. Then he sank. Snyder grabbed at something flesh-colored, held on, and lifted the boy by an elbow. The weight leveraged against Snyder's chest tore at the muscles of the left shoulder. Snyder let go again, and the boy, caught by a fresh wave, was propelled twenty yards to the side. The boy turned in the foam, reaching back. Snyder heard nothing, but read the boy's lips, "Don't leave me, mister!"

Snyder kicked hard against the feeble strokes of his exhausted arms. The boy clawed at his approaching face. Snyder seized the boy by the throat with his right hand, then smacked his face with his left. He knew the blow was weak, but the boy subsided. Now Snyder tried holding the boy while pushing with his legs, but he felt no forward motion. Suddenly in a rage, Snyder called to the boy,

"You're going to swim, you little fucker!" and the boy strained in terror. He shoved against Snyder, splashed forward, gasped, and sank. Snyder waited. The boy bobbed up and held on at Snyder's shoulder. Neither of them, Snyder knew, had anything left.

A looping wave raised them once more toward the sun. The beach appeared in Snyder's vision—as seen through the wrong end of a telescope. Dots of red and orange on the sand signified towels and blankets. Matchstick figures ran into the surf. Snyder thought they must be three hundred yards from the nearest swimmers. He knew he could not swim that far with the boy. He was almost certain that he could not even swim that far alone.

Holding the boy by an armpit, Snyder waved his free hand toward shore, shouting, "Help!"

His voice had quaked. It sounded feeble and hopeless against his own eardrums, even a little embarrassing. He had never heard himself cry for help. It was interesting. Certainly, no one could have heard. He shouted again, "Help!"

Without a word, the boy slid off Snyder's shoulder and sank. Snyder fished for him, caught his hand, and lifted. The boy came up coughing, water pouring from his nose. A wave crashed over and drove them down. Below the surface, a sudden lucky current carried them forward. Snyder yearned to stay under, to avoid the buffeting of the waves, and to rest his arms while the current carried them home.

When they surfaced, he inhaled quickly and ducked under again, at the same time pushing the boy upward. The lucky current was gone. So was their luck, Snyder believed. All strength had left him. He knew that he had no chance to save the boy, and the barest chance to save himself if he let go of the boy. That is the way it is, he told himself.

They surfaced once more. Snyder had the boy by the hair. He saw the beach again, perhaps fifty yards closer. He cried, "Help!" but, almost immediately, sank exhausted into the next wave. He shouted to the boy, "Breathe! Breathe!" and, holding the boy by the hand, let himself go under. He rested in the deep as long as he dared, 14, 15, 16, 17 seconds, exploding to the surface on the count of 21. The boy flung his arms around Snyder's neck. His eyes were screwed tight shut. His torso and legs stiffened. The boy knew he was drowning.

Snyder saw a wave rolling behind them and thought: this is for him. To the boy, he cried, "Catch it! Catch it!" Then Snyder lifted the boy by the back of the neck and the small of his back and threw him on top of the wave. The boy was virtually sitting on top when Snyder released him. Snyder sank down six feet, ten feet. There was no bottom. The water was cold and very calm.

Snyder floated quietly, amazed at the last show of his strength, seeing the boy on top, and then sliding forward. He counted 18, 19, 20, 21 seconds. He kicked hard at 24, forward and up, surfacing in a deep trough. There were no bathers, no beach, only the amazing boy —half out of the water, arms flapping.

The boy leaped at Snyder. He caught Snyder's hand and held on. Snyder lacked strength to break the boy's grip. Two tall waves rolled over them. With the third approaching, Snyder screamed into the boy's ear, "That's all! That's all!"

Snyder grasped the boy by the neck and his right thigh. Then without lifting, for he could not lift, he forced his own body up the wave, rising under the boy until they reached the crest. Snyder fell forward. His arms dropped away like spaghetti and the boy came down flat as the wave broke. Snyder took a deep breath, then sank, letting himself drift down into the peaceable deep, counting his own heartbeats.

A cold calmness enfolded him. He wanted to weep for the boy, for his own limitations. He kicked, forcing himself to go deeper, arms at his side, slowly paddling to resist the undertow. He rested profoundly. He wanted to rest more than he wanted to breathe. He counted 25, 26, 27. One more effort before you drown, too, he was thinking.

At the count of 29, a hand wrapped itself firmly around Snyder's right forearm, just below the elbow. The hand moved up to the biceps and pulled. A muscled thigh treading water knocked Snyder sideways. The surface broke into sunlight. He seized the shoulder of Reed Herndon. It would be Herndon, he thought. But the boy is lost.

"Hello, Ishmael," Herndon said.

Through a brilliant mist, Snyder saw Luther Wood behind

Herndon linked by their grip on a towel, and June Matsushida behind Wood linked by another towel, and other walkers and Peace Council members linked one behind the other by towels and shirts, forging a chain seventy or eighty yards long, through the sequence of breakers to Arley Broyle waist deep in the surf, anchoring all. And beyond the chain, there were two figures on the beach, surely Rachel and the boy she had rescued.

Snyder clung to Herndon as the chain pulled them both toward the shore. It is too bad, he was thinking, that your boy is lost, that you could not have saved your boy—that your all, more than you knew you had, was not enough.

Then, at the penultimate line of breakers, just as his foot touched bottom, Snyder saw his boy—the boy himself—handed from Ezra Little to Broyle and from Broyle to Rachel, and saw Rachel carry the boy above the high-tide line.

Gratitude surged through Snyder like a new fuel, an unnameable compound of pride and shame, and propelled his body from Herndon's grip into a breathless stagger toward the shore.

"He's all right," Rachel said as Snyder flung himself to his knees beside her on the beach. The boy lay face down on a yellow blanket. Gasping, Snyder beheld the pulse of life thumping against the back of the boy's rib cage. The boy opened his eyes, coughed, and licked at a ridge of sand around his lips. Rachel draped Snyder's neck with a dry towel and sat back on her heels. Snyder grasped the ends of the towel. His breath came fitfully. His spirit seemed to gather in his chest. His heart made a fist. He felt he should be crying.

Shadows fell across the sand. Snyder looked up to greet perhaps a dozen of his rescuers, including Herndon, who had led them from the surf.

Snyder closed his eyes. He willed his lungs to work. He was aware of Herndon kneeling beside him, Herndon's arm around on his heaving shoulders. It had to be Herndon, he thought once again, to block all escapes from self-contempt. In the end, luck saved the boy. The boy knows this. You only saved yourself.

Snyder could not speak. He covered his face with the towel and wept. Imagine, he was thinking, bawling in front of strangers!

"Come on, Jack," Herndon said. "You can't do that. We own you now, by right of salvage."

6

The Slaughter Beach outing, brought back to the campus at dusk, had paused for showers and clean clothes, and was to continue across the green in the Rathskeller. In his room, Snyder changed to a sport shirt and khakis. He could hear the walkers in the corridor, the voices he knew so well, Herndon and Amelia, Dorene, June and Sylvia, Wood and Broyle. Rachel knocked on his door. "Coming, Jack?" "A minute," he said. He really didn't want to go.

Snyder sat at the desk and opened his notebook. The last sentence he had written was by itself at the top of a fresh page. "Herndon: We own you now, by right of salvage." It was another something not to be used, only remembered. Herndon, of course, was joking, Snyder thought, cheering you over your moment of despair, the guilt of the survivor. Or was he? The subtext of morality is always ownership, to what do you belong and for what are you responsible. If the drowning boy were not a perfect stranger, were he a colleague or friend, or your daughter, would you have found more to give? Your life? Now here is Herndon himself drowning in your assignment. You have another chance at a rescue. Two days to go. How much do you give? Your story—your integrity—for his freedom? Snyder lit a cigarette. He thought of Rachel. She would ask all the right questions.

In the moonlit dark, he found Rachel sitting on the front steps of the dormitory. She wore her bosomy white dress, last seen in Fort Wayne.

"I'm glad you waited," he said.

"I don't mind."

Snyder sat beside her. He said, "I've been grieving about this afternoon."

"That makes two of us. The boy I took from you could swim."

"There was no telling. I gave up on the one who couldn't."

"He's alive, Jack."

"But I lost him."

"Don't say that."

"It was Herndon and the others that saved him."

"Please, everyone has limits."

"All right. But I wanted you to know."

"You have too much of a good thing, dear heart."

"Is that bad?"

"No answer."

Rachel kissed him. Her lips parted and they kissed again. Her arms came up over his shoulders. They kissed a third time. She pressed her face against his jaw and the clean smell of her hair was very moving to him.

Rachel took his hand. "I wish we could like ourselves as much as we like each other," she said.

"I'm working on it," he said.

They were silent. They could hear an accordion and a recorder playing campfire songs in the Rathskeller. Rachel leaned against him and he put his arm around her.

Quietly, Snyder said, "Next case, Ray."

"It's Reed."

"Answer me this: is he more important than the story?"

"We all desperately want the story. Reed wants it, too."

"But that's the question, isn't it?"

"How important is Reed's parole? Ask it that way."

"All right. So, imagine Reed drowning. Like that boy this afternoon. Is my life—the story—more important than his?"

"You can't ask that unless you've got a choice."

"I have a choice. Like this afternoon."

"You do your best, that's all. I suppose survival comes first—you can't help that."

"The choice is for me to leave the Walk until Monday," Snyder said, a plan forming as he spoke. "Reed gets the two days to decide on civil disobedience. Whether I abort the story will be up to him."

"How will you know his answer?"

"I'll be at the White House on the Fourth. If he's there, I do the story."

"If he's not? If it's just us?"

"I'll have to deal with Mr. Erlanger's expectations."

"But why do you leave the Walk, Jack?"

"So Reed will trust me only to write a story that has him doing civil disobedience. He'll know I can't write if we haven't spoken again."

"And the Walk goes on, either way."

"Yes—that's why he can drop out and still keep the faith."

"And if Amelia dropped out with him, we'd be six. Not much of a story anyway."

"A grand story, Ray, for sure. I just wouldn't be able to write it."

They were silent again. Snyder looked across the green toward the Rathskeller. He had not quite known his own thoughts until he heard them. Now he thought, why wait?

"I think I should leave tonight," he said. "If I write a note for Reed, will you see that he gets it?"

"Tonight?"

"In the morning, in confidence."

Rachel kissed him softly on the cheek. Then he felt her hands on his shoulders, lifting herself to her feet. Snyder stood beside her.

Gravely, she said, "I'll take myself to the Rathskeller."

"Okay," he said, "thank you."

They kissed again and their bodies came together.

"Damn you, Snyder," she whispered.

Snyder watched her walk down the steps and across the green. As she passed through the arc of light from the campus gate, he saw her turn and wave. Snyder waved in return, knowing he was invisible in the dark. It was all he could do to keep himself from running after her.

Over the common-room phone, Snyder called for the Baltimore–Washington inter-urban train schedule, a taxi, and a room near the White House at the Hay-Adams Hotel, where *Harrington's* maintained an account. He returned to his room and packed his gear. Last, he set up his typewriter and wrote to Herndon using the small pages from his notebook.

"Dear Reed:

"I am leaving the Walk this evening. Only Rachel, you, and I will know why. I'll be at the Hay-Adams Hotel all weekend and through the Fourth. Should you decide tomorrow or Sunday to lead the walkers in civil disobedience, anyone can let me know. I will rejoin you on the road and the article for *Harrington's* will proceed as before. Should you decide on the Fourth, I will be at the White House for the demonstration.

"If, however, you decide against it, not to worry. I will not write anything at all. I wouldn't be able to write without talking to you again, do you see? That's why I'm leaving now, so you can trust me. I have realized that I can give you a fair chance to make your decision according to your own lights and within the boundaries of what I do for a living. My own decision is that my story is not as important as your freedom; if you choose not to risk your parole, no story will be written. Watch out for yourself, Reed, as I'm trying to do. We both have our own dilemmas. Good luck to you and the rest."

Snyder signed his name and folded the pages. He printed Herndon's name on the outside. Then he let himself into Rachel's room, placed the note on her pillow, and made his escape.

A yellow radio cab waited for him at the campus gate. When the driver offered him the early-bird edition of the Saturday-morning newspaper, Snyder asked for a rear light. He read as they drove to the downtown station. A small item on page two caught his eye. It said that President Johnson would be spending the Fourth of July holiday at his ranch in Texas with family and friends. Snyder opened his notebook to the page bearing Herndon's last quote. He added: "When Walk reaches White House, there will be nobody home."

NINETEEN

The Good That Men Do

1

At the Hay-Adams, Snyder slept until noon. When he awoke, he turned off the room air conditioner and opened a window. He was on the fourth floor. Across Sixteenth Street, St. John's Church of the Presidents shimmered in brilliant sunshine. Snyder thought of the walkers, probably at that moment in the midday heat facing south on U.S. 29, struggling with the distance. He missed them, but not the struggle. Besides, he could use the time to advance the story. By phone, a patrolman named Leonard Miller gave him a three o'clock appointment with Lieutenant Anthony Caffuzzi, the public information officer on duty for the holiday weekend at Metropolitan Police Headquarters in the Municipal Center on Indiana Avenue. Then Snyder paid the hotel valet two dollars to put a rush on pressing his jacket and trousers, and sent out all of his laundry at a premium for overnight holiday delivery. He dressed, wearing a shirt with a necktie for the first time in seven weeks. No one, he was thinking, is more class-conscious than a cop.

At two-thirty, the hotel doorman whistled up a taxi with a weekend driver who instinctively proposed the scenic route. Snyder didn't mind; with the Walk on its way, part of any ending would be Independence Day color in the nation's capital. The driver tooled around the White House East Wing and down Fourteenth Street, crossing Constitution Avenue and onto Jefferson Drive, for a slow cruise along the Mall past the Smithsonian and the National Gallery. To his notebook, Snyder reported "a human flood on the Mall, some thousands of people almost all seemingly in motion, going to or from a picnic, a shrine, or a museum, feasting on freedom and ices, but taking their time in the weather—at 93 degrees, never saw so many red, white, and blue sun umbrellas."

The driver circled back and around the Washington Monument, where the flags hung becalmed in the humid air, and, returning to Third Street, passed north across the great white face of the Capitol, between Labor and the District Court, into Indiana Avenue. "It's right here," the driver said, "you catch our famous Municipal Center, famous above-deck for police headquarters, famous below-oh-oh for our central cell block."

In a zone of remarkable public buildings, Snyder saw before him one of the least remarkable of all. The Municipal Center was five stories high and almost twice as wide, a buff-colored stone shoe box set on a ridge so that from the front there was no hint of the unpleasantness below the main floor. To one side on the broad entrance plaza was an oversized bronze statue of one Albert Pike, described on his pedestal as "Poet Author Scholar Soldier." The statue added just the right touch; the Center looked like a bank or a post office—anything but a police station on top of a jail. In the foyer, however, the nature of the building's business was made clear with a large display of wanted posters and a memorial plaque in a glass case for Metropolitan Police officers killed in the line of duty. The latest was Martin J. Donovan, d. 1964.

From the foyer, Snyder went down a long, windowless hall to the public information office. Patrolman Leonard Miller, sweating through his gray-green summer uniform, registered Snyder's magazine credentials, New York State driver's license, and Washington address and seated him at a small conference table in an air-conditioned inner room. On each of the four walls hung a framed front page from the Washington *Post*, respectively commemorating high moments of the Kennedy years: the Kennedy-Johnson inauguration; the Cuban missile crisis; the March on Washington, led by Martin Luther King, Jr.; and the Kennedy funeral. Snyder thought someone in the office wanted to say those were already the Good Old Days.

Snyder smoked and, checking his watch at three, imagined the pilgrims' progress, the Walk at that moment perhaps entering Fairland, Maryland, with the Troubled Saint in the lead.

"Would you like a Coke, Mr. Snyder?"

Snyder stood up. Lieutenant Caffuzzi had come from an adjoining office to greet him. He was about thirty, tall and fair, and wore a yellow necktie and blue plaid summer suit with an aluminum badge pinned to his lapel. Snyder took out his notebook, putting the meeting on the record.

"No, thank you, Lieutenant," he said.

"Harrington's, right?"

"On assignment. I'm here for Monday."

They shook hands and sat down. Caffuzzi smiled politely.

"The anti-war demonstration at the White House, yes. How can I help?"

"Anything current on it? I've just arrived."

"Numbers? Deployment? No, I can't. Security. I'm sorry."

"I've been with a group walking from Chicago. They'll be here tomorrow to lead it, noon on the Fourth. I expect some will do civil disobedience."

"Yes, we hear. Not a big group, but leading a rally of local nonviolents. You'll need working press credentials to get close." Caffuzzi called to Patrolman Miller. "Lenny, please, w.p. temporary!"

"Thank you," Snyder said. "I'm interested in police procedure for civil disobedience. You understand, my story is about the people who've walked a long way to make their protest. This is the climax. So, I'm interested in the law."

"The law?"

"The D.C. law and the police procedure."

"Of course. Well, assuming non-violence, the offense is disorderly conduct. Specifically, under the District code, revised and so forth, 'obstruction,' or impeding free flow of traffic, is a misdemeanor. That's your routine civil disobedience, sit-ins, lie-ins, high jinks associated with free speech. Get that?"

Snyder looked up from his notebook. "Falling under whose jurisdiction?"

"Metro PD, usually, unless someone were to penetrate the White House gate and engage the federals. Routinely, we process White House sidewalk and street demonstrators at the Second Precinct station house on Virginia Avenue."

"Involving what?"

"You want all of it?"

"I need to know."

"Okay, there's a red-tape routine, record taking and fingerprint check, maybe a mug shot for a real rowdy. Also, we interview for criminal information, previous convictions, parole status."

"I'm sorry. Parole status?"

"Am I going too fast?"

"A little."

"Yes. Parole status—we hold parolees pending further information from a parole officer."

"Under local jurisdiction?"

"Nationwide. Do you have a parolee?"

"No."

"Well, so, assuming the perpetrators are squeaky-clean, Washington area residents may request release on personal recognizance. Out-of-towners may post bond, or stay with us until they have their day in court. Refusing release Monday means transfer in here, at the Center, to the central cell block until court opens Tuesday morning. No visitors. But, sure, lawyers. You get a chance to pay your fine or ask for a trial, which may get on the docket in a matter of weeks to a couple of months. That's about it. Routine, like on television."

"What's the damage?"

"Minimum's ten dollars or ten days."

"Not a lot."

"Deliberately. Taxpayers don't want our limited facilities filled with nice miscreants. It's the hassle that deters."

"Hassle," Snyder said, and wrote, and turned to a clean page in his notebook. "What else?"

"You ask."

"How's your jail?"

"Truth? Is there a good jail?"

"No."

"Overcrowded and understaffed. Don't quote me."

"I won't."

Caffuzzi beamed as Patrolman Miller brought in Snyder's temporary working press credentials. He signed a red card and two forms.

"Jack, this card gives you the run of the town for a week. You have the right to cross police lines, the usual press courtesies, and so forth, July four through ten. During a scene, wear it where we can see it."

Snyder countersigned the card and the forms. "Thank you, Lieutenant," he said.

"I've got an idea for a *Harrington's* story myself," Caffuzzi said. "We've got a special narcotics unit doing great things—maybe I could send you something on it."

"By all means."

"I do some free-lance writing. Pen name's Anthony Pike."

" 'Poet Author Scholar Soldier' Pike?"

"That's Albert, but you know where I got it."

"By all means, send me a query, to my office."

"I will! And just for that, you need anything while you're here, let me know."

Caffuzzi wrote his private telephone number in Snyder's notebook.

"Twenty-four hours a day at that number, they'll find me."

"That's a real favor, Lieutenant," Snyder said, smiling as he appreciated the secret of Caffuzzi's cordiality.

"Cops can't help it, Jack," Caffuzzi nodded. "They've always got a quid pro quo."

2

That night at the Albion Motel in Fairland, the letter that Reed Herndon wrote home said:

"Dear Mother:

"Tomorrow we arrive in Washington! You can guess how that satisfies us even though we are only eight. Now we don't even have Jack Snyder (he is the writer for *Harrington's* magazine).

"I must explain, so you won't be surprised by whatever happens. A national magazine story, of course, will magnify all we've done, so anticipation of it has greatly concerned us from day to day—and has become decisive now because the writer has given me to choose whether there will be any story at all. I don't want to trouble you with all the nuances, but it is an either-or situation, for which neither of us is to blame. It's just the way we are, the writer and me. And I like him very much. We all do.

"What's it all about? Well, I can decide right up to the White

House gate, but I do have to decide between civil disobedience (story) and parole (no story). I never wanted this much responsibility —yet, there it is.

"It's so personal! Just one walker is up to date on all this, Rachel Abraham, who can take over for me. But rest assured, either way, I will be all right. To be or not to be is not the question. It's time (prison) versus space (magazine)! Not an easy decision (when you know all the nuances), but either way, I can make it.

"Love, as ever, Reedy."

3

For Snyder, as a journalist, despite his bond with Herndon, the moment of their crossing the District line on Sunday afternoon was prime material—his Walk making the penultimate distance, setting foot in Washington, before there was a crowd to dilute the walkers' private appreciation of victory, surely an epiphany for the five (Rachel Abraham, Reed Herndon, June Matsushida, Dorene Quink, Luther Wood) who had walked all the way, for the driver (Arley Broyle), and even for the two (Amelia Pendergraft, Sylvia Vecchio) who came later! So at two o'clock, for insurance against professional temptation, he took himself to the David Lean movie *Lawrence of Arabia*, four hours with intermission, playing second-run at a neighborhood theater around the corner from Edgar's Pub, a place he knew in Georgetown. He stayed to the end.

Under the circumstances, he was thinking as the lights went up, the movie was a bad choice, reminding you, for one thing, of journalism's often sorry role in the fate of heroes. Worse, it occurred to him, was the point that the movie ignores, that Lawrence himself had lived to tell the tale, wrote *The Seven Pillars of Wisdom*, and taught lots of little boys growing up between the wars, even in Topeka, about the nobility of good causes. That writers write and thereby justify their existence was just the sort of argument that Bruce Erlanger might soon make. Did you need to be reminded of that, too?

That evening, Snyder ate dinner alone at Edgar's Pub, killing time in the air-conditioning with coffee and a complete reading of the early edition of Monday's Washington *Post*. He also clipped the *Post*'s

back-page box of cost-free holiday events, including midnight fireworks (Reflecting Pool), a dawn prayer service (Jefferson Memorial), a noon anti-war demonstration (White House, West Gate), an
afternoon pro-war demonstration (Capitol steps), and a sunset band
concert (Washington Monument). The fact, he was thinking, that the
Walk's effort is merely part of the Fourth's routine is something else
not to be forgotten.

Later, at the bar, Snyder ordered a Scotch and discussed American
League baseball with Edgar himself, in particular the Senators-Indians holiday double-header at Griffith Stadium. He declined a second
drink, but went yet another coffee with Edgar, and stayed on to
watch the eleven o'clock news on the television above Edgar's display of Irish liquors. He learned from the President's deputy press
secretary that surgical targeting by U.S. planners had minimized civilian casualties in the bombing of Hanoi. Snyder left after the news,
having managed by then to stay away from his hotel room most of
the day.

Deep in the lobby, Rachel was waiting for him.

He spotted her first, standing near the elevators. She wore her
other outfit, the sleeveless blue linen summer dress. A leather purse
the size of a saddlebag hung from her shoulder. She had just looked
down at her wristwatch. Snyder asked, "Waiting long?" and saw her
face, so tanned, rise toward him with a heart-stopping smile.

"Twenty minutes," she said. "We're here, on Military Road. I
took a cab."

They shook hands. Her eyes were very bright. She seemed breathless.

"I'm glad," Snyder said.

"I thought we should talk, so I came as soon as I could."

"The bar's downstairs. But closes at half past midnight."

"Feel like a walk? No eavesdroppers."

"Walking's what I do best."

They circled the lobby and left by the H Street door. A sudden
fresh breeze had begun to cool the night from hot to warm. Entering
Lafayette Park, Rachel said, "Everyone misses you."

"I missed you. Today especially."

They walked around the Clark Mills statue of Andrew Jackson,
who seemed dour and unfriendly in the darkness.

"We had a great day!" Rachel exclaimed. "We left Fairland to beat the heat at seven-thirty this morning. At three, oh, my, dripping, we stood squarely on the District line just below Silver Spring. Everyone stepped across together, right in the middle of the street. We laughed. We cried. We hugged each other. People thought we were mad. A man got out of his car and congratulated us. His son had burned his draft card. He was very proud of that. There was a photographer from the Associated Press, thanks to Mr. Katz. I thought of you, Jack. I knew you'd have made many notes."

"I wish."

"And Reed gave a little speech. He remembered all the walkers—Sam and Molly, Joe Rice and Vachel, Peter and George and Ellroy, Lester Kupferman and Reverend Nick, the Fishbeins, Frank Dunne, Jack Snyder, everybody."

"Sounds like a casualty list."

Snyder knew he had hurt her.

"I thought you'd be pleased," she said.

"I am pleased."

Rachel stopped Snyder under a park lamplight. There was a momentary traffic tangle on Pennsylvania Avenue and angry horns honked. A young couple quietly smoked pot on a nearby bench. On a shadowed patch of lawn, two couples shared a blanket, respectively entwined; each had brought along an overnight bag. Rachel took a sheet of onionskin paper from her purse.

"Then there's this," she said. "It's the final version of the petition, a carbon copy. Everyone wants your name on it, too."

"I can't do that."

"We know about your stiff neck, dear heart, but we thought you'd be pleased if we asked."

"I am, very." Snyder felt she wanted something for which she was not asking.

Without reading, he examined the petition. It ran four paragraphs, typed single-spaced, with a list of the names of the walkers who had spent at least one night on the road. "This is it?" he asked.

"It's for you. The original goes with all the signatures on Sam's petition sheet. Mostly, Reed and I revised the old draft, kept brief for the newspapers. We finished it an hour ago, and Sam approved."

"You spoke to him?"

"Reed called the hospital. Sam's all right, but not terrific. He knows about Frank Dunne. He asked about you and Reed said you were fine."

"Meaning?"

"Just that—I don't think Reed wanted to upset Sam."

Snyder folded the sheet and tucked it into his notebook. They walked on. Across the avenue, the White House was asleep. There were security lights on low voltage in the guardhouse at the West Gate. Snyder counted four guards on duty, three inside, one at the iron gate itself. At the curb on Jackson Place, he made a note. They continued along the north side of the avenue, passing Blair House, to the corner of Seventeenth Street. Here they were opposite the looming, gray-black fortress of the Executive Office Building.

Rachel looked back. "Was that the West Gate?"

"That was it."

"It will seem different tomorrow."

"Yes," Snyder said, taking Rachel's arm. "Tell me about Reed."

Rachel sighed, then paused, like a performer in the wings about to go onstage. "Okay," she said. "Well, I went to his room yesterday, early, before breakfast, with your note. He read it and handed it to me. It was a good letter, Jack. He didn't say much. You know Reed —sometimes he seems so utterly composed and yet so isolated. He said you were an admirable man. His exact word—admirable. He thanked me and asked whether I intended to tell the others. I said I didn't intend to discuss your offer with anyone. I told him I would tell people that you'd wanted to go to Washington and that's all. That would be no lie. He said he would do the same and that's what we've done. Everyone's curious, but they've just assumed you had work. Since yesterday, Reed has not mentioned your name except in his speech. And I don't think even Amelia knows what's on his mind."

"Do you?"

"He's into all the plans. Tonight at Katz's house, before he typed the petition, the walkers met together, with Mr. Katz and three local anti-war leaders. Reed was chairman. We heard from Mr. Katz that perhaps three hundred people will march with us."

"Three hundred!"

"It's wonderful, but Mr. Katz seemed restrained. It's about ordinary these days, he said. Maybe it's not a monster rally, Reed said, but it's more than eight walkers. And it's part of something that's growing—I said. Mr. Katz smiled. That's right, I guess, he said, and you have your story in *Harrington's* magazine. I looked at Reed. Not a flicker. So, the meeting went on. The White House, the police, and the press are all on notice. Mr. Katz's got a law firm here, so he knows how these things are done. He told us the President's gone to Texas, but plenty of press has stayed behind and, of course, the TV.

"After that, Reed laid it all out for us. Tomorrow morning, eight-thirty, walkers and supporters assemble at Military Road and Connecticut Avenue, march the seven miles to Washington Circle by eleven forty-five, then down Pennsylvania to the West Gate at noon. Reed wants all eight of us to stand at the gate and ask for a representative of the President to receive our petition. If someone comes, Reed will hand him the petition. There will be copies for the press. If no one comes, Reed will hand the petition to a guard. And if the guard refuses, he will lay it at the gate. I remember Reed's next sentence. He said, whatever happens, after the petition has been delivered, those who choose to bear further witness against the war will sit down at the gate and not move unless arrested."

" 'Those who choose'?"

"Yes."

"So he hasn't chosen."

"He said he would not ask any of us to pledge ourselves to civil disobedience until the moment comes. Tonight, he said, is the night to think about it, meaning himself, too, and tomorrow at noon, you decide, he said, meaning he will, too. Then he said, 'Let's do the petition.' "

"No word of advice, no recommendation?"

"None."

"What are you going to do tomorrow, Ray?"

"I don't know. How can I know? I think I will do whatever Reed does."

"So might everyone."

"Not Arley. Reed's put him on 'the post-Walk watch.' And not Mr. Katz, because he can't risk getting hung up before he's needed for legal matters. But everyone else might be arrested because they love Reed. Reed is conscious of that, too. For the first time, I feel sorry for him. It was actually easier for him when he expected you to write about the Walk, no matter what happened. He really had no choice. Your story meant too much."

"Seems to be coming out the same way."

"I wouldn't swear to that. I'm just saying, freedom to choose is no blessing for him."

"Does he know the procedure, Ray? If he's arrested and his parole status becomes known, his parole officer must be called. That's certain. I've checked."

"Yes, he knows. We all know. Mr. Katz briefed us on the law, the fines, everything."

"Mr. Katz is rough."

"Everyone knows the consequences of civil disobedience for Reed. But can Reed live with himself if there's no story? That's the question now."

"The trouble with him is goodness, Ray."

"Just him?"

They had been walking south on Seventeenth Street. At the end, Snyder knew, they would find the Reflecting Pool and, at its tip, the Lincoln Memorial. Now there was a scurrying of crowds in the dark on both sides of the street moving that way. And ahead, in the park, just then a string of fireworks exploded in rapid sequence, lighting up a throng celebrating the Fourth at midnight. People cheered. A battery of Roman candles shot a stream of colored balls into the night sky. The latecomers broke into a run toward the display.

Rachel stopped short. "I'm not up for this, Jack," she said.

"No," he said, turning with her against the crush.

"It would be nice to visit Mr. Lincoln at this hour, but not with a cast of thousands."

They retraced their steps along Seventeenth Street. Then again on the corner at Pennsylvania Avenue, they paused with the midnight celebration well behind them. Expectant taxis lined up across the avenue and brightened the corner with their headlights. Rachel nervously ran her hands through her hair. Buying time, Snyder lit a cigarette.

"What is it, Ray?" he asked at last.

"Where will you be tomorrow?"

"Watching from someplace."

"With the press?"

"Up close? No, I don't want Reed to feel I might betray him."

"He knows you wouldn't."

"Maybe across the street, where we were—Lafayette Park."

"I'll look for you." Rachel folded her arms across her chest. "I'd better get a cab now," she said abruptly.

Snyder waited. Rachel turned aside, then back, facing him.

"Say it, Ray," Snyder said.

"You were not wrong, Jack," she said. "Reed is Reed."

"I really don't want him to go back to prison."

"But the deal's not working. He's going to do it tomorrow."

"How do you know?"

"Just like I know you won't do all you can to stop him. He's a pacifist and you're a writer—both blind!"

Snyder met her eyes. "Ray," he said, "if there's a story, Reed's got to be in it."

"That's what I mean."

Accused, Snyder shook his head. "I can't lie, Ray!"

"Oh, I know. But if Reed's not in the end of the story, would that change anything?" Her voice was rising. "You're always selecting things to write and things not to write—your story's about the struggle of the Walk, not every damn detail about every damn walker!" Rachel's voice turned sharp. "You told me that yourself! An endurance story, you called it—you can leave him out!"

Snyder held her by the shoulders. Her skin felt cold to his touch. Sternly, Snyder said, "He's got to decide, Ray."

Rachel whispered a cry: "He's going to prison, Snyder!"

"He doesn't have to," Snyder said—too harshly, he knew—"but I can't stop him!" He released her.

"You can!"

"Okay, Ray, I won't," Snyder said, and smiled in distress.

Rachel flinched and then struck him hard with the flat of her right hand against his left cheek and ear. A light flashed behind Snyder's eyes and the inner ear twanged painfully. She did not raise her hand again. Snyder leaned away with his hand to his face. He was surprised to see that he still held on to his cigarette.

"I want you to feel that all night," Rachel said, seething.

Snyder watched her step off the curb and hail a waiting taxi. As if by well-mannered reflex, he followed and, when the taxi pulled up, held the door for her. He leaned in at the window. It was the release of the last angry word that he wanted.

"Tomorrow, Ray," he said bitterly, "pay your fine."

"Do us a favor," she shot back, "drown next time!"

As the taxi pulled away, Snyder slammed his fist on the trunk. The driver braked, then continued. Stepping backwards to the curb, Snyder kicked a trash basket. Blackmailing bitch, he was thinking, you blackmailing bitch!

He cooled off walking to his hotel. In Lafayette Park, he stood on a bench. From there, he saw that he could have a good view of the West Gate. He would need binoculars. He jumped down and continued toward H Street. He felt calm now. He imagined Rachel in the taxi, taking pleasure in her direct hits, physical and verbal. But his cheek felt no more than a slight sting. And if her mistake was subornation of perjury, his was revenge. He had left himself open, and she'd delivered the touch. A professional, he was thinking, should've known better; you should've been taking notes.

At the hotel desk, he left an eight o'clock wake-up call with the night clerk and went to his room. His laundry was back. He undressed down to his shorts, drank a glass of water, and sat at the desk with his feet on the bed to read the Walk's petition. It said:

"To the President of the United States:

"A few days ago, Americans bombed Hanoi and Haiphong. Our immoral and illegal involvement in the civil war of South Vietnam escalates into an ever-wider immoral and illegal war with North Vietnam. We fight, we are told, against 'aggression from the North,' for an 'independent South Vietnam,' to 'honor our treaty obligations,' for the 'credibility of our military,' to deny 'Chinese influence in Southeast Asia,' and, above all, to 'defend Western democracy against Communism.' Yet, given all these 'reasons,' our policy is to fight without a declaration of war by the United States Congress, and in contradiction of your own election campaign promises of two years ago, with dwindling support from the American people and our allies, and with no lawful justification other than your own executive powers, of dubious merit. Such a policy shames us all, Mr. President.

"In democratic protest against this immoral and illegal war, the undersigned have participated in a Walk from Chicago to Washington over the past seven weeks and six days. We have spoken out against the war and we have listened to the arguments, pro and con, of our fellow citizens. Now we bring you our petition on behalf of our group, the World Institute for Survival Education, and on behalf of so many other Americans who have helped us on our way, with one simple request—that you commence serious talks now with all concerned parties to make peace, Mr. President.

"Some of us believe all war is wrong. Some of us believe only war in vital self-defense can be justified. All of us hate aggression. All of us seek the renunciation of the use of force and violence in the affairs of nations. And all of us believe that this war, prosecuted by your administration in defiance of both law and morality, must cease, Mr. President.

"Mr. President, do not underestimate the tide rising in our country. Profound resistance to the war in Vietnam has begun here at home. It is non-violent, and only as such will it be decisive in confronting and contesting the immoral and illegal use of force by our beloved country, or any other. So therefore, in the name of democracy and our national pride, we call upon you now to join us on the frontier of a new era of non-violence for America and the world, an era in which war will not be inevitable, but obsolete. Mr. President, we call upon you, in the name of God, stop the bombing and start talking to end this war. Mr. President: Stop and talk!"

Snyder reread the petition and turned to the desk. It's no Gettysburg Address, he was thinking, but precise and persuasive, most interesting because the bombing of Hanoi has escalated the gentle walkers' theme from a "Walk for Talks" wish to a demand: "Stop and talk!" He moved his typewriter aside to make more room for his notebook. He labeled a page "Petition's Progress," and jotted down the genesis of the petition, recalling Rachel's account, and listed the names of all those "pilgrims" who had signed it. "Pilgrim's Progress" came to his mind again, became a plaything, and suggested itself as his title for the story, adjusted, for accuracy as well as irony, from the singular to the plural, apostrophe *s* to *s* apostrophe. He wrote "Pilgrims' Progress" in capital letters, knowing Bruce Erlanger was sure to add an explicit subtitle, say, "The Story of a Long Walk Against the War." Still, if it was good enough for John Bunyan—

Suddenly depressed, Snyder lit a cigarette.

Rachel has a point, he told himself. You have a title, yes, if you have a story.

He recentered the typewriter on the desk and removed the case. Then he rolled in a sheet of hotel stationery. He typed the title and, four spaces below, the subtitle. Yes, all right, he thought.

His hands rested on the familiar typewriter keys. Yes, a cover story, he was thinking, but only if Reed Herndon sits down at the West Gate and takes the consequences. Rachel's slap was for that.

With one finger, Snyder tapped the typewriter's space bar and tapped again and again until the margin bell tolled. He slammed the keyboard with the heel of his right hand and a dozen little hammers jammed together in the well of the machine.

No harm done—he could tell. Portables, unlike people, are not easily broken. But at least now he knew that he wanted Herndon to quit.

4

The hotel switchboard woke Snyder with a wish for a happy Fourth of July and a temperature reading; it was ninety-one degrees at 8 A.M., and climbing.

He left the hotel at nine, wearing his necktie for the police and his hat for the sun. He had pinned Lieutenant Caffuzzi's temporary working press card to his jacket's left lapel and was carrying the jacket. He taxied to Mount Vernon Square, where an Army-Navy store operated 365 days a year. He spent thirty-two dollars on a good pair of surplus GI binoculars. It was almost eleven o'clock when another cab dropped him back at the hotel. There were no messages, so he walked on to Lafayette Park, thinking he would have liked best of all a four-word message from Rachel about Herndon's decision: no arrest, no story. It was the message he wanted, even as he prepared to finish in style, and even as he wondered whether he had come to wanting that message only with the virtual certainty that he wasn't going to get it. You are good, he thought, both ways.

Over the park's open spaces, the sun shone bleak and brutal through a globelike haze. A crowd of about two hundred spectators had gathered so far, tending to seek the fringe of shade under the old elms along Jackson Place. An elderly Negro couple with a red umbrella and a picnic basket occupied about half of Snyder's chosen bench. They smiled with him as he draped his jacket over the backrest and climbed up on the bench to test his new glasses.

Snyder panned across the avenue along the elegant façade of the White House—East Wing to his left, living quarters straight ahead, and West Wing to his right, all protected by lawn and fence. He focused momentarily on workmen in khaki finishing the job of setting up wooden horse-and-beam barricades on the curbs along both sides of the avenue. Then he sighted past the West Gate to the Executive Office Building, across Seventeenth Street, and up the angle of Pennsylvania Avenue, down which the Walk was to come. The image of a bus rider getting out at the intersection came through large and clear.

Over the next thirty minutes, Snyder saw a police unit with four squad cars assume control of traffic on the avenue west of Fifteenth Street. A blue-and-white communications van with the letters MPD on its sides pulled up at Blair House. Approaching from H Street, a train of vehicles entered Jackson Place: ambulance, prisoners' van, and a patrol bus. A company of patrolmen wearing blue hard hats and carrying batons assembled in the street and marched quickly across the avenue to take up guard positions every twenty feet along the White House fence. A dozen federal security police in green fatigue suits and jump boots moved randomly behind the fence on the White House lawn. Busying themselves at the West Gate were six guards, smartly dressed in white caps with blue visors, white shirts, blue ties, and blue trousers with white stripes. Batons appeared to be their only personal weapons. And behind a sidewalk barricade just east of the gate itself, a cluster of reporters, photographers, and film cameramen and technicians from the three national TV networks arranged themselves for the action. It was as though the President's absence had combined with the usual scarcity of news on any holiday to favor high visibility for the Walk. "The press turnout," Snyder wrote, "is a surprise (to me)."

The growing numbers in the park surprised Snyder, too. With only minutes to wait, people now stood three deep at the curbside barricades and the inner walks were bringing more. Snyder guessed a crowd of five hundred, mainly couples, black and white, many with neatly dressed children waving small American flags. About thirty carried anti-war signs. One man dressed like Uncle Sam in a red, white, and blue plastic suit wore a dissenting sandwich board, "Kill Chicoms" on one side and "God Bless LBJ" on the other. But the flags and umbrellas outnumbered slogans of any kind. A holiday crowd, Snyder thought, and when it comes to liberty, more celebratory than expressive, for sure. But a real crowd.

Precisely at noon, the bells of St. John's Church began pealing for Independence Day. They rang out "God Bless America" and "America the Beautiful" in a churchly, almost somber tone. They fell silent at twelve-ten. The crowd stirred. Snyder saw an MPD van stopping at Blair House. Twelve more patrolmen stepped out. A sergeant assembled them on the center stripe of the avenue between Jackson Place and Seventeenth Street.

Snyder adjusted his binoculars. From the northwest on the avenue above Seventeenth Street, he saw two policemen on foot coming in slow step over a slight ridge through a shining mirage of hot air. A policeman at Seventeenth Street passed one last private car through the intersection. Two photographers left the press barricade at the West Gate and hurried west, across Seventeenth Street, toward the tips of the signs and flags of the demonstration appearing then behind the police vanguard.

"They're coming," Snyder said, and lent a hand as the elderly couple scrambled up beside him on the bench.

In sharp focus, Snyder saw Reed Herndon in the glow of the mirage. He carried the Walk's lead sign and seemed alone. Then, ten paces back, four walkers came on in a second rank: June Matsushida with her flag, Rachel with REMEMBER NORMAN MORRISON, Luther Wood with his recorder, and Amelia Pendergraft with one of the four photographic placards, unseen since Chicago, "Marine Zippo Torches Viet Village." After a gap of another five paces came a third rank of three walkers, Sylvia Vecchio, Arley Broyle, and Dorene Quink, each with a new one-word placard, combining to make the Walk's final, three-word point: STOP AND TALK. And at their heels marched two men in black suits like twin undertakers, Joe Rice carrying the Walk's trident with his white cane in the crook of his left elbow and Vachel Rice holding his father's right hand. Snyder felt a rush of tears to his eyes.

Still he watched. The Walk stopped in place on the avenue about fifty yards above the Seventeenth Street intersection, where now four photographers and a TV film cameraman knelt in anticipation. Then through the mirage came the first rank of supporting demonstrators, and then another and another, strung out across the avenue in ragged lines of ten or twelve, until at last about thirty ranks topped the ridge with scores of signs and American flags seemingly afloat above them. Thin but distinct, the sound of voices chanting "Stop and talk!" reached the park. Four hundred marchers, Snyder guessed, and again fastened his glasses on Herndon, who appeared to wait on a signal that a certain close order had been achieved.

Standing next to Snyder on the bench, the elderly man said, "Oh, my, a ship with a hundred sails!"

Snyder smiled. He would remember that. He's right, Reed, Snyder was thinking, so how's the old agony, Reed? Not the greatest outpouring today, as crowds go, but above expectations. The Walk won't be ignored! It's become a ship with a hundred sails! Walk away, Reed! You've walked on the water. You can walk away!

Snyder saw Herndon step off again with slow and deliberate steps, so that the demonstration moved together like a single organism, the Walk at one with its supporters. Never assume a goddamn thing, but —he was thinking—Rachel is right: Reed is Reed.

Snyder turned to the elderly man. In a decisive instant, he said, "Please save my place."

"Of course," the man said. "It's the best view."

Snyder jumped from the bench. He shoved his arms into his jacket, and pressed himself through the crowd at the corner of Jackson Place and the avenue. When he cleared the barricade, his jacket and tie were in order. He jogged along the north lane to the sergeant commanding the center-stripe patrol. The sergeant stood at an angle, one eye on the approaching demonstration, the other on the approaching civilian. He was a trim, blond young man, wearing a blue hard hat with the chin strap, guardsman style, under his lower lip. His name tag read: "L. Scott, Sgt."

"Can't come through," Sergeant Scott said. "This is a crowd-control zone."

"Working press," Snyder said, pointing toward the intersection. "A photo story. I'm supposed to be there, with my photographer."

With timeless deliberation, Sergeant Scott examined the card on Snyder's lapel. "A Caffuzzi card," he said.

"An original."

"Okay. They're moving. Don't get trampled."

Snyder crossed directly to the south side of the avenue, slipped between two barricades, and took to the sidewalk just above the gatehouse. A patrolman eyed him, but let him go on, seemingly because he was aimed away from the White House. He began to jog again as he saw the Walk within the Seventeenth Street intersection. The photographers were already retreating to the press barricade.

Snyder passed another patrolman on the sidewalk about fifty yards beyond the gatehouse at the quirky corner separating the White House grounds from the Executive Office Building. "Wait," the patrolman said. Snyder turned. They were both dripping sweat. The patrolman said, "Hot, isn't it?" Snyder sighed. He had no ready excuse to proceed.

"Working press," he said, hand to his left lapel.

"Reporters by the gate, sir," the patrolman said, indicating the press barricade. "Petitioners are coming this way."

"I know. It's my story."

"Just wait, sir," the patrolman said, with finality.

Though the patrolman paid no more attention to him, Snyder waited as though in custody. He watched as the walkers cleared the intersection and saw that, in fact, Herndon was tacking south toward the sidewalk on which he stood. At the same time, the larger procession of supporters had veered north toward the crowd-control zone at the center stripe. Sergeant Scott's patrol had formed a channel to the street side of the barricades, where, Snyder realized, the supporters would become an audience of four hundred for the Walk's drama on the sidewalk at the West Gate.

In the lead, Herndon marched toward Snyder with military serenity, carrying the lead sign high and steady. Behind respective gaps of about ten paces each, making each Walk sign clearly visible, the three ranks of walkers followed. June seemed to see Snyder first.

Above the din of chanting in the street, Snyder heard her call out "There's Jack!" Dorene and Broyle exclaimed "Jack!" in unison. Joe

Rice through wired, clenched teeth: "Hey! Hey! Jack!" Though no happy cry came from Rachel, Snyder thought there was more than anger in her startled look, dismay if not regret. But it was Herndon who most counted and who, after a glance of human recognition, gave him only a taut nod. His dauntless manner suggested more than ever to Snyder that he had made peace with himself. Snyder asked himself, shouldn't you respect that?

Ten yards separated Snyder from Herndon. Strange, he thought, no sounds of walking feet, those wondrous scrape and shuffle sounds of the highway days; of course, someone's turned up the volume on "Stop—talk! Stop—talk!" Herndon won't even hear you.

At last, Herndon was so close Snyder could see the whites of his knuckles as he clutched the lead sign. What do you have from now to the gate, Snyder asked himself, thirty seconds? Skip the hellos.

As Herndon came abreast, Snyder fell in beside him, next to the curb. He realized the cadence was faster than it had looked. Make it twenty seconds, he told himself, in medias res.

"Reed, listen," he said. "We're beyond my letter now. I want you to know that the story is aborted. Canceled."

Herndon kept his pace, staring straight ahead, and asked, "What about 'right of salvage,' Jack?"

"Not for this story, no matter what, never. I give you my word. I won't write it."

"After all?"

"After all! On my honor—no matter what you do, whether you sit down or stand aside, I am not writing about any part of the Walk."

"It's the walkers' story, Jack. Mine, too."

"It's my assignment and I have aborted it. You know I'll keep my word, even if you spend a year in jail. I swear it to you."

Herndon glanced at Snyder. "All right, but why?"

"It's not a necessary story."

"For me, it absolutely is."

"I know. That's 'why.' "

They were a few paces from the gatehouse. Snyder saw a blur of waiting guards, exulting crowds, and pointing microphones and cameras. You have not said it straight out, he was thinking—that he is more important than the story. But surely, he understands you!

"We're to halt here," Herndon said, "we close ranks, get out the petition, and go on."

Behind them, on the edge of Snyder's awareness, the walkers were closing in. He registered Rachel's white blouse and the big leather purse on her shoulder. Snyder looked for Herndon's eyes, to try for a knockout.

"Let it end without you, Reed! Nothing's going to be written!"

"The story's the end, Jack. We need the story. You know that."

"Hear me! I won't have you on my conscience."

Snyder had delivered his hardest blow. He sensed rather than saw that the ranks of walkers were upon them. There is too much noise, he was thinking, too much intensity, and nothing left—failing the miserable argument of "conscience"—except perhaps this: that actually seeing you yourself walk away might yet move him. Snyder waited only for a last word. He saw sweat on Herndon's glasses and an aching smile on his face.

"Then do civil disobedience with us," Herndon said.

"I won't even watch," Snyder lied, and abruptly turned his back on Herndon.

Louder than ever, the Walk's crowd chanted, "Stop—talk! Stop—talk!" and Snyder slipped between the barricades into the anonymous midst of it.

5

Snyder knew he must not only watch but find out how the Walk was going to end. With no story to write, there was still a story to be told, if only in self-defense, to Erlanger. He hated this last, but it was true: the man who really owned him would have to know the outcome. He jogged across the avenue on a straight line toward his benchmates' red umbrella rising above the spectators in Lafayette Park. Somewhere, his hat had been lost, which, he thought, will be just as well. Hatless, he was most probably unrecognizable at a hundred yards should any walker glance his way. The elderly couple were saving his place. "Thank you," Snyder said as he regained his perch, bathed in sweat.

"You're a reporter," the elderly man said, reading Snyder's lapel card.

"Yes," Snyder said. "But I'm off duty now."

"My, my," the man said, "but it gets you into places, doesn't it?"

"Yes, it does."

Snyder adjusted his binoculars. The sun-bleached tableau across the avenue and over the Walk's crowd seemed close enough to touch. Snyder panned with care, west to east, through the flags and signs. Sergeant Scott had moved his patrol onto the sidewalk about twenty yards above the gatehouse. The ten walkers held their signs aloft in a tight group next to the fence outside the gatehouse. Snyder thought Herndon would be announcing his decision at last.

Snyder saw a lone guard in blue-trimmed white, taller than any of them, step up to the Walk with his palm extended toward the West Gate. Between white brick pillars, the double-door vehicle gate was shut, with two guards at the ready, one centered on each door. The pedestrian gate in the fence beside the gatehouse was also shut, but unguarded.

There was Herndon meeting with the tall guard, listening, nodding, apparently agreeing; Herndon speaking to Arley Broyle; and Broyle collecting the walkers' signs. June clung to her flag. Awkwardly, Broyle stacked the signs against the fence just above the gatehouse. Rachel opened her purse. The sheaf of white papers in her hand would be copies of the petition. Behind the press barricade, there was a flurry of waving hands. Dorene took petitions from Rachel to the reporters. An envelope passed from Rachel to Herndon. That would be the original petition with the signatures.

At last, Herndon led the other nine walkers through the remaining fifteen paces and into a single rank facing the vehicle gate. Like a ringmaster, the tall guard had moved with them, confronting Herndon at dead center. Herndon's back arched and his shoulders lifted. The crowd at the barricades fell silent. In the park, Snyder suddenly heard the murmur of voices and a child crying.

The elderly man asked, "What's the boy doing?"

"Presenting a petition for the President," Snyder said.

"Oh, glory—they'll say, son, send it by mail."

Snyder had to remind himself that he was not working. It was a quotation he might have used.

In that moment, the tall guard had spread his arms, shook his head, and smiled. He would be saying that there was no one inside prepared to accept the petition. Herndon bent below Snyder's line of sight, presumably placing the envelope at the tall guard's feet. The cameras pointed down with him. The tall guard returned the envelope to Herndon. The Walk's crowd groaned its disappointment.

Herndon faced the press to read the petition. Microphones reached for his voice. Reporters behind cameramen slipped out toward the curb for a better view. There was a short, sharp cheer from the Walk's crowd, a fifteen-second pause, then another cheer, another pause, another cheer, each cheer apparently following the end of a sentence, until a high, loud cheer with applause sounded conclusive. The Walk's crowd waved flags and punched the air with fists and V signs. Herndon waved the petition to the crowd and the walkers themselves applauded him. He can walk away even now, Snyder was thinking, even now, Reed, even now. The way out is walking away.

June stepped forward. Snyder watched her shove her flag between the bars of the vehicle gate and onto the White House drive, where an inner guard stood unperturbed. Slowly, from front to back, a wave of silence overtook the Walk's crowd, which seemed to Snyder to understand that the civil disobedience had begun. June turned and her body sank so that Snyder could see only her head and shoulders as she sat with her back against the gate. At once, she was joined by Sylvia, Dorene, and Amelia. Joe and Vachel Rice moved to the gate and disappeared from sight, presumably lying flat on the sidewalk. Rachel and Luther Wood exchanged a glance and let themselves down, and must have been kneeling. Herndon had stepped back. Now he looked right and left as though to satisfy himself that all were in position. Then he, too, disappeared. Only Arley Broyle remained standing, hands folded at his chin, the sole survivor surveying the field of honor. So the police would arrest nine out of ten.

The tall guard bent toward the walkers. The shadow of his visor hid his expression. He would be explaining the consequences of the Walk's misdemeanors. The Walk's crowd began a new chant: "No! No! No!" The tall guard straightened. He glanced left, an arm raised, and Snyder panned right. Sergeant Scott and his patrol were walking slowly toward the gate.

Snyder lowered his glasses. The prisoners' van had pulled out from Jackson Place and was circling behind the Walk's crowd toward a guarded parking space at the curb paralleling the press zone. As the driver adroitly backed into the space, the van's rear door slid open. And on the sidewalk between the press barricade and the curb where, a moment before, several reporters and photographers had stood, there was a clear path manned by two policemen from the fence guard.

Snyder checked his watch. It was minutes before one. Still with his naked eye, he again looked to the gate. A 20/20 view of his perfect failure—Herndon's arrested and he has no story—was close enough: two of Sergeant Scott's men were lifting Herndon as though he sat in a chair. Herndon seemed limp, but they carried him easily through the path and into the rear of the van. They seemed deaf to jeers and blind to shaking fists. Two-man police teams rapidly followed with Wood and Rachel in the same chair-carrying grip, and another two-man team carried Joe Rice, prone and stiff as a steel beam, with his cane on his chest, while Vachel Rice walked just behind. In close order, the four teams returned to the gate for June, Amelia, Dorene, and Sylvia. The bus departed, in slow motion east toward Fifteenth Street, as the clock struck one in the bell tower of St. John's Church. The MPD had arrested the nine walkers in less than ten minutes. Snyder thought he might have made a note of that, too.

Snyder found Arley Broyle with his binoculars. Broyle was already trudging toward the signs. The Walk's crowd was staying to sing "We Shall Overcome," flags waving in rhythmic accompaniment. A word passed to Broyle from Sergeant Scott. Broyle turned away, then with sudden purpose turned back. He was questioning Scott, who pointed west to the Seventeenth Street corner and vaguely south. Broyle collected the Walk's signs and headed off as directed— no doubt, Snyder thought, to the Virginia Avenue station house.

It was an old three-story brick-and-limestone pile on the shady side of the avenue at Twenty-third Street. A neat small lawn in front and hedges along the driveway to the rear gave it a touch of the residential that suited the neighborhood. Nevertheless, it was unmistakably a police station, with squad cars at the curb, outside green lights, barred windows, and worn steps leading up to scuffed front doors.

At first sight, about two that afternoon, Snyder imagined the fear and nausea he might have felt, were he Herndon, as the prisoners' van drove up. Then, shamelessly, he allowed himself a wild hope—at that, not such a wild hope, he told himself—that some bureaucratic error might yet cause the system to pass Herndon by. You would not write the story even then, word of honor, Snyder was thinking, but at least Herndon would be free.

Snyder paid his taxi and went inside. The public room was bright and well kept. The air smelled of metal polish. There were a dozen policemen at work in shirt sleeves, but none seemed in haste. Clearly, the business of booking the walkers was elsewhere. On a long bench at one end of the room sat several reporters and still photographers. A Negro police matron came from the visitors' bathroom leading two lost white children. At the communications desk with his back to the room, a lieutenant spoke on the phone while cooling his face two feet from an electric fan. A sergeant examined Snyder's press card, which registered in the man's eyes as a lifelong grievance against journalists.

"You can wait over there with the local Fourth Estate," he said. "We're all waiting for the counselor."

About three, a red-cheeked, gray-haired man in his sixties, wearing a seersucker suit and carrying a briefcase, entered the public room. Only Snyder among the reporters was not on a first-name basis with Milton Katz, the activist lawyer and Walk host, who had been around Washington since the days of the Truman Commission on national defense, for which he had come up from Charleston to serve and after which he had never left. Snyder remembered July 1964, when Katz's gentlemanly resignation after only six months on the White House staff was reported as the first whiff of Vietnam policy dissent within the Johnson inner circle. His anti-war motives were widely believed and never confirmed, a combination that preserved much of his influence in the government and testified to his skill at public relations as well as the law. Forthwith, and with a flourish, Katz approached the reporters staked out on the Walk story before so much as a nod toward the desk sergeant or his overheated lieutenant.

"Troops!" he said.

"You're late, Milt," a reporter said.

"My driver went to the demonstration."

"Arrested?"

"No. He brought home the signs of my clients."

"Arley Broyle?" Snyder asked.

"Yes. Are you Snyder?"

"Yes."

"I heard about you. Staying long?"

"After court tomorrow."

"Interesting."

"How long do we have to wait, Milt?" a reporter asked.

"Yes, lots to do here. This being a holiday, everything takes time —time! Thus the whirligig of time brings in his revenges. And I expect my people will refuse bail, at least some of them, and suffer detention for the night over at the Municipal Center, an unfriendly place, until morning's light opens the court. My clients are a very determined and dedicated lot. So, you see—it all takes time. But, yes, give me fifteen minutes and we'll talk."

As the reporters laughed, Katz smiled. Snyder couldn't decide about him, he was too much a star; but for p.r., if not professionalism, he had lived up to his notices.

Outside, Snyder saw the Walk truck parked at the curb. The signs were neatly stacked in the rear and weighted down by a corner of the tarp. He found Arley Broyle at the wheel, sweating and ashen-faced. Broyle's smile of greeting barely lifted the corners of his mouth. Snyder slid into the front seat beside Broyle and they shook hands.

"Are you making it, Arley?" Snyder asked.

"I'm waiting for Mr. Katz."

"Are you okay?"

"Sick feeling. You missed it, Jack."

"No, I saw it—from the park."

"Last minute, Reed said he was going to do it and I wanted to do it with him. He wouldn't let me, Jack. So I went to Mr. Katz's to be here with the truck and Mr. Katz came, too. Are they getting out, Jack?"

"Maybe some today, some tomorrow."

"What about Reed?"

"I don't know, Arley. Mr. Katz is having a press conference in a few minutes. He'll tell you what he tells us. I wanted to say hello."

"I missed you the last couple of days, Jack."

"I missed you, too."

"It all means something, doesn't it, Jack?"

"Everything has lots of meanings—but you never know until later."

"Reed wouldn't go to prison, would he?"

"I don't know. It doesn't look so good."

"Something terrible in a country that would make him go."

"That's what I think, Arley."

"You think that, Jack?"

"Yes."

Broyle stared through the windshield. No tears came, but to Snyder he seemed to be weeping. His shoulders shook and his hands made fists in his lap.

"Cigarette, Arley?" Snyder asked, offering his pack.

"Yes."

They smoked together quietly.

"You don't want to miss the press conference, Jack."

"No, Arley. Maybe I'll see you tomorrow, if they are in court."

"Well, I'll have to stay with the truck."

"I forgot—the truck."

"I'd like to say goodbye to you, Jack. Thank you for everything."

"Goodbye, Arley. Thank you for everything."

Snyder stepped down from the cab and slammed the door. He looked in at the window and shook hands with Broyle again.

"So long, Arley."

"So long, Jack—be looking for your article."

Snyder hesitated. He felt stifled. He did not want to tell another lie.

"I've got your address, Arley. I'll write you a letter."

"Will you, Jack!" Broyle smiled full, and color rose to his forehead.

"You blush like me, Arley," Snyder said. "I'll write for sure."

"You do! And I'm going to read every issue of *Harrington's* anyway."

Snyder waved stiffly and plunged up the steps into the station house. To be pushing back tears twice in one afternoon is some kind of a fucking record, he told himself; you might actually choke on self-disgust.

Milton Katz appeared at the reporters' stakeout precisely on schedule. He had flung his seersucker jacket over one shoulder and his shirt was transparent with sweat. He was well muscled for a man of his age.

"Well, sirs," Katz began, "my clients are downstairs, in good health, and we thank you for your attention. Tomorrow morning in court, we will answer all charges. The District, in its wisdom, alleges obstruction plus refusal, one count more than is customary in these situations, a twin count that slightly increases the range of fines and punishments. In the meantime, all but one of my people will be facing a long night in the Municipal Center, inasmuch as they are, for the time being, refusing bail, a citation release, or any other instrument of exit from the toils of the law."

"But they'll plead, won't they?" a reporter asked.

"The First Amendment notwithstanding," Katz said, "and there are First Amendment issues inherent in every political protest by civil disobedience, the answer is yes—we do expect to plead."

"And pay fines?"

"That depends. Obstruction, which is the usual charge, is ten dollars, at most twenty-five. But refusal, a count heavy-handed to say the least, meaning refusal to clear a way or some such dubious legalism, is fifty to one hundred dollars. Is the court compassionate? Do I expect understanding? As you know, boys, it has always been a showing of earthly power most like God's when mercy seasons justice."

"Do we credit you or Shakespeare, Milt?"

"As you wish, professor."

"Milt—why not make bail this afternoon? Is it masochism or publicity?"

"The bondsman is ready, sir," Katz said. "But by a night's repose in the District of Columbia's jailhouse, our stop-and-talk walkers intend to express more strongly than ever their demand for a change of policy in Vietnam. Why, you ask? How is an ideal served, a goal reached, by enduring both the hardship of a walk of seven-hundred and fifty miles and the pain of imprisonment? What, in short, is going on here? In court tomorrow, friends, I will take as my text Martin Luther King from Birmingham's jail, answering so: 'Why direct action? Why sit-ins, marches, and so forth? Isn't negotiation a better path? You are quite right in calling for negotiation. Indeed, this is the very purpose of direct action. Non-violent direct action seeks to create such a crisis and foster such a tension that a community which has constantly refused to negotiate is forced to confront the issue. It seeks to so dramatize the issue that it can no longer be ignored.'"

"Bravo, Milt!" a reporter cried.

Katz raised his hand. "If you read your own newspapers today," he said sharply, "you saw that President Johnson is expected momentarily to announce yet another increase in troop levels for this dreadful war. And if you were at the White House today, you saw nine valiant Americans, backed by a growing host, confronting this issue so that it can no longer be ignored. Refusing bail continues that confrontation, for which we hope you will find generous space in your sheets, with special reference to the text of our petition."

"You're making bail for one?"

"Rachel Abraham of Chicago and Northwestern University, a Ph.D. candidate, represents WISE for the Walk. The Municipal Center will receive her as well as the others and I go there now to facilitate not only their comfort but her release. You readers of Dickens know about the law's delay."

"Who's paying?"

"Tonight's meeting at my home to raise bail and pay fines is called for ten o'clock to make certain Miss Abraham is available to speak. She is a very fine speaker. You are all welcome."

"Enough is enough, Milt," a reporter said, and closed his notebook.

"I would not tread upon your patience," Katz said, and turned to Snyder. "Her message is, she would like Jack to take her call."

"All right," Snyder said, "of course."

Trailed by the photographers, Katz strode from the station house and posed for pictures in the still-bright sun beside the Walk truck.

Snyder watched in the shade at the top of the steps. Sam Lucas, he was thinking, chose the right lawyer for the Walk. Then he decided to walk back to the hotel, knowing that the rest of his day was committed to waiting for Rachel's call.

6

The phone in his hotel room rang, one long, one short, at ten minutes to six during the bottom of the ninth inning of the second game of the Senators-Indians double-header. Carefully, Snyder set his glass on the desk next to two empty and four unopened two-ounce room service bottles of White Label Scotch and turned down the volume on the TV. He was not feeling drunk, only precise. The phone rang again, once, and, by the ring, he knew she was in the lobby.

"Hello, Ray," he said.

"Hello, Jack," she said. "I'm downstairs. Arley and Mr. Katz brought me. Mr. Katz loves to ride in the truck."

"Katz was good today."

"May I see you?"

"I'd like you to come up. The news is on at six-thirty, TV."

"I'll send them home."

More coldly than he felt, he said, "Do that."

"Jack?"

"Yes?"

"I'm sorry, Jack."

"It's okay, Ray. Room four-oh-six."

"I've got that. In a minute."

Snyder took the bath towel from his waist, and put on skivvies, a clean T-shirt, khaki pants, and shoes. That done, he finished his glass and prudently cleared the little bottles into the desk drawer. He lit a cigarette, dragging deeply. When he heard a knock, he turned off the TV and opened the door.

"Come in," he said.

Rachel smiled uncertainly. Her face was lined with dry marks of the afternoon's sweat. Her hair was tangled and there were stains of street dirt and motor oil on her white blouse and blue jeans. "Arley took Mr. Katz," she said, passing into the room. In one hand, she carried the big purse, its strap dangling.

Snyder closed the door and indicated the room's lone armchair, which faced the darkened TV console. Rachel sat down. Snyder sat on the bed.

"You broke your strap?"

"In the sit-down. Did you see us?"

"Yes."

"Reed said you'd left."

"I watched from the park."

"No more story?"

"No."

"We didn't know what you'd done till Reed told us in the van."

"What did he say?"

"He said you'd decided you didn't want to take responsibility for him."

"I did say that."

"That's all he said."

"Not that I don't give a damn about him?"

"No."

"Do you think I care about him?"

"More than what?"

"Myself."

" 'Myself,' meaning your story?"

" 'Myself' means myself."

"I know you think you've done the right thing. I was way out of line last night and that's why I'm sorry."

"Did any of the others understand? Joe Rice? Dorene?"

"Joe and Vachel arrived this morning. They understand. Everyone understands, Jack. You walked from Chicago. You were a hero."

"But not now?"

"Is that how you feel?"

"I don't know."

"Perhaps nothing would've made a difference."

"Nothing I could do did, Ray."

"Vietnam, Jack."

"Is that it?"

"We're in the war, Jack." Her eyes filled. "Reed's been separated and taken away already."

"Oh, Ray!"

"Five o'clock."

"The paperwork—it's not possible!"

"He saved them the trouble. First thing at the station, he told them two phone numbers for his parole officer. And at the Municipal Center, they just suddenly took him away. Mr. Katz found him in an isolation cell for Federal prisoners. Mr. Katz sees him at eight tonight and they plan to hand him over tomorrow, maybe Wednesday on account of the holiday."

"Why did he tell?"

"Reed? I guess he wants to get it over with. He's been through it. He knows what's coming. He knows how they've designed the whole setup to humiliate people. Jack, here's the central cell block! It's noisy, hot, and overflowing from the long weekend. Luther's in a cage with Joe and Vachel, two auto thieves, and a boy who went swimming naked in the Reflecting Pool. They gave us, the women, a dormitory cell with three other women, all three innocent of prostitution. I have to appear in court with the Walk at nine A.M., but we're not even on the docket yet, and may not get a judge to look at us until Wednesday, maybe Thursday!"

Rachel lifted her hands, palms up, and continued. "Oh, but, Jack," she said, "the meanest thing is they let none of us say goodbye to Reed! When we first arrived at the Center, we were all in this big, ominous, concrete room, almost interested in the change of decor— the really evil modern fortress after the breezy old lockup on Virginia Avenue. It was a lesson in psychology, architecture and the denial of identity. So we should've expected the worst when a guard called Reed's name, like he had a visitor. Only we didn't and he didn't. Reed went and was gone, the bastards took him. And Amelia is beside herself!"

Snyder assimilated the details slowly, deliberately separating Herndon's drama from the others'. Among those at the Center, he cared most, perhaps only, about Herndon. He could not have said he had expected a miracle, but he realized that his absurd hope for a rescue-by-mistake had done more to sedate him than the White Label. Absurd, absurd, he told himself, when you yourself could have saved Herndon by drowning.

"Someday a story on prisons, Ray," Snyder said obliquely.

"Can you imagine Reed after another year?"

Snyder shook his head in answer, a vision in his mind of Herndon's last look, an aching smile, at the West Gate.

"Mr. Katz thinks maybe longer," Rachel said. "Escalation tends to push imprisonment for resistance toward the maximum. There's a fund-raiser tonight—he's speaking about it."

"You're speaking, too?"

"Begging is a better word."

"I can give something personally now."

"I forgot you could. I wasn't asking you for money."

"I want to. I mean it."

Snyder looked around for his whisky glass, remembered he had finished it. "Fifty bucks for the kitty?" he asked. There was an emergency blank check folded into the postage pocket of his wallet. Swiftly, he made it out to the World Institute for Survival Education.

"It's too much," Rachel said with an uncomfortable frown. "Does this mean we can fall in love now?"

"Put it in your saddlebag," Snyder said. "I owe it."

"It's too much money."

"Jews and philanthropy, Ray."

"So then, thank you. You wouldn't come tonight?"

"No."

"Are you leaving tomorrow?"

"I know a lieutenant at the Center. I want to try to see Reed in the morning."

"You're a nice man, Snyder."

Snyder checked his watch. "Then home to face reality," he said. It was 6:17. "Well," he said, "I have Scotch, no ice. Would you like a drink?"

"A weak Scotch."

"Shower? I can let you have a clean shirt, my hairbrush."

"Yes to all that."

"News in twelve minutes?"

"I'll make it."

He was dialing from station to station, commercial to commercial, to locate the start of the networks' news as she came back barefooted from the shower. She wore his blue shirt, tails out over her jeans, and sat again in the armchair. Her hair was brushed back tight behind her ears. Snyder divided a single room service whisky between them and filled their glasses with tap water from the bathroom sink. In a corner by the tub, her blouse, brassiere, and socks lay in an orderly bundle on top of her shoes. He heard her call, "Hurry!"

Snyder viewed the half hour sitting on the floor by the console, flipping the stations to catch the Walk according to the networks' respective news menus. He was never unaware of Rachel sitting above him, breathing, sipping her drink, but it was as though they had produced the news programs themselves. They did not speak, watching in a state of absorption, hers seemingly complete, his in the nature of one both involved and detached who routinely watched life and watched himself watching.

All three networks had topped the day with the war and the nation's heat wave. At 6:37, NBC broadcast ninety seconds on the White House demonstration to close a cross-country roundup of holiday events, games, picnics, and prayer meetings. At 6:44, CBS cleverly offered the demonstration as counterpoint for a feature from Saigon about an Independence Day celebration for U.S. troops in South Vietnam. At 6:49, having been delayed by an earlier technical failure, ABC presented President Johnson's Fourth of July in Texas with a thirty-eight-second cut from the scene at the West Gate, introduced by a reporter who said, "Meanwhile, back at the White House, the beef goes on." Film of the Walk's crowd and the arrest of Reed Herndon appeared in all three reports. NBC mentioned the Walk's 750-mile "ordeal" and CBS used footage of Herndon's final "stop-and-talk" appeal. ABC seemed least impressed by the protest, "no injuries, only nine arrests," and moved on to a fireworks display, hailed by a former congressman as a patriotic reminder to "certain Americans who give aid and comfort to the enemy." But, of the three, ABC was the only network to reprise the demonstration under its closing titles, signing off as the Walk's crowd chanted, "Stop—talk! Stop—talk!"

The Walk delivered, Snyder was thinking, and with newspaper stories yet to come, they are entitled to satisfaction.

He looked up at Rachel, trying to hold on to that thought, even as he realized that the publicity, folded into the networks' holiday themes, had diminished the investment in its achievement and missed entirely the year to come in Herndon's life—the pilgrims' progress. Rachel still stared at the black-and-white images scuttering on the tube. The station's break for commercials—soap, automobiles, and breakfast foods for sale—seemed to absorb her as much as the news.

Finally, Rachel turned to him. "No matter what grief appears on television," she said with bitterness, "it's always bracketed by commercials that put everything right." She turned off the console and took a step to the view of St. John's Church. As Snyder had once done, she shut off the air conditioner and opened the window. She ran her hands through her hair.

"Should I feel so rotten about the TV, Jack?" she asked.

Snyder joined her at the window. The incoming air was warm and moist and hinted of rain. Sunlight reflected from clouds lowering in the east cast the church tower in a lavender glow. Snyder leaned back against the wall, facing her. "Assume the absolute minimum you can say for the coverage," he said, "without the Walk, there might have been no peace news on the tube tonight."

"I've thought of that."

"That's something, isn't it? With sixty million people watching."

"They watched the commercials, too."

"And tomorrow, they read the newspapers, then the magazines—theoretically, there's no ending."

"Oh, Jack, I hate the way it's ending for—"

"It's messy."

"—Reed, you, even me!"

"Take some pride, anyway, Ray."

"I'm sick of pride, Jack. That's what the war's about. That's why Reed's going back to his joint. Why you've got no story to write"—her eyes remained fixed on the view of St. John's—"why I feel wasted."

Snyder touched her hand. "Okay, Ray," he said, "but tell me it wasn't something to walk all that way."

"Jack," she said, turning to him, "will you hold me?"

Rachel narrowed the gap between them and lifted her chin. Snyder kissed her and embraced her. He felt her lips respond and they kissed softly. Rachel's arms came up over his shoulders. Her hair smelled very clean. Her hands tightened on the back of his neck, and her breasts, high and free, pressed against him. Yet he sensed in her a reticence not unlike his own. For the moment, it was the unfinished business of the Walk. With one finger, she touched the scar on his lip. Then she rested her forehead against his jaw.

"I was scared today," she whispered. "The batons frightened me."

"They were meant to."

"When I saw you, I had this waking dream that you'd returned to the Walk, that you'd take out your notebook, and last night would be forgotten."

"It was too late to return."

"Did you know that you and your notebook always made us feel safer?"

Snyder shook his head and kissed her hair. "I've been believing involvement was something you chose."

"I could've cried when you left again. Then Reed told us they would arrest him and I knew they would arrest me, too."

"You couldn't step aside with Arley?"

Rachel raised her face to his. "You know the answer to that," she said. "I wanted your gift."

"My gift?"

"Immortality."

Rachel had smiled with her perfect word. It was also a wise smile, Snyder thought, proposing that the lost gift mustn't matter anymore. The work of both of them was to accept it. He wondered, who then is consoling whom? Is this letdown or buildup? The end of their friendship or the beginning of their love affair? She had left it to him to decide.

He glanced outside. The clouds were moving faster and the light had gone gray. The air felt heavy with rain. Rachel took his face in her hands.

"Where are you?" she asked.

"Here," he said.

"I don't want to be hurt, Jack."

"You should go, if you should go," he said. "You've a meeting in a couple of hours."

"You're excused," she said. "You gave fifty dollars to the kitty."

"Where are you?"

"I'm all right as long as I know the ground rules."

"You know my life."

"You were very good on the Walk."

"I don't want to hurt you, Ray."

"We'll have an advantage over most people. We start out as friends."

Snyder covered her hands with his and kissed her lips. She kissed the palms of his hands. Then they sat down on the foot of the bed. Rachel brought up her legs and turned so that her body crossed his. Rachel took off their wristwatches. They helped one another undress. It had been too long for both of them to wait or experiment. Snyder came over her long body. She took his eager sex and guided him, slowly at first, into her flowing self. They made love quickly. Afterwards, Snyder sat above her, smoking as she lay on his pillow, holding him. He took delight in her pink-tipped breasts stark white below the tan of her chest.

"Did you think about this?" she asked.

"Often," he said.

"I did."

"It's raining."

"Pay no attention."

But they listened to the soft rain and the room turned dark.

Later, Snyder lay beside her, and they caressed one another, and they inverted, and their sexes rose against one another's lips. Rachel became athletic, noisy, and fierce. At last, Snyder lifted her above him until she could kneel, her breasts on his palms and her body gliding in harmony with their needs. When they rested, Snyder lay on his back and Rachel curled at his side. He thought of the length of her.

Snyder awoke with a start. The room light had been turned on and the rain had stopped. Rachel sat at the foot of the bed, dressed again and waiting. She looked sleepy to him, and very young. Snyder reached for his watch.

Rachel smiled. "It's nine-fifteen," she said. "Are we saying good-bye now?"

"I will see you in court tomorrow."

"I like that."

"Good luck, tonight."

"I've had mine for tonight."

"We'll have to discuss it."

"I did something wrong?"

"Like Helen."

"Helen who?"

"Of Troy."

"I like you, Snyder."

"Friendship and love, we have to discuss them."

"Do we love each other, Jack?"

"I don't know. I have no reservations. Just the reticence of a misspent youth."

"There's nothing I'd take from you, dear heart, that I would not give back if we don't make it."

Rachel kissed him on the knee, the shoulder, and the mouth. The fullness of her blue shirt lightly touched his chest. She took his hands and placed them on her breasts.

"I want you to feel that all night," she said.

"I like you, Abraham," he said.

"Don't get up," she said.

After she had gone, Snyder sat up in bed. He was famished. In due time, he thought he would order up some dinner. Outside there was the muffled pop-pop-pop and echoing rumble of fireworks somewhere among the monuments. The room was warm and muggy. Another scorcher tomorrow, he thought. He wondered if it would be so hot in New York.

Once you're there, he was thinking, the only thing you can do is tell Erlanger the truth about Herndon.

TWENTY
The True Thing

I

In the holding cell for Federal transfers, before Katz arrived that night, a letter home was written by Reed Herndon on the back of the original Walk petition and the signature page, which together the White House had refused, and two pages of yellow foolscap bearing the MPD seal. It said:

"Dearest Mother:

"You can guess by my makeshift stationery that I chose civil disobedience this afternoon. This is the petition and the envelope (I've crossed out President Johnson's name so the mail goes to you, not him!) that we took to the White House. My isolation (they are holding me for the Federal parole authorities—tomorrow?) means I won't see how it plays at six-thirty tonight on the television. Hope the newspapers will pick it up. Anyway, you have it to read in full.

"You must understand that the situation got out of my control. As I told you in my last letter, my decision about my own personal commitment for today had an unexpected effect on whether the Walk would receive a major story in *Harrington's,* one of the most important magazines in the country, by its top writer. If I were to leave the Walk before the Fourth of July demonstration, the story would not be written. If I chose to sacrifice my parole by civil disobedience, it would be. I don't blame the writer, Jack Snyder. I just didn't know him.

"However, there was always a third alternative, involving dishonor for me, but requiring neither civil disobedience nor the cancellation of the article. That is, I could stand aside at the White

House gate and let others take the risks of civil disobedience while I looked on.

"But, here, you have to understand that about half of the walkers (without my problems!) were undecided about civil disobedience and would, almost certainly, follow my lead. Perhaps all would follow my lead just to protect me, do you see? Whether ten or five or even none of us did civil disobedience at the White House made little difference to Snyder's story, because he would understand it, but quite a bit to the type of coverage on July 4–5 from television and the newspapers.

"Still, this morning (I didn't sleep last night), as I led the Walk along Pennsylvania Avenue (wish you'd been there!), I decided on this third course, knowing that my reputation, and no doubt my future usefulness as a leader of the anti-war movement, would be damaged, perhaps lost.

"Jack Snyder, being Jack Snyder, would have written of my choice and, even if only by indirection, he would've had to humiliate me. Still, I'd become ready for that because, in the end, shame seemed to be a better solution (marginally) than no magazine story or no parole. There would be a story in *Harrington's*! And I would be on parole! Just no soul.

"However, I waited too long. As I approached the White House this afternoon, Snyder came out of the blue. And, in order to persuade me to reject civil disobedience and remain on parole, he was, as he said, 'aborting' his assignment, no matter what action I was about to take. He assumed, of course, civil disobedience. And my instant reaction was, okay, then I'm going to do it after all. I wanted to show him!

"It was over then. I know he thought he was saving my life. But if his word of honor meant his story was dead, I was not going to kill our chances with those cameramen and reporters at the White House gate, setting a coward's example for the walkers, and ending with only a few or even none doing civil disobedience, not after such a big buildup. No way!

"Or maybe I was just looking for that excuse to do the true thing, like Gandhi said. Don't forget, the memory of Norman Morrison walked with us every step of the way.

"The fact is, I believe, that Snyder became disgusted with me. He did not stay for the civil disobedience, and expects to return to New York tomorrow after the others have been to court.

"Snyder finally felt, I think, that I had put my life in his hands (alternatives one, two, or three—no matter) and he would not accept this. Perhaps one should always beware of this and take care of oneself, because you never know what the other guy is going to do with the power over you that you give him. Especially when he's a professional like Snyder. Our lawyer, Milton Katz, said this afternoon, 'To do a great right, do a little wrong,' but not Jack!

"And now Snyder must be more disgusted than ever because I went ahead with civil disobedience and, having sworn to me that he would not do the story, he goes home empty-handed after nearly two months' work.

"My uselessness is complete tonight. The Walk's best chance to forward the anti-war cause has been foiled and here I am facing what I have prayed and prayed I would never have to face again, the joint. At least the *Harrington's* story would have given this next year a decent meaning.

"Handled Jack Snyder wrong from the beginning. A little hubris can get you into a lot of hot water. I see that. But it fills me with enormous regret that the others who walked with me from Chicago, Sam Lucas and Joe Rice, who were ready to give their lives for the Walk, have been denied a very meaningful projection of their sacrifice just because I have Snyder's word he won't write about them. Talk about irony! Perhaps if I were to just disappear, taking his word with me, he might tell the Walk's story after all. I'd like to ask him about that!

"Well, the lawyer is due here any minute. Well-connected, I gather, but even he told me, first thing, that the atmosphere in the country makes it certain I will have to serve out the rest of my sentence, and may even lose my good time. Swell! But meanwhile, I want you to believe that all I've done and must do is for peace.

"Hope this letter (longest ever!) explains things so that my follies will make a little sense and never shame you. I feel bad enough for one family.

"I send you all my love, Reedy.

"P.S. Good night."

Herndon's letter addressed to Mrs. Adele Herndon in Decatur, Illinois, was mailed later that night by Milton Katz.

2

At a minute or so before eight next morning, a voice had awakened Snyder, at first unrecognized by him save that it was not the usual switchboard operator.

"Hello, Jack. This is Caffuzzi."

"Lieutenant?"

"You better get down here quick. My office."

"What?"

"It's not for coffee."

Click.

Later, Snyder would remember Lieutenant Anthony Caffuzzi's call and believe he had known then, and pretended not to. Otherwise, he would have tried to call Rachel.

He dressed fast and, on the drive to the Municipal Center, calmly appraised the Washington *Post*'s two-column report on the Walk's demonstration, enhanced by a photo of the arrest of Reed Herndon and the headline "Anti-Vietnam Protest Grows. Nine Arrests at White House Rally." It was just page twelve, but eighteen column inches, plus a box for the complete text of the WISE petition. The tiny group of surviving walkers could not have asked for more and, unless the Walk had grown en route to a mighty torrent of many thousands, probably could not have received more. Snyder tore out the entire page, thinking it is something to show Erlanger at the truth meeting. He realized he had forgotten his notebook.

Lieutenant Caffuzzi was alone in the public information office, seated at his clerk's desk drinking coffee from a porcelain cup. He wore the same blue plaid suit and yellow tie. Snyder did not recall the blazing pink shirt. Caffuzzi had only just shaved; blood from a nick coursed down his neck in a thin, wet stream and threatened his collar. They shook hands.

"You're bleeding," Snyder said.

"Shit," Caffuzzi said. "Thanks."

Caffuzzi patted his neck with a handkerchief and poured coffee for Snyder. Snyder lit a cigarette.

"Funny how things happen," Caffuzzi said. "My relief's sick, so I get in at seven-thirty, and the official word's out at seven-forty, so I can give you a jump on the police beat. The usuals will see the captain and the coroner at ten, maybe eleven, depending. The Federals are hopping mad and all over the place, so we have to relax them before we go public. But you don't need to wait, Jack. We can get it all for you."

"Is it Herndon?" Snyder asked, hearing the quake in his own voice.

"He stole a water glass, used the shards. The temporaries in the federal holding cells don't get the same surveillance. That's off the record. Those high-class prisoners are usually so happy to get out of the central cell block, they don't worry anybody."

"Is he dead, Lieutenant?"

"Both wrists. Guards discovered him at six something this morning. Rush to the infirmary. Cause of death—heart failure due to loss of blood. God-awful loss of blood."

"What time?"

"Five A.M., maybe. Probably happened at dawn. It often does. No note. No nothing."

"He was alone in the cell?"

"Oh, sure. No doubt about that. We're listing it suicide pending an autopsy, but 'pending' is just a technicality for lawyers. They like to tell families and insurance companies everything's according to Hoyle. It's suicide to us. Always hard to predict, but easy to detect."

"What about the autopsy?"

"Minutes ago, I heard they sent a squad car for the lawyer, Milton Katz. Pretty famous, eh? He'll attract some press! He's got to sign a release, so they'll buzz me from the captain's office when he's in the building. But you don't have to wait, Jack. Body's in the infirmary. Want to see?"

Snyder knew he had known.

"Wait a minute, Lieutenant," Snyder said.

"Not a nice thing," Caffuzzi was saying. "Young guy, too."

Snyder turned away and wept. His chest ached. He held his face with one hand and reached for a nonexistent handkerchief with the other. He wept through a chain of reactions, grief, then regret, then an overpowering remorse that captured his glands and poured bile into his throat. You knew, he was thinking, but when did you know? Yesterday's aching smile? Last week's confessional? The first week's negotiation? The moment you saw him in Chicago? Why the fuck did you let him get away with it? The right answer was no compromises from the word go. Talk about shit!

Caffuzzi tapped his arm. "Use this," he said, offering his handkerchief. Caffuzzi's blood spots were already turning brown.

Snyder collected himself. He returned the handkerchief.

"Thank you," he said. "I'm sorry."

"No problem, Jack. You all right?"

"I'm fine. Thanks."

"You must've known him pretty well."

"On the assignment is all."

"Who was he? We can always use a motive."

"I wouldn't have one, Tony. I'd like to see him now, please."

They took the security elevator down one flight to the first basement. The infirmary was at the far end of a corridor lit by wirecovered ceiling lamps. A vent above the door filled the corridor with an odor of disinfectant. A Negro male nurse in whites opened the door. "This is Louis," Caffuzzi said. Louis led them past a dispensary cage into a small, windowless consultation room, fluorescent light overhead. Snyder attributed a slight dizziness to the lighting.

As from a great height, he saw a form lying on a mobile stretcher covered by a green plastic sheet from its blond hairline to its ankles. It was Herndon dead. A pink identification tag hung on his right big toe. Louis folded the sheet down to Herndon's waist. Someone had crossed Herndon's arms on his chest and wrapped his wrists in clean bandages. His chest below the tan line of the neck seemed remarkably white to Snyder. The few curly yellow hairs on his chest seemed pointless.

Snyder stepped around to the side of the stretcher. Herndon's face was blue-brown, smaller and narrower than in life. Herndon's eyes were closed, unfamiliar without glasses. Nothing about Herndon seemed lifelike. Even Herndon's jaw was locked in an uncharacteristically stern line. Snyder put the palm of his hand alongside Herndon's jaw; the skin felt damp and cool. The least Herndon could have done, he was thinking, was explain. He felt warm tears on his cheeks and a flaming sob in his throat.

Snyder returned to Caffuzzi's office. Patrolman Miller had come to his post, so they sat in the conference room. There were yellow foolscap tablets and pencils on the table. Snyder folded six sheets in half to make a notebook. He loosened his tie and began to write.

"So?" Caffuzzi asked.

"So," Snyder said.

"Looked like a nice young guy."

"He was."

"Go ahead, work."

As Snyder wrote, Caffuzzi took a call on the intercom.

"Katz is in the building, Jack," he said. "The captain's got him and a woman, R. Abraham, who speaks for the group. You know her? They're going to the infirmary now. Seeing it's Katz and all, I probably ought to be there."

Snyder looked up. Caffuzzi was rising.

"Deliver a message for me, Tony?"

"A quick one, yes."

Snyder removed a sheet from his make-shift notebook.

"Dear Ray," he wrote. "I want you to know I am here and have seen Reed. I know why he did it, so how can I refuse to write the story of the Walk? I'll wait for you on the steps outside. We can talk. The only other thing I'm sure of now is that the kitty can keep my fifty dollars. So much for integrity. Love, Jack."

Snyder folded the note and Caffuzzi touched it to his forehead in salute. "I'm working on my drug story," Caffuzzi said.

When Caffuzzi had gone, Snyder put his foot on a chair and lit a cigarette. His watch read 8:55. He looked from wall to wall at the front pages of the Washington *Post*, circa the Good Old Days. He thought how much he disliked rooms without windows. Then it occurred to him that he had neglected to notice the weather. It must be hot, he was thinking, but never assume. Oh, yes!

He thought he could allow himself another ten minutes with his notes, drawing back from memory the facts of the past three days. The Walk demonstration as seen through binoculars appeared first on his mental screen and he knew the rest could appear with a few hours of recall. *Pilgrims' Progress!* It was all there.

Patrolman Miller looked in from the outer office. "Caffuzzi phoned," he said. "On your horse. They're coming up."

Snyder folded his papers and straightened his tie. He walked from the office past the security elevator. A red light indicated that the car had not left the basement. He continued into the foyer and glanced at the collection of wanted posters. The alleged outlaws looked like anybody, even like some of the people coming to work through the foyer.

Beyond the front doors, the sun glared harshly. For the second day in a row, he had no hat but he went outside anyway. He looked for shade on the top step and found none. It was all sun and moist, heavy air. So he gave the sun his back and faced the doors dead center. He lit a cigarette and waited, imagining the next moment when Rachel would come through the doors to meet him—Rachel: dark, long-legged, and mourning. They would embrace, he was thinking, but now again only as friends, at least for the time being.